BILLION-DOLLAR DATING

ALLY BLAKE

MARIAH ANKENMAN

MILLS & BOON

First published in Great Britain 2025 by Mills & Boon, an imprint of HarperCollins*Publishers* Ltd, 1 London Bridge Street, London, SE1 9GF

www.harpercollins.co.uk

HarperCollins*Publishers*, Macken House, 39/40 Mayor Street Upper, Dublin 1, D01 C9W8, Ireland

ISBN: 978-0-263-41760-9

11/25

MIX
Paper | Supporting
responsible forestry
FSC
www.fsc.org
FSC™ C007454

This book contains FSC™ certified paper and other controlled sources to ensure responsible forest management.

For more information visit www.harpercollins.co.uk/green.

Printed and Bound in the UK using 100% Renewable Electricity at CPI Group (UK) Ltd, Croydon, CR0 4YY

FAKE DATING
THE ITALIAN HEIR

ALLY BLAKE

MILLS & BOON

For my wondrous and endlessly adored daughter, Bridget, whose own next chapter is unfolding before us. Thank you for all that you are, and for finding my hero his name. (Is there a nod to a certain Collingwood player in there? Good chance.) And for all the Book Clubbers in all the world—here's to stories shared, connections made, and understanding one another better through words on a page.

CHAPTER ONE

"NICO! OH, THANK GOODNESS. Everyone, back away. Nico is here!"

Niccolo Rossi had been ambling down the main street of Vermillion, enjoying the mid-autumn sunshine on his face, drinking in the scents of eucalyptus and wild rosemary from the front garden of the Barrels & Blooms Garden Centre, notes of fresh sourdough and preserved summer fruits wafting from the Yeast of Eden bakery, when he heard his name on the breeze.

Then he was halfway across the road, bounding towards the strip of golden elms that cleaved Main Street in two by the time Mrs. Constantine—the wiry, septuagenarian owner of the Savvy Sausage Butchery—had waved back the small crowd.

"Oh, Nico!" cried Mrs. Constantine, as he sprang up onto the verge.

"What seems to be the problem?"

"It's Basil." Mrs. Constantine pointed a crooked finger to a branch halfway up a tree where a tuxedo cat sat licking its paw; clearly unperturbed by all the attention.

"Is she serious?" murmured Aurora, Nico's younger sister, as she pulled up puffing beside him.

Nico didn't bother looking at his sister; the A-grade eye roll was patent in her voice. For while Aurora was only back in Vermillion from her European adventures for a visit, this was Nico's town. Literally and figuratively. Not only did he oversee the entirety of the Vermillion Hill vineyard, but he was also heir to the Rossi family estate, which owned half the commercial property in the picturesque town at its feet.

"Mrs. Constantine," said Nico, as he squinted through the rays of sunshine darting through the imposing branches above. "You do know Basil spends quite a bit of time in this particular tree, do you not?"

Mrs. Constantine demurred, "I worry. He is all I have."

Nico glanced across the street to where Mr. Constantine stood in the large window of the butcher shop, wiping his hands on a towel. The older man flapped a "she's all yours" hand Nico's way before disappearing from sight.

So, Nico rolled up the sleeves of his shirt, allowed himself a brief moment to wonder how he got himself into such follies, looked up in search of the path of least resistance, and hauled himself into the tree.

"They swooned!" said Aurora, once Basil was back in Mrs. Constantine's cooing embrace.

"Hardly," said Nico, brushing leaves and twigs from his clothes as they rejoined their earlier mission, checking in with the last of his family's tenants; Laila Vale, owner of the town's lone bookstore.

Had he deliberately left her till last? Most definitely. Did he do so each and every time he did the rounds? Absolutely. Was he looking forward to introducing Laila to his sister? Hell, no.

"One woman swayed," Aurora went on. "Another gasped. Yet another tugged on my sleeve, asked if I could set you up with her daughter."

Ignoring the question in her tone, Nico moved around behind Aurora, so that he ended up streetside.

"Come on!" she cried, hands beseeching. "You *must* have noticed."

Fine, Nico had noticed. It just wasn't all that noteworthy. As head of the family that owned much of the town, as well as the renowned winery that remained the linchpin of Vermillion's success, Nico was used to being leaned on. And cheered. And, well, adored profusely on occasion.

It wasn't why he did what he did. That came down to a sense of duty to this place, as it had to his father before him.

Aurora bumped him with her shoulder. "Do you think if they knew you wore a Superman cape everywhere as a kid it would mitigate the hero worship? Or ramp it up to Harry Styles–level idolisation?"

Nico lengthened his strides. "How long did you say you were staying?"

Aurora jogged to catch up. "Someone in this town has to keep your ego in check. I consider it a public service."

As luck would have it, they had reached the one place in town where augmenting his ego would not be a problem.

At the front of the bookshop, a white picket fence drooped under the weight of a mass of wild, deep purple bougainvillea. The front garden leading to the small weatherboard cottage in which the shop resided was a luscious, overgrown abundance of green. And yet it was the only shopfront on the entire block without a single iconic grapevine trailing over a trellis or an eave.

At first glance the aesthetic of the bookstore appeared to fit with the wholesome, tourist-friendly Vermillion brand; take one step inside and it soon became clear that the proprietor was not on the same page as the rest of the town.

Beside him Aurora yawned.

"If you've had enough," he said, seeing an out, "we can head home now."

Aurora linked her elbow through his. "I want to immerse myself in all the unhinged grandeur this town relishes. While I can," she added, sending a quick, complex glance his way.

Nico squeezed her hand against his side. For the night before, only hours after Aurora's arrival, their mamma had dropped a bomb.

They had barely sat down with a glass of predinner wine when she'd said, "*È giunto il momento per me di tornare a casa.*"

The time has come for me to go home.

After twenty years in South Australia, Celia Rossi planned to move back to the Rossi family estate in Siena, where their father was buried. Leaving the future of the Rossi family holdings in that corner of the world—the fate of the vineyard, and the town that relied on its patronage—entirely up to Nico.

"Oh wow," said Aurora, eyes widening when she noticed where they had stopped. "I can see why you saved this place for last!"

Tiny pink lights twinkled through the panes of the front picture window, bouncing off a bright array of pansies waving happily in planter boxes below.

A flash of movement behind the glass sent a spike of electricity down Nico's spine. The surfeit of battle-ready energy, normal preparation for coming face to face with the bookshop owner.

"I can't believe this used to be the Vine and Dime," Aurora said, pressing open the flower-laden front gate Laila refused to let him fix. "I'd half expected the place to be condemned by now."

Narrowing his eyes at the building, Nico had to admit it was much improved since the bookstore had moved in. The little old couple who had leased the cottage from their father had run the place like a hoarder's haven. Insurance and health and safety concerns aside, Aldo Rossi had kept rent low, taken care of maintenance himself, and dropped off the occasional pasta bake to make sure they ate well. Showing

Nico what it meant to not only speak to a strong sense of comfort and community, but to mean it.

Then, when the little old couple had retired, moving to be near their daughter in the Adelaide Hills, the very next day a stranger had rumbled into town; a vision of blonde waves, big blue eyes a man could get lost in, va-va-voom curves stepping out of a bright red MINI Cooper. And for Nico nothing had felt quite so comfortable since.

"Forbidden Fruits Story Emporium." Aurora read the shop name written on the hanging sign next to the pale pink front door. "That's awesome."

"Is it now?" Nico muttered under his breath, as he forced himself up the front steps.

For of all the ways his relationship with this tenant was contentious, the most frustrating was her refusal to give her shop a name that fit with Vermillion town lore—every place on Main Street having a *wholesome* name that included a wine-adjacent pun.

While the celebrated Vermillion Hill vineyard was a draw on its own, the kitsch store names were the extra something that sent tourists flocking down the hill into the town proper. Yet, from the moment Laila had signed the lease, they had been embroiled in a tug of war over what the name of her romance-only bookshop might be.

Nico had offered up dozens of ideas. Bubbly Bibliophile. Rosé Romance. After suggesting Harvest Hearts, Laila complained it had an "organ donor chop shop" vibe that was likely best avoided. After which she'd come back him with Tipsy Tales and the Bound Brut, before she'd settled on Forbidden Fruits, which, by then, had felt like the lesser of many evils.

That was eighteen-odd months ago now. Had he admitted defeat? Not a chance. The town's success was just that important. And if that meant visiting her shop once or twice a week, with new options in tow, then that's what he had to do.

"Come on." Aurora grinned over her shoulder as she opened the front door.

A bell tinkled to herald their arrival. It always made Nico feel like sneezing, as if the thing was sprinkling fairy dust. And while Aurora spun in a circle, mouth agape in clear delight, Nico's shoulders lifted up around his ears.

The walls were now a cotton-candy pink, the floor covered in such a large black-and-white-check tile it gave *Alice in Wonderland* vibes, and the ceiling was draped in enough fairy lights to make a guy squint. Under the front picture window sat a jade-green velvet couch big enough to lie on, covered in an excess of fluffy throw blankets, and by it was a large coffee table strewn in vintage magazines with glamorous old movie stars, or buff moustachioed dudes on motorbikes on the covers.

Then there were the books.

Floor to ceiling, lined up neatly in a mishmash of thrifted shelves, alongside what his mother might call "collectibles"— gilt-framed art, packs of cards, fancy book ends, all of which teetered just on the edge of propriety.

For the Forbidden Fruits Story Emporium didn't just sell romance novels, it sold *romance novels*. The kinds with bright, cheeky cartoon covers, or couples who looked a moment away from tearing one another's clothes off. Then there were the men with hooves in lieu of shoes, with tentacles, with kilts suggestively split to the upper thigh.

When Aurora reached a hand towards a cover with a sombre-eyed, shirtless beefcake, Nico muttered, "Don't. Touch. Anything."

Aurora glanced back at him. "Do you think I'll get cooties? Or *ideas*?"

Nico shot her a look, and, arms in the air in surrender, she disappeared deeper into the store.

It wasn't the books he had a problem with, or the "ideas" within. He was Italian after all; an appreciator of wine, women, and song. And while he wasn't seeing anyone—not since ending things with a travelling sales rep when she moved to the Adelaide Hills, a little too close for comfort—chances were he'd gotten up to much of what went on between those covers at one point or another in his thirty-one years.

It was the fact that the store so overtly refused to meet the Vermillion promise. All of which could have been ameliorated if the stubborn, frustrating, intentionally obstructive owner listened to his suggestions. Denying him, *defying* him, seemed to be the highlight of her week. Now he could no longer walk past this part of town without feeling a scratchy kind of heat banked inside him; like a match waiting to strike.

Speaking of the owner, he usually didn't get much further than a step inside the door before she appeared, as if from a pink puff of smoke that smelled both sweet and tart, like hot apple crumble.

As if he'd summoned her, a sardonic voice drawled, "Well, if it isn't Constable Goodboy."

Nico took in a bracing breath, then turned to find Laila standing, arms crossed, by the door to the storeroom at the very back of her store.

"Here to actually buy a book?" she asked, a single eyebrow rising to a point. She picked up a book from a shelf and turned it over in her hand. "They are an excellent means to learn how actual humans interact."

It was astounding how quickly she got under his skin. For one thing there was so little of her compared with a whole lot of him—five and a bit feet to his six-three. Though she had personality enough to take up twice as much space as she ought, she always made him feel like the Hulk.

As she walked towards him light sprinkled over her from the fairy lights. Her top was soft, and pink, and sheer, or near enough to hint at lace beneath; the neckline a near perfect heart. Pale jeans hugged her from her cinched-in waist to her ankles, and glittery heels brought the top of her blonde waves to just under his chin.

A profuseness of pastel contrasted with the colour of her lips; the same bright, lustrous red that she wore every single day. He even knew its colour was called Kiss Me, for she left tubes of the stuff everywhere. He'd seen her use the one she kept in a little "not sure where this stuff goes" bowl on her counter, and he'd once had to follow her down the street to return one that had rolled out of her bag.

His gaze was on her mouth as it quirked, before she said, "No? Must mean you're here for your bi-weekly harassment. Big shock."

She stopped at the far edge of the counter. "No 'look at me I'm a volunteer firefighter' uniform today?" she asked, looking him over, pausing briefly to blink at the front of his jeans, before her gaze swiftly rose back to his.

For a brief second, he imagined regaling her with the tale of Basil the cat, making it clear how brave he had been. But then she plucked a pencil from a caddy on the desk, one with a big fluffy white pompom on the end, and began pulling it through her fingers, over and over again, and he lost his train of thought.

"I know it might seem like a missed opportunity," he said, "but I tend to save my kit for when there is an actual emergency."

"How disappointing for the rest of us," she shot back as she cocked her hip against the bench. When she realised what she'd intimated, her blue eyes widened. "No emergency is a *good* thing. Just… You know what I mean."

What he knew was that he'd scored a point. Only when he opened his mouth to double down, Laila looked over his shoulder, her bearing shifting from darkly disenchanted to pure delight with such haste his head swam.

Bright as a morning in May, she said, "Well, hi there!"

And Nico's eyes drifted closed as he realised who was behind him.

He turned, slowly, to find Aurora slipping out from behind a bookshelf, a book in hand, her smile wide, her gaze shifting from Nico, to Laila, to Nico, to Laila.

"Is this your place?" Aurora asked.

"Sure is," Laila sing-songed.

"It's marvellous! I honestly feel as if my entire life could have gone on a completely different trajectory if this shop had been here sooner."

"Never too late to change things up," said Laila.

"See," said Aurora, moving up beside Nico to bump him with a shoulder. "There's still plenty of time for you to become less you."

With that it became Laila's turn to look from him, to Aurora, and back to him.

Only before he could explain that Aurora was his sister, Nico noted the book Aurora was holding. Or, to be more specific, the headless man with his fly half undone on the cover.

Nico ran a hand through his hair in an effort to comport himself, then motioned to his side as he said, "Laila, this is my sister, Aurora Rossi. Aurora, this is Laila Vale. Aurora is home for a quick visit. Laila is…"

A beat slunk by while he tried to find a rejoinder that wouldn't bring on more questions. In the end he went with "Laila has turned this place around in an impressively short time, making it one of the most popular new destinations in town."

Laila blinked at what, between them, amounted to gushing. Then she snapped her gaze back to Aurora, and said, "So you're the *sister*. Huh."

Nico wondered for a moment what the "huh" might mean. But *no*. Trying to untangle the twists and turns of Laila Vale's thoughts would never be a good use of his time. She was a thorn in his side, a pebble in his shoe, an itch he'd never scratch, and that was the end of that.

Laila nodded at the book Aurora held. "You want to grab that?"

"Um…"

"Can I suggest an alternative?" Laila picked up the book she'd been tapping against her hand earlier. In lieu of a half-naked man this one was a happy green colour with an apple on the cover.

Nico breathed out in relief.

Till Laila added, "There's a jetty scene that will alter your DNA."

Aurora laughed. "Done!"

Laila wrapped the book deftly in hot pink tissue paper before slipping it into a carry bag. She glanced at Nico as she added a hearty pinch of pink glitter, then another, and he knew he'd find specks of the damn stuff in the house for years to come. He'd see it and think of her.

When Aurora held up her phone to pay, Laila waved it away. "On me. Like any good pleasure pusher, I know you'll be back for more. So, you're just back for a flying visit?"

"Seems so." Aurora shot Nico a quick look, their mother's declaration no doubt at the front of her mind too.

Nico half winked in encouragement, and Aurora perked back up. "Spending some family time with Mamma and this guy."

"We're putting her to work while she's here," he said, "so if you need anything, feel free to lean on her as you would me."

Laila's snort was delicate, but telling. Unlike just about every other person in town, she'd never leaned on him. Not once. In fact, he'd put money on the fact that she'd be happy for him never to darken her pink door again.

"I do hope to see you again while you're here," said Laila, holding out the shiny red bag, not quite the same colour as her lips but damn close. "Feel free to come alone next time."

"I will," said Aurora, stifling a half laugh, half yawn.

Nico, seeing his chance, said, "Come on, let's get you home," and turned Aurora towards the door.

Then, remembering what he'd actually gone there to do, he turned back. "Any building issues that need tending to? Anything you need me to grab you from a high shelf?" he asked, turning back and expecting to find her watching Aurora, instead finding Laila's big blue eyes on him.

Maybe it was because he'd been thinking about the first time he'd seen her, remembering the kick in his chest when those eyes had met his—wary, and skittish, and so very blue—that he held on. Gazes caught, far longer than either normally allowed, he noted a shift therein. A swish of something dark and slippery, like a fish beneath the surface of a lake.

He felt a tug deep inside, like a claw snagged on some sequestered part of himself he kept far out of reach. As a matter of self-defence, he brought out the big guns and cracked a smile. Not just any smile; *the* smile. The one that made the wily sisters who ran Swirl and Purl Craft Corner pay their rent on time. The one that had grandmothers readying to offer up their granddaughters on a plate forget their mission mid-sentence. The one his mother called both his sword and his shield.

Laila blinked first. Then, plucking a seemingly random

pile of papers from her counter and shuffling them for all she was worth, she said, "I don't need anything from you, Nico. As ever, I am fine and dandy all on my own."

Not moving lest he spook her—for seeing Laila Vale ruffled was like spotting an endangered species in the wild—he said, "Any more thoughts about a fresh name for the shop?"

The shuffling stopped, and her bright gaze lifted back to his. "I can promise you, with all my heart, that the moment you leave, the thought does not cross my mind."

"Disappointing, because I have a ripper."

Botheration poured from her in waves, but, interestingly, she didn't stop him.

Nico waved his hand across the sky as he said, "Once Upon a Wine."

She pointed to the front door. "Get out of my shop."

"Wait. How about… Read Between the Wines?"

"Go," she said, "now. Before I call an actual man in uniform to come arrest you."

"On what charges?"

"Unlawful possession of…painfully terrible puns."

This time his grin was real. And this time he saw it hit. Like a crack of lightning had lit up the air around them, sparking in her eyes, sending shards of pink into her cheeks, and—

"Are you guys done flirt-fighting yet?" Aurora called out from the doorway. "This girl needs a nap."

Laila turned her back and began rearranging one of the shelves behind her counter. While Nico looked to the ceiling and dragged his hand over his mouth before turning to glare at his sister.

She shrugged; *What?*

"Hey, Aurora," Laila called, turning to press her hands to the counter. "If you find yourself in need of feminine energy to balance out your time with Boy Scout Fever over there, I run a number of book clubs. There's the Once Upon a Book Club for lovers of historical romances. The Plot Twisters—romantic suspense. The Booze and Bonkbusters are the biggest, and they love the really dark, hot stuff. You'd like that one, Nico."

Nico's mouth opened but no sound came out.

"The wine reference in the name," she explained, smiling angelically. Then, "They're not to be mistaken for the Blushing Boomers, who are the spice-loving over-seventies—"

"Okay," said Nico, holding up his hands in surrender as he backed away. "We're going."

Laila's smile widened, as she waggled her fingers, shooing him out of her store.

Once the door shut behind him, Nico dragged in a fresh breath, grateful for the clarifying burst of wood smoke and car exhaust. Last thing he needed was to be smelling apple crumble all day.

"Home now?" asked Aurora, sleepily clutching her shiny red bag close to her chest.

"Home now."

They made it halfway down the path before Nico had to say, "Just so you know, that, back there, was not…flirt-fighting. Yes, we differ in opinion at times, but other than that we enjoy a perfectly civil, landlord/tenant relationship."

"Sure," said Aurora through another yawn. "Whatever gets you through the night." Then, "I do like her though. She's like a post-feminist, pin-up Polly Pocket."

Nico had no clue what that meant, so he just wrapped an arm about Aurora's shoulders in order to keep her from tipping over and guided her out onto the footpath.

The sun had begun to set, bathing the town in glowing afternoon light. Soon the tiny solar lights wrapped around trees all over town would flicker to life and the temperature would drop dramatically from one minute to the next.

It was his favourite time of day, a lull between all the town things he had to do during the day and all the vineyard things he had to catch up on at night. It was a fulfilling life—busy, challenging, varied, doing work of which he could be proud.

It was enough.

The fact that it wasn't a life he had chosen, rather one that had been thrust upon him when his father had passed, had never been an issue. Until his mother had looked him in the eye, said, "I'm making changes in my life, and you can too."

Nico guided Aurora to the passenger door of the Land Rover, then waited till she was buckled in before pulling out into Main Street, to head home to Vermillion Hill.

As the road curled and wound up the rise, Nico thought back to the last time his family suffered such an upheaval—the accident that had befallen his father, forcing his mother to change from wife to carer overnight, leaving Nico, at age fifteen, with a level of responsibility he'd not been close to being equipped to handle.

Yet those years spent supporting his mother, learning the industry from the phenomenal Vermillion Hill team, helping keep Aurora on track, moving to online learning so he could matriculate early, and finishing up his business degree in record time, meant that by age nineteen, when his father—who had fought so valiantly to stay with his family—had died, Nico had been ready to protect his own, and protect this town.

Now, with his family scattering to the other side of the world, he had to decide—would staying *still* be a matter of family duty? Or was it the path of least resistance?

He made the right turn into the Vermillion Hill private driveway. And as they rode the first in a series of low-speed bumps, Aurora, half asleep, murmured, "Booze and Bonkbusters. Classic."

Nico huffed out a laugh. Then, in his mind's eye, he pictured the shape of Laila's mouth as she'd said, "They like the really dark, hot stuff".

When a glimmer of heat sparked to life in his belly, he shut it down fast.

Sparks weren't intrinsically bad. Nico was more than open to exploring a spark when out of town, or via the occasional long-distance situationship. But sparks with someone local, someone he saw every day, someone the townspeople might invest in, someone *he* might invest in... Out of the question.

Since he was old enough to know what a lasting romantic relationship meant, he'd never wished for what his parents had had. How could he when he'd seen, up close and personal, the ravages of losing it?

So inseparable had they been, when his father had become incapacitated, his mother had checked out. Not in such a way that anyone would know from the outside, but for himself, and for Aurora, who had been so young, it had felt like they'd lost both parents in one hit. Even the strongest, most wonderful people had only so much to give.

As such, Nico made the decision to focus on what he could control—his work, his family, his town. Leaving nothing left over for some fantasy future someone, who could as easily take his heart as break it into a million little pieces.

As he pulled up near the house, he paused a moment to look out over the western vineyard, the vines glowing a tawny gold as the sun set.

There were big changes coming, meaning his focus, his foundation, had to be stronger than ever. The very last thing he needed was a distraction in the shape of a hostile, bombshell bookstore owner whose own mission seemed to be to slowly drive him out of his mind.

CHAPTER TWO

LAILA WOKE AS she normally woke—curled up in a ball, sheets twisted and tucked around her like a burrito, arms and legs wrapped about a pillow she'd most definitely *not* been cuddling when she fell asleep.

She squinted through one eye as she checked the time. It was a little after seven. Not too bad considering she'd had a restless night. She always did after a certain someone visited her store, leaving her all riled up and wanting to kick something.

Lucky for her then that she ran her own business, meaning she could open and close when she wanted. Where Old Laila's bedside table would have been plastered in Post-its reading "confidence is currency" and "don't wait for doors to open—kick them down in heels," now she didn't even set a morning alarm.

Disentangling herself from her sheets, she rolled out of bed, plucked her slinky satin robe off its hook on the wall, and got ready for the day ahead.

Power suits and an eye-wateringly large expense account having gone the way of her Post-it mantras when she'd quit her career in crisis management, she flicked through her carefully curated new wardrobe, choosing a fitted yellow vintage tee she'd picked up at the fabulous Closet Reserve vintage clothing store up the street. While the curling *l* over her left breast had been embroidered for her by Beryl from the Swirl and Purl Craft Corner. Next came high-waisted, checkered pedal pushers, platform espadrilles, then finally her favourite, kick-ass, Kiss Me red lipstick.

Slipping a book into her bag—for what true reader ever left the house without one?—Laila flipped through the signs hanging on the back of her front door and chose Shhh… Characters Sleeping. Back in a Bit!, locked the door, then headed out onto Main Street.

It was a beautiful day in Vermillion. The sun was out, the birds were chirping. It was the kind of fresh you simply could not find in the city. Laila slipped on dark, cat's-eye sunglasses—it was still a smidge early to stop and chat, so the armour never went astray—and headed off in search of strong caffeine.

Small-town life was a balancing act, she had found, between being friendly enough and guarding one's privacy like a hawk. Too standoffish and it hurt sales, too open and everyone wanted to know where you were from, why you were there, and what football team you followed.

At least she had two areas where she felt she had it worked out since settling in Vermillion: her bookstore and her personal life.

Not only was her beautiful bookshop the most perfectly, gloriously, lusciously wondrous space, but from the money invested, the clean-up and redesign, to every hour worked, she'd done it all on her own. Crisis management proved daily how illusive any real control could be, but, so far, she was keeping things afloat.

As for her personal life, it was the complete and utter lack thereof of which she was most proud.

She'd wasted years dating, chasing some blissful, picture-perfect future—everything her chaotic childhood was not. She chose men who called her savvy, whip smart, claimed to find her aloofness beguiling, only for them to soon back away the moment they realised it wasn't a front. That she didn't want to be softened or moulded, unlike her fey, romantic-movie obsessed, hot mess of a single mother who pinned her hopes on Mr. Right and was always left disappointed.

Then her mum had died suddenly, and the hours every week Laila spent helping her out of some scrape or another became a great empty void. During that blur of a time she'd met Rufus. He was so savvy, so whip smart, so aloof—she'd been certain she found someone who finally understood her.

A month later he proposed and it had felt like fate. No, like relief.

She'd sold her apartment in readiness to move in with him. They'd visited a rescue shelter, as he'd always wanted a dog. Then, the week they had been meant to marry, he'd taken her out for coffee, reached for her hand, and she'd known what was coming before he'd delivered his speech: she was a cracking girl, but all locked doors and no key, so he'd decided to go another way.

Another way. Like she was a tux he'd hired before considering buying. *You look great, and feel amazing, but you're a little much for everyday.*

The casual cruelty in his words had been the last straw. Swearing off men, cold turkey, after that had felt like the smartest thing she had ever done. And she'd not regretted her decision for a single second since.

Who needed a hairy, opinionated, emotionally defunct flesh-and-blood man when book boyfriends never dumped the heroine the week of their wedding, or scratched themselves in public, or left their towels on the bathroom floor?

The fact that she pictured one particular flesh-and-blood man as she thought it, was by the by. Though she wouldn't necessarily consider Nico Rossi "hairy." He was always rolling his sleeves up, so she knew his forearms were smooth, bar long roping veins running from wrist to elbow. And he was perennially clean-cut, all granite jaw and cheekbones carved by the gods, with that ridiculous dark curl that fell down over his forehead.

Not that it mattered. While every other person in Vermillion acted as if he was so terrific cartoon mice likely darned his socks while he slept, no chiselled, broad-shouldered, weekend-firefighting, matinée-idol-handsome Gaston wannabe would ever get the best of her again.

His only saving grace was that he'd not once requested an inspection of her back storeroom. Sleeping there was not, officially, allowed under the terms of her lease. Alas, when a "pay now or else" letter, a final account for her defunct wedding that had gone missing in the move, had found her a couple of months back, paying rent as well as the shop lease had become touch and go.

Sleep in the storeroom, crisis averted. For now.

Her phone buzzed. She glanced at the screen to find a message from her best friend, Sutton Mayberry, a supercool, English indie band manager who'd dipped in and out of Vermillion all too soon.

Sutton had sent a picture of her current view—some gorgeous river, colourful old buildings lining the banks, taken through a hotel window.

Laila tucked herself against a lamppost to get out of the way of what looked to be a couple of dozen elderly tourists who'd just started piling out of a bus in front of the Vine.

LAILA: Where are you?

SUTTON: Copenhagen! Heading home tomorrow.

Home being a sun-drenched, hillside vineyard in Umbria that belonged to Nico's far more likeable cousin Dante, who

Sutton had met and fallen for in Vermillion the past spring. Considering Dante was a complete and utter grouch, that was saying something.

SUTTON: What news from Vermillion?

Other than a recent attack of navel gazing?

LAILA: Selling books, changing lives.

SUTTON: *drop mike emoji*

LAILA: You planning a visit again soon?

SUTTON: *fingers crossed emoji* You know how it is. Dante's time is determined by crops and seasons and wine stuff. Why don't you guys come here?

LAILA: We guys?

SUTTON: You and Nico.

Laila knew Sutton meant it as a catch all—Laila being her friend, Nico being Dante's cousin—and yet seeing the words "you and Nico" made her want to wave smoking white sage all over her phone.

LAILA: All that hazy sunshine and fresh air? I'm an indoor girl, remember.

SUTTON: Ha. How is our Nico? Leaving broken hearts in his wake, clueless he's done it?

As Laila had no clue what Nico did to other people's hearts, Sutton would have to ask him herself.

LAILA: Nico's sister is here.

SUTTON: Aurora!

LAILA: That's the one. They came into the shop. Seems she got all the normal genes.

SUTTON:...

While Sutton typed, Laila looked up the street to find the bus line had cleared. Moving away from the lamppost, she made her way to the pub's front door. Until Sutton's next message stopped her short.

SUTTON: Nico INTRODUCED you to HIS SISTER?

LAILA: It wasn't like THAT.

SUTTON: He is ITALIAN. It was ABSOLUTELY like that!

Laila looked skyward, and prayed to Jane Austen to send some Lizzie-type burn her way. The man had been taking his sister around town to meet with the tenants, that was all. The fact he'd said one nice thing about her shop was a momentary lapse. But she'd read enough books to know that the more she protested, the more Sutton would think it true.

So long as *she* knew there was nothing there, that was all that mattered. For while Nico Rossi, with his bite, his height, his heart-aching good looks, the way he moved with such easy confidence as if used to everything going his way, was so her type she was certain the gods had put him in her path to test her, her vow would not be vanquished.

She lifted her phone and took a photo of the broody exterior of the Vine and Stein, then sent it to Sutton.

LAILA: Heading in for a coffee.

SUTTON: Say 'hi' from me!

Laila waved to the building and said, "Hi, Vine."

SUTTON: And give Nico a big squishy hug and kiss from me when you see him next. *side eye emoji*

LAILA:...

SUTTON: *laughter emoji*

Allowing herself a brief moment to miss her friend, and her sweetly hopeless mum for good measure, Laila collected herself, popped her phone in her bag and slipped inside the pub.

With its rustic decor, matte black walls and floors, cool staff, and excellent food and drink, the Vine and Stein was the one place in Vermillion that made Laila feel as if she could be back in Newtown, Sydney, where she was from.

Meaning it had taken her some time to step foot inside the place. That and the fact that she knew it was yet another Rossi-owned establishment.

In fact, it was Sutton's and her desire to help Dante drag the pub into the twenty-first century that had forced Laila to first step out of the sanctuary she'd built for herself since moving there. Organising a banger last-minute event—the Starry Starry Singles Night—had turned the pub's fate around, and hers, by introducing Forbidden Fruits to a new, young, hungry, romance-loving crowd.

She might not attend local council meetings, or agree to call her bookstore the Love You Mer-Lot, but when it mattered, she stepped up. She just didn't strut about town expecting flowers thrown at her feet in gratitude, unlike some people.

Laila glanced around for a table, only to find the busload had snapped up the bulk of the spots. Spotting a cocktail table at the back of the room, near the currently quiet stage, she headed that way.

She sent a quick text to the barista, Kent—currently behind the coffee machine, flirting with some guy in a flannel shirt.

LAILA: tall, sweet, strong iced coffee, drizzled in caramel and topped with a mound of sweetened cream.

Ten seconds later, he checked his watch, clocked her message, looked up to find her pointing to the back of the room. He gave her a thumbs up.

Okay, she thought. *It's going to be a good day.* Only to come to a screeching halt when she saw Constable Goodboy himself sitting at a table right in front of her.

Nico had his back to the double-storey street-side window. Sunlight poured over his broad shoulders, making art of the natural creases in his blue button-down as it attempted to contain his bulk. A neat silver laptop was open on the table, a pile of papers, notebook, and pencil at its side, and he wore a pair of dark-rimmed glasses she'd never seen before.

But it was the dark shadow covering his jaw that kept Laila's feet stuck to the floor.

The man was always pristinely clean-shaven. *Always.* Yet that morning, brutally dark stubble lined the edge of his hard jaw, created deep shadows in his cheeks, and edged the top of his strong throat.

He was a good-looking guy. That was not up for debate. But it was a preppy kind of handsome—a little too tall, a mite too broad, with thick, dark, wavy hair and an impossibly perfect forehead curl. Add gentle, dark brown eyes that creased at the edges, and a smile that glinted in the sun, and he might as well have been made by AI.

But stubbled, and broody, and frowny, his face in shadow, one side of his collar bent and a little askew, one big blunt-fingered hand lightly holding a pitch-black espresso, the other running across his mouth, back and forth, as he concentrated hard on what he was reading, the man had her knees turning to water.

"Laila!" said Aurora, appearing out of the ether beside her, espresso in hand.

Laila flinched so hard she pulled a muscle in her neck.

Nico flinched harder. Hard enough his coffee sloshed over the side of his glass. When he looked up, Laila was caught in a beam of laser focus, and it cut through her like a blade made of smoke, leaving a sweep of heat in its wake.

"You spilled some," Laila blurted.

And when he spied the drops of coffee on what looked like a prospectus of glossy images of hillsides covered in grape-vines, he swore in gruff Italian before mopping them up.

"Are you joining us?" asked Aurora.

"Me? No! I'm sitting over—" Laila looked up to find her spot had been taken by a pair of young women who were already scrolling on their phones.

"Come," said Aurora, gently hustling her forward. "Sit."

Wishing she could come up with a better excuse than "I don't want to," Laila took the seat Aurora pulled out for her. Only for her toes to bump against something hard. Nico's shoe, she realised when it abruptly pulled away.

"Can I order you a drink?" Aurora asked, as she settled herself in her own seat, between theirs.

"Thanks. But I've got one coming."

Nico, tossing his clean-up napkin into a saucer, lifted his gaze back to her. His eyebrow flickered, the slightest of movements. A silent, private query. And she realised she'd been staring.

Laila's pulse kicked up a notch, but years of practice meant she held herself together ably. She tilted her head slightly, putting the same question back on him.

A smile started in his eyes, glints of molten chocolate within the previously hard brown, then he laughed; a low soft chuff that skittered down her arms and settled in her belly.

"Here we go, gorgeous," said a voice before Laila's drink, condensation already beading on the sides of the takeaway cup, landed on the table before her.

Taking the opportunity to break eye contact, she looked up at Kent. "You're a gem, thanks."

Kent gave her a quick wink. He looked to Nico as if he would happily eat him up with a spoon, sighed, then headed back to the front of house.

"Now, Laila," said Nico, moving on from having been devoured with a glance as if such things happened to him every day. "What on earth is in that drink?"

"Iced coffee with a few fun additions," she said, far preferring to face Nico the Virtuous than the wholly unsettling Nico the Slightly Rumpled. "You should try one. Looks like you could do with a little pick-me-up this morning."

She motioned to his collar, his stubble, the mussed hair.

Nico's hard gaze stuttered before a glint of light, of fight, sparked in his eyes. Then, as if he could read her mind, he lifted a hand to fix his collar, and a quick swipe of fingers through his hair settled it back into a perfect coif, forehead curl and all. As for the stubble, there was no amending that.

"Wow," Aurora added, the word drawn out and suggestive.

And Laila snapped out of what felt like a trance, glancing up, away, anywhere but at Nico, while wondering how long she had to sit there before she could excuse herself.

"Anyway," said Aurora, "Laila, tell me what brought you to this darling little corner of civilisation? You don't scream small-town to me."

"Don't I?"

"Are you kidding? You're way too cool for a place like this." While she said "place," Aurora motioned to Nico, who shook his head, nostrils flaring, as if in silent communication with his sister.

Then, less silently, he added, "I don't think Laila came here this morning for an interrogation."

"Oh shoosh, Niccolo. It's called conversation. How did you get into books, why romance only? I want to know everything."

Laila opened her mouth, then let it shut.

She liked Aurora. She especially liked how easily Aurora riled her older brother. But she was not about to tell the tale of how she'd burned down her old life, spent her savings paying all the nonrefundable wedding bills herself so she wasn't beholden to her ex, left her furniture on the verge with a sign for anyone to take whatever they wanted, got in her car, and drove.

Or how by the time she'd reached Vermillion she'd been driving for two weeks; through coastal towns and outback dots on a map, places well-known and some a million miles from anywhere. Until she'd driven beneath the arched sign leading into Vermillion, and something magical had come over her.

She still remembered slowing to take in Main Street with its avenue of gargantuan elms, the golden sunshine bouncing off clean shop windows, the glitter of soft pollen floating on the air. It was so wholesome and sweet, so contrary to the grief and rage and exhaustion that had kept her going for so long, something in her had broken free.

So much so, she'd had to pull over, nudging her car into an angled spot so she could stop her heart from trying to beat its way through her ribs.

When she finally calmed down, she'd looked up to see an overgrown garden outside a small run-down cottage; a For Lease sign out front.

"Aurora," Nico chided, less gently this time. And Laila could feel his gaze on the side of her face, along with his unfurling curiosity.

Aurora sat up. "What? Sorry. I didn't mean to pry."

"Yes, you did," Nico said. "Laila might not want to spill her life story so early on a Wednesday morning."

Laila, grateful for the moment to collect herself, said, "Tuesdays are the day for spilling, so you just missed it." With that she lifted her iced coffee and took a deep suck on the straw. Full stop.

"And," Nico added, "since Main Street opening hours start—" he checked his watch "—two minutes from now, Laila has to head off."

Laila choked on her drink, the cold burning her throat. When Nico leaned forward, his hand moving to cover hers, she whipped it back into the safety of her lap a half second before touchdown.

"I'm fine," she gritted out. Then, glancing at her bare wrist, she said, "While a rarity, your brother is right—I'd best be off."

When Laila pushed back her chair, Nico went to stand. She held out a hand, shaking her head just once. With a flicker of a furrow between his brows, he did as he was asked.

Then Aurora said, "Ooh," before pulling *Welcome to Temptation* from her bag.

"You started it?" Laila asked, narrowing in on the one thing that always gave her her land legs back.

"It kept me up half the night! The banter in that first meet? *Sigh*. And chapter five, am I right? And on that I need more coffee."

Aurora stood, held out a fist for Laila to bump, then she was off, slipping between tables, her long brown ponytail swinging, as in true Rossi fashion she looked like she had not a care in the world.

Laila knew she should leave too, but the need to thank Nico for helping her avoid having to tell her story—just so she didn't owe him in any way, of course—had her turning to find him watching her.

"What happens in chapter five?"

"Hmm?"

"Chapter five," he repeated, "of the book you gave to my little sister."

Laila couldn't remember the exact details, but had a good feeling it had to be the jetty scene. "Do you really want to know?"

He held his big hands up in surrender. "I take it back. On this, ignorance is very much bliss."

When he sat back this time, he looked solid, self-assured, perfectly put together, as if Mussed Nico had never existed. And with that came a wave of vexation.

"You know what?" Laila said pointing her finger right at him. "Maybe that's the problem."

"What's the problem?"

She waved a hand in front of his face. "*This*. This dedicated obliviousness so many men have as to what makes a woman tick."

Nico stilled. Then blinked. Obliviousness personified.

"Why is it you've never bought a book in my store, Nico? Despite the hundreds of times you've found some excuse to come in. And why is it the only other men who come in are dragged there by their significant others?"

While it had started as a rant, a light bulb turned on in Laila's mind. While you could take the crisis manager out of the big city, you couldn't take the crisis manager out of Laila. Her mother's daughter, she'd been doing the job since the day she could talk.

Step one: identify crisis. *Men don't read romance.*

Step two: create plan and mobilise team.

"That's it! I need to be getting more books into the hands of men. Not only because it's a huge untapped market, and I like pretty shoes and need to make a living to be able to afford them, but men could absolutely learn a thing or two about what women really want, if only they read more romance novels."

Heck, if any of her exes had taken the time to read a book *at all*, they might have had more empathy. Might have realised that what they saw as aloofness was a result of watching her mother go through rejection again, and again, and again, which made Laila constantly wait for the other shoe to drop. Then they might have even asked her why. Then they might have treated her less like something entertaining to bring to parties, and more like a person of contradictions and longings—flawed and worthy of patience. And love.

Then Nico, without a lick of irony edging his deep, mellifluous voice, said, "I've never had any complaints."

Laila came back into her body with a thwack. "You want to know *why*?"

As if sensing he was about to become an insect pinned to a board, Nico shifted on his seat. But he did not back down. "I assume it's because they've had nothing to complain about. You have a different theory? Enlighten me."

Laila itched to say that it was because the women he'd been with had been conditioned to tell him he was a good boy, as his emotions were underdeveloped. So if he didn't feel constantly appreciated, he would fall apart. But when she realised the words were coming to her in her mother's reassuring voice, like pearls of wisdom, she stopped.

After a few loaded beats, Nico leaned forward, rested his forearm on the table, the hint of a vein roping up the inside as his fingers flexed and unflexed. "Then tell me this, Laila—what is it that *you* really want?"

The way he said her name, that latent Italian accent making it dance on his tongue, had her longing for someone who lit up when she walked in the room. For a place she felt safe and secure; where she belonged. All of which had been offered to her on a lure, then whipped away, time and again till she'd not been able to take it anymore.

"What I want is to have my coffee and get to work." With that Laila grabbed her takeaway iced coffee, spun on her heel, and walked away.

"Laila—"

She waved a hand over her shoulder.

"Laila!" he called. "Come on."

Letting out a hard breath, she stopped, turned, and found him standing a few feet away, having pushed back his chair till it tilted against the window, and followed her.

His right eye scrunched as he said, "I'm sorry. It's been a morning and I took it out on you. Which is wholly unfair. If you have something to say, I'm here to hear it."

Laila's heart thumped dramatically against her ribs. Was the universe kidding when it made this guy?

"You know what?" She rustled through her bag till she came up with the goods. "Here."

She held out the book she'd slipped into her bag before she'd left the store. When he looked at it as if it might bite him, she waggled it at him, till he moved in close enough to take it from her hand.

He turned it over, his eyebrows flickering ever so slightly as he took it in.

Steeling Harts was written across the top in solid black military-style font, the author's name—DeVante Gray—in thin elegant white at the bottom. Pink-and-blue clouds, hints of planets, a fairy-tale castle, and glittering starfall made up the backdrop, as the hero and heroine, Tyrrano the battle robot and Elvie the space farmer's daughter, looked potently past the reader's shoulder.

"What is this?" Nico asked, a hint of *this isn't quite what I meant when I said I'd listen* in his tone.

"It's a book, dummy."

"I know it's a book, but—"

"I take that back. It's not just a book. It's a wonder, a delight, an adventure, a love story, a life-changing experience. And for our purposes today, consider it a how-to manual."

His gaze slid back to hers, held it for a long, intrigued moment, before he said, "Well then," and tucked the book under his arm.

And Laila wondered what the hell she'd been thinking. Had she really just given this man insight into the soft, vulnerable places inside that she'd never shown anyone? Ever. And told him so?

"Okay," she said, glancing at the book to find the only way to get it back would be to tackle him. All she could do was hope it all went over his head, if he ever even looked at it at all. "Well. *Ciao*. I guess."

"*Ciao*, Laila," said Nico, a smile in his eyes.

Once outside, Laila tossed the remains of her iced coffee in the nearest bin and made a beeline for Forbidden Fruits Story Emporium—her safe island from any storm.

Some kids wanted to be astronauts when they grew up, some wanted to be ballerinas. Laila's dream job had been opening a bookstore. But, in the chaos of her childhood, it had always felt as far away as the moon.

Then, for all that her mother had lived on the breadline her entire life, she'd somehow kept up a small life insurance policy, of which Laila had been sole beneficiary. And the moment she'd seen that shabby little building she'd known what she had to do.

Her love of love stories was one thing she'd inherited from her mother that she'd never wanted to give back. Opening a romance-only bookstore had felt like an ode. It had also felt like a screw-you to those who'd made her certain she'd never have a love story of her own.

Then, by some strange twist of fate, it turned out she was really good at it. She'd worked hard to build up a plethora of regulars, her social media accounts were constantly ticking up, her eye for new break-out books was spot-on, and her book clubs were flourishing. Add her ability to quickly pull together a book-release event that always sold out, *and* her ability to flout her lease to save on overheads, and she was doing okay.

If having to deal with a hunky, chisel-jawed, chocolate-eyed man who was progressive enough to apologise was the price she had to pay, then that was the way it had to be.

Determined that by the time her first customer walked in the door she'd have shaken off the tingles in the backs of her knees, the curls in her stomach, the thorny brambles in the back of her mind, Laila fixed her lipstick and flipped the front door sign to Come On In: Your Meet-Cute Awaits!

CHAPTER THREE

LAILA TACKED THE final title card to a book on one of the new displays she'd set up at the front of the shop. It read, Warning: Explosive Chemistry Inside. The one next to it said, You Could Lift Weights, or You Could Lift Her Expectations. She nudged the A4 framed sign entitled Real Men Read Romance so that it faced the front door, then stepped back and admired her handywork.

"Looks great," said Aurora, who had come into the store pretty much every day since her first visit.

"You think it will work?" Laila asked.

"Meh. But good for you for trying." With that, Aurora lay on the velvet couch beneath the window to read *Red, White, and Royal Blue*.

It seemed that hanging out for no particular reason was a Rossi family trait. Though while any time Nico stepped foot over the threshold Laila felt scratchy for hours afterwards, Aurora's company was a breeze. With Sutton off overseas, Laila had missed the constancy of having a proper girlfriend to just hang with.

Nico, on the other hand, obviously meant it when he'd told her to look to Aurora for any landlord issues, as since the whole "what is it you want, Laila?" conversation, he'd not darkened her door once. Every now and then she caught herself staring at her front door, wondering if he'd fallen down a well, or been abducted by aliens—but only in the way she hoped any person would not befall such ignominies.

"Missing your adventures while stuck here in Smalltownsville?" Laila asked, as she piled up the books that had not fit on the display tables and went to put them back on the main shelves.

Aurora flicked the page. "A little. But it's nice to all be together again. We have a little tricksy family stuff to sort out at home, then I'll be off and away again."

Laila paused at the way she'd said "family stuff." For, to be honest, it had never occurred to her that Nico could have family problems. Or problems, period.

"Though not back to Rome, I don't think," Aurora went on, frowning a little. "Though don't tell Nico. He'll just worry."

"Why would he worry?" Laila asked, as she slipped an India Holton book back with the rest.

"It's what he lives for—brooding over me, our mother, his grapes, the Vermillion Hill staff, this whole dizzy town. Now I hear he's joined up as a volunteer firefighter. It's a miracle he doesn't spend his nights rocking in a corner muttering incoherently, the amount he has on his plate." Aurora sighed, then, perking up, added, "That's why I'm so obsessed with the whole love/hate thing you two have going on."

Laila coughed on her next breath in.

"It's so good to see him loosening up," Aurora went on regardless. "He was such a rascal when we were kids, running around in his Superman cape, getting up to mischief. Then after what happened to our dad the Superman thing kind of became real, and he became so impossibly focused on protecting us, I thought his fun side might have been lost for good. But with you he gets to be kind of…playful, you know? Messy."

Laila did not know any such thing. In fact, it seemed there was a lot she was unaware of where Nico was concerned.

Superman cape? Something happening to his dad? Laila was certain none of this was new news, the way Aurora was blurting it all out as if it was public record, making her feel slightly bad about how little she actually knew about the guy.

That said, she was hardly one to give up much about her own situation either. And it wasn't as if they were friendly. They were friends of friends—Sutton and Dante—with the vibe of nemeses. Neme-friends?

"Enough about Nico, let's swing back to you, shall we? Ready to tell me what brought you to Vermillion?" Aurora asked.

Laila narrowed her eyes, then said, "Okay fine," but only because she was ready this time. Step three in a crisis—control damage.

"I worked in crisis management, helping politicians, corporate interests, celebrities, and the like get themselves out of a pickle. I survived on a cortisol high for ten years, and the only thing that gave me any respite was coming home, running a bath, and disappearing into the pages of a romance novel. So, when I had the chance to change things up, I took it."

All of which was true, while as holey as cheap Swiss cheese.

"Oh, I love that," said Aurora. "Though I was hoping for a little more drama."

"Drama is for dabblers," Laila posited. "This shop, for me, is as serious as it gets."

Then the bell over the door tinkled, and the two of them looked up to find a pair of young women, male friends in tow, their expressions quickly turning from delighted to dazed.

Aurora rolled off the couch gracefully then went to chat to the women, and show them the book she was reading, leaving Laila to take on the men.

Just a friendly, neighbourhood pleasure pusher, at their service.

* * *

Nico's nailbeds were caked with soil and leaf matter, his shirt stuck to his skin with sweat, and he felt the kind of bone-deep exhaustion that came from days of honest outdoor labour.

Vermillion Hill's vines were bare, bar crooked tendrils holding onto a smattering of shrivelled grape skins. Any remaining leaves would soon drop, leaving a carpet of vibrant ochre, and the ghostly scent of fermenting juice lingered in the air. For after three long months, the harvest was finally complete.

Alongside Vittoria, his esteemed head viticulturist, Nico and the vineyard crew had walked or driven the entire estate over the past week, discussing each varietal's harvest results, and agreeing to plans for the coming winter.

Leaving Nico's passion project—a hybrid cross between Sangiovese from his cousin Dante's estate in Umbria, and the century-old Grenache that had come with Vermillion Hill when his family had moved there twenty-odd years before—for last.

"E il baciami?" Nico asked.

Vittoria's gaze roved resolutely over the elevated block. "Vines look woody, a little tired, but in robust health. Soil is in perfect condition. And the crop…" Vittoria kissed the tips of her fingers. *"Gloriosa."*

Nico let go a hearty breath, then laughed, relieved, as he ran a hand over the back of his neck. *"Grazie.* Well done, everyone. Now go, enjoy your time off."

The crew patted one another on the back as they made their way to the dusty four-wheel drives awaiting them at the end of the rows of vines. After a final quick chat with Vittoria, Nico sent her off too, a well-deserved holiday ahead for them all.

But not for him.

The Vermillion Hill yield was now in the hands of the

other half of the business—the winemakers. Nico would meet with them the next day. Then it would be time to check in with his tenants, again, to follow up on the plumbing issue at Tendrils Hair and the faulty back door hinge at the Bubbly Crust Pizzeria, then the cycle would repeat.

It was just the way he loved it. Meaning his mother's assertion that he should use her departure as an opportunity to consider his own future was unwarranted.

Then there was his *baciami*. Of all his obligations, it was the one thing that was his alone. He'd done the research, he'd curated the original base stock, he'd hand pollinated the first crop, personally winnowing the vines down until they consistently produced a beautifully balanced grape, smooth and full-bodied, with dark, aromatic undertones. And one day, from it would come a wine of pure epicurean decadence. A drink that made people hum.

He'd been working on it nearing a decade now, and it was finally starting to show results. Both there, and on the Serenità estate in Napa Valley—his favourite of the Rossi vineyards, bar Vermillion Hill. For he'd convinced the Vitali family, who ran the Californian operation, to lease him a plot on which to test how his *baciami* would grow elsewhere.

When his father had passed, and the extent of his mother's ambivalence towards running the vineyard alone had become clear, the Vitalis had been the ones to encourage him to finish his business degree and had taken his calls anytime he needed advice. He'd visited Claudio and Rosetta twice a year since planting his crop on their land, until their daughter, Savannah, had taken a rather effusive shine to him. And he'd not been back since.

He just needed to figure out how to let Savannah down without causing a breach in the crucial relationship he had with the Vitalis, or getting his mother involved. For they would all no doubt be overjoyed at the prospect of joining their two families, neither understanding why it would always be a blanket no.

The fact that his mother was the reason *why* could never come out.

He had witnessed her pain after his father's injury then death firsthand—how ravaged she had been, how enraged, enough that she'd pulled away from her own children, making them feel forgotten for years, all while they were also grieving the loss of their father.

Nico ran a hand down his face. Things were much better now. But it was still so close to the bone the thought of ever being in that position again was untenable.

It was why he had long since kept his personal life parallel to the rest, never within. Separate, uncluttered, uncomplicated. No locals, no long-term. No one who gave him even a glimmer that he might one day want more.

The moment he thought of glimmers, only one woman came to mind, and if she had a single clue that he thought of her that way she'd laugh him out of town.

It had been days since he'd visited Laila's store—the longest he'd gone since she'd moved to Vermillion. After the new-found intensity of their last couple of run-ins, space had felt judicious. Niggling was fine; that he could handle. But when he'd asked her what she wanted, and her gaze had dropped to his mouth, her teeth clamping down on her full bottom lip, he'd felt parts of himself begin to unravel.

Then there was the book. The self-professed "how-to manual" that currently lived on his bedside table. Unopened as yet. Even if acting on them was not in his future, knowing Laila's desires might eat a man alive.

When the *Superman* theme chimed from his phone, Aurora clearly having changed his ringtone, he saw the number was the local emergency services.

"Rossi," he said, quietly grateful something had snapped

his thoughts back to reality as he jogged towards his Land Rover.

"Hey, Nico. Smoke spotted coming from the Moss barn."

He recognised the voice as Jane, a local dispatcher. "Anyone home, Jane?" he asked, the car already bumping and jostling up the rutted path.

"No one answering at the house." Didn't mean there was no one in the barn proper.

The Moss farm was about five kilometres up the road, deeper into the Barossa than the nearest firehouse, which was twenty odd minutes in the other direction.

"I'm first responder?"

"If you're able."

A quick glance over his shoulder showed his pack was in the back seat—fire-retardant uniform, helmet, water, first aid ready to go.

"I'm on it," he said.

Adrenaline kicking in, sweeping away all other concerns, Nico went to the rescue.

Laila grabbed snacks and cups from her storeroom/bedroom, readying for that month's session of the Main Character Energy Book Club, then with a quick glance to make sure no one could see into the room, she ducked back into the store proper and locked the door behind her.

She glanced to the corkboard covered in pink Post-its to double-check that month's books—the RomCommers had picked an Amy Andrews delight, the Wild at Hearters a Clare Connelly cowboy romance, and the Booze and Bonkbusters crowd were reading *Riders* by Jilly Cooper. The Main Character crew preferred to go with authors over single titles and that month was all about the fabulous Talia Hibbert.

At the front of the store a dozen young women were curled up on the large couch, or stools she'd brought out of storage, with throw blankets and cups of hot tea, taking photos of their book piles, or taking selfies together.

Laila's heart—cold, hard, embittered lump of meat that it was—gave a little flutter at the sight of them. Not only because the Forbidden Fruits socials would light up that night with no work from her, but because how could some guy compete with all that beautiful, happy, pleasure-positive, feminine energy?

As if reading her mind, Kelly, a bumptious delight of a human whose family owned a dairy farm on the edge of town, said, "Laila, when are you putting on another one of your singles' nights?"

"Sorry," Laila said, not sorry at all. She nudged a socked foot off the table so she could put down the snacks. "It was a one-off, I'm afraid."

"Awww," came the chorus of sad voices. Apparently, she was alone in her thoughts regarding date night versus book club nights.

"But I want one of these," Kelly lamented, pointing at the chisel-jawed cartoon character on the cover of *Take a Hint, Dani Brown*.

"He's all yours," Laila assured her, flicking at the annotated tabs poking out from between the pages.

"Do you think it's possible?" asked Jane, who worked in her parents' florist as well as manning the local emergency dispatch phones a few days a month. She nodded to the book. "That kind of love?"

Hannah—black hair, black clothes, several nose rings around each nostril, worked in the local barbershop—said, "Absolutely. These stories don't come out of nowhere."

A dozen heads nodded in enthusiastic agreement.

Jane sighed. "Imagine—a book boyfriend come to life."

"Whoa," said Kelly. "Is it possible we just manifested the real thing?"

A ripple went through the group as they climbed over one another to look out the front window, straining to see what had Kelly up on her knees on the couch.

"What on earth…?" Laila muttered, before spotting Nico Rossi standing outside her front gate, positioned just so beneath the decorative streetlamp, talking to Meryl and Beryl from the craft store, while decked in his firefighter uniform.

Despite the jokes she made at his expense, no man should look as good as Nico did in a tight black T-shirt, blocky yellow high-waisted pants with fluorescent chevron patterns at the knees. And now, after Aurora's revelations, Laila experienced an uncomfortable moment—seeing the uniform, and the man in it, in a different light.

"Oh, my goodness, that's Niccolo Rossi!" cried Jane. "He's a first responder. I had to call him a few hours ago about a fire at the Moss farm."

"Shut up!" Kelly cried, smacking poor Jane on the arm.

Blushing, but clearly enjoying having an audience, Jane leaned in. "My mum calls him the town catch."

"How is it he's never been caught?" asked Kelly. Her face dropped. "Could he be gay?"

Laila snorted, then hid it behind a cough. They might be combative as hell, but she'd seen the way Nico Rossi looked at her. Felt it, like warm honey tracing her body. The man was definitely interested in women.

"Oh, he's totally straight," Hannah resolved, completely confident in her appraisal. "My cousin went to school with him. He was school captain, or soccer captain, or something, and he was a total lad."

The crowd were in rapt awe. Laila, trying not to listen, but unable to help herself, thought Meryl and Beryl and their crew had the pulse of the town, but this lot? They had the goods.

"And now?" asked Kelly, eyes wide.

"Classic confirmed bachelor."

They all nodded in understanding, having read about a *lot* of those.

"But *never* locals anymore. Not since school. I overheard my mum once joke that there was a force field around the town, and anyone trapped inside was doomed where he's concerned."

As one the group turned to look forlornly out the window, right as Nico lifted a hand to scratch at his opposite bicep, fingers pushing the fabric up to his shoulder, showing off mounds of muscle.

Someone giggled, someone squealed, and as Laila winced at the noise, she realised it must have carried as Nico looked up, right at the window. Right. At. Her.

She held her breath, hoping against hope the light outside was brighter than inside, but then a smile tugged at the corners of his mouth before he lifted his hand in a wave.

As one, the book clubbers fell over till they ended up in a decadent sprawl of cushions and twisted blankets, arms flung over foreheads, legs askew.

Leaving Laila in the window, alone.

Nico said something to Meryl and Beryl, who turned to walk back in the direction of their store, then he took a step as if he might come up the path.

"No, no, *no, no, no!*" Laila muttered under her breath. Then, things moving too fast for her to formulate a crisis plan, she had to run on instinct.

She turned to the book clubbers, pointed at each one, said, "Stay. The lot of you." Then bursting out her front door she met Nico halfway.

"Hey," he said, glancing from Laila to the window.

"Ignore them," she said, clicking a hand in front of his face.

He brought his gaze back to hers and she considered taking her last command back. For with the light from the streetlamp creating a glow around his big shoulders in that tight T-shirt, he looked huge. Didn't help that she'd slipped out of her usual high heels and into slippers with bunnies on the toes the moment the store had closed.

"What's going on in there?" he asked, his voice a little rough and a whole lot tired.

"Book club," she said, unable to tamp down a funny little flicker of concern as she wondered where he'd been, what he'd seen. "And they're in a mood."

Laila glanced over her shoulder, and a dozen faces ducked back out of view. When she looked to Nico, his dark gaze was still on her.

"So, you didn't want me?" he asked, low voice intimate in the quiet of night.

"I didn't want you," she managed to say through a sudden clog in her throat.

He nodded, a slight wince flashing over his face. And now that her eyes were more used to the light outside, she noticed the smudges under his eyes, an abrasion on his neck, the slightest air of smoke wafting off his skin.

"Hey," she said, taking a small step closer, her fingers reaching for a suspender before curling back into her palm. "What happened?"

"Barn fire at the Moss farm. Then a lost kid on Stringybark Loop Hike. It's been a night."

She swallowed, her gaze roving over his features, trying to ascertain if he was hurt elsewhere, or just tired. "Everyone okay?"

"All fine and accounted for." The corner of his mouth lifted, more slowly than normal, which only made her feel it more. "Careful though. You're starting to sound as if you might care."

At that, Laila's heart lifted and fell with a mighty thud.

"Go home and shower, Sergeant Smoke Show," she said,

backing up a step, then another. "Before the wind changes and that smugness sticks."

"Sergeant *Smoke Show*, is it?" he lobbed back. "That's a new one."

"Careful," she managed through the buzzing in her head, "you're starting to sound as if you care."

Nico's grin was sudden, the laughter that came on the back of it so loose and low it felt like a warm, rough hand moving slowly down her spine.

Figuring it was best not to say any more words, lest she get herself in real trouble. she lifted a hand to shoo him away.

Nico gave her one last smile—the kind that promised he'd see her again soon—before he turned and ambled down her front path.

Then, at her gate, he spun on the spot, lifted a hand before bending into a deep bow for the crowd. A cheer rose up from behind Laila's front window, then Nico sauntered down the road.

Laila needed a beat to collect herself. Only once she was sure her cheeks were not pink with heat, did she jog back up the steps and into the shop, where the Main Character Energy Book Club was in hysterics.

"That was amazing," said Jane, her face the picture of awe.

"Why didn't you invite him in?" Kelly implored.

Laila looked to her. "You'd have eaten him alive."

"Can you imagine?" said Kelly swooning atop a half-dozen legs.

Watching them coo and titter, all hope and heart eyes, Laila wondered if she ought to just give them the tough love her mother had never given her.

Her mother's entire existence had been built around the certainty that one day her prince would come, which had most definitely spilled into Laila's subconscious, adding impossible pressure to every relationship she'd ever had.

While Laila had loved her mum, difficult as growing up in such chaos had been, she didn't want to *be* her. And didn't want to see these young women make those same mistakes. Yet those faces—so sweet, so dreamy. She couldn't do it. Couldn't kill their hope.

Instead, Laila took the book from Kelly's hand, and said, "Book boyfriends are so much easier, right? They don't leave their undies on the bedroom floor, or make weird noises when they shift on the couch."

"Or leave the toilet seat up," Jane added. "My brother does that all the time."

Once they had moved on to all the reasons why real men might yet have some evolving to do when compared to book boyfriends, then finally moved on to talking about the books, Laila slumped back against her counter in relief.

CHAPTER FOUR

BREATHING IN THE scents of basil, oregano, and chilli curling up from the stovetop, Nico added a splash of wine to his pasta sauce, wincing only slightly as his shoulder twinged again. Whether it was wrenching open the Moss's barn door, or lifting the kid from the gully into which he'd fallen, he'd pulled something. Add the day on the estate, and he felt as if he'd been sandbagged.

If someone asked him at that exact second if he might consider selling up, and moving to live on a beach in Bermuda, he'd have said…not a chance. For the vineyard, the town, the people—it was what *he'd* signed up for.

What he hadn't signed up for was Laila Vale jogging down the steps of her shop in bunny slippers, hair tied up in a small bouncy ponytail atop her head, lips bare of her usual Kiss Me red. Remembering how hulking and rough he'd felt compared to all that clamorous femininity had him breathing out long and hard.

Or the moment when she'd stepped towards him, eyes flickering with concern, hand reaching for him before she'd remembered herself. Remembered that they were combatants, not… What? Acquaintances? Familiars? Something entirely new? Trying to pin down who he was to Laila, who Laila was to him, was not a good idea. But, *dammit*, in that moment he'd wanted to. As if naming it would make it easier to put into a box that he could pack away someplace quiet.

He gripped the edge of the counter.

With Meryl and Beryl on the spot, he probably should have just waved and walked away. But after the day he'd had, seeing her face in the window had released something inside of him. Because when Laila was near, the weight of his responsibilities had no choice but to take second chair.

When the pasta sauce began to spit and hiss Nico turned it down to a simmer and brought his thoughts back to where his responsibilities did lie. Despite literally dragging his feet he was so exhausted, he'd cooked the sauce from fresh the moment he'd cleaned up. Otherwise, he could not be sure his mother would have eaten at all.

She'd always been lean, but he'd not noted how frail she had become till Aurora had quietly pointed it out. She'd tried to take the edge off his shame at not noticing by insisting it was the time she'd spent away that made it obvious. But of all the spinning plates he could have let fall, that was the most important one of all.

It was why when his mother had been so vehement in her decision to go back to Italy, he had not demurred. If that was what she felt she needed in order to be happy, then he would make it happen.

As for him? He was content, wasn't he? In such a privileged position, doing work he loved, surrounded by people who looked up to him, there was no reason not to be. And yet a constant, uncomfortable thrum had taken up residence in his chest—like the rumble of an oncoming storm.

Wooden spoon at his lips, he stopped, ears pricked, when he heard voices coming from the patio beyond.

Specifically, his mother saying, *"Chi è di nuovo questa 'Laila'?"*

"Laila?" Aurora answered. "She owns the local bookstore. Where the Vine and Dime used to be?"

"Ah. *Si.*"

A teasing note entered Aurora's voice as she added, "Why do you ask?"

"The local Country Women's Association visited me today and several of them are in a book club this Laila runs," Celia went on. "The Blushing Bloomers?"

"Boomers," Aurora corrected.

"*Si*. They raved about a book she had recommended to them. Something with dragons and...*molta sensualità*."

Much sensuality? Nico translated, then dropped the spoon in the sauce before heading to the patio.

A bottle of Vermillion Hill Red Velvet had been decanted at some point, and glasses showed signs that they were a couple of drinks in. While Aurora was laughing so hard she couldn't catch her breath, it was the smile on his mother's face, the first of that kind Nico had seen in some time, that stopped him in his tracks.

Spotting him, Celia Rossi held out a hand, drawing him to the outdoor couch on which they sat.

Aurora looked to Nico. "So, it wasn't your beloved first-born who made mention of Ms. Vale?"

When his mother's eyebrow rose eloquently, Nico said, "Surely, at some point. Several months back she was instrumental in the turnaround at the Vine and Stein."

"She's remarkable," Aurora extrapolated. "Used to have a hotshot career in crisis management then one day just decided to change things up."

Did Nico know that about her? Searching his memory banks, he was certain he did not. What else did he not know? A lot, he realised, as once again he felt that ominous thrum of thunder.

Aurora went on. "She's also the only person in town who doesn't think your son walks on water. You should see them bicker. It's priceless!"

"Niccolo," his mother chastised. "One does not *bicker* with one's tenants. One tends them."

Nico steadied himself at the edge in his mother's voice. For she was quoting his father, word for word. Gone near twelve years now and *still* she mourned. Witnessing her pain was tough, yet fortifying. Things might be changing around here but he could, and should, be the one to stay the course.

For the town, for the business, and personally.

While Nico had been busy fortifying, he'd forgotten how Aurora had her own agenda.

"Maybe *bickering* was the wrong word," said his sister batting her lashes his way. "It was more like watching them circle one another—Niccolo, all doting chocolate lab energy, Laila staring him down like a well-groomed house cat."

He glared at Aurora. *Seriously?* Did she not remember how their mother could be? She was constantly assuring them that one day they would find a love as great as hers. As if that was their wish, not Nico's worst nightmare.

"Is that so," said his mother, a twinkle back in her eye. "Is it possible my son is no longer trawling the outer edges of the universe for love?"

While Aurora let out an "Oh burn!" Nico choked on his next breath.

His mother lifted her shoulder in an insouciant shrug. "Do you think I do not know how you live your life, *caro ragazzo*? Do you think the entire town has not kept me up to date on that score? Let me see, there was the Spanish flight attendant you would see on occasion."

"The sales rep from Adelaide," Aurora added. "We were all a little saddened when we heard you'd let her go."

"*Si*," his mother agreed. "Though I had high hopes for the vet from Port Augusta. Italian mother, correct? Meryl showed me a photograph someone had taken when you were spotted having coffee together. In public, no less," she whispered behind her hand.

Nico held up both hands, beseeching his mother to stop.

"*Uffa, va bene,*" she said. "Though I could have left this place, followed my Aldo home, a long time ago, if only you had..." Her voice drifted off.

Nico's blood ran cool. "If only I had what?"

"Had you fallen in love," Celia said, imploringly. "Had you married, and started a family of your own."

Somewhere nearby a tree scraped against the roofline, a breeze whistled through the eaves.

Celia gentled her expression and reached for Nico's hands. "Why will you not allow someone take a hold of that *enorme bello* heart of yours? Did your father and I not show you how wonderful love can be?"

Nico didn't move. Didn't even breathe as he fought the urge to say something he could not take back. Then he felt Aurora's knee knocking against his in support.

Counting backwards in Italian from ten, he schooled his expression, and squeezed his mother's hand. It was cool, skin and bone, yet the life force flowing through it was strong.

"You've said your piece," he said. "And I appreciate it. Now how about we focus on Aurora's love life instead?"

Aurora pinched him in the side as she whispered "*traitor,*" in his ear.

Celia waved her spare hand through the air. "Aurora will be fine. She is young, full of life. One day she will look up and bam. That will be that."

Aurora stopped her fussing and stilled.

"As for you, my dear boy," Celia said, taking Nico's face between her hands. "Promise me you won't always be so guarded. Promise me, when it comes to love, one day you will be selfish and demanding and welcome it with all that you are."

Of all the hits he'd taken that day, that one bruised most of all. For it was something he just could not give her. The potential price was just too big to pay.

Instead, he kissed her on the cheek, and said, "The sauce will be ready. Eat outside?"

Celia frowned, then nodded, allowing Aurora to help her to her feet.

Nico watched them amble over to the large outdoor table. Chosen by his mother to be big enough for several families, it had never extended beyond their small group.

Because his father had said the wrong thing to some drunk guy in a taxi line, and a second later had hit the pavement like a sack of flour.

Because his mother had loved her husband too much to see beyond her pain when he was taken from her.

Because Aurora had been young enough to disconnect herself from this place and leave before her roots had sunk too deep.

And because of all the duties Nico had taken on, he'd refused only one—to fill that table with wife, children, a family of his own.

The rumble in his chest easing, Nico went inside to sort dinner.

It was late by the time Laila closed up shop.

Lights off, bar a single downlight over a shelf of gold-foiled titles in the front window, she padded to her back room, brushed her teeth, washed her face, lathered her face in an overnight mask, and fell into bed.

Then she looked to her bedside table to find the book she was after wasn't there. Dragging herself up again, she slipped back into the bookstore, and came back with a fresh copy of *Steeling Harts* by DeVante Gray.

Back under the covers she readied herself to fall headfirst

into the story of Elvie Hart, sheltered farm girl with a secret identity, and Tyranno, the towering, battle-hardened, alien combat robot who had been sent to protect her. A tale of insatiable longing and forbidden love, *Steeling Harts* was the most gloriously, unashamedly romantic story Laila had ever read, and she'd read plenty.

She ran her fingers over the hero's "face," hidden though it was by the scarred silver battle helmet. The rendering was so stoic, so blank the reader could choose what they imagined he looked like beneath. When Laila pictured him pulling off his helmet to reveal a chiselled jaw, wavy dark hair, and deep brown eyes she let the book fall to her chest and looked up at the ceiling and breathed out through a small gap between her lips.

She could usually shake the after-effect of seeing Nico well enough, but there had been a moment that night when his voice had dropped, and his gaze had roved over her face as if it grounded him somehow. A moment when she'd felt cocooned by his focused attention. When she'd not seen him as some cardboard cut-out, Disney-prince version of all the men she'd ever been drawn to, but as a good guy who was doing his best under trying circumstances.

Realising she was gripping the book hard enough to crack the spine, she attached her mini–book light, turned off her bedside lamp, tucked herself up under the covers, squished her soft feather pillow up around her ears, and flicked to the first page.

If tonight she decided to flesh Tyrrano out with a little stubble, a narrowing of eyes in promise, the scent of smoke and forest and warm male skin, it didn't have to *mean* anything. And nobody had to know but her.

Laila sat hunched in a window seat in the Rosy Crumb Cafe nursing a sickly sweet strawberry thick shake, hoping bright morning sunshine and oodles of sugar might make her feel more human after a night of dream-addled sleep.

She'd read *Steeling Harts* before bed a hundred times. And while the lyrical language and the glorious sensual tension could linger, leaving her feeling second-hand heartache for days, this wasn't lingering.

This was something else.

This was *Nico Damn Rossi*.

Why had she added Nico's smirk to Tyrrano's arsenal as she'd read herself to sleep, his scent, the particular deep rumble of his voice? She'd woken so tangled in her sheets, for a second she'd thought she might be stuck there forever. And now she couldn't even go to the Vine for a much-needed coffee as she was not about to risk bumping into the man.

When the front door of the Rosy Crumb sprang open, and a crew of SES volunteers sauntered into the small cafe, adrenaline sparkled along her veins as she searched the group and—

Half a head taller than the rest, Nico stood out instantly. His hair was mussed, dirt dusted into the fans around his eyes, and it was clear by the way he moved that he'd been through something. Meaning even after the barn fire and the lost boy the evening before, he'd gone out again through the night.

It was becoming clear to her that he didn't do this stuff to make the uniform look good, or to *act* like the town nice guy— to him it mattered. And dressed in the same vibrant orange as the others, while they looked like walking traffic cones, Nico looked—her teeth clenched against the word—*heroic*.

Careful, he'd told her, and she wished she'd listened.

As, when he ran a big hand through his hair, tugging for a quick second as if resetting himself, and glanced unseeingly around the room, she couldn't move, couldn't hide. When his eyes found hers she stopped breathing.

After a slow blink he raised his hand, his mouth lifting into a half smile. It wasn't the charmer he used on other people, it was slow, it was gentle, and it was real. Making her feel as if, in some small way at least, she mattered to him too.

If this realisation had hit her on a normal day, she would have scoffed at her fancifying. But after their "moment" on her front path the night before, and the hours spent dreaming of the man, her chest began to hurt.

When she finally remembered to breathe, Nico's nostrils flared, mirroring her, in perfect unison—as if he knew what she was feeling, or was feeling it too.

A wave of panic came over her and she pushed back her chair, gathered her things, and took off around the small cluster of tables.

Beyond the blood rush in her head, she heard Nico's voice above the chatty din.

"Laila." Then, "Laila, wait!"

But Laila did not wait. Looking at the floor, she pushed the door open and burst into the Vermillion sunshine. It was so bright outside she shielded her eyes like a vampire. Then, rather than turn left towards the store, she turned right and walked so fast it was almost a run.

Not that he'd follow. Why would he follow? She wasn't living inside a book. This was a regular day, in a nice small town, and—

"Laila!"

Oh, boy. He'd followed.

Knowing she'd never outrun him in her tight jeans and high-heeled ankle boots, she slowed, dragged in a deep fortifying breath, and turned.

Nico was slowing to an amble a few metres away. The top half of his kit was unzipped, hanging from his toolbelt at his waist, a dark navy T-shirt clung to his broad chest.

Remembering her thick shake, she lifted it to her mouth

and took a long drag to cover up her desperate need to swallow. Then, tired and furious with herself, she blurted, "What do you want now, Nico?"

A frown formed between his eyes, highlighting the dirt in the creases of his laugh lines, the exhaustion in the deep brown depths. It was enough to snap her out of what had been a truly impressive spiral of self-indulgence.

"Sorry," she said, closing her eyes for a beat. "Let me try that again." She squared her shoulders, offered up a broad grin, and sing-songed, "What do you want now, Nico?"

Nico huffed out a laugh as he took another couple of steps her way. She somehow managed not to sway as he towered over her.

"I'm glad I caught you," he said. "I was coming to see you today."

"Oh?" she managed, even as a strange bubble of intimacy curved around them once more, in the middle of the footpath, in broad daylight.

"I was hoping you might be able to recommend a book."

Laila blinked. A book? A *book*. The guy hadn't chased her down the street because he was feeling all swoony and discombobulated the way she was, he wanted a book, and she sold books, and that was that.

Which was just *great*. Much better than…the alternative. There was her no-men deal to consider, and his apparent no-locals rule, so in the end it was all moot anyway.

"Brilliant," she said. "It seemed my speech the other day about men reading romance hit home. What are you after? We can ease you in—historical, maybe, or romantic suspense."

A flush came over his swarthy cheeks, as he lifted his hands and said, "Ah, no. It's not *for* me."

If he was about to tell her he wanted to buy a book as a gift for someone he was *seeing*, she might throw herself in front of a car. Well, no, she wouldn't do that. In fact, maybe that would be the best outcome of all. Cut this now near-constant awareness off at the knees.

Then, gaze obscuring, as if he had overdone things—not only the night before but perhaps for quite some time—Nico said, "It's for my mother."

And Laila's damn knees nearly gave out. "Right. Well, that's…really nice. Um, do you know what kind of romance she might like?"

"Uh," he said, blinking furiously.

"Relax. I'm not asking if your mother is into tentacles and love triangles."

"*Madonna*," Nico moaned, then leaned forward, hands braced on his knees.

Laila's laughter came from nowhere, and a good portion of the tension that had been twisting her in knots all morning eased away. Apparently chatting with Nico helped where sunshine and sugar could not.

"Might she like a family saga?" Laila asked. "Something set in Italy?"

Nico looked up, his gaze near level with hers. Close enough she could see the ridges of his strong neck, the tangle of his dark lashes. Then his gaze shifted, considering her a moment, and on a slow breath out it traced her cheek, the neckline of her fluffy, periwinkle-blue sweater top, before his eyes lifted to her mouth and stayed.

Something warm and soft and ancient seemed to shift and spin about them before settling deep inside her.

When he slowly pushed himself back to standing, Laila took another long drag of her shake. The sooner this conversation was over the better.

"A book for your mother?" she reminded him.

"Right. The thing is I'm at a loss. On several fronts," he added, softly enough she almost missed it. "I'm sure you've already heard, the grapevine being what it is around here, my mother is heading back to Italy soon. For good."

"Oh! No, I hadn't, actually. But then I'm not really a grapevine type."

"No," he said, a glint hitting his eyes as they once again found hers. "You're not."

Then he lifted his hand, ran it across his mouth once, and said, "Okay, some background. I was around fifteen when my parents decided I was old enough to stay home and look after Aurora when they went into the city to see a show. They were lined up for a taxi outside a restaurant when a bunch of drunk guys came by, causing trouble. Dad, a big, genial bear of a man, attempted to draw them away, one took offence and took a swing, he was out before he hit the ground."

Laila didn't realise her hand was at her mouth till she gasped.

"A woman in the line was an EMT, a first responder—she performed CPR till the ambulance arrived. Saved his life, no doubt. But he was never the same after. Skull fracture. Traumatic brain injury. Mum was his carer for the next few years, till one day he went to sleep and didn't wake up."

Oh, Nico. Oh, Aurora. Even while she'd never known her own father, the loss of her mum and the raw note in his voice tugged at a jagged spot behind her ribs.

"And now my mother wants to go back to Italy, where they lived when they were young, where he is buried…" Nico's looked out towards Vermillion Hill. "And I'm not sure why I just told you all of that."

"We were figuring out her perfect book."

"Right," he said looking at the ground, before looking back at her. "We were."

"Leave it with me," she said, her voice catching, just a smidge, at the way he'd said "we."

"Are you sure? If it's too much to ask—"

"It's what I do. I'll find her something lovely. Something that might help her through this transition. Just give me a day or two then come by the shop."

"Okay. Though that might be the first time I've ever been invited."

"First time for everything."

When he breathed in deep and breathed out hard, she wondered what kind of everythings he might be imagining. Then gave her own imagination a good talking-to.

Looking out across the street, where autumn leaves fluttered from the branches of the elm trees like confetti, Laila said, "I know it was a while ago, but I'm still sorry about your dad."

"Thank you. I appreciate it."

When she looked back, Nico was watching her. So big and handsome, wry and capable, so her type she could have built him in an app. Yet while she'd spent months telling herself how alike he was, on the outside, to the men who'd let her down, now when she saw Nico, she saw only him.

Filling her lungs in a deep fast whoosh—after having forgotten to breathe, yet again—she then had to fight back a yawn.

Nico's brows rose. "Late night with book club?"

"Mmm," she said when the yawn kept on keeping on. "Rubbish night's sleep, that's all."

"Bad dreams?" he asked.

"Ah, no," she said, blinking a little too fast. "Just… dreams."

"Did I make an appearance?"

While it was clear he was joking, he hit the mark so precisely Laila baulked—for a half second at most. But he saw it; his eyes widening in delight.

"Well, how about that?" he drawled, the tightness around his shoulders loosening immeasurably.

Laila glared at him for a good long moment before she muttered, "Oh for Pete's sake," as she stalked past him, heading for Forbidden Fruits; any kindly thoughts she'd been feeling towards the guy sizzling like mist on a hot morning sidewalk.

Nico was beside her in a beat, long legs easily keeping up. "I know most people don't like hearing other people's dreams, but I'm here for it. Be as detailed as you like."

"I have literally nothing to share with you on the matter."

"Just one scene. A crumb. A nibble. Actually, was there nibbling involved?"

She shot him a glare that would have burned down entire forests, if she'd had the power. Yet Nico remained unfazed.

The worst of it? Amidst her mortification she noted that the smoke and sadness was gone from his eyes. And she'd done that. The thrill that alighted in her was not good. Not good at all.

When she reached her shop, Laila heaved the bougainvillea-laden front gate between them so she was on one side, Nico on the other. He was tall enough he could just step over the thing if he wanted to. If he had reason to. But he stayed where she'd put him.

Then his gaze dropped to her mouth, to where her top teeth were dragging over her bottom lip as she tried to hold in the breaths coming thick and fast.

And time seemed to still. Flecks of pollen fluttered in the buttery beams of sunlight falling over his shoulders. Native bees wove daintily around the flowers draped over her fence.

"Laila," Nico said, his voice rough, as if he'd hit a level of such exhaustion, and pressure, the mental ropes keeping his good sense in place had finally snapped.

Laila felt it too. A deep, red, swirling need to tell him exactly what he'd done to her in her dream, or yell at him for being so freaking beautiful it hurt to look at him, or ask if he was ever going to damn well follow up on the way he looked at her.

Dammit. Just *dammit.* And *no.* And *not here.* And *not now. Not ever.*

And, finally, *not him.*

Not him because he was a man and she'd sworn off men, indefinitely.

Not him because this town had become her home, and if anything happened between them, when it ended, which it surely would, she'd be the one left on the outer again.

And not him because of all the men she'd ever met, if big-hearted town hero Nico Rossi stomped her heart into the ground it would never recover.

Laila peeled her fingers from the gate, and took a big step back.

"You are the devil," she said, "and I hope you trip over your shoelaces on the way home. Consider this your weekly landlord check-in." She turned to walk away, then, swearing under her breath, turned back. "And I'll have your mum's book ready by the end of the day."

"Thank you, Laila," he called, while she jogged up her front steps on wobbly legs.

She shot him the international sign for "get stuffed" over her shoulder as she opened her door, closing it on the sound of his deep, sexy chuckling laughter.

When she went to bed that night she'd be listening to a true crime podcast.

CHAPTER FIVE

WHISTLING A HAPPY TUNE, Nico pulled his Land Rover to a halt outside the villa's quintuple garage, only to find a big white truck in the way.

Vehicles coming and going weren't uncommon on the Hill, so he ignored it as he headed into the house, until the packing boxes leaning against the back of a chair in the sunken lounge, and the gaps in the entryway wall where a credenza and artwork had once been, stopped him short.

"Aurora," Nico called. Then, "Aurora!"

"Niccolo. Cease your caterwauling."

Nico turned to find his mother exiting the hall that led to the family wing. "Mamma," he said, moving in to kiss her cheek. "What's going on?"

She tilted her head. "I am moving. Home. To Italy. I thought we had put this subject to bed."

"Yes, I know. But now? Today?"

He had accepted it was happening, but he thought he had time. Time to smooth out the rough edges that had appeared between them again last night. Time to make sure *she* was sure. Time to find the perfect way to assure her that staying behind was the right thing for him.

"I'm getting the process started," she said with a blithe wave of her hand. "Putting items into storage until I am ready for it to all go into a container to send across the seas. We organised it all online."

"We?"

"Aurora and I," she said, moving into the kitchen to start emptying drawers.

As a kid he'd loved the size of the villa—it wasn't as old and drafty as the places he grown up in in Italy, and it had twists and turns and add-ons and extensions that made it fantastic for hide-and-seek. Today, as he stalked the halls in search of his sister, not so much.

"Auroraaaa!"

"Whaaaaat!" Aurora finally called back.

Nico found her in a random guest bedroom, leaning against the bedhead, reading yet another romance novel she must have picked up from Laila. She took her sweet time finishing up a scene before sliding in a bookmark with For-bidden Fruits written down the centre in gold, closing the book, and looking up at him.

"As I said," she said, "whaaaaat?"

"Mamma is packing. There is a truck."

Aurora crossed her legs and leaned towards him. "This is not new news." Then, her gaze softening, she said, "Appar-ently, she has been talking to the family in Siena every day for months. They have set her up with a suite in the main house. She will have her own driver. She's already made plans to catch up with old school friends. It's happening, Nico. So, I figured I should probably help her make sure it happens as smoothly as possible."

She swallowed, then said, "She also told me to tell you that she feels immense guilt that you were forced to step into Papa's shoes so young, without being given the chance to decide if it was what you wanted."

That's where her guilt lay?

"She's still on that?" he asked, rolling out a shoulder.

"She is. And if you don't take this time to truly decipher

if it's what you really want, she will never forgive herself. Never ever."

Nico sat, fell back on the bed with a *whumph*, and pressed into his fists into his eye sockets.

"Could you be any more dramatic?" Aurora asked.

"The situation calls for it."

"I think it's a pretty good deal. Like the gift of a midlife crisis long before you have all the other midlife stuff—beer belly, sore knees, thinning hairline etc."

"*Brilliante*," Nico muttered.

"It's pretty simple, Nico. Stay, or go." Aurora patted him on the arm, and shuffled off the bed. "I'm going to check on Mamma. Make sure she doesn't pack all the saucepans."

Nico let her go without another word, while his mind ran in circles around one central thought. *Stay or go.* And while it had never occurred to him to consider such a choice, and while the women in his life were being as manipulative as all hell, Nico gave himself a minute to imagine what leaving Vermillion might look like.

Would he want to work in wine? Yes. No hesitation.

Would he like to work someplace bigger, with amazing new tech? Perhaps. He certainly loved the time he'd spent at Serenità in Napa over the years.

Or would he prefer to take on a more boutique set-up, such as Dante's vineyard outside of Montefalco, so that he might focus solely on his *baciami*. At that, the thunder that had been rolling in his chest the evening before roared.

Hell.

Nico slowly sat up, let his feet fall to the floor by the bed, and looked unseeingly through the plantation blinds at the rolling landscape out the window.

They'd had offers for Vermillion Hill over the years. Only six months earlier, a local conglomerate had come to town, "sniffing around," as Meryl and Beryl had put it, and their pitch had been impressive. It would protect the label's name, and the vineyard's staff—those who had guided him, taught him, supported him as he'd learned the ropes.

Only then he pictured himself telling the locals that the Rossi family's twenty-year connection with Vermillion was over. People whose rents had not gone up in that time, who would rightly fret over new ownership. Leaving his SES mates in the lurch.

And then there was Laila. The thought of leaving and never knowing what might have been made him feel as if he had a fist gripped around his insides.

Growling, he launched himself off the bed, and stalked to his room to scrub off the night. Yet, as if in even considering leaving, something had been unlocked inside of him, and the tension only grew.

Leaving a message with Sandrino, his head winemaker, moving their meeting to the afternoon, Nico walked past the white moving truck, got back in his Land Rover. Instead of heading towards town he hooked a right up into the hills.

Nico got about three kilometres out of town before his phone rang—a pipe had burst at Tendrils Hair. *Dammit.* He'd been meant to get onto that days before. Then a message came through looking for helpers to move a felled tree blocking a mountain road. Followed by a calendar reminder to hire a new maternity coverage admin assistant for the winery.

Three hours later, having barely caught up with the backlog, he was striding down Main Street, when his phone rang again.

And for the first time ever, he considered not answering.

Grabbing his phone from his pocket, he checked to find it was Claudio Vitali, who ran the Serenità vineyard in Napa; the second test site for his *baciami* hybrid.

Slowing, Nico took a breath and answered. "*Ciao, Claudio. Come stai?*"

"Bene. Bene."

As Claudio went on to give an abbreviated update on his family, Nico felt the flicker of a plan. Harvest was done. Once plans for the crop were agreed upon, his chief winemaker needed no oversight. Aurora would be home helping their mother. It was the perfect time for a trip to Napa.

"We've had a small problem," said Claudio. "A warm spell followed by late frost. Early bud break followed by sudden temperature drop. We've lost around a quarter of the young shoots."

Nico slowed to a stop and closed his eyes.

"We are so sorry, Niccolo."

Nico's phone buzzed with another call. Ignoring it, he said, "It's not your fault."

"What do you need me to do?"

Nico rubbed at his temple. What he needed was perspective. If not for the unresolved issue of Claudio's daughter, Savannah, having thrown herself at him the last time he'd visited, the perfect place to get some was Napa aka *anywhere* but Vermillion.

"Leave it with me for a day."

"Ma certo."

"*Grazie, Claudio*," said Nico. *"A presto. Arrivederci."*

After ringing off, Nico let his head tip back, the warm Vermillion sun brushing the backs of his eyelids, the whoosh of the breeze rustling the leaves of the great elms across the way. And he let out a rough, sorry laugh.

Legs leaden, Nico started back for his car. Only when he passed by the Swirl and Purl Craft Corner, and saw movement behind the window, he knew they were coming for him.

Meryl, or Beryl, likely both. It would be nothing of import. Some morsel of local gossip they just had to share. And while he usually—no, always—gave them whatever time they required, something came over him. The need to know that he *could* step away.

Before he knew it, he'd picked up pace. Then he was jogging, and ducking through a wonky front gate laden with bougainvillea.

The bell tinkled over the door and Laila—high up a big wooden ladder, her arms filled with books—rolled her eyes.

After returning from the discombobulating run-in with Nico, Laila had been overcome with the need to rearrage the entire store. Changing into her favourite "get stuff done while no one is looking" outfit—Magnolia Blossoms tour tank top, ancient denin cut-offs, and UGG boots—she'd gotten to work. Only while she'd turned the sign to Swept off my Feet. BRB! she must have forgotten to lock the door.

When no one called out, or appeared around the side of the shelf, she hefted the pile of books into the crook of her arm, grabbed the edge of the bookshelf, slid the rolling ladder sideways, and peeked out to find Nico pacing before her counter.

She whipped herself back behind the shelf so quickly she nearly kept going, teetering a moment before righting herself on the ladder. Biting her lip, Laila looked to the heavens and called on the book gods to help her heart settle.

Not that it had settled yet since Nico followed her out into the street that morning, calling her name for the whole town to hear.

Once upon a time she'd faced down infamous politicians, panicked celebrities, race car drivers on the far end of the narcissism scale without her heart skipping a single beat. Nico Rossi just had to *be* and her heart was aflutter for hours.

When she heard Nico clear his throat, she plonked the books onto a random shelf, then stepped carefully down the ladder. She fixed her top, tugged at the hem of her shorts, considered pulling the band out of her hair and giving it a quick fluff, then gave her high messy ponktail a yank instead.

For who was she trying to impress? And why?

Chin up, shoulders back, she strode around the corner of the shelves only for any quip she might have tossed his way to catch in her throat.

Nico was leaning against the counter, eyes closed, head tipped back. Deep furrows were etched his brow that she was almost certain weren't there that morning. The hollows beneath his eyes were filled with shadows.

The urge to go to him was so strong she tucked her hands into fists, and said, "I said I'd have the book ready by the end of the day."

Nico blinked his eyes open, dropped his chin, and took her in. At least that's how it felt—as if by the power of his gaze alone he was pulling her close. His gaze roved over her hair, traced the edge of her shoulder where she could feel the cut of her hot pink bra strap, and he breathed out hard when he hit the hem of her short shorts.

"Nico," she said, trying to snag his attention, but it came out far more plaintive than she'd have liked.

When his gaze moved slowly back to hers, as if time was moving through molasses, she could have gathered enough fantasy material to last her a decade, but it was clear something wasn't right.

"Come sit," she said, motioning to the couch in her picture window.

When he didn't move, she went to him, took him by the wrist, and carefully pulled him away from the counter. His arm felt heavy. His pulse beneath her fingertips strong and steady.

Then Nico's eyes opened wide, he growled, "Dammit," and his hands grabbed her at the waist as he spun her around and shoved her deeper into the store.

"What the hell, Nico!" she cried, even as her hands landed

over his. His skin was so warm, and slightly rough under her palms. His body hard and hot, as he loomed over her, hustling her towards the back room.

"Wait!" she said, braking and spinning to face him. Only to have to look up and up and up into his deep brown eyes, his hands on her hips, her shirt twisted against her body.

Heat moved through his gaze, like fire along an oil slick, before he ground out, "She's coming."

"She's…" Laila looked around him through the window but all she could see was one of the Swirl and Purl sisters heading up the footpath. "Do you mean Meryl?"

"Yes," he whispered.

Laila laughed. Sure, it was slightly hysterical, but the situation called for it. "But she's harmless."

With a groan Nico leaned forward, and Laila's hands went straight to his chest before he could move them another step closer to the back room. Under the soft give of his shirt, his chest was rock hard, his skin warm, the thump of his pulse not so steady anymore.

Every time she'd seen the man these past days, it was if another layer of the onion had been torn away. Like Dorothy peeking behind the Wizard's curtain, she was discovering he was all too human after all.

The messiness of being human was so in her wheelhouse, when she looked past him to see Meryl now halfway up her front path, going on gut instinct Laila took one of Nico's hands in both of hers and dragged him down the aisle between the second and third bookshelves.

To the left there was a person-sized gap where the shelf didn't meet the wall. It led to a clever void space she'd created where she usually kept her stackable bench seats, spare cushions, and cosy throws, but since she'd put them out for the Blushing Boomers book club, who were coming in that afternoon, the space was now empty.

"Come on," she said backing into the gap and dragging him with her.

She was yanked to a stop.

"Do you trust me?" she asked.

A muscle flickered beneath one eye, one that told her that it was a *maybe* at best. But then he nodded, twisting his shoulders and edging his way into the gap.

By the time she realised it was smaller than she remembered, especially for someone Nico's size, it was too late. The bell tinkled over the front door, and she grabbed him by the shirtfront, yanking him with her, as far as they could go.

When her head hit the back of a shelf, she winced. While Nico, in order not to end up bodily against her, braced a hand beside her neck. The shelf behind them rocked the tiniest amount, but it was enough for Laila's gaze to snap to his. And while the light from the store didn't quite reach them down there, its glow traced the edges of his strong features in a pale pink outline, though his eyes appeared danger dark.

Adrenaline surged through her, in a hot shimmery wave. And when Nico breathed in, she realised her hands were still gripped in his shirt.

She tried to back up, but there was simply nowhere to go. Nico was more than a head taller than her, twice as wide, and in that moment, she felt every inch. But it was the scent of him—fresh-cut grass and winter air, tangled sheets and salty skin—curling against the back of her tongue, that had her stilling, all bar the stammering of her heart against her ribs.

And after two long years without holding a man, kissing a man, touching a man in a way that veered anywhere close to sexual, her body betrayed her in a heartbeat. Restless with the need to curl closer, skin prickling with awareness, she needed to get out of there right now before she climbed the man like a tree.

She opened her mouth to tell him to move, but Nico lifted

his hand and placed a finger a millimetre from her lips. And the invisible bubble that had been closing around them for weeks snapped tight like cling wrap.

"Ms. Vale?" a voice called, from *just* the other side of the bookshelf. "Niicooo?"

Laila, in alarm, yanked Nico closer and buried her face in his chest.

When the hand that had been hovering near her lips moved to cup the back of her head, Laila felt every ridge of his palm—big, warm, gentle, protective. Senses having flicked to high alert, only then did she note his knee wedged between hers, her fingers holding so tight to his shirt her knuckles hurt, how hard their chests rose and fell—breaths so loud they were lucky Meryl's hearing was fifty-fifty or she'd have heard them for sure.

Feeling woozy now, her neck like rubber, she lifted her head to find Nico's face right there. Jaw clenched, eyes half closed, brow furrowed for all its might. As if it was taking every bit of self-control not to…

What? Pull her closer? Press his lips to hers? Lift her into his arms so she could wrap her legs tight about his waist?

She wanted all of those things with such ferocity she reared back and hit her head on the back of the shelf again. She let out a small sound of pain, then bit her lip. While Nico, expression instantly switching from heat to concern, lifted the hand at her neck to feel for a bump, his fingers catching in her hair. And spot-fires broke out all over her body.

"Nico," she whispered; asking him to stop, asking him to go, who knew? Then, finding some last vestige of strength, she mouthed, "Is she gone?"

Nico's gaze dropped to her mouth and stayed. It was a few seconds before he shook his head, the heavy curl swaying back and forth on his forehead.

Then Meryl called, "Ms. Vaaaale? Are you heeeeere?"

When a bark of laughter crawled up Laila's throat, she lifted a hand from Nico's chest to slap it across her mouth.

"Young people today," Meryl muttered. "So, lapse in their duties. I ought to steal a book just to teach her a lesson."

Nico's hand dropped to her shoulder, giving it a light squeeze, as if in apology. Only before she could revel in the lovely weight of it, tuck the feeling away in case it was just as long, or longer, till she felt such a sweetly intimate touch again, Nico stilled, seeming to hover on the edge of something, before his hand slowly, *slowly* ran down her bare arm.

As if he was a conductor and her nerves a song, she rolled into the touch, then away, like a cat finding a patch of sunshine. By the time his hand reached hers, tracing the edge of her fingers before sliding around her to land on her lower back, she was pressed up against him, one foot curled around his calf, one hand still gripping his shirt for dear life.

Then the bell tinkled over the front door before the door closed with a soft snap.

The huff of the air-conditioner whispered into the heavy silence, along with the Caro Emerald playlist humming gently through the heart-shaped speaker behind her counter. And it was clear they were alone, in the shadows, pressed up against one another where no one could see them.

If she tugged, he'd come to her. If he leaned in the tiniest fraction more, she'd lift to her toes and swipe her tongue alone the length of that strong neck. And it wouldn't have to mean anything bar dissipating the aching tension that had been building between them for months.

Only it would. It would mean that the vow she'd made—not only to put men on the back-burner, but to choose herself first—would have unravelled at the first true test.

Whether Nico's hand moved first, or hers, Laila could never be sure, but they were both unpeeling, uncurling, untwisting all the bits of themselves that had become intertwined.

Then, after one last, hot look, Nico edged his way back out of the void.

While Laila took a moment to breathe air that didn't smell entirely of him, her skin felt as if it was on fire, her hair had stuck to the nape of her neck. She allowed herself an extended, all-over body shiver before following Nico out into the store.

She found him by the front door, pacing, a hand tugging at his hair, his dark gaze following her every step, and while it ought to have made her feel better, to know she wasn't alone in feeling utterly off kilter, it shook her anew.

Making her way behind the counter, putting something concrete between them, she said, "Now that the big bad lady is gone do you want to tell me what that was all about?"

The man's cheeks—his damn carved-by-the-gods cheeks—began to pink. And then he laughed, a gorgeous self-deprecating sound that made her heart clunk rustily in her chest.

Pacing no more, he ambled over to lean his elbows on the countertop, dropping his head into his hands. "I honestly don't even know if I can," he said, voice muffled.

"Try."

Letting his hands drop, forearms braced on the counter, he said, "I was on the street, doing my thing, then like some crack in the space-time continuum just opened up before me I didn't have it in me to be Niccolo Rossi."

"Mmm," she said, remembering the times her mother's name had come up on her phone and for just a second she'd considered not answering. "It's funny how you can be so good at something and yet drown in it at the same time."

He lifted his eyes to hers in surprise.

"My mother," she said, surprising herself now too, "wasn't the most organised person in the world." Putting it mildly. "Meaning I had to be. And while taking up the slack was my love language, I cursed her for it too."

"Is that why you went into crisis management?"

"How—" she started, then, at the same time as Nico, said, "*Aurora.*"

Yet another "moment" passed between them as they found themselves on the same side for once.

Breaking the spell, Laila said, "Short answer, yes. The experience came in very handy when it came down to fixing things for others. Not so much for myself. Till I came here."

Nico's gaze was so absorbed, so honestly interested, Laila felt even closer to him than during their minute in heaven behind the bookshelves.

Then, shaking his head as if he too fell into an unexpected fog, Nico stood, clasped his hands behind his neck and stretched, his T-shirt lifting and exposing a sliver of warm brown skin, before thankfully letting his arms drop, his thumbs hooking into the front pockets of his jeans.

And it hit her how effortlessly Nico knew when to push, and when to back away, in order to draw someone out, but not unnerve them. It spoke to his maturity. Something that probably came of having to step into a grown-up role at such a young age.

And while having a big, strong, hot, well-groomed man up all inside her personal space had nearly unravelled two years of good work, she was just as hot and bothered by the fact that he listened. That he asked questions. That he paid attention.

Two years of celibacy and she'd developed a competency kink.

Only while she was battling yet another way Nico Rossi got under her skin, she noticed Nico's gaze was no longer on her. He was looking over her shoulder, down the length of the store towards the back room.

She followed his gaze and felt the blood drain from her face.

Meryl must have done a more thorough search than she'd

imagined, for the door to the storeroom, the room in which she'd secretly made herself at home against the express rules of her contract, was wide-open.

The view of her unmade bed was clear as day.

Like water dripping into a bucket, slowly filling till that one final drop would make it overflow, seeing the edge of a bed, sheets mussed, soft white blanket bunched at the foot where Laila's storeroom ought to be, sent Nico into a slow, but inevitable, meltdown.

"Hey so, that was pretty funny, right?" said Laila, leaping out from behind the counter, and waving her arms. "Meryl and the hiding and all."

When he caught a waft of apple crumble, putting him right back in the dark, tight nook with Laila's hand gripping his shirt, her forehead tipped against his chest, it was enough for him to pace past her and down the length of the shop.

"Nico," she said. "Nico, wait!"

But Nico was on a mission. Missions were far simpler and more straightforward than dealing with anything related to Laila Vale.

When he reached the door of the storeroom, he felt her move in behind him, but he was too distracted by the tall tasselled pink lamp in the corner, the pink velvet chair in the other corner covered in strips of lacy underthings. This wasn't set up for the occasional late-night sleepover. Laila was living there.

"You know you're not allowed back here," she said, "without advance written notice."

Nico looked over his shoulder. "Are we really arguing about what's allowed and not allowed?"

Her teeth dragged over her bottom lip and he had the sudden, primal need to growl like a wolf with the scent of prey in his nostrils. "Correct me if I'm wrong," he said, his voice amazingly calm, considering, "but aren't you back staying at the Grape Escape?"

He knew, from her lease, that she had stayed at the quaint little bed and breakfast for a few weeks before finding herself a small rental just out of town. Then, he'd received notice that she was back at the Grape Escape two, maybe three months back.

"Not exactly," she said, her voice carrying none of its usual bumptiousness. "Though it is where I collect my personal mail."

Nico had no words.

Thankfully Laila did. "When I opened this place, I went all in. A few months back, I had a big bill pop up, so paying rent on two places became difficult." A beat then, "Barry at the Grape Escape lets me use his address and I keep him stocked in Minotaur romances."

Nico opened his mouth to ask what the hell a "Minotaur romance" was, then instantly thought better of it.

"This isn't zoned residential, Laila." That, and it hadn't been safely set up for human habitation for decades. They were heading into winter and the insulation wouldn't be up to scratch. Imagining her sleeping back there, shivering under her bedclothes—

Then Laila's hand curled around his forearm and his thoughts scattered like ash on the wind.

"The electrics have all been checked and tagged," she said. "I've had the plumbing serviced, paid for by me. I don't plan to stay here forever. Just till I have a buffer. A safety net. I…" She swallowed, then lifted her chin a mite higher. "I won't put myself in a position where I'm financially unstable. I can't."

The tightness in his chest lifted as her words came back to him. *Crisis management. Taking up the slack. Till I came here.* What had happened to her in order to leave behind what must have been a very different life, start afresh, with just enough capital to have a red-hot go at something, but not enough to feel entirely secure?

Curiosity warred with the desire to put his arm around her, and promise her it would all be okay, so he deliberately veered to the inane: "Where do you even store the things you need to store?"

She blinked. Then, hand trailing away from his arm, slipped past him and into the room, where she pointed out a nifty shelving system, boxes of spare books stacked in one corner, before she bent from the waist to haul out two large drawers from under her bed. At least he assumed they were drawers, as Laila's backside was suddenly pointed his way, the edges of pockets poking out the bottom of her frayed shorts.

When she stood back upright, arms crossed over her band shirt, cheeks pink in a pale face, she looked like a ferocious Tinker Bell. Ready for a fight. Only now he saw she wasn't fighting for the fun of it, but because she had something to fight for.

"So now you know," she said, and made to sweep past him.

Without thinking, he reached out and wrapped his fingers around her wrist. He did not want her to leave. Whether that meant the conversation, or his vicinity, he couldn't be sure.

As his thumb caressed the soft skin on the inside of her wrist, just the once, and she let him, he knew there had been a shift. Before the bookshelves, or the conversation about his parents, something had fundamentally changed between them over the past few weeks.

"Laila, you're not in trouble."

"You have no idea what trouble is." Eyes bright, she wrenched her arm from his grip and headed back to the front of the store.

Watching her fuss behind the counter, Nico pressed his thumb into the palm of the hand that no longer held her, as his mind whirred.

Yes, she was erratic. Yes, she rarely made his life easier. But when he'd felt things closing in, he'd gone to her. As if knowing instinctively, of all the people in Vermillion, she'd not be disappointed in him if he admitted that he was struggling under the load.

She needed time—so she could get to a point where she could feel secure.

He needed space—to find perspective, and to not have to watch his mother decide which wooden spoons she'd take and which she'd leave behind.

The plan formulating in his head might be the most foolish thing he had done since he'd jumped off a shed believing he was Superman, but in that moment it felt like it might be his only choice.

"Okay," he said. "How about this—and keep in mind I am flying by the seat of my pants here. We renegotiate our contract—you can stay, temporarily, and I have a duty of care to make sure it is up to code as a living situation."

Laila stopped fussing and stared at him.

"After which I will petition council, requesting rezoning this area as semiresidential. It was clearly a cottage at some point, so that might help."

"If council finds out I am already here, is there a chance I could be evicted?"

"Not if I have any say in the matter."

She nodded, as if that was good enough for her, and it felt as if he'd been given a gold star.

"And what do I need to do in return?"

"Not a thing," he said, even while the plan kept formulating. A plan that had both merit and mess written all over it.

"That's unacceptable," she said. "If you're doing me a favour, then I need to do you a favour."

"You're choosing a book for my mother," he said, giving himself a final out.

"That's commerce."

That didn't come close to what it meant to him, and he was certain she knew that too. Then his phone buzzed. It was his mother, messaging to ask if he wanted the nesting tables in the second hallway, or if she could take them with her, and his decision was made.

"Do you have a current passport?"

Laila blinked. "Ah, yes, I think so. Why?"

"How does a trip to San Francisco sound?"

After the silence had stretched a smidge too long, Laila repeated, "San Francisco."

"Big red bridge, fun slanty streets, west coast of California. Or, to be more precise, Napa Valley."

"Yes," she deadpanned, "I am familiar."

"I need to take a quick trip. A week at most. A Rossi family winery in Napa has been working on a new hybrid of mine, testing how the latitude, weather, soil, etc., affect the result, and it's past time I check in."

"What does that have to do with me?" She was, rightly, baffled. But, interestingly, she hadn't said no, or ordered him out of her store.

"A plus one would be beneficial."

"Wouldn't you take Aurora?"

"Not for this," he said. "It would make the trip far easier if my plus one could pull off the aura of being…into me."

Laila's expression was incredulous. Rightly so.

"Actually, you know what, forget it—"

"Oh no no no," she said, clearly aware that he was now the one in the firing line. "Please explain in excruciating detail."

Nico lifted a hand to squeeze the back of his neck. *Here goes.* "The last time I was there, the daughter of the Vitali family, who own and run the Napa estate, stole a key to my lodgings and climbed into my bed as I slept."

Laila's hand flew to her mouth so that all he could see was her big blue eyes. "What did you *do*?"

"I rolled out of bed so fast I sprained my wrist as I hit the ground, then I gently shooed her from my room."

Laila's laugh was pure evil.

"I spent the rest of the night on the couch, eye on the door, ready to throw myself against it if the doorknob so much as rattled."

Laughing so hard she pressed a hand to her side, Laila asked, "What did her parents say?"

"As far as I know they still have no idea it even happened. Though, I do wonder if they quietly harbour hopes that we one day end up together."

"Well, of course they do," she said, her eyes still bright. "You are a menace to the public peace in this town, how could you possibly expect it to be any different over there?"

This, he thought, feeling energy surge through him. The flirt-fighting Aurora had pegged from the very first moment was what he needed to get him through this next patch. The way things were before the "moment" during book club night, before she'd dragged him behind her bookshelves, before he'd been in her bedroom. When it had felt spikey, but under control.

"So," she said, "you want me to come to Napa and pretend to be 'into you' so you can do grape things with people who you don't want to let down. And you're asking me, as opposed to anyone else because…"

There was the rub.

He was asking her because if he asked for her help, she gave it. He was asking her because the Vitalis would believe that Laila was the kind of woman who could knock him out for good. He was asking because—

She clicked her fingers. "You know I won't spill the tea

to the rest of the Vermillion gang. Or get the wrong idea and climb into your bed one night."

Nico stopped breathing as he did everything in his power *not* to imagine that happening, but he wasn't that strong. And he knew in that moment, if it ever happened, there was no way in hell he'd turn her away.

"I can see the panic in your eyes," she said. "Relax. I get it. The fact that this entire town is obsessed with you, and your 'I don't date locals' rule, it does rather thin the herd."

"My *what* now?"

Her eyes flared. "Um, well, as the story goes, you leave broken hearts in your wake, but only far and wide."

"Aurora?" he asked, deciding having a sister really wasn't worth the hassle.

"My book clubbers. They know things."

"Mmm," he said, neither confirming nor denying. "What say you? You coming to Napa? With me?"

Laila looked at him for a long hard moment, then pressed her hands to her cheeks so that her mouth squished into a fish pout, while her vision blurred. She looked so damn adorable. And knowing how she smelled up close and personal, knowing the small sounds she made when his hand ran down her arm, made things far messier than he preferred. But things were changing, and fast. All he could do was roll with it.

"A week?" she said.

"At most."

"What about the bookstore?"

"Aurora could manage it for you." She owed him, after all. "And I'll do what I can to see how to find a way around the commercial zoning for the cottage."

"*If* I go with you to San Francisco."

"No," he said, making sure she heard him. "One has nothing to do with the other. I will do what I can to help you have all you need to run your business. That's done. You're the one who offered to do me a favour."

He saw the moment she realised she'd been hoisted by her own petard.

"San Francisco," she said.

"Napa Valley."

"It's been so long since I've been *anywhere*."

Nico held out both hands, leaving it entirely up to her.

The wheels and cogs were in full flight behind her bright eyes, and having seen how fast she was able to make things happen when she wanted to, he knew his answer would be imminent. Either way.

He didn't realise he was holding his breath, till she said, "I think I have to go, just to watch you navigate the mess you've gotten yourself in."

"So, it's agreed."

She held out her hand. He shook. Their hands held a beat too long, then another, before as one they let go.

"I'll get the details to you this arvo," he said.

She nodded.

Nico, figuring he'd better leave before anything else unfolded, shot her a quick salute then headed for the door.

"Wait." She ducked down behind the counter and pulled out a book. *A Room with a View*, by E. M. Forster. "For your mum."

"Right. You sure?"

She smiled. "Worth a go."

He tapped it to his chest in thanks, then left.

He somehow got through the rest of his day. Though what he achieved he could never have said; his head so full of thoughts of bright blue eyes and the frayed hem of denim shorts.

CHAPTER SIX

AND THAT'S HOW Laila found herself on the Rossi family jet, flying from Adelaide to San Francisco, wondering what on Jane Austen's green earth she'd been thinking when she'd agreed to this madness.

While she was certain Aurora would be able to open and close the store—the extra incentive of a week's free rent and Nico agreeing to pay Aurora a hefty wage helping that pill go down easier—it was absurd to think she and Nico could spend an hour together without squabbling, much less a week.

There was also the fact that she now knew how it felt to have his hand run down her arm, or cradle the back of her head, or caress the side of her wrist. Picturing what else it was capable of kept her up nights.

Several hours into the flight not even her favourite Lisa Kleypas book was enough to hold her attention, as sitting across from her in a creamy leather seat patterned in imprints of delicate grapevines, Nico was in full "international vineyard boss man" mode. Meaning her competency kink was getting a full workout.

His cuffs had been rolled up, revealing those strong suntanned forearms, a chunky watch sat rakishly askew on his wrist. He was wearing glasses again, large dark frames that did all the right things for his face. He ran his thumb over his bottom lip. Over. And over. Hypnotic. And the fact that he'd printed out whatever he was reading on paper brought on hearty tugs of unwieldy affection.

Needing to get a grip, Laila honed in on his crisp, corn-flower-blue, button-down shirt, the uniform of every alpha corporate bro she'd ever dated, only to find herself staring at the straining button at his chest. Anticipation building inside her at the thought of it popping free.

Dammit.

Nico Rossi had the confidence, the swagger, and the self-awareness that had made it easy to convince herself he was the small-town version of every man who'd broken her heart, but now not even those warning signs were enough to snap her hormones back into line.

Meaning she just had to work harder.

When he looked up, a single eyebrow nudged north, making it clear her face was telling him something she probably did not want him to know, she blurted, "Are the glasses real, or do you wear them to appear smart?"

Nico's smile was far too knowing, and she wondered if she brandished her butter knife on the guy, would the pilot have to turn the plane around.

Taking off his glasses, he leaned his cheek against his hand—two fingers to his temple, the tip of his ring finger notched between his teeth. "I was just thinking—"

"Good for you."

His eyes narrowed raffishly, and she had to press her knees together to stop the shimmers that started in her chest from travelling any lower.

"I was thinking," he began again, "if we are going to pull this off, we need a story."

"This?"

"Us."

The shimmers kicked up a notch. She gave her body a good, silent talking-to, then pulled out her phone and opened up her notes app. "Lucky for you then I've decided to treat this week much the way I would a pop-up book club, a midnight book release, or our much-vaunted Starry Starry Singles Night. We prep. We prop. We disaster plan."

"So nice to see you're taking this so seriously."

The shimmers were *not* doing as they were told, Laila thought, as she went to cross her legs only to bang her knee against the underside of the table.

"I made a list of things we should probably know about one another if we are going to fool anyone into thinking we are…" She waved a hand between them.

"Smitten?" he asked.

"I was going to say 'together just enough to let a lovely young woman down easy.' That'll be enough of a stretch."

"You really think so?"

Laila knew he was baiting her, only it felt far more like flirting than flirt-fighting. That rumble in his voice, the way his hand framed his face, the slight hood of his eyes. It had to be deliberate. No man was that effortlessly fanciable.

"Or," Nico said, "we can do what normal people do and just talk."

Laila pressed her lips together as she felt herself losing control of the conversation. She knew if she made a case for project managing this thing, he'd acquiesce. Not because he was Constable Goodboy, but because he was so damn comfortable in his own skin he didn't have to win all the time. He was rather evolved, for a man.

But maybe talking like "normal people" was worth a shot.

Laila turned her phone over and lay it face-down on the table between them. "What do you want to know?"

"Let's start at the beginning. You know my parents' story, tell me about yours."

For a second she considered making something up. If she had to play the part of doting girlfriend, why not take it the whole way, and invent an entire character? But in the end she gave him the truth.

"Fine. I never knew my father. My mum claimed not to know who he was either. We were tight, the two of us against the world. But it was complicated. Then she died a little over two years ago. Reaction to anaesthetic." Her mum would have been livid not to have died falling off a cliff. Or in the arms of a lover. Something tragic and memorable. "Next question."

"Complicated how?"

"I said, next question."

"That is my next question."

Laila glared at him, and he glared right on back; an immovable object meeting an unstoppable force. While she did not want to talk about all she'd left behind, she'd told clients a zillion times that sometimes the best way to get past something uncomfortable was right through the middle.

"My mother," she said, "would melt chocolate onto waffles for dinner. Wake me at two in the morning to look for shooting stars. Whisk me away from school to see old movies in the middle of the day."

She brought her hands into her lap, and picked at her thumbnail. Finding the spirit, and despair, of her mother was always hard to put into words.

"While that sounds magical, and it was at times, I didn't know a person needed to brush their teeth till the school nurse gave me a lecture. My nights were so unstructured, I'd fall asleep in class—and that was if I made it to school, which I figured out how to do, on my own, when I was eight, maybe nine. By high school I bought the groceries, I paid the bills, and had two jobs while she could never hold one down."

After school it had become about picking her mum up from seedy motels after her latest beau had done her dirty, or paying off loan sharks when her mum was hustled by some guy.

"Homemade crisis management?" Nico asked gently.

Laila lifted her eyes to his. "Every day of my life."

There was no way she'd have left the city if her mother was still alive. Meaning she'd have been stuck there, cleaning up her mother's messes, doomed to keep repeating the same mistakes.

Leaving, she'd put a line under all that—thick, and deep, and permanent. If she was going to make mistakes they'd be her own.

"Anyway," she said, a shiver running through her, "that was my mother. She ran into life headlong. Then she was gone."

"Thank you for telling me," he said.

She nodded.

Then with one eye squinting at her asked, "Now tell me this—how does an expert manage a crisis?"

And she could have kissed him for so blithely changing the subject. Well, not *kissed* him. Slapped him heartily on the back.

She talked him through the steps, gave him glimpse of some of the wilder cases she'd worked, leaving out enough detail to keep it anonymous.

And he told all the reason why going to Napa was so important to him—his *baciami* hybrid grape. His dream to create something that tasted like fields of the bright orange red of Sangiovese vines in autumn made him feel. Of red berries with a dash of pepper. Of spice and liquorice, going down smooth.

When, hours later, the lights in the cabin dimmed after they'd eaten dinner, and sleep was creeping up on her, Laila wished it didn't have to end.

So, through the start of a yawn, she allowed herself one more question. "Tell me the story of the Superman cape."

Nico's gaze slid to hers. "Aurora?"

"Aurora."

His mouth lifted at one corner, and the mix of brotherly

annoyance and patent adoration for his sister in his eyes made Laila yearn. For family? For consistency? Or simply knowing there was someone in the world who would think of her, know her foibles, and still smile?

Last question, she thought, most definitely.

"I was six years old. We were staying at the family vineyard in Siena. My father had set up a screen on the east wall of the villa and as the sun set we all watched *Superman*. I don't remember much about the movie, but clearly it made an impact as what happened next has gone down in family folklore."

Nico lifted his hand and swept it through the air. "Picture a dozen grownups and twice as many children sitting around a table one summer evening, drowning themselves in antipasto and wine, when a small, dark-haired boy bursts from the kitchen door, a tea towel tied around his neck like a cape. Before anyone realises, he has climbed atop the feed shed, declared himself *Superuomo!* and jumped before anyone sees it coming."

"You did *not*."

"I most certainly did. I still remember my mother's scream as she came running towards me; Aurora, a babe in arms. I landed in a crouch, the ground jarring my bones for a second, but not a scratch on me. I remember looking up to find my aunts all aflutter, uncles reeling, but my father was cheering, a huge grin on his face. The rest was drowned out by the wind in my ears, and the adrenaline pumping through me, as I bolted for the hills. After that it was Superman lunch boxes, Superman action figures. I was quite the little collector."

Laila laughed through a much bigger yawn. Then, when their gazes locked for longer than was in any way sensible, she said, "And if that's not the perfect way to end our fake 'getting to know you' session, I don't know what is."

Nico's forehead creased. But before he had his say, their flight attendant appeared.

"Sir? You asked me to let you when it was ten local time."

Nico sat up tall, and shook his head. "Yes. Thank you. You've set Laila up in the suite, yes?"

"Correct."

"As I said earlier, I'm more than happy to sleep anywhere," Laila protested, even while sliding out from behind the table.

"It's all good," said Nico, laughing at her move. "I still have work to do and the divan convert is more than adequate."

"Okay. Well good night, then."

She lifted her hand, spread her fingers in a well-known salute.

Nico blinked.

Laila looked to her fingers. "Wasn't that a Superman thing?"

"Spock," he corrected her dryly. "From *Star Trek*."

"Close enough. Good night."

"Good night, Laila."

With that she followed the flight attendant, who led the way to the suite, the feel of Nico's dark gaze watching her the whole way.

After a quick shower and change into silk pyjamas, she slid under the soft sheets of the double bed; her heart squeezing painfully, enough she thought it might actually bruise, when she saw, on a shelf, a small but purposefully curated supply of romance novels.

Laila woke with a start, as if she'd literally just closed her eyes.

Even with the hum of the engine in her bones, and the burr of the captain's voice telling her they were nearing San Francisco, it took her a minute to remember where she was.

Stretching, she checked her phone, realised she had no clue if it was on South Australia or California time, then padded to the sliding door of her suite and gently pulled it open.

Only to be met with the perfect view of Nico Rossi, sitting up in bed.

His hair spiked up in all directions, his face was soft with sleep, he was making grumbly, stretching noises, and while a sheet curled low around his hips, he wore not a stitch of clothing above.

His chest was glorious, all hard planes and slabs of muscle, his pecs covered in a smattering of curling dark hair. The definition—holy hell; from the ridges of his abdomen to the hard curves of his arms there was not an inch of him that wasn't utter perfection.

"Good morning."

Laila's gaze snapped up to find him watching her, a sleepy smile in his eyes. A morning-after smile. A smile of a cat that got the cream.

"Is it morning?" she chirped, tugging her robe tighter about her neck. "Who can tell?"

"Clocks. They say it's around eight thirty San Fran time," he said. Then, "Sleep alright?"

When he lifted a hand to scratch at his belly, she lifted her gaze to the ceiling, counted in threes, and gave him a thumbs up.

"Great. So, we can eat now, or shower first." He pointed past her to the suite beyond. "Then we have an hour or so before we have to be buckled up for landing."

The fact that it had taken Laila a few seconds to realise he meant eat together, but shower *separately*, had her backing back towards the suite. "I'll go first."

When he scratched his belly again, and her eyes fell to the spot, the man laughed. For he *knew* exactly what he was doing.

"You suck," she said.

"Nah," he said. "I'm a delight."

If she repeated those words, from that mouth, in that voice, several times as she ran soap over her body, then it was his own damn fault.

* * *

"There are around five hundred wineries in Napa," said Nico as the car that collected them from the foggy San Francisco airport swept them off to Napa Valley. "While on a similar latitude, Californian climate and soil differ from South Australia, which differs from Italy. This means the same grapes can have different flavours dependent on weather, hang time, nearby flowers, bee population—"

"Fascinating," said Laila, failing to hold back a jaw-cracking yawn. For while she had slept, she'd also dreamed. Only having gone to bed reading *Austenland*, this time the star had not been Nico cosplaying as Tyranno the battle robot; it had been Nico cosplaying as Mr. Darcy, and she honestly didn't know which was worse.

"You asked," Nico said.

"I did?" Laila glanced across the back seat of the car; his beautiful old leather briefcase thankfully playing chaperone on the seat between them. "Sorry. It's been a while since I arrived in one place *before* I left another, and I'm not sure my brain has quite caught up."

Nico, on the other hand, had come up peachy. Clean-cut, well pressed, his glasses sparkly clean, Clark Kent incarnate. Which, along with competency kink, was apparently a new "thing" for her.

"Maybe, rather than giving you a brief history of wine, we could practice." He held out his hand.

"What do you expect me to do with that?"

"How about you try holding it."

Her deadpan gaze rose back to his.

"I have a sister," he said. "I've seen *The Proposal*. I've seen *Green Card*. I understand how arrangements such as ours work. We agree, in advance, how physical we will be around one another. My two cents, holding hands is a fair place to start. And end, if that's what you'd prefer."

He was right. In fact, she was disappointed in herself for not having 'agree to PDA boundaries' in her own notes, as the number of fake dating books she'd read would put his movie list to shame.

Palm up, he curled two fingers her way, beckoning.

Laila slapped her hand into Nico's and held on tight. Which was fine, until Nico loosened his grip, moved so that their fingers intertwined, his sliding along the edges of hers, sending little tremors in their wake.

"There," he said, voice even, smile in place, as if he felt nothing at all, "this isn't so hard."

Hard? It was torture. Laila's knee began to jiggle as a surfeit of energy washed through her.

Then Nico slid his fingers from hers, turned her hand over, and cradled it. Then, with his spare hand, he ran his fingers down her palm.

"How long are we doing this?" she asked.

"As long as it takes."

"For?" Her voice sounded far away, mesmerised as she was by the shape of his big hand holding hers. The curl of his blunt fingers, the scars and the toughness and the strength. The intimacy, the sweetness.

Forget sex, this was heaven.

"Long enough for it to feel normal," he said, "so you stop looking like you're on the verge of running from a bear."

Laila glared at him, and commanded the heat to leave her cheeks.

"All I ask," said Nico, his voice calm and warm, "is that you stay by my side when we arrive, be your usual charming self, and stand guard outside my bedroom all night long."

Laila snorted a laugh. And a measure of the tension curling tightly inside her dissipated.

Until Nico's finger ran gently down her lifeline. Or was it her heart line? Whatever it was, it tingled wildly beneath the calloused scrape of his broad finger.

"Okay, Valentino," she said, drawing back her hand. "Any more of that and I'll think you have a fetish."

Nico laughed. *Laughed.* As if this was a lark. As if they weren't blithely hurtling headlong into something neither of them had thought through, while waiting for the other to flinch first.

"Okay," he said, leaning to look out the window as they passed a road sign. "We're getting close."

"Look at you, all giddy at seeing your little *batch-ee-army* friends again soon."

"I assume that was your attempt at *baciami.*"

"*Baciami,*" she attempted, exaggerating the second *a*. "Please tell me that doesn't translate to something like *bug resistant* or *batch number twelve*."

His gaze dashed across her mouth as he said, "It does not."

Before she could ask what it *did* translate to, the car turned, bumped over a cattle grate, and began the trek up a long, cypress-lined Serenità Estate driveway.

"Now," said Nico, "before the hordes envelop us, I brought you a gift."

"Oh." Curious, she opened the brown paper bag he'd slid form his briefcase to find a hefty hardback monolith entitled *Vineyards of the Napa Valley*. "You shouldn't have," she deadpanned, groaning under the weight of the thing.

The edge of his mouth kicked up. "You gave me a book. Now I've given you a book. I know you don't like to feel beholden, so consider us even."

A book? She'd given his *mother* a book, not—

Oh. Oh no. *That's* where her bedside table copy of *Steeling Harts* had gone. She'd tossed it into her bag a few weeks earlier on the way to the Vine, then forced it on Nico while ranting about how different the world might be if men read romance novels.

"You *kept* it?" she asked, pulse beating in her throat.

"Better than that, I brought it."

With that, Nico reached back into his briefcase, pushed aside his sleek laptop, and pulled out her favourite book in the whole wide world. The book she turned to when nothing bar great big dollops of delicious banter, and grand romantic gestures, and love scenes that made her toes curl could assure her that the world didn't completely suck.

Her self-confessed "how-to-manual."

"I rarely have spare time to read," he went on, opening the book to a chapter or so in, "so thought this would be the perfect week to give it a go."

"That's…amazing," she said around a gulp.

"Sorry," he said. "Couldn't find a bookmark."

She ought to have felt grateful that he mistook her panic that he'd actually started *reading* the book for disappointment that he'd dog-eared the page. She who used popsicle sticks to mark pages, placed cups of coffee on her books in lieu of coasters, and loved the sound of a cracking spine. She believed in leaving her mark on the books that left their mark on her.

"Heathen," she said.

"I try."

Their gazes met and held, combatants in their respective corners. Only the zing that usually sparked between them now seemed to curl about them, like an electric rope.

Then the car eased to a stop.

"You ready for this?" Nico asked, sliding the book back into his briefcase.

Not in the least, Laila realised far too late, as out of the corner of her eye she saw people spilling through the front door of a huge hacienda-style home.

What could she do but offer up a big, fake smile, and say, "Game on."

CHAPTER SEVEN

ONCE INTRODUCTIONS TO CLAUDIO, Rosetta and family were made, Nico stuck close to Laila as they moved through the house to the back patio, where lunch awaited.

"So, she's your *cousin*?" Laila murmured, leaning into him so his hand hovering at her lower back was forced to make contact. And once there it stayed, savouring the connection.

Feeling Savannah watching them, he let his hand slide around Laila's waist, and kept his voice low. "She's not my *cousin*. The estate is Rossi adjacent, but the Vitalis are chosen family."

"Ah," Laila said, craning to smile up at him, her eyes extra blue in the bright, Californian spring sunshine. "I figured inbreeding was how your family had stayed on top of the wine world for all those years."

That smile, he thought, that private, intimate, irreverent smile, the Kiss Me red lips a siren song, a lure to certain oblivion. He knew he ought to bite back, but all he wanted to do was use the hand at her waist to haul her close.

Claudio insisted Laila sit perpendicular to his spot at the head of the table. Nico took a seat across from hers. Rosetta positioned everyone else, saving space for Savannah with her down the other end, and when she placed a gentle hand over her daughter's, and Claudio sent his wife a brief, doleful nod, Nico wondered how much they *did* know about his last visit.

Then the scent of smoky cheese hit the back of Nico's nose

before platters of spicy salami, stuffed peppers, and sun-dried tomatoes, bowls of salad, and slippery penne, and spaghettini with prawns, and rolls and loaves of fresh bread were swept from the kitchen to the long wooden table.

After Claudio shouted "*Mangia!*" the table erupted in conversation and clinking cutlery, as food and wine moved like a well-choreographed dance.

Nico felt a bittersweet twinge—once his mother arrived in Siena, she would have all of this once more, while he'd have a villa, all to himself.

Leaning to fill his plate, Nico noticed Laila was sitting back. And it hit him that while fighting jet lag, and surrounded by strangers, she was also the only child of a woman who often forgot to feed her. He'd always found her formidable, if not a little intimidating, now knowing how it had been earned only made her more impressive.

Catching her eye, Nico motioned to the bowl of salad in front of him—lettuce, tomatoes, avocado, red onion dripping in lemon and olive oil—then mimed lifting his plate. She handed hers to him and he loaded her up.

"Pasta?" he asked.

She nodded.

He ladled a big scoop of penne onto her plate, and added a crusty bread roll. Pouring each a glass of Serenità Estate Zinfandel, he toasted her, then ordered, gently, "Dig in."

When she took her first bite, eyes closing in bliss, Nico felt it deep in his gut. Her pleasure. Her comfort. For a moment it was overwhelming. Thankfully, it eased up once the food and wine did their thing and Laila settled, charming Claudio as Nico knew she would. The older man laughed till he cried as she regaled him with tales of Vermillion—how Nico couldn't walk through town without people swooning in his wake.

When she told the same stories to Nico, she tossed them at him like live grenades; here she made it all seem enchanting. Golden. A place one might wish to not only visit but stay. And he wondered how much was acting, and how much of it was her.

Deep down he'd always assumed that one day he'd wake up to find her gone, the bookshop empty bar a few stray pink feathers and sparkles of glitter all over the floor. Leaving in a blink, just as she'd arrived.

But the light in her eyes, when she talked of his town, made him wonder. Maybe he'd created a version of her in his head and stubbornly held onto it, as it suited him.

Maybe he had Laila Vale all wrong from the start. And maybe this would be the week to get it right.

Once the long, long lunch was done, Rosetta and Claudio—with Savannah dragging her feet at the rear—walked Laila and Nico to the converted carriage house where they would be staying for the duration.

"Not your usual suite," Rosetta said, putting an arm around her daughter. "But we thought you could do with some privacy."

"*Grazie*," Nico said, glancing beside him to find Laila blinking slowly, as if she might fall asleep on the spot. "With that, I think we'll turn in early. This one is upright by way of stubbornness alone."

He held out his hand and Laila, barely holding back a yawn, took it without pause. So utterly spent was she, she leaned against his arm, her spare hand crooking gently around his elbow. And he had to fight the urge to scoop her up and carry her through the door.

Claudio's weathered face crinkled with delight. "Remember when we used to be like that?"

"Mmm," Rosetta hummed. "Like it was yesterday."

"Like what?" Savannah asked, a note of youthful petulance in the first words she'd spoken in Nico's vicinity since they'd arrived.

Her mother said, "So mad for one another we all but levitated."

While Nico wasn't sure they'd put on that good a show, he watched as Savannah looked from him, to Laila, then him, then Laila, and the rose-coloured feelings she had harboured for him for years *finally* lost their lustre.

When the Vitalis wandered back to the main house, Nico breathed out in blessed relief. "Come on, Sleeping Beauty," he murmured as he guided Laila inside.

"I could fall asleep where I stand," she said, her head tucked into his chest.

"First, pyjamas," Nico said, wondering what that might mean. Something frilly and pink? Or long and loose? Or nothing at all?

He attempted to pry Laila from his side, but she was having none of it. So, she came with him as he searched for their luggage only to realise it would be in the bedrooms. Or one of them, since the Vitalis had been led to believe that's all they would need.

"Follow me," he said, his voice a little rough with the effort of not thinking of beds and twisted sheets and bare limbs and warm skin while Laila was leaning into him, making little sleepy noises, her arms now wrapped around his waist, her body a dead weight.

Then he opened a cupboard in the first bedroom and found their clothes hung up side by side, the way his parents' clothes *still* hung in his mother's closet even after all these years, and ice shot down his spine.

Beside him, Laila none the wiser, groaned, "If there's only one bed, I might cry."

Through the sudden tightness in his throat, Nico laughed. If his ego wasn't as healthy as it was, her line might have made *him* cry.

Instead, her directness was like a light in the dark. Bewitching. Wildly, deeply, impossibly, regrettably, wholly. Feeling her against him, the scent of her burning the back of his throat was the sweetest of tortures.

There was no denying it. Not anymore. And what was the point? It was there, just under the surface; when he was with her, and when he was not. When he woke and saw the book she'd gifted him on the bedside table, when he heard others in town talk about her store. All the damn time.

The important thing was—it didn't matter. For he and Laila could never happen.

The ice in his chest at seeing their clothes all tucked up together had been a timely reminder why. *That* life, his parents', that depth of entanglement, terrified him. For he'd lived, firsthand, the aftermath of despair when forced disentanglement felt akin to erasure. And he'd not put himself, or anyone he loved, through that again.

And yet, there was Laila. Soft, and hard, and warm, and cool, and forthright, and generous. Pretending his attraction to her didn't exist had been futile. Fighting it hadn't done a lick to make it go away. Maybe acknowledging it, and *then* staying clear on his refusal to act on it, would be the answer.

It had to be.

"Lucky for you," he said, a raw note entering his voice, "there are two bedrooms. Two beds."

"That's nice," she said, opening her eyes long enough to see the bed right in front of her. And with that she slid her arms free, and crawled onto the bed, and landed face first on the pillow.

Nico watched her for a moment, and when she didn't move, he unzipped her boots and slipped them off her feet; gritting his teeth when her toes curled happily in her dotty pink socks. He found a throw blanket and laid it over her, and she instantly rolled on her side and wrapped herself up tight. When she reached for a spare pillow and wrapped arms and legs around it, Nico had never wanted to be an inanimate object more in his entire life.

Moving to the door, he flicked off the switch, the lamps around the room turning off.

"Nico," Laila said, her voice barely audible.

"Yes, Laila."

"Did we do okay so far?"

"We did great."

"Knew it," she murmured, nestling deeper into the bed. Then she fell instantly asleep. Breathing softly, eyes closed, lashes lying gently against her cheeks, making his heart squeeze so hard he rubbed his fist into his sternum as he left the room and closed the door.

He let his head hit the wood with a thunk.

The fact that, for whatever reason, Laila seemed just as determined to fight this thing between them, had probably been his saving grace. It had also allowed him to indulge it, knowing she'd always push back. Only this time when he'd pressed her to do something plainly ludicrous, she'd said yes.

Wired, Nico knew sleep was not an option. Casing the joint, he found the second en suite bedroom, a small kitchen, coffee machine, well-stocked fridge, a second filled with chilled wine.

He made himself a strong espresso, then moved to the couch and sat. Needing a distraction, he reached into his briefcase and pulled out *Steeling Harts*.

He opened it to the end of the first chapter where he'd left off the night before, after Laila had gone to bed. From what he could figure, Tyrrano, the battle robot, had been hired to protect Elvie, the space farmer's daughter, and she wasn't happy about it.

Lying back on the couch, propping a cushion behind his neck, and crossing his feet over the armrest, he read on.

* * *

"Morning."

Laila looked up from her spot by the window in the small dining nook where she'd been reading *Vineyards of the Napa Valley*—figuring it was the safest thing she could read right now—to find Nico at the front door of the carriage house, nudging off muddy sneakers.

His hair was a mass of damp dark curls, his bare arms were slick with sweat as he'd clearly been for a run.

She worked to swallow the piece of toast that had become stuck on her dry palate, and said, "Morning."

Then watched, in rapt silence, as he moved past her into the kitchen and opened the fridge. There he grabbed an apple, let it roll down his forearm before flicking it in the air and catching it. When he stood tall, and stretched out his back, trackpants that were too large hung low on his hips, while a shirt two sizes too small rode up his belly.

"I hate to be reductive," said Laila when she finally found words again, "but what are you wearing?"

"My clothes are all in your room, so I had to wangle what I could find in the other room."

"Oh," she said, gaze roving over him, not entirely sure she'd heard what he said. Then, after a long beat, he lifted his hand to his belly and gave it a scratch and she knew— *knew!*—he was doing it deliberately.

Her scrambled brain fought for purchase. *Bed. Other room. No clothes.*

"Your clothes are in my cupboard. Yes, I saw that this morning. All hung and pressed by some magical elf. You're welcome to leave them in there, or—"

"May I?" he asked, walking towards her bedroom door.

She waved a hand in the affirmative, listened as muffled sounds came from the room, then watched as he brought out his suitcase, clothes half hanging out the sides, then stalked into a room on the other side of the lounge.

She blinked at the half-closed door, her breath tight, a Pavlovian response to what felt like disengagement—the fear he was about to brush her off, now that he didn't need her anymore. For she swore he'd told her she'd done a good job, after seeing her to bed, alone, the night before.

Then Nico stuck his head through the door, his face hard, grumpy even, before he seemed to shake it off. "Ready for phase two?"

"Sure," she said, breathing out in relief.

"Want to check out my grapes?"

"Well, that's not one I've heard before."

His mouth tugged so quickly she nearly missed it.

"I'm meeting with Claudio in half an hour or so. If you're ready, you can come."

A minute later, the shower started up, and Laila decided she quite liked the fact Mr. Impeccable had a grumpy side, hummed as she finished her toast then went into her room to get ready.

"Unlike Nico's precious *baciami*, which we hand harvest, our Shiraz is machine harvested," Claudio was saying, "as are the Cab Sav and Chardonnay. High yield, fermented in bulk, aged in oak, our bread and butter."

Laila bounced around in the passenger seat of the ancient, doorless Jeep, hanging on for dear life as her host told tales of advancements in vineyard technology while also driving at ludicrous speeds up hill and down dale.

"We use drones now too," said Claudio, looking over his shoulder at Nico, who was in the back seat, "for seeding and visuals."

"Look!" said Laila, pointing out the front window at nothing just to get her host to turn to look front.

"Ah," said Claudio, thankfully slowing. "You are right. Here we are."

When the car pulled to a jerking stop, Laila held out her hand to stop herself from jackknifing. By the time she collected herself, Nico was at her door. When the ground was just too far to jump, she put her hands on his shoulder, his hands moved to her waist, and he lifted her down as if she weighed nothing at all.

To think a few days earlier the idea of holding this man's hand would have seemed ludicrous. Now, as he held it out to her, she took it without thought.

"Righto," said Claudio, waving his kerchief towards the plot. "Let's see what we can do to save your vines."

While Nico and Claudio stayed back, discussing the crop, Laila wandered the aisles between vines. Compared to others they'd passed—delicate, pretty things—Nico's were much sturdier. Gnarled with flecks of copper on the reddish-brown bark. They were also budding with tiny white flowers.

She reached out to touch one, then pulled her hand back.

"Go ahead," Nico said as he came up behind her.

When she baulked, he cupped a hand at her elbow, the rough scrape of his palm sending a shiver right through her as he nudged her hand forward. Her fingers brushed the leaves, serrated and slightly sharp, the petals so soft she barely felt them. Leaning in she sniffed, and the fragrance was the most delicate mix of citrus and honey. Sweet, slightly musky. Beautiful.

"Kiss Me," Claudio said.

Laila blinked, and glanced Claudio's way.

Claudio smiled broadly at the expression on her face. "Never fear, I was not propositioning you or your young man. We were just discussing Nico's new wine. Whether to name it after the grape or go another way."

"His grape? *This* grape?" Laila spun to find Nico looking

at his shoes, his cheeks blotchy, his jaw tight. "But it's called something in Italian. Batch…"

"*Baciami, si.* It was to be Incanto for a while. Scirocco—*warm wind.* I was partial to Rosavita—*rosy life.* But his final choice*, baciami*, was *perfetta.* It translates to…"

He held out both hands to Nico, who was looking to the sky as if hoping it might swallow him up then and there.

"*Kiss me*," he eventually said, his voice a low rumble that only just reached Laila's ears. "It means *kiss me.*"

Laila tried to swallow but her throat had gone dry. Not only because hearing those words, in that voice, made her head go all swimmy, but because Kiss Me was the name of *her* lipstick, the one she wore all the time, the one she was wearing right now.

Did he know that? Was it possible? And even if he did, would he— Surely not. For that would mean… No. Just no.

Claudio, who'd clearly had enough of the silence, filled it with talk of frost protection, and accelerated-growth techniques, while Nico still refused to look at her. She could tell he was only half listening to Claudio, as he rocked slowly on his heels, his hands shoved into his jeans pockets, his brow hard.

Then, as if he could no longer stop himself, his gaze moved to her mouth. And stayed.

When Laila's tongue darted out to swipe quickly over her parched lips, heat rose in his cheeks, and a rush of longing swept over his eyes. Leaving no doubt in Laila's mind that Nico Rossi had named his pride and joy after her.

After another night of rubbish sleep, fuelled by the Kiss Me conundrum, and having to watch Nico read her favourite book on the couch after yet another long dinner with the Vitalis, Laila lay in bed the next morning, waiting for Nico to go out for his morning run.

The moment the door shut she quickly showered and

dressed, wrapping her out-of-control hair into space buns, and dragging on jeans and a top, and some flip-flops she'd tossed in last minute.

When she went to the mirror to touch up her make-up, she lifted her Kiss Me red lipstick to her mouth by instinct, then paused. After a beat, she tossed it into her bag, swiped a clear gloss over her lips, then grabbed her stuff and hot-footed it to the front of the hacienda, where she waited for the ride-share car she'd ordered.

She tapped out a message to Nico, letting him know she was off to do some local sight-seeing and would be back for more "pretending" in the afternoon.

Glancing up the long driveway, she noted the sky was no longer the bright blue it had been the last couple of days; heavy-set clouds over the mountains in the distance looked ominous. Irrelevant—she needed to be elsewhere for a while.

When she heard the sound of a car engine, her tension eased. Until footsteps scraped on the gravel behind her.

She knew it was Nico before she even turned.

Time seemed to slow as he ambled her way. Not decked out in running clothes after all, he looked like an absolute dreamboat in an olive-green henley over mid-blue jeans, one hand in a pocket, dark sunglasses hiding his eyes.

"Hey," he said, brow furrowing over his sunglasses.

"Hey. No run this morning?"

"Meeting with the head viticulturalist. Going some-where?"

She lifted her phone, and said lamely, "I was just typing you a message. Thought I'd head into the local town. Check things out." *Et cetera.*

He lifted his chin in acknowledgement. "Want company?"

She lifted a hand to shield her eyes from the sun. "Don't you have to help your grapes make sweet sweet love to one another?"

His mouth lifted *achingly* slowly into a half smile. "That's not how it works."

"No?" she asked, all innocence.

She felt the smile light his eyes, even though she couldn't see them. She just knew his face so well. Knew the crinkles at the edges, the exact molten-chocolate shade, the way they looked a little hooded anytime he bit back.

She needed that car to arrive, right now.

When it did, she nearly whimpered with relief.

After a quick hello to the driver, she went to open the back door. Then paused and closed her eyes tight, a very small but very loud part of herself raging at her for what she was about to say.

She turned, pinned Nico with a look, and said, "So are you coming or not?"

Where. Is. Your. Willpower? Laila shouted inside her head as she swiped a hard finger over her phone, looking through images of Redwood Glen, the local town. The architecture was different, the cars on the wrong side of the road, but it might as well have been Vermillion.

"Where to first?" Nico asked.

"Shush. I'm deciding."

"I'm more than happy to follow your lead," he said, "but if you'll allow me, I know the area well."

She counted to five inside her head then, smiling sweetly, said, "Okay, fine. You choose."

Nico leaned forward, and to Pietro, the driver, said, "How long can we have you?"

"If you can pay, as long as you want me."

"Then let's start with the Little Literary Bookstore and go from there."

"Yes, sir," the driver said.

While Laila sat back, and tried terribly hard to remain

upset with herself, the fact that Nico had picked the most perfect place to visit took the edge off her censure, just a tad.

After spending a good hour following Laila around in the bookstore, Nico took Pietro's advice and they found a vintage record shop, where he picked up a Gigliola Cinquetti vinyl for his mother, then a letterpress print shop, where Laila forced him to help her choose stationery and co-write a letter to Sutton and Dante.

After which he asked the driver to swing them to Clover-Dale Farms.

As they wandered through the gates of the boutique farmstead, Nico knew he'd chosen well. For all that she'd lived in Vermillion for over eighteen months now, Laila was still a city girl, so from the petting zoo, to the maypole, to the ten-minute baby-goat yoga, she threw herself at it all.

He herded her to the Farm Shop, where they collected the large picnic basket and large checkered picnic blanket he'd called ahead and organised earlier, then he directed her to the edge of the farm, where they hit a marigold field—hectares of bright orange flowers around three feet high, as far as the eye could see.

"Nico, this is stunning," she said. Then, as if she'd given herself away somehow, she added, "I mean, not baby-goat-yoga-level great, but quite something just the same."

"Go on then." Nico motioned to the field.

"Are we allowed?"

Nico raised an eyebrow. Laila glanced back over her shoulder to see if anyone might be watching, then with a grin took off into the maze.

They soon found a thatch of soft green grass where the flowers hadn't taken. Laila shook out the blanket, Nico set down the basket, and they gorged themselves on mortadella and goat's milk cheese on fresh sourdough, iced tea, goat's milk fudge, and of course a bottle of local wine.

"And I thought the Vitalis put on a spread," said Nico, as with a groan he rolled to his back, legs and arms akimbo. The flowers swaying overhead a vibrant contrast against the grey sky.

Then a face appeared above him. A pair of bright, judgey, blue eyes.

"Can I ask you something?" Laila asked.

Nico moved his hand behind his head. "Of course."

"Did you name your grape after my lipstick?"

A rumble of thunder echoed in the distance, electricity crackling in the air, a swift breeze fluttering at the ends of the hair Laila had twisted into rolls either side of her head, but neither broke eye contact.

Then Nico said, "Yes. I did."

He waited for her *why*, and had no idea how he might answer. Though reasons aplenty whispered at the edges of his mind.

Only she said, "Okay then," and moved to lie down on her back beside him, her legs crossed at the ankles, hands clasped over her belly.

After a few long moments spent lost in their respective heads, she said, "Today has been a good day."

"Glad I came?"

"I'd not go *that* far," she said, then rolled towards him; her body curled into a comma, her knees an inch from his hand. Glittering in weak rays of sun slicing through the clouds above, making her eyes such a warm, welcome blue against the orange of the marigolds.

His hand moved, almost of its own volition, his little finger running down the seam of her jeans. The rise and fall of her chest proof she felt it. The sudden heat in her eyes proof she had no intention of asking him to stop.

"Well, I'm glad *you* came," he said. "I'd never have been able to focus on what I needed to do here if I was concerned I might hurt the Vitalis."

"You're too nice for your own good," she said, her voice soft, and a little raw.

"Is that what you really think of me?" he asked, fingers lifting to trace over her knee.

Her eyes moved between his, as if contemplating her answer.

A snap breeze lifted around them, sending the marigolds swaying overhead. Petals fell; dappled sunlight wavering over their hollow.

Before he could stop himself, Nico lifted up onto his elbow and plucked a petal from Laila's hair. Her breath hitched at his touch, the blue in her eyes turning to smoke.

Then a splash of water hit the back of his neck. Another hit Laila's cheek. Then the heavens opened and the rain began to fall.

Too far from the farm proper, they quickly gathered their things and ran beneath the canopy of a nearby fig tree that gave them enough shelter to decide what to do next.

Nico pulled his shirt from his skin, the fabric sticking like glue. He knew if Laila was doing the same, he might spontaneously combust. Literally. For while the rain came down cool, he felt like he was burning from the inside.

Ten more seconds back there, five even, and who knows what might have happened. If he'd run the back of a finger down her cheek as he'd so wanted to do, would her mouth have opened on a sigh? Would she have pressed her hand against his heart, her fingers gripping his shirt the way she had behind the bookshelves? Would she have drawn him to her, or would he have curved his mouth over hers, as they lost themselves in a kiss?

Too nice for his own good? The things he wanted to do to her, with her, for her... Hell. He wanted her. He wanted *Laila*. He wanted her with a vehemence that now, unleashed, threatened to consume him.

Rules be damned. Past be damned. *He* was damned.

But the thought of wanting her, of having her, then *losing* her; it tangled up inside his head like chains and knots and barbs.

Distance, self-control, deliberate choices—that was how he had stayed true to his responsibilities all these years. Though imagining a future in which he never kissed Laila, never held her, never touched her, made the rules he'd set for himself feel scooped hollow.

Laila made a sound as she shivered beside him. He glanced over to find her running her hands over her face, flicking the rain drops into the air, as she shivered from top to toe.

"Here," Nico growled, pulling her close and rubbing his hands over her arms. And she let him. For several long minutes they huddled together as the rain bucketed down.

When it started to ease, Laila was the first to move. With a quick dark glance, she leaned away just enough to pull her phone from her back pocket, and said, "We should call Pietro."

Of course. Nico had kept their driver on retainer for the day, meaning he was likely sitting in the car park at the entrance to the farm.

Laila shouted against the rain. "Pietro! It's Laila." She laughed at something Pietro said, her gaze scooting to Nico. "Yes, him too. If you don't mind a couple of drenched, goat-and-marigold-scented swamp creatures in your car, how about giving us a lift home?"

Her eyes stayed on Nico, roving distractedly over his face, as she listened. She continued to shiver, make-up rimming her eyes, but her energy was bright. All vitality, and mischief, and dogged determination. Just watching her be her was enough for Nico's heart to tumble over on itself so thoroughly he was left feeling bruised.

She gave Nico a thumbs up, and as soon as the rain cleared to a gentle mist, as one they ran out into the haze.

CHAPTER EIGHT

SITTING IN THE back of Pietro's car with Nico—windows fogging, skin steaming—had been bad enough, but the walk back to the carriage house was pure agony.

Every swing of her arm Laila imagined her fingers brushing his. Every glance sideways she imagined her gaze finding his, heat burning in his eyes. As from the moment his touch had grazed her knee, her body had been aflame.

But she couldn't. *Wouldn't*. If anything actually happened between them, she'd regret, instantly, losing the hard-won self-control that set New Laila apart from Old Laila, taking her back to square one.

The moment Nico unlocked the door to the carriage house, Laila all but ran to her bedroom, muttering something about staving off a deathly cold. Then she got straight into a long hot shower, and didn't get out till her inside felt cooler than her outside.

Hair air dried, face scrubbed clean, changed into baggy trackpants and an oversized sweatshirt, Laila lay on her bed and read the same page of a book she couldn't remember until she could no longer stand it.

Peeking out her bedroom door, she found the place quiet. Then her phone buzzed and she nearly leapt out of her skin.

NICO: I'm spending the afternoon with Claudio and his head winemaker. There will be much talk of maceration, and pumping, and *bâtonnage*, which I would not wish on anyone. There's a nice pinot gris chilling in the wine fridge, and I'll bring dinner back for the two of us.

The man printed out his work on actual paper, read books she asked him to read, and used correct grammar and punctuation in his texts—was he *trying* to seduce her?

Needing a distraction, she moved to the couch and checked in with Sutton.

LAILA: Snail mail incoming.

SUTTON: Mail! How vintage!

Then Aurora.

AURORA: all going swimmingly at the bookstore. reading *the hating game* as kelly said I had to before I die. so good.

A while later, Laila went back to her room and ate leftover goat's milk fudge. Then woke from a dreamless nap and felt more discombobulated than she had before.

Only to find Nico was back.

NICO: Lasagne is in the oven. I'm on the patio.

Heart skipping madly, she thought about dragging her hair into a messy bun and wrapping herself in a blanket in the hopes of staving off any more hot looks from the man. But her ego won out, and she changed into white tank, cream cardigan, and soft grey yoga tights.

Checking her face to make sure it wasn't creased from her pillow, she left her mouth Kiss Me free. To think she'd started wearing it as a form of resistance, and now *not* wearing it felt that way. Sometimes it was hard to be a woman.

The scent of cheese and herbs wafted from the oven as she made her way outside.

The patio of the Carriage House was a smaller version of the main house—elegant terrazzo tile, and columns holding up the canted ceiling overhead. To the right a fire had been lit in a large fireplace. To the left the space was closed in, private by way of a stuccoed wall covered in creeping vines. Tiny lights lit a path out towards the nearest vineyard, all of it bathed in gold as the sun began to set.

Nico stood leaning against the balustrade, gently swirling a glass of red wine—all loose limbs, and broad shoulders, as if ready to break into song, or fight a gnarly beast, if the moment hit.

Only now when she looked at him, she no longer saw some cartoon character with a hero complex. Now she saw a man too kind to tell the daughter of a close friend that he would never be romantically interested in her. A man who wasn't into wine for the cool factor, but because he was a true believer. A man who spent his life trying to be the kind of man his long-gone father would be proud of. A man with facets and flaws, and the cognisance to admit to them.

Her wariness around him was no longer tied to a healthy mistrust of confident, good-looking men, but due to very real feelings she had for him. And only him. Meaning if he ever disappointed her it would be due to something substantial. Something genuine. And it might break her in a way she couldn't put together again.

She cleared her throat, and Nico started, turned, and shot her a smile that was filled with such honest-to-goodness joy at seeing her, her poor wayward heart fluttered up into her throat.

Down, girl, she chastised gently.

"For a second there I didn't recognise you," he said. "I was on the lookout for a drowned rat clutching a bag of fudge as if her life depended on it."

"Ha-ha," she managed. "You look a tad more human than you did a few hours ago too." By *human*, she meant absolutely delicious in his navy sweater and dark chinos and, if she wasn't mistaken, freshly shaven. As if had put in some effort too.

As some kind of last resort, she tried to come up with a book boyfriend who might compare—Phin Tucker, Rhys Penhallow, Lord St. Vincent? But none came close, mostly because none of them were there, right in front of her, looking at her the way Nico did.

Pulling her cardigan tight across her chest and folding her arms, she moved to the far left of the patio, near the safety of the vine-covered wall. The rain had cleared, leaving a deep blue sky, with a smear of pink-and-gold cloud in the distance.

"Magic, isn't it?" said Nico, who had moved up beside her.

She turned to find him holding out a glass of wine, which she took; telling herself to have a sip and leave it alone. She needed her wits about her tonight.

"How do you think our great deception is going?" she asked.

He leaned his forearms beside hers and looked out into the growing dark. "I think we're managing to pull it off. You?"

"Totally," she agreed, lifting her glass.

He gave hers a clink, snagged her gaze over the top of his glass as Laila brought hers to her mouth and took a fortifying glug.

"Lucky," she said, "as without me here, I think you like these people so much you might well have come back engaged. And then what? Would she have moved to Vermillion, or would you have had to move here?"

Nico's short "hmm" was unexpected. Surely, a brisk "Vermillion, without doubt!" would have been more in keeping with Nico's relationship with that town.

Before she could press him, he motioned to the glass in her hand and asked, "So, what do you think?"

"Of the wine?" She took another sip, and paid attention rather than simply pouring it down her gullet. "Oh! I really like this one."

The smile that came over Nico's face nearly undid her.

"Wait," she said. "Is this…?" The Italian was lost to her. "Is this Kiss Me?"

Nico nodded, but not before his gaze dropped to her mouth for a beat before rising once more. "Unfortunately, Serenità lost around a quarter of next year's crop due to a late frost. Winemaking is not for the weak of heart. But *that* wine is from last fall's harvest. And it's pretty damn good."

"I'm no expert but it really is."

"Traditionally, Vermillion Hill makes wine for experts, but *I* make wine for intimate dinner tables, and long lazy summer lunches. For celebrations and commiserations. For people to laugh over, and learn over, and listen over, and enjoy."

"If that's not on your website, you're doing yourself a disservice."

Nico turned so that his back was to the view, and crossed his feet at the ankles; his face all hard angles and warm glints in the firelit near darkness. "Now, tell me what you taste."

"Might as well learn something while I'm here," she tossed back. "Tell me what to do."

Nico gathered the bottle at his feet—no label, just a sticker penned with Baciami, the date harvested, date bottled, and date opened—and he topped up her glass.

"Step one," he said, "look."

"For?"

"Colour. Clarity." He held the glass by the stem, and at an angle.

Laila did the same.

"Step two, smell." Nico swirled the glass once, with an adeptness that set her competence kink alight before he lifted the glass to his nose. When Laila followed suit, he said, "Catch anything in particular?"

She tried. Truly. But all she could catch was grape skin, grape flesh, a little dry feeling in the back of her throat.

"Look for layers. Is it fruity? Earthy? Spicy? Woody?"

"Yes," she said.

Nico laughed softly. "It's warmer back home, not as close to the sea, meaning the grapes harvested there are jammier. Think plum, fig, liquorice. The same vines grown here accumulate notes of lavender. Mint. And something more mineral." He sniffed again. "Graphite."

"If you say so. When do we get to taste it again?"

"Now," he said.

Laila lifted the glass and the wine slid smoothly into her mouth. She closed her eyes as it coated the back of her teeth, her palate, under her tongue. When she swallowed, she let go a surprised "Oh! I think I caught something spicy. Bell pepper?"

Nico tipped his glass her way. "Great catch."

"Ha." Laila took another sip. Chasing the pepper, and some kind of tang, and a cool lingering sharpness at the end that she really liked. Then, "Oops. Was I meant to spit it out somewhere?"

Nico brought his own glass to his mouth. His voice a raw growl as he said, "Don't you dare."

Laila already feeling a buzz in the back of her head, and self-aware enough to know it had little to do with the wine, put the half-empty glass on the balustrade.

Then she took a step back only to get caught up in vines curling down the stuccoed wall behind her. She bounced forward with a squeak, her cardigan and her hair covered in loose, dry twigs.

"May I?" Nico moved towards her.

"I've got it," she said, madly brushing herself down all over, remembering how it had felt when he'd lifted a marigold petal from her hair.

"There's one… Laila, just let me."

Laila held her hands out between them, balanced on a mental precipice. Protect herself at all cost. Or give a little.

She looked up. Nico was so steady, rock solid, as he waited for her to decide. That honest forbearance the one thing that could tip her over the edge.

"Please," she said, her voice barely a whisper.

Nico took another step closer and pulled a twig from her hair. He showed it to her, knowing she'd want proof. Knowing, because he knew her, that she found it so hard to trust.

He tossed the stick over the balustrade, then, brushing her hair off her shoulder, came up with another. "You really did do a fine job of de-twigging the wall. You don't do anything by halves, do you, Laila Vale?"

When he breathed in deep, as he brushed her hair from her other shoulder, his hand lingering at her nape, she knew deep in her gut that there were no more twigs. He was touching her now because he could.

His nostrils flared as his thumb traced the line of her jaw, running over her earlobe, down the side of her neck, sending a shower of stars falling inside of her. When his hand delved into her hair, and she did nothing to stop him, he leaned in till his forehead met hers.

Her hand lifted to press against his chest, before grabbing hold of a hunk and tugging him closer. A hand at her waist slid around her back, his thumb catching the hem of her top so that he could lift it to find skin. As if now he had her, he wasn't messing about.

He lifted his head, and his nose bussed the end of hers. His lips traced her jaw as he murmured a string of deep, rough Italian nothings that she knew in her bones were dirty as hell.

If they stopped there, she could probably still tell herself nothing had happened—they'd not kissed, they'd barely done more than hold hands. But the moment her hips rocked forward to meet his, a soft moan leaving her lips, she knew there was no going back.

When the hard ridge straining against the front of his pants brushed against her, as she wrapped her leg around his calf, it was the exclamation mark that sealed that deal.

His hand moved up her back, and her body sang beneath his touch.

Laila didn't even know she was on her tiptoes, a hand tugging at his hair, till she felt his groan against her neck. When his teeth scraped gently along the slope between her neck and her shoulder, a shiver wracked her entire body.

This, her heart whispered. *This this this!*

She knew people talked about her—the romance bookseller who doesn't have a fella. Perhaps they thought her cold, or strange, or mercenary.

She wondered if any of them twigged that she had surrounded herself with so many love stories because the total opposite was true. Vale women loved love so much, they became slaves to it. While for her mother hope sprang eternal, when Laila fell, she broke. Every damn time. She was a lover of love who was a complete disaster when it came to the reality.

And this, *this*, had her in its complete thrall.

"Nico," she breathed, as her last living speck of sense broke through the haze. "Wait."

The moment he felt her hesitation, Nico stopped on a dime. One hand so far up the back of her shirt, her stomach was exposed, the other curled up in her hair. Her leg was around his thigh now, their bodies pressed together with heat and need. Yet he slowly pulled back, and took a moment to collect himself, before his eyes met hers.

She knew how she must have looked—hot, wild, undone—because a satisfied smile tugged at the corner of his mouth. He'd done that to her. And he liked it.

She shook her head, refusing to give in to his impossible confidence, his strident charm. But what could she possibly say? That she was *celibate*? That if any man could make her break her vow it was clearly him? If she explained her whys, she feared it would all sound so small to anyone but her, and he'd never see her in the same light again.

She *liked* how Nico saw her. Liked the awe she sometimes caught in his gaze. But who did she wish to be most true to, the feelings whipping inside, or some unremitting facade she'd created so she'd never be hurt again?

"Laila," he said, the hand in her hair shifting to cup her jaw, his thumb stroking along her cheek. "Talk to me. If you want us to put the wine away and have a nice dinner, then that's what we'll do."

She bit her lip; body warring with head, past warring with right now.

"Whatever you want," he said, "I'm there for it. But you're going to have to tell me."

Laila read all kinds of heroes—alphaholes, lone wolves, boys next door, bad boys, protectors, shadow daddies—but until that moment she had no clue that "a good man" could be such a deeply, ethic-loosening turn-on.

When she let out a sound that felt like twisting metal, Nico's gaze darkened. "Now you're starting to make me worry. And you know what I'm like when I worry."

The thought of Nico going all Superman, or Gaston, even Constable Goodboy right now made her knees near go out from under her.

"I…" Oh gods, was she really about to let this man so deep behind her defences? Apparently so. She licked her lips, closed her eyes, and said, "I haven't done this in a long time."

"Okay," Nico said. Then, "And by *this* I assume you mean drink excellent wine, and fall into a grapevine, only to be rescued by a handsome vintner?"

Laila laughed, the sound catching in her chest. But this was better. This was *them*. "Handsome? I mean, in the right light, I guess."

The glint in his eye made it clear he knew his own worth.

Filling her lungs in an attempt to clear just a little more of the hazy fog that still enveloped her, Laila said, "By *this*, I meant…man-woman stuff."

Nico pulled back a fraction, his gaze widening. "And by *that* you mean…"

Laila laughed. "Do you want me to draw a picture?"

"If you would." He made to step back as if clearing the way to pen and paper, but she reached for his jumper and held on. With an out-shot of breath, the kind that felt like relief, Nico moved back into her personal space. Filling it with his durability, his forbearance, his substance.

"You have nothing to worry about with me, Laila. I hope you know that. I have no expectations when it comes to… *this*." His mouth lifted in a half smile, while his eyes remained serious. "That said, I would very much like to kiss you. And I believe you want to kiss me too."

"Nico," she said, the word a whisper, a question, a wish.

Because he was right. She wanted to kiss him. She wanted it more than she wanted air. Or books. Or to keep any other promise she'd ever made.

Surely, after all this time, the many *many* months of abstinence, of self-denial, of living in constant fear of misinterpretation and heartache, her instincts had been honed. Maybe even reset.

They told her that this man was unique among all men. And that *not* kissing him, far from home, under a wide foreign sky, would be her biggest regret of all.

"Kiss me," she said.

His throat worked as his gaze dropped to her mouth.

"Kiss me, you big galumph."

As if he had been holding on by a thread—made of pure steel, no doubt—the moment it snapped free, Nico gathered her to him, gave her one last hot ravaged look, then pressed his lips to hers.

For one brief second the world around her seemed to hold its breath. The air hushed, the wall behind her disappeared, time and place became irrelevant.

The next second her senses splintered into starlight.

The kiss was pure languor; all lazy spring afternoons and pollen in the breeze. Her bones melted with every slow sweep of his lips over hers. All enchanting pleasure, and sunbursts, pleasure pouring through her like honeyed wine—heady, golden, and achingly slow.

Laila dived her hands into Nico's hair, revelling in the textures, the give, the roughness against her fingers. The friction of her breasts bussing against his hard chest felt like pure potential, like the rasp and hiss of an unlit match. While his arms around her were bands of hot muscle and strength, holding her wilted body upright when it felt as if nothing else could.

When the edges of her vision behind her tightly closed eyes began to close in, only a pinprick of light keeping her tethered to here and now, she took a breath and the fresh cool air of night felt like ice against her lips.

As if fearing she might abscond, Nico scooped her closer, arms wrapping her so tightly she could feel his fingers caressing the very edges of her breasts. A whisper of a touch, setting off a wildfire inside her. And when he kissed her again, their mouths met more deeply. More urgently.

His tongue slid along the seam of her lips, echoes of berries and rich red wine. Once she opened her mouth to his, wildness whipped through her and she was in freefall.

"Nico," she said against his lips. Unsure why. To slow down, to speed up, to make sure this was real?

Kissing the edge of her mouth, her cheek, her eyelids, he said, "Tell me what you need."

No want this time, but *need*. That's what this was. Primal, beyond thought.

"I *need* you to touch me."

"Where?" he rumbled, his kisses moving down her neck.

"Anywhere."

He didn't wait to be asked twice.

Thank the gods for soft yoga pants, for his hand at her back dived below the elastic top to palm her cheek. Kneading, caressing.

Laila wrapped her leg tightly around his thigh for purchase, for nearness, to feel a part of him. Till she no longer felt corporeal. She was breath, and impulse, and demand.

"Touch me," she said, her face tucked into his neck as he lifted her, pressed her back into the wall, her feet no longer touching the ground.

Her mouth opened on a gasp, her eyes closed, her hands gripping whatever part of him they could find as his hand slid further, deeper, curling beneath her, fingers sliding, between her legs, glancing over the nub at her centre.

She cried out at the intimacy of his touch. How had she denied herself this? Only none of *this* had ever been on the menu. The care, the focus. The *accuracy*.

Her breaths came high in her throat as his big, rough fingers moved over her with such delicacy, swirling back and forth and around and into her. *Hot damn*.

"Stop?" he asked, when her breaths became little more than short sharp pants. "Slow down?"

"Don't you dare," she said, parroting his earlier words, then sinking her teeth against his neck so as not to scream.

The cocksure rough of his laughter against her cheek was like feathers brushing over her sensitive skin. Too much. Yet she clung to him still, now riding his hand, the slow, insistent, cruel, perfect motion of his fingers, the deliberate press of his palm, matching the roll of his hips against hers in intentional liquid rhythm.

"*Non ho mai desiderato nessuno come te. Mi fai dimenticare il mondo,*" he whispered to her; a string of deep, husky words, all cadence and heat that coiled deep inside of her.

And he kept her there, right on the edge, as her mouth dropped open and her head fell back, her hair catching on the vines. Her mind a swirl of colour and light, her body the most beautiful, all-over ache.

Then, hovering on the crest of a wave of the most intense pleasure she had ever known, she clutched around him, before tumbling over the other side.

Shaking around his touch, gentle strokes that brought her back to earth, she gathered herself to him, wrapping her arms about his neck.

When he pressed one final kiss atop her head, it was so sweet, so tender, reality crept in. With nothing to stop them, she waited for all the bad thoughts to tumble in, remorse snapping her mind into crisis mode. But while she knew she'd capitulated, it hadn't *felt* that way. It had felt like a choice, a decision. Time.

Book boyfriends might not leave towels on the floor, but they could not give her what Nico had just given her. A gift so personal she'd never forget it for the rest of her life.

Breathing in deeply, she grabbed the front of his shirt and gave it a half-hearted shake. Taking it as instruction, he lowered her to the ground. And the cold air of early evening rushed between them.

Laila drew her cardigan tight about herself. "So that happened."

"Hell, yeah it did," he said, awe very much intact.

Her heart pulsed a happy extra beat.

"Nico," she said, her hands dropping to her sides, fingers curling and uncurling restlessly, not at all sure what she might say next.

More? Again? Your turn? What now? How did they go back to normal life after that? But they had to, didn't they? It was the culmination of a whole lot of flirt-fighting, and now it had passed. Hadn't it?

Then his hand dropped to the front of his jeans, to make things more comfortable, and she saw the ridge standing out in proud relief against the front of his pants, and despite the fact parts of her still trembled, her thighs clenched and her mouth began to water.

"Nico," she said again, her voice plaintive, raw—

And the oven alarm went off like a racket in the kitchen.

"That would be dinner," he said, his voice only a mite above subterranean.

"But…" She glanced at his zipper.

"No expectations, remember," he reassured her, reaching to brush his thumb over her cheek. "We're all good."

Laila nodded. Though even after what had just happened, even after he assured her he was "all good," disquiet flickered to life in the back of her head.

She'd told him to kiss her, begged him to touch her, *anywhere*, and he was still able to walk away.

"You get the lasagne," she said, nodding vociferously now as she eased herself away from the wall and backed towards the house. "I'm going to freshen up."

His gaze, still hot, still dark, flickered. "Sounds like a plan."

She turned then, legs still not quite right, and headed for the door.

"Laila."

She stopped at the door and looked over her shoulder. "Yep?"

"Hands down the best damn kiss of my life."

The laugh that wavered out of her ended with an ache deep in her chest. Aflush then, with delight, and late-blooming daze at what had unfolded, she showered for the second time that afternoon.

All the while picturing Nico, hours from now, leaning his big hand up against the wall of his own shower, thinking of her, of her mouth, of her body, as he finished what they'd started.

CHAPTER NINE

WHETHER BY DESIGN or accident, during their final day in Napa every time Nico looked for Laila, she was elsewhere. Back at the bookstore, or helping Rosetta, taking a row boat out on the local lake with Savanah, of all people.

She was clearly trying to make some point, but he still wanted to get her alone, sink his hand into her soft waves, and kiss her till nothing else mattered.

Maybe that's what he should have done after dinner the night before. Rather than giving her space, give her the choice to finish what they'd started. Maybe then he wouldn't feel wound as tight as a steel drum. Itch scratched. Move on.

"Young love," Claudio had sighed, during their final visit to the *baciami* plot. "As fraught as it is fine."

Not love, Nico thought later that night as he packed his bags, everything in him pushing back against the idea. It could never be that. No matter what else changed, the lessons of his past remained a constant.

It *was* something though: her voice, husky and light as she'd demanded *kiss me, touch me*, would haunt him forever. But while what had happened had felt inevitable, necessary even, and only half finished—he'd seen in those wildly expressive blue eyes of hers that she'd felt the same way—it was just too damn bad.

For while he'd gone to Napa looking for clarity, instead he'd found triumph. His Californian wine was ready for market, meaning he had real decisions to make. Not only for his family, or the town, but for himself.

To do that he'd need every ounce of mental space he had at his disposal so that he would get it just right. Meaning, they went back to Vermillion, everything had to go back to the way it had been.

While turning up at her shop with a list of alternative names, or happening to be at the Vine the times he knew she got her coffee, felt so transparent now, they'd managed to get through the past year and a half wanting one another on the quiet.

Surely, they could do it again.

When they drove under the Welcome to Vermillion archway it was early evening, the street its usual fairy-tale gorgeous, but Laila was far too wired to notice.

Not only from their whirlwind trip, but because she'd spent the sixteen-hour flight back waxing lyrical about books, movies, sport, politics, even religion, so she didn't have to hear Nico say the words, *Look, Laila, you're a great girl but...*

She knew it was coming. She could sense it the way snakes sensed rain. He'd be lovely about it, couching it in kindness, but it would still hurt. For while trying to tap into the exact pain she'd felt when Rufus put an end to things was muted now—like knowing it hurt when you kicked your toe, but trying to recall the exact feeling was near impossible—she knew that being cast aside by Nico would be so different it was not even the same thing.

When the car pulled to a stop outside Forbidden Fruits Story Emporium, Laila glanced up at the window and felt a flash of relief. She had missed her little haven, the place that had saved her from herself all those months ago. It would be fine company again.

But more than that, she'd come back from California with

something other than an even more complicated situation with the man sitting in the back seat of the car beside her. The realisation that she was not the island unto herself she'd tried to be.

Too afraid to let *anyone* close, she'd convinced herself that her regulars, her neighbours, her book clubbers were there for the books alone. But they had become her friends, whether she'd wanted them or not. And, it turned out, she really did.

When she saw Nico was already out of the car collecting her luggage, she hopped out, stretched, then slung her soft bag over her shoulder, knowing if she tried to wrangle the big one, Nico would fight her for it.

"I can take it from here," she said when they reached her front gate.

"Let me help."

When their gazes snagged, she wondered if he too was re-membering his offer to help remove the twigs from her hair. And all that came after.

"Not this time," she said.

He ran his hand over his mouth, a move of frustration, as if he too wasn't ready to end things, though knew he must, and such sweet warmth trickled through her it felt like the first sign of a waterfall after spring rain.

"I'll take it from here," she reiterated. "We don't need to give this town any reason to talk."

Confusion flickered over his beautiful face, then, meaning dawning, he said, "Right. Of course. Smart move."

"So, we agree—what happened in Napa stays in Napa."

A long slow moment beat between them. Nico's gaze roved over her with a thoroughness of a man going off to war, perhaps never to see a woman again. And for a second, she thought he might refuse her. But he nodded, and said, "If that's what you want."

What she wanted was to stop feeling this much. This wild.

This want. It would be crushing if she didn't cut it off at the pass. The longing she was feeling wasn't healthy, or sustainable. For either of them.

"It's what we both want," she said.

Nico nodded, then took a step back so that light from the streetlamp created a golden halo around his broad shoulders. "One last thing. I got a message from council. They've agreed to allow me to table a proposal to make the old cottages on Main Street semi-residential at the next quarterly town planning meeting. So, you can relax. No rush to make any changes."

"Brilliant," she said giving him a thumbs up. Though it had taken her a beat to remember what he was talking about—only the entire reason she'd agreed to go with him on the trip.

"Well, good night, Laila. And thank you again."

"My pleasure," she said, then felt heat scoot up her neck into her cheeks and she remembered exactly how much of a pleasure it had been.

And would be no more.

Then she gave Nico a small wave and went inside the safety of her darling little store.

The next few days life went back to normal, or as normal as life could be in Vermillion.

Laila woke when she woke, went to the Vine for coffee, and hawked books to anyone who passed over her threshold. Which turned out to be quite a lot, for the shop had been extra busy since her return. Especially with local foot traffic. She'd met the haberdasher and the pizza shop owner. Hannah's folks had come in to rave about how much their daughter had opened up since starting book club.

She put it down to them sensing that she had finally opened up to being one of them now. Though it could also be the cooler weather making people want hot books to warm them up at night.

Either way, it had given her the final push to organise an outing in a month's time to the local botanical gardens for *all* of her book clubbers. A way for all the women of the area to feel more connected.

But even with all that, everything felt a little grey.

Nico had clearly taken her at her word, as he'd not come into her store once since they'd been back. And she missed him. Missed teasing him, missed catching him watching her like he was imagining all the things he could do to make her sigh. She should have known it would be that way, for the man Nico Rossi followed through.

Kiss me, she'd asked. And he'd kissed her.

Touch me, she'd begged. And he'd certainly done that.

Keep your distance, she'd insisted. And well, that's what she got.

Then, one random Tuesday morning, the core of the Main Character Energy Book Club dropped by en masse.

"We cannot believe you!" Kelly cried as they burst through the front door, nearly knocking the bell from its hinge.

Laila, who had been leaning on the counter, engrossed in *The Devil in Winter*, flinched so hard she knocked over a stack of The Book Was Better bookmarks. "What can't you believe?"

"The Book Boyfriend dropped you home the other night," said Hannah, accusingly.

Jane, breathless, eyes bright, said, "I heard it from Maggie from Corker of a Deal, who heard it from Mrs. Constantine, the butcher's wife, who saw it happen with her own eyes."

Laila opened her mouth, then closed it. So much for discretion. Not that it mattered to her *so* much, for the tea had clearly not gone beyond a car ride. But Nico? With his infamous "no dating locals" rule—if this got out, they would eat him alive.

Then Aurora, lying on the couch in the window reading Kate Clayborn's *Love at First*, piped up with "Probably the night you both came home from Napa."

Aurora, Laila thought.

"Oh my heavenly heart," said Kelly. "Is that where you were last week? Napa? With Nico 'Future Father of My Unborn Children' Rossi?"

While it took a good few seconds of heavy silence before Aurora dragged her gaze away from the page, once she realised what she'd said, she curled up and hid her face behind her book.

"Okay," said Laila coming around from behind the counter. "This is as far as this conversation goes. If we are all friends here, real friends, that is the deal. *Capiche*?"

"That's Italian," Jane whispered to Hannah, as if it was the final nail in Laila's coffin.

While Kelly, looking a little chagrined now, said, "Our lips are sealed. But I don't know how that'll help, because *everyone* is talking about it."

"Everyone?"

"Everyone," Jane whispered.

And suddenly the extra foot traffic made a whole lot more sense.

"Don't worry though!" said Jane, reaching out in empathy. "Not everyone is up in arms. Gerald, from the menswear shop, had a go at Meryl when she was trying to claim winnings from the betting ring. She said..." Jane looked to the ceiling as if Meryl's words might be written there. "Since it was now clear the two of you were up to no good, the kitty should be hers. Gerald told her the whole thing was in poor taste."

Kelly nodded in agreement.

"There's a betting ring?" Laila looked to Aurora, who was now peeking out from behind her book, her eyes on the front door as if she too was worried how her brother would take all of this.

But Laila moved first. "Aurora, honey, can you…? Can you watch the shop?"

Auroa nodded in understanding. "I'll stay till close."

"Us too!" the other three called out.

Laila grabbed her phone and her keys, then looked down at her dress—a fifties pale pink covered in embroidered cherries—and grabbed her cardigan from a hook by the door.

She had no idea if Nico would be home, or off rescuing a llama trapped in a well, or reading *The Hungry Little Caterpillar* to local toddlers in the Vermillion library, or whatever the heck he did on a Tuesday morning. All she knew was that she had to find him.

Not quite sure what she was going to say, not having seen the man in days, Laila felt as invigorated at the fact she finally had an excuse to see him at all.

Nico was finishing up a chat with a seasonal gardening crew when he heard a car engine, then what looked like a red MINI Cooper flash past fence posts and craggy brown winter vines as it hooned its way up the winding driveway.

When it reached the edge of the lawn, it slowed as quickly as if the handbrake had been yanked, and the driver's door was open before it had bobbed to a full stop.

Then there was Laila, storming his way, a sundress covered in apples, no cherries, cinched at her waist, the skirt fluttering about her thighs. An oversized cream cardigan that looked a hell of a lot like the one she'd been wearing that night on the carriage house patio hung half off her shoulders. Her hair moved in soft pale waves, her cheeks were flushed as if she'd run all the way there, and he'd never seen anything more beautiful in his entire life.

While part of him wanted to leap in the air and shout

Huzzah, another part thought, *Dammit. What the hell am I going to do now?*

He'd managed to fill the hours since he'd last seen her and then some, finalising six months' worth of plans with the winemaking team, taking on every volunteer call, all in the effort at keeping himself away from her.

Firstly, because he'd promised it.

Secondly, because she'd asked it of him.

But mostly because he knew that if he saw her, he'd do everything in his power to convince her to let him kiss her again.

"We need to talk," she said, clearly clueless that she'd brought him to his metaphorical knees simply by being there.

Nico thanked the gardening crew, told them they were excused, and waited till they were out of earshot before he said, "Good, thanks. And you?"

She rolled her eyes and said, "Peachy."

He laughed, because hell she was something. Then, when he saw the gardeners looking back over their shoulders, he held out an arm and guided her inside.

She'd never been up to the house before, though there had been times he'd considered inviting her for dinner, or a drink, a friendly game of strip Scrabble. Only to stop before he stepped over that line.

He watched her as she took it all in—the wide front entrance with the vaulted ceiling, sculptures and art, or gaps where art had been. The large chef's kitchen on the left, halls leading to the family wing, the guest wing, and entertainment spaces. The huge sunken lounge on the right that led to the patio, and beyond that views directly over Vermillion.

"Nico," she gushed, "this place is gorgeous." Then, "Half your stuff is gone."

"My mother," he explained, "is cleaning house. Taking everything that's meaningful to her when she leaves."

Apparently, that meant all the dinner ware and cutlery, bar a single set for him, a passive aggressive move on her part. *This will be your life, my boy, alone in this big house, if you keep going the way that you are.*

"Here," he said, motioning her down the step to the large modular couch, big enough to fit a dozen people.

When she sat, he sat near, but not too near. When her cardigan fell an inch, revealing a creamy bare shoulder, he managed not to move to her, tug it all the way down and scrape his teeth over her warm, tender skin.

Holding himself together with pure dogged grit, he said, "We have to talk?"

"We do?" she asked as her eyes moved between his, oceans of deep blue, tangled lashes, sparks of light.

Her vitality had been a shock to his system the day they first met, like a bolt of lightning hitting the ground at his feet. Now, up close and personal, he felt no less awe.

Then she shook her head and said, "We do. Though I don't know where to begin. Okay, suffice it to say, the plan to leave what happened in Napa…"

She waved a hand between them.

"In Napa?"

"We failed. The entire town thinks that something is going on between us, they have opinions, and apparently have been taking bets for some time. And I know that that's probably a good reason why you have your 'no locals' rule, all that intense focus on something that can be so delicate, so complicated. So I'm sorry."

"What do you have to be sorry for?" he asked, moving closer.

"You make it look so easy," she said, and she moved closer too. He wondered if she even knew it. "Holding the town on your back the way you do. But I also understand what it's like to constantly feel judged."

Her mother, he thought, had done some real damage. But she'd also been the seed for so much of Laila's chutzpah and strength. Much the way his own circumstances had shaped who he had become. The trick was figuring out which things to allow to build you and which to let go.

"It's not that," he said. *Not only that.*

"Oh," she said, blinking several times in a row, before she looked down at her hands clasped tightly in her lap. "Then... okay. Maybe I shouldn't have come."

"Laila—"

"I mean you stayed away, signal enough that that was how you wanted things. Which is fine. I get it."

"Laila. If you think my staying away from you was easy, you're wrong. I was doing as you asked, because what you want is important to me."

Laila swallowed, hard. And he could see her inner demons telling her that what he was saying couldn't possibly be that straightforward.

Someone had clearly hurt her in the past. Some damn fool who'd not realised what he'd had. While for the life of him he could not imagine how anyone could be that much of a putz, it was clear Laila suffered because of it still.

And the looseness with which Nico had appeared to treat her feelings, telling himself it was what she wanted in order to save himself from making a hard choice, had clearly played into that. The damn fool that time was all him.

"The town," he said, "is only a small part of why I've never dated anyone from around here, but it's not the main part. I told you how when my father died, my mother struggled."

Laila blinked in acknowledgement. For a big talker, she was an incredibly active listener. Which made him want to get this next part exactly right.

"Aurora and I were lucky; the staff here knew the work, so

they could run the vineyard with minimal supervision, and the town loved us and kept tabs on us. But we all but raised ourselves. While Mamma was here, she was not here, not really, for a good number of years.

"I'd never want to put anyone through what Aurora and I went through. Rolling out from that, the thought of being with someone I saw every day, and it not working out, turning my back on them, yet still seeing them all the time? To me that just feels cruel."

Laila shuffled forward on the seat, her hand coming to rest softly on his knee.

"I'm fine," he said with a self-deprecating laugh. "I promise. I've found my own way to deal with it. And Mamma and Aurora and I are good now. It's just…"

You, he thought, sitting up straighter. *The only difference is you. You muddy the water, and make me want to rethink the way I look at everything.*

What he said was, "I've never really said any of that out loud before."

Her smile was slow, and sad, and real. "Thank you for telling me."

"Thank you for coming all the way here to try to save me from the big bad town."

She lifted a shoulder, then tugged the cardigan back onto her shoulder. "I know how you get sometimes. If you need a place to hide, you know where to find me."

Yeah, he thought, *I remember. I remember how you clung to me, the feel of your hands tugging at my hair, the tilt of your hips against mine.*

Now what the hell was he meant to do with all of that?

Laila wasn't merely local; she was a whole new ball game. She was a listening ear, a port in a storm, one of his favourite people. And the town already thought she and he had something going on. How could his rules even apply?

"So," he said, turning so his knee brushed hers, "who's winning?"

"Winning?" she asked, the bob of her throat proof that the slightest of touches affected her too.

"The town bet."

"Ah. Meryl, I think."

"And what was her call?" he asked, taking the hand she'd placed on his knee, and lifting it to his mouth. Slow enough she had every opportunity to pull it away, which she did not. Darkness swept into her blue eyes as he turned her hand over and pressed his lips to her palm.

She tasted of apple crumble and fresh paper. Her skin was warm and soft. She was so beautiful and vital, and to have come there to warn him was gutsy and kind.

"Laila?"

"Hmm."

"The bet?"

"Right," she said, shaking her head. "That we are up to no good, I believe were the exact words."

Nudging his nose over the soft pad of her palm, then along her wrist, and down the sweet pale length of her inner forearm, he said, "Doesn't seem fair that they might pay out. Unless…"

"Unless it was true." Her gaze lifted to his. And whatever she saw in his eyes was enough for her to lean in and kiss him.

Her lips were cool and soft, her eyes fluttered gently closed. With her hand in his, their knees just touching, it was the single sweetest moment of Nico's life.

But he'd been craving this for days, dreaming of it, aching for it. And considering how changeable the both of them were, he was not going to let it go to waste. Sliding a hand behind her neck, he pulled her closer, slanting his mouth over her to kiss her back. Properly. Deeply. His tongue entangling with hers till a sweet moan trembled through her. And the knots holding Nico's self-control in place dissolved like dragon fire through silk.

Only before he could move, Laila grabbed his shirt in both hands, lifted herself up and straddled him, her knees either side of his thighs, her hands in his hair. As if she too had made the decision not to waste time.

He rolled her cardigan down her arms, then tossed it away. Her arms wrapped around his shoulders, and his hands went straight to her backside, bunching her skirt, as she sank down over him.

Only for her to lift back to her knees as if electrocuted, gasping, "Your mother!"

"My *mother*?" he repeated. If that was her attempt to cool him down it would take more than that. He'd watch the house burn around him if it meant having her right there, right now. "What about her?"

"Is she suddenly about to appear from… I don't know, the billiard room, or the secret hidden underground pool?"

Nico tipped back his head and laughed. "God, I hope not. As far as I know she's in Adelaide on a bus trip with the local Country Women's Association, choosing replacement furniture for this place."

"Why can't you get your own furniture?" she asked, genuinely curious.

"Try asking any son of an Italian mother the same question and you'll get the same answer. It's just easier."

His hands had gently moved beneath the fabric of her skirt, till he found the skin of her thighs. As he stroked from beneath her knee up to the edge of her underwear, she let out a huff of breath.

There, he thought. No more town, no more family, no more anyone but him.

When her hand tugged at the hair at his nape, and she

began to roll into his touch, Nico took his chance, finding the top of the zip at the back of her dress, hauling it down, then flipping her onto her back on the couch.

She let go an effusive *whoop,* followed by a flutter of laughter; it and the fire in her eyes banking to a mellow heat as he shifted, settling his body along hers. Giving her room to curl a leg around his.

"Hey," he said, brushing her hair from her face, as he braced himself on an elbow, not wanting to crush her.

Her smile was fast and bright, as if surprised to find herself there. Surprised but delighted. The delight shifted into something softer, warmer, as she lifted her hand to touch his face, the angle of his jaw, the column of his neck, before she brought his mouth back to hers.

Setting himself over her, Nico took her kiss and made it his own. Chasing the soft sounds of pleasure when his tongue traced hers, when he sucked her bottom lip.

He found the strap of her dress, and tugged it over her shoulder, the fabric catching on her taut nipple, the moment mirrored with a tug deep in his gut, before slipping free.

Beautiful, he thought, as heat coiled inside him. The creamy soft skin, the dusky pink of her nipple, it was too much and not enough. Her pleasure as important to him as his own, he ran soft kisses over the rise of her collarbone, nipped the tendon leading to her shoulder, lathed the rise of her breast with a long wet sweep of his tongue, before his mouth closed over the peak.

She rose to meet him, writhing, clawing at his back, as he sucked gently, then more thoroughly, till her rhythmic whimpers sent pulsing heat rushing through him.

Easing the rest of her dress down to her hips, he smoothed his hand between her breasts, his thumb catching on the fresh peak before taking it between his teeth for a gentle tug. Her skin was pink from heat and attention, her eyes closed, her mouth open as she panted in short sensuous breaths.

"*Non ho mai conosciuto una bellezza come la tua,*" he whispered as his eyes adored her, as his mouth devoured her. This woman. This dream. This challenge. This attrition.

When he bent to kiss her mouth once more, she wrapped her arms about him, her legs parting, and she gasped into his mouth at the feel of him pressing against her core.

He rolled into her and she cried out.

"Nico!" Then, on a sob this time, "Nico, please."

Taking a moment to imprint her on his mind, knowing that any second now he'd not remember his own name unless he heard it called out in her ragged voice, Nico murmured, "*Si, tesora?*"

"I want you," she said, her hands roving frantically over his back.

"You have me already. Now tell me what you *need.*"

"You, Nico. I need you."

His mouth moved to hover over hers, not touching, but close enough to feel the tremble in her lips. Her eyes opened with a languid flutter before they found his as she said, "This is cruel and unusual treatment."

"I can make it better."

Her arm flopped over her eyes, as he moved down her body, brushing soft kisses over her breasts, dipping his tongue into her navel, washing hot breath over the trembling skin of her belly.

"I thought you were meant to be a nice guy," she said, her hands in his hair.

"We'll see about that," he growled, before lifting her dress over his head, dragging her underwear to one side and going to town.

So ready was she, so wanton, several strong, long swipes of his tongue, and she was crying out. Tracing her nub with slow deliberate strokes, he tugged it into his mouth and sucked it, as she rocked up into his mouth.

When she came her cry emptied her lungs, pleasure bowing her off the couch. Nico pressed her back down, holding her wide, lathing and nibbling and tasting and sucking as she trembled under his touch before bowing off the couch again.

While her body went lapse, boneless, her breaths short and soft, like she might well fall asleep, Nico moved back up her body, tasting everything he'd missed.

When his mouth met hers, she lifted to her elbows and kissed him fully, before gentling, her kisses mere whispers, like butterfly wings. Then, as he felt himself drowning in tenderness, her hand went to his jeans, pulled down his zip and slipped inside his pants. Gripping and palming the length of him.

"Hell, Laila," he said on a hiss of breath, his hand moving to hers.

But she shook her head, and said, "What do you want?" Her thumb stroking along his length through his underwear.

What did he *want*? He was in no mind to be answering that question in that moment.

"What do you need?" she asked, her voice soft as she ran her tongue between her lips. "What do you need from me?"

Her. He needed all of her.

He shucked off his boots till they went flying across the room, then yanked off his jeans. Then tugged his shirt and jumper over his head in one smooth move.

Breathing out hard, she ran her hands down his chest, over the flat planes of his pecs, the hard ridges of his ribs, the rows of muscle beneath. When she licked her lips he had to hold his breath so as not to come on the spot.

Reaching for his jeans, which he'd thankfully not tossed across the room, he pulled his wallet from the back pocket, and came up with the goods.

She grinned, motioned for him to give her the condom, then ripped the packet open with her teeth, before sheathing him in one long deft movement.

This woman, he thought right before she gathered his balls in one hand, the other running up his ridge, and every thought fled. Then she drew him down, positioned him just right, grabbed his backside in her hands and as he drove into her she cried out in pleasure.

He swore ten different ways at how good she felt, how right. Growling, he said, "No matter what, I'm keeping this couch."

Her laughter rang through the house, before her touch, her heat, her kisses, her sex, dragged him under.

And as her body tensed, her mouth open on a gasp, a mighty pleasure rose inside before he shattered, like stars scattered across a midnight sky.

When Nico ran his hand over Laila's back, her skin was so soft against his work-roughened paws, he lifted his hand away so as not to graze her, only she made a sound.

"Don't stop?" he asked.

"Don't stop," she murmured sleepily, draped over him in his bed, a sheet half covering them, her fingers playing with the hairs on his chest.

Nico did as he was told, tracing the curve of her shoulder blade, and asked the question constantly running over and over in his own mind these days.

"Of all the places in all the world, why Vermillion?"

For a while he thought she might not have heard him, then she lifted her head and rested her chin on his chest, and blew a blonde puff of hair from in front of her eye.

"It's not all that exciting a story," she said.

"Doesn't have to be."

"Hmm," she hummed.

Then she took a deep breath and told him. How she'd been headhunted by a crisis management firm right out of university. How she'd become a bit of a legend in the field. How that was balanced out by a constant state of crisis with her mum. How, in search of stability, she dated men who seemed to have it all figured out, only to realise that they needed to be top of the call sheet, meaning while at first she'd been a trophy, she was soon competition. How her mother's sudden death was followed by a broken engagement.

"A fresh start felt like my only option," she said. "So, I got in my car and drove till one day I saw a threadbare little cottage with a lease sign out front."

Nico could tell she'd only shown him the tip of the iceberg. And where he'd had Aurora, and the Vermillion Hill staff, and the people of the town who treated him like their favourite son, Laila had faced it all on her own.

"You are an impressive person, Laila."

"I know," she said, batting her lashes.

He smudged his thumb down her cheek. "Truly."

She swallowed then, as if wanting to believe him.

"And if you thought," he said, "even for a second, that I asked you to Napa to be some girl on my arm, while I think you're gorgeous, you're also a pain in my ass. So there had to be a better reason for me to bring you than the desire to look at you all day. True?"

"True," she allowed, then she wriggled higher up his body, to scrape her teeth over his collarbone. Then she lifted her gaze to his. "There's one more thing."

"Okay."

"When I came here, I made a vow to never let anyone fox me like that again. And I stuck to it. For a long time. You're the first man I've been with since that day."

"Really?"

"You don't have to sound quite so pleased with yourself. I could reset my vow again, in a heartbeat."

"That so?" said Nico, his hand trailing down her back and flicking the sheet away from her backside so he could palm her lovely ass.

Her gaze flickered with a burst of heat, as she whispered huskily, "No doubt."

He slid a finger beneath the tuft of hair that kept tipping over her eye and tucked it back into her hair. Then, holding her gaze, he said, "You do know it was never about you. You were far too good for them, and they knew it. They also knew that one day you'd wake up and wonder what the hell you were doing with them. So, they took the coward's way out."

"They really did. And you know what?" A glint sparked in those beautiful bedroom eyes, before she pressed herself up to straddle his hips, her hands flat on his chest, beautiful body bare to the world. "I'm glad. Without them I'd not be here. Never have opened a romance bookstore. Never have met my book clubbers."

Her gaze shifted back to him, but while she refrained from saying *Never met you*, he felt the truth of it.

"This is wild!" she said, giving her hair a happy fluff. "I'm a small-town girl who found out by lucky accident." Then she collapsed against his chest as if her revelations had released some glorious weight.

Ironic that while Laila had realised how settled she was in Vermillion, at the very same time Nico was considering what he might possibly achieve if he was anywhere else. And while for him it felt like jumping out of a plane without a parachute, Laila had leapt, and never looked back.

Nico ran his palms down her, curving them around her adorable backside, then swept them up her sides, slowing as his thumbs traced the swell of her breasts. With a sigh, she lifted back to sitting, taking one of his hands with her and holding it over her breast, as she rocked gently against him.

Palming her breast with one hand, his other roved over the dip at her waist, the swell of her hip, before his thumb delved to the cleft between her thighs. With a gasp, she rolled into his touch. A hedonist. A giver and taker of pleasure. Biting down on her lip, taking it all.

And while the urge to lift her up and plunge himself into her, to kiss her till every other man she'd ever met became dust on the wind, he had something to clear up first.

One hand slid north, the other south, both landing on her hips to steady her. And her eyes fluttered open—dark, smoky, drenched with displeasure that he'd dared stop.

When a blast of adoration whipped through him so fast it made his head spin, a small strident voice in the back of his head told him to end this, after this night, put a final line under the whole thing. Till, frowning, she leaned back, her hands moving to his thighs, her back arched, breasts begging for his touch, and he overrode every defence mechanism he'd ever had like it was nothing.

"You know that I'm not one of your clueless alpha dolts, here to muck you around."

She nodded as she rolled against him. "I know."

"But neither am I some two-dimensional paperback hero onto whom you can work out your demons."

Her eyes flared at that one, but she said, "That's fair."

"And my responsibilities are still what they are. There are many who rely on me and my focus has to remain on my family, and my work, and this town—"

Laila lifted a hand from his thigh, traced a finger around her nipple, then down her belly, before taking his hand at her hip, unfurling his middle finger, and sliding it between her legs. She moaned softly, then rolled her backside against his rock-hard ridge.

Smoke-filled eyes finding his, she said, "Sorry, were you still talking?"

With a growl, he rolled them both over, till she was beneath him, and her hands found his backside, as her legs wrapped around his hips.

Then, eyes dopey but serious, she said, "I'm not asking you for anything, Nico. Just don't lie to me, okay? Don't make promises you have no intention of keeping. I'm a big girl. I can survive anything. I'd just rather not have to."

Nico dropped his head to kiss her but she tilted her face away.

"Agreed?" she said.

"Agreed."

Then he kissed his way down her lush body. And he was soon lost to her taste, her moans, and her glorious wanton heat.

For now, the rest of the world could damn well wait.

CHAPTER TEN

A WEEK LATER, it was Celia's last night in town, so while Nico was at the villa having dinner with his mother, Laila went to the Vine. She'd not offered to join him, and he'd not asked, which was fine. Totally normal for two people *not* in a relationship.

Though the way they'd sneaked around town, finding whatever time they could to be together—lunch in his office in the winery, five minutes up against the bookshelf in their secret space—one might begin to wonder.

Not Laila, of course, but someone else.

"Laila!" Jenny from the Bubbly Crust called as she and her family came in looking for a table for dinner. "Can I come by tomorrow for that book you mentioned?"

"*The Love Hypothesis*?" Laila said, then, to Jenny's husband, Garth, "You'll thank me."

He smiled, cluelessly.

"No pizza tonight?" Laila asked.

Jenny's youngest pretend-barfed.

"I get it. Too much of a good thing," Laila said on a laugh. "Have a good night."

Laila turned back to the bar.

Kent was watching her with a cheesy smile. "Look at your being all helpful and neighbourly," he said. "It's so Nico coded I might die."

Laila opened her mouth to tell him that Nico had nothing

to do with it, but there would be no convincing him. No convincing any of them. She was practically a town celebrity now. Locals no longer waved politely as she passed, they stopped to chat. Or they came into the shop for a "proper look around" before spending up a storm. She had come back from Napa decidedly friendlier, but the Nico factor could not be denied.

Nursing her Shirley Temple, she shook off a familiar gut feeling that it was all leading to something, some chaos just over the horizon. That was an Old Laila thing, and New Laila was rolling with life these days. Seeing a guy without strings or expectations. Not constantly waiting for the other shoe to drop.

When her phone buzzed, and it was Sutton sending a photo of the beautiful recording studio they were building by a lake on the vineyard, the frisson of disappointment that it wasn't Nico had her telling herself to get a grip.

SUTTON: Have you read the latest Christina Lauren?

LAILA: Have you?

SUTTON: Well, no, but I heard some women talking about it on the plane.

LAILA: Philistine.

SUTTON: Ha. What news at your end?

She typed: If I had one of those signs they used on construction sites, it would say Zero Days Since Falling Off the Celibacy Wagon. Then remembered she'd not told Sutton about any of it, as there was, officially, nothing to tell. She deleted it letter by letter.

LAILA: Same old same old.

SUTTON: And what about your Nico? Celia's moving tomorrow, right? Is he doing okay?

Laila hovered her thumbs over the screen readying to type again, before she saw what Sutton had written.

"*Your* Nico."

With a flash of cognition Laila scrolled back through old messages and saw that Sutton had *always* referred to him that way. While Laila had always read it as "*our* Nico," and had vociferously rejected the moniker even then.

Sutton had known Laila had had a thing for Nico all this time.

Kent, who saw them accidentally bump into one another most mornings when she got coffee, had probably had an inkling.

Meryl had clearly known, as she'd bet a hefty sum on the supposition.

And while Laila had been fighting it tooth and nail, until very recently of course, they'd all been right.

From the moment Laila had heard his voice—a deep, intimate "Hey"—then looked along the path outside the cottage that would become Forbidden Fruits to see a hulking cartoon hero of a man sauntering her way, there had been something magical fizzing between them.

Meaning while she'd been telling herself she was celibate, off men, putting her own interests front and centre for the first time in her life, she'd been emotionally cheating on herself the entire time.

SUTTON: Hello?

Kent walked behind the bar, pointed to her drink, and gave her a look to see if she wanted another. She blurted, "Kent, say hi."

Kent said, "Hi?"

LAILA: Kent says hi!

SUTTON: Hi Kent!

Soon after they signed off, and Laila took off out the bar door. A few steps later, her phone buzzed in her pocket, and checking she wasn't about to walk into a tourist or a light pole she had a quick look.

It was Nico, and such warmth and relief swept through her, her knees nearly gave out.

NICO: What are you wearing?

A laugh shot out of her. Though it also felt kind of like a sob. This stuff—the banter, the teasing, the magical fizz— had been the sweetest fun of her life, but the rest was an emotional rollercoaster.

LAILA: New phone, who dis?

NICO: Funny girl.

LAILA: I think you mean strikingly beautiful, incandescently brilliant, witty-as-all-hell woman.

NICO: I stand corrected.

Then he paused, long enough she wondered if he was okay. Considering the years Nico and Aurora had spent in the wilderness after their father died, this night might be more fraught than he had let on.

LAILA: I really hope you have the loveliest dinner with your mum tonight.

NICO: It'll be strange.

NICO: But good, I think.

NICO: She seems happy, which is all we could ask.

Another pause.

NICO: Can I see you after?

Oh Nico, she thought as her belly pitched and butterflies lifted in her chest. For it felt as if he was asking her to be his safe place to land.

It had to be projection on her part—this burgeoning hope that maybe he actually saw her as more than a neme-friend, or a fake girlfriend, or whatever they were to one another. And she knew all too well where hope led.

She licked dry lips and considered her words carefully.

LAILA: Did you honestly just send a prebooking for a booty call?

NICO: Hell, yeah, I did.

Dammit, she thought as her heart—that big dumb ball of meat—twisted in her chest. How had she let herself get in this deep?

Nibbling at the inside of her lower lip, she thought hard. Thought clearly. And typed:

LAILA: It's been a big day. Heading to bed now. Raincheck?

She pressed Send before she could take it back.
His response was instant.

NICO: You bet. Whatever you need. Sweet dreams.

Laila let the phone drop to her side and she looked up. Silvery clouds had been brushed across the sky, a smattering of stars in amongst them. With nothing awaiting her at the cottage, bar a thousand book boyfriends she no longer had the urge to see, she walked back home.

Nico sat atop the bonnet of his Land Rover looking out over the vineyard to the town below. During the day, the vines were king, striations of lush green and gnarled brown rolling off into the distance. At night, golden street lamps creating a glow on the horizon, the town of Vermillion was the jewel.

Moments like this had made it easy to see the good. To feel pride in what he and his team had achieved. While the years spent watching his bear of a father wither, his mother fading before his eyes, had forged him in fire, the past eighteen months had been the most taxing of his adult life.

As if he'd known the minute Laila Vale drove into town, she would be his reckoning.

He turned his phone over in his hand. Wondering if he ought to message her again. Or call. Make it clear that just seeing her would be enough. Maybe he should just go to her now, knock on her door like some lovesick fool.

Not love. Though he was spending a lot of time convincing himself of that these days. But something. Something restless, and unceasing.

Rather than rushing in like a teenager with his first crush, he could have slowed things down. Now there he sat, wanting her, wondering if *she* was pulling away.

It would be all he deserved for having one foot out the door. No matter that he'd made it clear that was how it had to be, she had every right to reject it at any point. Only his insides squalled at the thought.

Maybe the fact that the foundation on which he'd built his life was crumbling at every point was a sign that it was time for the entire Rossi family to take their leave from Vermillion, gratified to have left it far better off than it had been when they'd bought it.

Maybe that would be best for Laila too. Without him in the way she could have a true fresh start. Meet someone less choked by his own past, who took one look at her and didn't hesitate before sweeping her off her feet and carrying her down Main Street. Like the final scene in the book she'd given him.

His watch beeped, telling him it was time for dinner with his mother.

Compartmentalising, but knowing he had big decisions to make and soon, he slid off the bonnet, gave the thing a single bump with his closed fist, then took himself home to say goodbye.

Having gone a whole thirty-six hours without seeing Nico, Laila felt as if she'd finally crawled out of the rabbit hole down which she'd fallen at the Vine.

Yes, they'd messaged several times, and an hour-long call during which he instructed her to get naked, lie back on her bed, and do everything he wished he could do if he was with her. But still.

In celebration—and in the hopes she might bump into him at the Vine getting coffee the way they had in the old days— she zipped herself up in a bright red dress with teeny straps and a sweetheart neckline, added a double layer of Kiss Me red lipstick to her pout, and headed out into the Vermillion sunshine.

Feeling like a sassy Little Red Riding Hood—which was doubly perfect as the Cosy Chaos Book Clubbers were coming in that evening—she made a quick stop at the Pressed & Blessed New Age store.

Foraging through the crystals for gifts to give the book clubbers who bought copies of *The Ex Hex*, their next month's read, she looked up as the front door opened, taking the edge off the warm patchouli-scented air inside the shop.

"Morning," called Sabrina, the shop owner. "What treasures are you in mind for today?"

"A good-luck charm for the whole town might be the go," a quavering voice called back.

Laila glanced down the aisle to see Mrs. Constantine, the butcher's wife, her tuxedo cat, Basil, sitting in a custom cat backpack strapped to her chest.

"How so?" Sabrina asked, leaning against the counter, eyes bright with curiosity.

"Oh, I bet I know what this is about," said Riley, one of the Wine Down Day Spa employees who came slinking around the corner.

Then Beryl appeared from nowhere, saying, "So you've all heard the news then?"

Having clearly met this way before, they huddled together, like a foursome of witches around a cauldron.

"The town mob who came sniffing around Vermillion Hill a few months ago are back," said Beryl. "A half-dozen cars arrived yesterday, and spent the day on the hill. Meaning it's on the market. The Rossis are selling up."

Laila ducked back around behind the shelf, heart hammering against her ribs as she tried to make sense of what she'd just heard. Celia was leaving yes. Aurora soon too. But Nico?

"That would be such a shame!" cried Sabrina.

"Apparently Nico's recent trip to Napa was not a romantic tryst with the bookseller after all," said Mrs. Constantine. "It was a scouting mission. He's planning to move there once the deal is done."

"See," said Riley, "*I* heard the whole family are moving to Italy after the sister had some disastrous fling with an Italian count."

As the assertions became more and more ridiculous, Laila's heart stopped beating in her throat. But having lived the life she lived, and had the career she had, she knew that such gossip always sprang from a kernel of truth.

"So sad," said Sabrina.

"Meh," said Beryl. "It happens every couple of decades or so. Out with the old, in with the new. And yet the town survives."

"I guess," Sabrina said on a sigh. "I will miss watching that man walk by."

As the women went on to list all the things they'd miss about Nico Rossi, Laila knew the only way to be sure was to hear it from the source.

So, she dumped the crystals back into their wooden boxes and scarpered.

As she drove up the hill towards the villa, Laila battled an all too familiar sense of dread.

It was the instinct that fueled her when helping clients through crises they were certain had ruined their lives. The cold sweat that came over her every time her mother's name lit up her phone. The metaphorical piano that hung over her head during every romantic relationship she'd ever had.

Till this one.

From the moment they'd agreed to "get up to no good" it had felt like no relationship Laila had ever experienced.

They'd been honest, they knew one another, they were aware of one another's flaws, and had not been deterred.

But what if she'd been wrong? The pieces were all there—his mother leaving, Aurora too, the success of his *baciami* in Napa, the laser focus of the town his cross to bear.

No, she thought. That wasn't how Nico operated. He'd never keep her in the dark that way. Then in the back of her head, she heard Old Laila thinking the same just before she was sideswiped. Again.

Pulling up outside the villa, Laila did a quick lipstick check in the side mirror, then knocked on the front door.

Only for a tall, lithe woman to open it, with an elegant smile. *"Si?"*

"Mrs. Rossi?" Laila said, for this had to be Nico's mother.

"Celia," Celia said in the most musical accent, "please. And you are?"

"Laila Vale. Nico's…friend." That she was able to hide her wince at labelling herself was testament to the fact she was running on pure adrenaline.

"Ah," said the older woman, her face softening. "You are the owner of the bookstore who has been making my Nico earn his supper. It is so nice to finally get a look at you."

Which she did. Look. While Laila just stood there feeling like a mannequin on display.

"Mmm," Celia finally said. "I see fire and I see ice. You'll do. You'll do very nicely indeed. Come come." She then walked into the villa, leaving Laila no choice but to follow.

There were packing boxes everywhere now. A pair of designer suitcases at the front door. Marks on the floor where furniture had been removed. Laila noticed the couch in the lounge had remained, and couldn't help the bittersweet feelings that tumbled through her.

"I thought you were heading home yesterday," Laila said.

"Something important came up," said Celia. "I am now off and away this afternoon. Anticipation is half the joy, *si*?"

Something? Such as an offer they couldn't refuse? thought Laila, heart surely beating outside of her chest now.

Celia reached to pick something up off a nearby table, then turned back holding *A Room with a View*, the book Laila had given Nico. "This came from you, correct?"

"It did. But the idea was all Nico's." Then, because she hoped she'd chosen well, she asked, "Did you enjoy it?"

"I have read it before. Several times in fact. My husband, Aldo, read it to me, when we were courting."

Laila huffed out a soft sigh. "I honestly had no idea. Though I will say your husband had impeccable taste."

Celia smiled. "He did at that. As do you, Ms. Vale."

Then, as if Celia hadn't just told Laila she was aware that she was more than her son's "friend," she turned and walked away, waving a hand over her shoulder. "Nico is in the west vineyard, keeping himself busy, as he does, before our final goodbyes."

Goodbyes. Laila's heart lurched as if she'd been shoved.

"It was nice to meet you!" she called, but Celia was already gone.

Laila's heart stammered *thank-god-thank-god-thank-god* as she saw Nico amble towards the house between two rows of vines, looking every inch the dashing grape grower in a button-down shirt open over a crisp white T-shirt, faded jeans, a battered cap on his head.

For, despite her subconscious taking a smattering of gossip and running with it, he was still Nico Constable Goodboy Ranger Heartthrob Rossi. He was dust motes dancing in a beam of sunlight on Main Street. He was music strummed on a vintage guitar outside the pizzeria on a Friday night. He was earthy, robust, and warm like the first sip of wine.

He was Vermillion.

If he left...

Nico looked up, and as a slow delicious smile eased onto his face, her heart tripped and tumbled, landing in the dirt at her feet.

Because, dammit, she loved this man. This wry, wonderful, complex, ungettable dream of a man. A man who'd told her, explicitly, that while he adored her, wanted her, trusted her there could be no real future for them. And not as some line, or an excuse for not treating her right, but because that was his deep, hard-won, indelible truth.

Meaning this current ache in her heart was all her fault.

It was her fault she'd tried to convince herself that she was okay with a casual affair. That it fit with her cool, unflappable, new-found independence. But *her* deep, hard-won, indelible truth was that she was a lover of love who, despite all the books she'd read showing how people could do it right, was a complete disaster when it came to her own reality.

Breathing deeply, she walked towards him on shaking legs, her heels sinking into the soft ground. She stopped a few metres away, knowing if she got too close he would go to her, slide an arm around her waist, haul her against his hard body, murmur something dirty and fabulous in Italian, and kiss her senseless. And while she wished he would, so very much, the moment she thought it might be taken away from her, she realised she wanted it forever.

Nico's gaze flickered, as if he could sense her reticence, but gentleman that he was, he stayed put. Then took off his cap, tucked it into the back of his jeans, and ran a hand through his hair, releasing the single dark curl.

"Wow," he said, gaze roving over her red summer dress, before settling on her mouth. Then, "Please tell me we had plans."

Swallowing hard, Laila shook her head, and said, "I just met your mother."

"Really?"

"We're besties now. Me and Celia. Fo' life." Needing some kind of gauge as to where his head was at, as hers was all over the place, she added, "I'm pretty sure she even gave me the seal of approval."

Nico *laughed*. "Why am I not surprised?"

So, he wasn't freaking out that she'd met his mother, which, according to Sutton, should be a huge deal. Was that a good thing? A bad thing? Or simply a Mr. Confidence thing?

"Laila," he said, taking a step her way.

She held out both hands to stay him. "I came here because I need to ask you something."

"Okay."

"I was in Pressed & Blessed and a group of people were talking about the vineyard, saying you've had potential buyers visiting, because you are considering selling Vermillion Hill."

Nico's nostrils flared, then he looked in the direction of the town, shaking his head. Making her wonder if it was all a big mistake—gossip twisting into half-truths. But when he looked back at her, his jaw hard, his eyes shuttered, she knew better.

"It's true?" she demanded, her voice cracking.

"It is. We met with a group who have been making us offers for some time, along with an independent appraiser." Then, in case she had one last shred of hope, "I was the one who asked them to come."

"You're *leaving*?" Laila asked, skin now prickling all over.

"I'm…considering all my options."

"I don't understand. Why? Why would you even want to leave?"

Releasing a long slow breath, he said, "It's not that I want to leave. More that I wonder, if I'd had a choice back at the start, if I'd have made the same one. This might be my only chance to figure that out."

Lungs suddenly too tight, as if they'd forgotten how to work, Laila bent at the waist, hands on her knees. This was really happening. Nico was actually debating leaving Vermillion. Leaving her.

When he took a step her way, hand reaching for her, she called out, "Stop."

And he did. "Ask me anything you want, Laila. About the meeting. Anything at all."

Pressing herself back to standing, she pinned him with a glare. "This isn't even about the meeting." *It was.* "Why did I have to hear about it from everyone else in town? At the woo woo gem store, of all places."

"Everyone?" he asked, his voice gentle, his feet shifting.

"Everyone!" she shot back. Then, "And please don't take another step. I need… I need you to stay where you are."

Stilling, Nico slid his hands into his pockets, his eyes growing dark. "What do you want me to say, Laila? That once a decision is made, you will be the first person I tell?"

Laila swallowed, thinking *Yes!* What she said was "It won't matter then. It'll be too late."

Nico's jaw ticked. Laila's nostrils flared with every hard-fought breath. It had been a while since they had been like this—on opposite sides.

"I'm not sure what else I can say," he said.

"I'm not sure there is anything to say." Then, "I know that you have no expectations of this, of us. You made that patently clear. But I only asked one thing of you; not to make me promises you couldn't keep."

Nico's brow furrowed. "And what is it that I promised you, Laila? What promise do you believe I have broken?"

Oof. Her hand moved to her belly as the truth of his words hit. He was right. He'd been clear from the start. It was his touch, the way he gathered her to him after they made love, the way he listened to her stories with endless patience, that had felt like a promise.

That had felt like love.

But what the hell did she know?

"Can we just go inside," said Nico, frustration now coming off him in waves, "talk about this?"

Laila shook her head, and once she'd started she couldn't stop. "You've clearly an important decision to make, Nico, so that's where your focus should be." Then, feeling as if layers of her heart were peeling away, she said, "We both got caught up in something neither of us was looking for, so this seems like a good time to slow down. Take a step back."

Nico, stoic and strong as a breeze whipped his shirt against his sides, said, "Which is it? Slow down or step back?" Then, reading her face, he said, "This is neither. This is over. We are over."

No longer able to feel her extremities, as her heart was squeezing so hard it had taken up all the leftover blood in her body, Laila nodded.

"If that's what you want," he said, voice now a rough, subterranean burr. "If that's what you need."

What she wanted was for Nico to love her as she loved him.

What she needed was for him to laugh off any suggestion of ever leaving this place.

Since neither was going to happen, she took the final few steps his way, placed a hand on his chest, lifted onto her toes, and laid a kiss upon his cheek. His skin was warm, fresh stubble growing in, and she breathed him in knowing she'd never get the chance to do so again.

Then she turned, the wind now whipping up around her, walked back to her car, drove away, and didn't look back.

* * *

Nico stalked into the house, nearly tripping over one of his mother's suitcases. He breathed through the desire to kick it across the room, tossed his damn cap on the damn hall table, and strode to the kitchen.

He went to the fridge, shut it. Went to the pantry, shut it. Then gripped the kitchen bench, feeling as if he'd been hit over the back of the head with a plank.

Aurora, coming out of the hall that led to the family wing, said, "What's with all the door slamming?" Then, not waiting for a response, she said, "Mamma says Laila was just here. Does that mean what I think it means?"

Nico highly doubted it.

"She was here," he growled, "now she's gone."

"Gone?" Aurora stopped short, her ability to pick up on his nuances second to none.

"Gone," he said, leaning his forearms on the counter when his strength simply ebbed away.

"What did you do?"

"Me?" What had *he* done? Only disregarded every single rule by which he had lived his life in order to have her, when not having her had become unbearable.

"*Yes*," Aurora deadpanned. "Because unlike the other women you've happily let waft in and out of your life, Laila is a sensational, top-drawer, grown-ass woman who has no time for fools. So if something has happened to burst your little love bubble, then it's all on you."

Love bubble? Nico ran a hand down his face, then left it there. And while he tried to dredge up his usual mantra— *not love, not love, not love*—it sputtered into nothingness.

Creating boundaries, being honest to a fault, making smart choices around who to date, had meant his determination to never fall in love had proven easier than he'd expected. But then along came Laila Vale.

He'd convinced himself it would all be fine, because even while his ramparts were being smashed, piece by piece, Laila was so damn cool. So gloriously disenchanted. So scintillatingly immune to his charms.

But out there, among the vines, when she'd accused him of breaking a promise—there'd been no indifference, no nonchalance. He'd all but felt her heart bleed. In doing everything in his power to never hurt her, he'd hurt her all the same.

"What happened?" Aurora asked, her voice gentler now. Finally sensing he was going through something big.

What happened?

He'd fallen for Laila Vale. Then he'd watched her walk away.

Aurora picked up a teatowel and smacked him across the arm. Then did it again. And again.

Nico brought up his arms to protect himself, swiftly snapped the towel out of her hand, then slumped against the bench. "Can you just leave it alone? Please."

At the "please," she stopped still. A soft "Awww," coming his way. Then she moved in to hug him tight around the waist.

Nico lifted his arm to let his sister in and they stayed that way for some time before she finally let him go.

"So what are you going to do about it?" Aurora asked.

There was a lot he'd gotten wrong over the past couple of months, but on this one thing he was absolutely sure—he wasn't going to do a goddamn thing.

He had fallen for her, but he had to let this go. Even while the thought of not having her in his life, in his arms, hurt like nobody's business he had to let *her* go.

For one thing, she'd *asked* it of him.

For another, she was right. He had the biggest decision of his entire life ahead of him. If he put her in the consideration, chances were he would do as he'd done the first time round, and choose for love. Not for himself.

Lastly, if the past eighteen months were anything to go by, he'd only grow to love her more every day. And if something happened, something terrible, or if she finally realised she was too good for him too…

The very best thing, for the both of them, the right thing, was to leave things as they were.

His watch buzzed, and it took him a moment to realise why.

"You ready?" he said, pushing away from the bench. "It's time to get Mamma to the airport."

He felt Aurora's eyes on his back as he somehow managed to get his feet to take him down the hall.

CHAPTER ELEVEN

DAYS LATER, AS rain drizzled and dripped from the eaves of the shop, Laila sat on the stool behind the counter of her bookstore, bouncing the pompom on the end of her pencil against her nose, wondering when things might start to feel normal again.

Though she struggled to imagine what normal might be, without Nico in her daily life.

She'd only seen him once since she'd ambushed him in the vineyard and that was in the distance, chatting with a group of tourists who were taking turns shaking his hand as if he was Mayor Fabulous. But he had messaged her every day, like clockwork. With shop questions, landlord questions, storeroom questions, and just the once, Hope you're doing okay.

So, while she felt like sludge, she knew that all the choices that had brought her to that point had been the right ones. Liking him, teasing him, trusting him, choosing him, loving him, and letting him go.

Though it would have been nice to *feel* it, in place of the swirling grey void of sorrow that had taken up residence inside her. She'd had one of her comfort reads, *The Seven-Year Slip*, open on the counter in front of her and it was still on the page it had been at an hour before.

When the bell over the door tinkled for the first time that day, as if her sombre mood was keeping people away, she looked up and saw Sutton Mayberry walk through the door.

After a moment of shock, Laila burst into tears.

"Oh!" said Sutton, rushing around behind the counter. "Oh, honey bun!"

Sitting, for who had the energy to stand anymore, Laila lifted her arms and let herself be hugged by her rain-flecked, sunshiny, leather-clad friend.

"What are you doing here?" Laila managed through a slew of tears.

"I told Nico to keep it a surprise, which clearly he did. Dante is here too. He's up at the villa right now. He's come to chat business, and to be a sounding board for Nico, so I had to come along as his general mood enhancer. And because I miss you guys, so much."

Laila sniffed and pulled back, wiping a hand over her face. When it didn't come up smeared in mascara and red lipstick, she realised she must have forgotten to do her make-up. No wonder customers had been scarce; they'd probably looked through her front window, seen a maudlin ghost at the counter, and run away.

"So, you know, then?" Laila asked. "About Nico and—" *And me.* She couldn't finish the sentence; it was still too raw. And no longer true.

"That he's been weighing up his future here?" Sutton asked, misunderstanding. "I know, wild, right! Though Celia and Aurora heading off makes it the smart move."

When tears started rolling down Laila's cheeks in big fat rivulets, Sutton took her by the arms and looked deep into her eyes. Then understanding dawned.

"You and Nico?" Sutton laughed a gentle understanding laugh. "That is so like you both. So stubborn and dramatic, you leave it for the worst possible time to finally sort yourselves out."

Sutton looked around, saw the place was quiet, then moved

to the front door, flicked through the signs till she found the one reading To Be Continued… Tomorrow. "Yes?"

Laila hiccupped and nodded.

Front door locked, Sutton asked, "Silly question, I know, but you got any wine back there?"

Laia wiped her hands under her eyes. "You don't drink wine."

"I *didn't* drink wine. Living with a wine-nerd, in the middle of a vineyard, in Italy…it changed me. I am officially a convert."

Laila pointed in the direction of her bedroom, and while Sutton went searching, she dragged herself off the stool, stretched out her arms, and wriggled her backside, which had gone numb from moping.

Sutton, back with two mismatched glasses and a bottle of Vermillion Hill red, said, "Now, tell me everything."

"Is she okay?" a voice asked.

"She looks terrible," said another.

"Is it contagious?" a third stage whispered.

"Out, out, out!" Sutton's voice commanded quietly.

Laila—lying curled on her bed—blinked grittily into the semidarkness, noting someone must have put a blanket over her. That same someone had let *people* into her store.

Sutton, standing over her, wringing her hands, said, "Sorry. They wouldn't take no for an answer."

"They?"

"Your book clubbers? When I told them you were indisposed, they said I could be an axe murderer for all they knew, and needed to see for themselves that you were okay."

Of course they had, Laila thought tearily. They were her people. Her friends. From her town. And, she thought, a single tear curling its way down her cheek, didn't that make her the luckiest person on the planet?

"You guys go have your meeting." Sutton's voice, a little further away now, said, "As for Laila—I've been there, so I can safely say that the nice thing about hitting rock bottom is the only way is up!"

Laila sat up, then crawled to sit on the end of her bed. Through the gap in the doorway, she saw the shop was lit by fairy lights and a distant lamp. Noises at the front of the store meant the book club had started their meeting without her— like the band on the *Titanic*, they were not to be deterred by something so small as their intrepid leader catatonic in bed.

Sutton came back in and sat beside her. "Well, Aurora is adorable."

"Aurora is *here*?"

"She's hosting so you can mope."

Laila had assumed Aurora had left by now. Was it possible she'd stayed because Nico was moping too? She felt a smidge perkier, till she remembered Dante had come all that way to "be a sounding board for Nico."

Sutton looked around her. "To think, when we first met, you were hustling to build a newsletter list, now you've become a part of the fabric of this place. I'm so happy for you."

Laila hadn't realised how much she'd missed the feeling of belonging to something, to someone, since losing her mum. This place, these people, had given that back to her. Meaning by the time she'd broken it off with Nico, rather than burn everything down and run again, it never occurred to her to do anything but stay.

And Nico had been the beginning of it all.

Accidentally bumping into her at the Vine each morning had forced her to regularly engage with the community. Nudging her to choose a name for the shop was his way of trying to make her feel a part of something bigger than herself. He'd given her the time and space she needed to claw her way back out of her shell.

Laila leaned her head against Sutton's shoulder. "When do you think he'll go?"

"Who go where?" said Sutton, patting Laila on the knee.

"Nico. Leave Vermillion."

Sutton looked at her as if she was speaking another language. "What on earth are you talking about?"

In the fog that was her heartache brain, a flare of light pierced the dark. "Isn't that why Dante is here? To work out how Nico can move back to Italy with you guys and live out his true dream of being a poor but dedicated *baciami* grape farmer?"

Sutton placed a hand over Laila's forehead. "Dante didn't come here to bring Nico *home* with us. Can you imagine! They'd drive one another bonkers. He's come here because they are joining forces. Creating a superconsortium of their own. Our Sorello, some place in Napa—"

"Serenità Estate?"

"That's the one. And Vermillion Hill. It's quite a big deal, apparently. When I left them earlier, Nico was bouncing around like he'd taken an upper, and Dante wasn't looking like he wanted to throttle him, so I take that as a good sign!"

Laila blinked. Nico was staying? *Staying.*

She thought back to their last conversation and remembered the word *considering* had been bandied around quite a bit. Had staying been a possibility all along? Or had something changed his mind? And was he going to tell her this time, or assume the gossip mill would give her the news again?

The urge to grab her phone and passive aggressively flirt-fight message him was overwhelming.

Until it hit her that Nico was doing exactly what she'd asked him to do. She'd made a hard choice in order to give him what she thought he needed. Wasn't it probable, knowing him, he was out there doing the same for her?

Only what was best for her was him.

Meaning it was possible she'd been wrong. It was possible that the best thing for Nico wasn't giving him the space to indulge his "I will never love" ambitions. Maybe the best thing for Nico was her.

Laila ran her hands through her hair, to find it a tangle of fine knots. "Okay," she said, "that's it. I'm done."

"With the bookstore?" Sutton asked.

"No! I'm done leaping straight to the end of a crisis, using all my energy to guesstimate what people need, rather than straight up asking. I'm done accepting scraps and thinking myself lucky to get anything at all."

"Yeah, baby!" said Sutton reaching up for a high five.

Laila smacked her friend's hand, the sting reverberating through her. Waking her up. She wasn't a moper, she was a lover of love. While her poor mum had spent her life thinking love came in the form of external validation, Laila had been lucky enough to have the chance to learn to love herself first. That way, when true love had come for her, she'd been able to see it for what it was.

True love. *Nico.* Oh boy.

Feeling as if she'd drunk something so high in sugar she'd end up in a diabetic coma in an hour, Laila kicked her way out of the sheet still half wrapped about her, leapt off the bed, and turned in a circle, looking for some shoes.

"What are you doing?"

"I have to go. I have to explain. I have to make him see… everything."

Sparkly heels in place, she went to head out the bedroom door, only for Sutton to haul her back. "Whoa there. Why don't we start with a shower. Pop on something other than pyjamas. Then we can get you where you need to go."

Laila nodded. Then her gaze zeroed in on her cherry dress lying over the tub chair in the corner, where it had lived since that day on the couch with Nico. She snatched it up, then rushed into the bathroom.

For if Laila Vale was about to start her life over again, again, she'd be doing it in style.

Nico signed his name with a flourish, waited for the swishing noise that intimated the online contract had been sent to his legal reps, along with Dante's and Claudio's, then he breathed out a long hard breath and rubbed both hands over his face.

The deal was made; providing each access to plots, staff, tech, know how, and bargaining power across all three locales, while offering Nico the international reach and reputation that would give his *baciami* a solid chance at becoming something truly special.

And with it he had inked himself to Vermillion Hill for life.

"This is a good thing," said Dante, his voice gruff.

Laughing hollowly, Nico let his hands fall, then held one out for a shake. His cousin, offering up a rare smile, clasped it, nearly crushing it in the process.

"Toast?" said Nico.

Dante tipped his chin in agreement.

Nico pushed back his chair and moved to the wine rack, where he took his time choosing a drop. For while this was a seminal moment in his life—having conceptualised, pitched, and penned the deal that would give him the future he wanted—it felt like something was missing.

Not something, someone.

It was laughable the number of times he'd picked up his phone over the past week and gone to call Laila, or text her, to ask for her take on what he was planning, only to message asking if she was happy with her recycling bin instead.

Though it didn't make him feel like laughing. Not when there was a big hole inside of him that only her smile, her glare, her snark, and her fierce support had ever truly filled. For she made him feel more capable than anytime he'd run into a burning barn, or brought in a successful harvest under trying circumstances.

Hell, she just made him *feel.*

And while feelings—the big, unwieldy, emotional kind over which he had zero control—had for him been akin to a visit from the bogeyman, they were her superpowers. Now, without her, while he ought to be celebrating, all he felt was her lack.

Nico pulled out a bottle of the Vermillion Hill Signature, a single-barrel shiraz. Then, pouring each a glass, he passed one to Dante. *"Salute."*

"Salute."

They drank in silence, giving the drop the respect it deserved.

Nico broke it. "You look like a caveman, you know."

Dante, who had once again grown out his hair and beard since the last time they'd seen one another, eyed him. "That is what happens when one is in love."

"One lets oneself go?" Nico asked, holding a hand to his flat belly.

"One has other cares."

Nico let his hand drop, and sat back in his chair with a thud.

Dante cleared his throat, before saying gruffly, "Sutton tells me that you and the bookshop owner—"

"Laila," Nico reminded him, rubbing at the back of his neck. "And yeah. But no."

Dante grunted.

"You're much easier to talk to about this than Aurora," said Nico after another quiet minute. "She's full of opinions. And you're less likely to hit me."

Dante raised his glass in understanding.

While Nico swirled the liquid within, looked unseeingly at his.

Then, through the glass, he saw something sparkle on the coffee table. Leaning over, he pressed his thumb to the spot and came up with a single speck of hot pink glitter.

He huffed out a laugh, remembering when Laila dumped the stuff into Aurora's shopping bag how he'd known it would linger, that he'd see it and think of her.

Dante downed the rest of his drink, and said, "Do you mind if I take a minute? I promised I'd let Sutton know when we were done."

Nico waved a nonchalant hand. Then stopped, as his own voice came back to him as an echo. He had news. Huge news. And he'd made Laila a promise that when he had such news, she'd be the first person he would tell. He'd also assured her that he would never make a promise he might break.

Nico was on his feet, grabbing his phone, turning in circles trying to remember where he'd put his keys, only to find them the same place he always kept them, before Dante had even started his call.

"You're off?" Dante asked, as he waited for Sutton to pick up the phone.

"I am. You'll be okay here?"

Dante lifted a single dark eyebrow, as if to say, *You've finally figured out what you need to do, so go do it.*

With a nod, Nico bucketed along out of the house, leaping into his Land Rover and planting his foot as he rutted the car down the curving driveway.

Laila had been right to cut him free. He'd kept one foot in and one foot out the entire time they'd been together. When in every other part of his life he went all in. Now he just had to convince her he was all hers. If she'd have him.

Because without her beside him to enjoy the good, and face the bad, what was the damn point?

* * *

Laila fluffed her clean hair, tugged the bust of her cherry dress into place, ran a finger under the lower lip of her Kiss Me red lips, then, patent red high heels clacking against the checkered floor, made her way to the front of the shop.

"Oh my gosh, you look amazing!" said Jane.

"Much better than earlier," Hannah agreed.

"Not too much?" Laila asked, giving them a twirl.

"Depends what for," said Kelly thoughtfully.

Laila caught Aurora's eye, only to find she had both hands to her mouth, her eyes sparkling with tears. As if she knew what Laila was planning to do—aka find her big brother and tell him what for.

She would also be telling him that whatever dreams he might have for his future, he would simply have to factor her in there too. Because she loved him and she wasn't going anywhere.

Nerves twanging in anticipation, Laila spun in circles by the counter, looking for her keys, only to find them where she always kept them.

Then the front door of the Forbidden Fruits Story Emporium whipped open so fast the bell was almost knocked off its hook. And there stood Nico—his hand splayed on the door, feet wide, hair lifting and settling as if a strong wind had brought him there.

Golden fairy lights sparkled over his handsome face, her favourite forest-green henley T, the dark jeans that clung to all the bits of him that made her mouth go dry. But it was the stubble that got her, the dark smudges under his eyes. There had been definite moping, she thought with a frisson of hope.

"Nico," she said, her heart beating so hard it physically pressed her towards him.

"Laila," he said, his voice raw, his gaze hungry and repentant and so lovely her heart ached.

"What are you doing here?"

"I've come to buy a book."

"A *book*? But I only sell romance. As in sweeping tales of longing, and compromise, and forgiveness, and bravery, and sexy times and—"

"That's what I'm here for." While his eyes were inscrutable, his mouth ticked at one corner, a dimple flickering to life before disappearing into the beautiful angles of his face.

She reached for the counter, as her knees threatened to give way, only her hand met fresh air. Then Nico was there, his arm at her back, and she settled on her heels, her hand fluttering to his chest, where she could feel his heat, his heart, and his restraint.

The book clubbers sighed as one.

"What kind of book are you after?" Laila's fingers curled into his top.

"You choose," he said. "You choose a book you think would give me the most insight, because it's clear I still have a lot of learning to do."

At that, one of the book clubbers whimpered, and while Laila didn't blame them, she said, "Can we...take this...?"

"Outside," he finished for her. Then, using the hand at her back he guided her through the door and onto the front porch, where their audience had to at least work to hear what was said.

Away from the fairy lights, and the flirty book covers, and the raging hormones inside the shop, Laila's chutzpah shook, just a little.

"I have news," he said. "And I promised you that when I had news you'd be the first to know."

Laila nibbled at the inside of her lip, then admitted, "Sutton may have let the cat out of the bag about the deal you made with Sorello and Serenità. So, you're staying?"

"I'm staying."

Laila breathed out hard, and followed up with a relieved laugh. "I'm glad."

"I'm glad you're glad. But that's not the news I came here to share."

Nico reached for her hand and brought it to his chest. She came with it, her toes nudging up against his, his body heat filling her with sparks and hope. Then right as she felt as if her life might be about to change, from one beat of her heart to the next, Nico's eyes narrowed.

"You know what?" he said. "I'll get to that. But first I have to do this." Then he slid one arm behind her back, and the other went behind her knees, as he swept her into his arms.

With a whoop, Laila's legs flailed, and she quickly wrapped her arms around his neck and cried, "Put me down, you big galumph!"

Nico carried her down the steps. "Not happening."

"Do as I say," she said, looking back to the window where her book clubbers were jumping up and down and hugging.

"Not anymore," he shot back, his voice dropping a good octave as he carried her down her front path.

When her gaze snapped to his, he looked right on back. "If I agree with you, I might. If I don't, then you can expect some push back. Fair?"

Laila, not in a position to argue, as the man she loved carried her through her front gate, said, "Fair."

Nico hitched her higher in his arms, then set off down the footpath.

Clueless as to where he was going, or what he had planned, Laila decided she was there for it. Settling more comfortably in his arms, she wondered if Aurora had been onto something—suggesting verbal combat was their love language. So was touch, she thought, as Nico pressed a kiss to the top of her head. And acts of service for the man who was literally carrying her down the street.

"First thing I'm going to do is fix your gate."

"I like it the way it is," she argued, glancing back at the bougainvillea that was strangling the thing whole.

"Too bad. It's a safety hazard. And I won't have you in danger."

"Danger," she scoffed, but she also kind of totally loved that about him. He was so dramatic.

"I can look after myself, you know." This said while she was in his arms, legs kicking merrily, as he carried her past the Wine Down Day Spa, then the Swirl and Purl Craft Corner.

"I know," he said, slowing just a tad so he could look at her.

"So it's not enough that you have a whole town melting at your feet, you need me there too?"

"I do need you," he said, as they passed by the Vine and Dandy, and left it at that.

While Laila couldn't remember a single more perfect moment in her entire life.

"Are we there yet?" she asked.

"Where?"

"Wherever it is that we're going?"

Nico slowed as if only just remembering that he couldn't simply carry her off into the sunset. "I had a plan."

Curling her hand into the thick waves at the base of his neck, Laila said, "You do know I love a plan."

Then, gifting her a hot, intimate, you'll-keep smile, the kind that usually meant some part of her was about to get his full attention, Nico stepped out into the middle of the street.

"Nico!" Laila cried, hauling herself higher in his arms, as a car that had been cruising slowly towards them pulled to a stop, then beeped its horn several times.

The doors to the Main Street shops began to open as people spilled out onto the footpath to see what the fuss was all about.

Right as Nico shouted, "Vermillion! I have news! And I figured I might as well share it with you all at once! Vermillion Hill is staying in Rossi hands, so you can shut those 'Nico is moving on' rumours down."

Somewhere in the crowd Mrs. Constantine, the butcher's wife, let out a happy cry.

"Not sure why I had to be here for that," Laila teased. "But okay."

Then Nico shouted, "For anyone who's not met her yet, this is Laila Vale—owner of the spiciest damn bookstore you'll ever be lucky enough to frequent!"

A mother walking by put her hands over her daughter's ears. Laila gave her a grin and a wave and she waved back before her mother hustled her away.

Laila, eyes back on Nico, said, "You are out of your mind, you know that, right?"

Voice booming as if he had a megaphone, Nico continued, "Her shop is called the Forbidden Fruits Story Emporium. It's the one with the broken front gate and the pink front door."

"So, head there now!" Laila shouted, taking up the cry. "And buy yourself a book! Heck, buy yourself a dozen!"

"That's my girl," Nico said, as he began to spin them in a slow circle.

And Laila's breath caught as it hit her what Nico was doing and why. The street, the spin, the crazy public declaration was straight out of the wildly romantic final scene of *Steeling Harts*; the moment when Tyrrano declared his love to Evie and the entire galaxy.

Nico, watching the realisation finally dawn, lifted her higher so he could place a gentle kiss on her lips. When he pulled back, a light smudge of her red lipstick touched the bow of his mouth.

Kiss me, it whispered, but it would have to wait.

"Shall we give them a big finish?" he asked.

Laila nodded, and felt every inch of her body come alight as he slid her down his front, till her shoes touched the ground. Then, hand in hand, they took a deep bow, and the people of Vermillion whooped and cheered.

When the car horn beeped, longer this time, Nico and Laila waved their apologies before holding hands, and hastening back to the footpath. Realising the show was done, the crowd disappeared back inside their respective shops. Leaving Nico and Laila all alone.

It was a beautiful evening, as if the recent rain had washed the town sparkling clean. The sky behind Nico's head was a russet sunset over autumn blue, the branches of the elms in the centre of the street swaying gently through it all.

"Hey," Nico said. Then when he had her full attention, he once again said, "Hey."

In that "hey" Laila felt the entire universe expand then contract, as if its heart beat for her.

"I hope that made a whole lot of things clear," he said, his voice rumbling through her.

"What kind of things?"

"Regrets, apologies, wishes, feelings."

As her pulse skittered and danced in anticipation, she said, "That's not how this works. You're gonna have to say the words, Big Boy."

"Big Boy?" he murmured, tucking her hand behind her back as he lifted her to her toes.

"That one's just for you."

Nico shook his head, then said, "I'm sorry for letting you think that walking away from this, from us, was what I needed. When all I ever needed was you."

"That'll do it," she said on a light bright laugh.

"And yet there's more." Moving in closer, he wrapped her up tight, the heat of his body taking the edge off the cool of the close of day. "Now the town knows they'd better get used to us; this next bit is just for you. I love you, Laila. I've loved you for so long I can barely remember a time when you did not have my heart."

Laila didn't know it could feel like this; her mind flying, her heart revelling in the sweetest kind of ache. Yet the fact that it was happening, *had* happened to her, felt so unreal she had to make absolute sure.

"But I'm contrary."

"So contrary," he agreed, easily, leaning down to nudge his nose against hers.

"And wilful."

"I'm aware."

"I hog the sheets, and the pillows. All of them. And I add sugar to everything. And I think most wine tastes pretty much the same—"

"Some of my favourite qualities," he said. "Meaning despite my clumsy attempts to go it alone, I fear this loving-you thing is gonna stick."

Laila had more. She had a whole thing about his handsome face, and charming smile, and choir boy goodness, and smoking-hot bod, but when he looked at her that way, with such patience and heat, what could she say but "I hope so, because I love you so much I can hardly breathe."

Nico cradled her face and he kissed her. And kissed her. And kissed her. And when his kisses petered out, a minute— or maybe a thousand millennia—later, when he pulled away his mouth was smeared in Kiss Me red.

"Here," she said, laughing as she rubbed the back of her hand, then her thumbs, over his face till she'd cleaned him right up.

"You're looking well kissed yourself," he said, his thumb tugging at the corner of her mouth to come up with a pale red smear.

"Time to retire the red?" she said on a sigh, figuring that the trade-off would be well worth it.

"Don't you dare," he said on a growl, kissing her, thoroughly, once more.

When she came up laughing, he took her hand, kissed her knuckles, then led her on a promenade down Main Street, where the street lamps flickered on as they passed, as if just for them.

She looked up to find him smiling down at her, and she held onto that moment as long as she could. Aware, even then, it would become one of her most favourite memories.

After a few quiet minutes, where they both seemed happy to simply be, to revel in what they had overcome to be there, to find one another, to demand one another, Laila gave his hand a squeeze, and said, "I love you so much."

And Nico stretched her out to the tips of his fingers, before twirling her into his arms and slanting his mouth over hers, bending her into a long slow dip, kissing her till she felt her bones melt away.

"Okay," he said, when they came up for air, "enough of that. Time to get you somewhere I can do this properly." Then with a heave, he lifted her up and tossed her over his shoulder in a fireman's hold.

Laila scrabbled at the back of his shirt, then grabbed a hold of the loops of his jeans. "Is this one of those times where you're not going to do as I say."

"Yep."

Laila laughed till her voice cracked. Then, finding his phone in the back pocket, she slipped it out. The man had no passcode, for who would dare steal Nico Rossi's anything, so she found Sutton's number and sent her a message.

The phone buzzed back a few seconds later.

SUTTON: What the what?

Laila checked the message she'd sent.

LAILA: ive been kindpped . xan you lokc up when you don

Rather than try again, she twisted her head towards Nico and called out, "Can you take me back to the shop first? I still have a business to run, you know. And my landlord is this huge pain in the ass, so, if I don't close up within the hours allowed in the town ordinances..."

Nico ignored her, though his hand shifted over her dress to grip her backside in a way that was entirely purposeful, sending pleasure rolling through her.

"Two butt slaps for yes, one for no?" she tried.

Muttering something deep and sonorous in Italian, something she would insist he say again when she finally got him *alone* alone, Nico kept his hand right where it was and carried her back to her golden little shop, filled with love stories, and the most wonderful friends, who were about to give them what would no doubt be the best reception two people who'd just declared their love for one another had ever received.

EPILOGUE

NICO AMBLED DOWN the main street of Vermillion, taking in the scent of fresh apple pie wafting from the Rosy Crumb, and the camphor from the Corker of a Deal thrift shop.

When a crisp wintry breeze ruffled his hair, and he felt Laila shiver beside him, he stopped to open the vintage coat she had bought for him when they'd joined Aurora on her flight to Siena, surprising his mother for her welcome-home party.

Kelly and Jane, two of Laila's most dedicated book clubbers, had run the shop while they were away, and Laila had kept them on as part-time help after their social media takeover had gone viral, and the new book-box subscription service they'd insisted she start became more than she could handle.

As he wrapped Laila in the warmth of his coat, it flared out for a second before settling around them. Did it have the air of a cape? Perhaps. The best part though was what was happening now; Laila snuggled up against him, making happy noises, her arms tight about his waist.

"Wait," she said, taking little steps to keep him as close as could be while she dragged him to the window of the Savvy Sausage Butchery. "Look."

A sign in the large window read The History of Vermillion Hill in brightly coloured letters. With it a display of collages and drawings, narratives written in confident young scrawl; a project put together by a local primary school.

Nico's gaze roved over the display. There were old black-and-white images from long before his family had arrived, including one of Main Street when the now-fifty-foot-high elms were mere saplings. Along with plenty more recent photos showing how the town had evolved.

"Nico, look, is that…?" Laila asked, moving out from under his coat to draw him closer to the window.

And yes, it was. His mother and father, in dungarees and gumboots. His father holding a shovel, his mother hugging him tight, both grinning from ear to ear.

Nico braced himself for familiar waves of grief, of loneliness to come at him, but when his focus changed, and he saw Laila in the reflection, soaking in the town's story that was now also her story, he found the trauma had shifted into something more manageable. It was just…life.

In the reflection, he watched himself find the curve of her waist. Watched her grab his hand, drawing it around her.

He leaned in to whisper in her ear, asking if she was wearing any underwear under the dress that hugged her from neck to knee, and if she couldn't remember he'd be happy to take her somewhere where he could find out.

Her breath hitched as her dusky pink lips popped open on a sigh—the colour his new favourite, and he was already thinking up a new hybrid to match.

Then Mrs. Constantine's face appeared in the window and they both reared back with a gasp. Laila, coming to more quickly, gave her a big friendly wave, but Mrs. Constantine pointed at the sign in the window Laila had made for her— No Loafing, Just Loins—and shooed them away.

"I think the town's hero worship has officially worn off."

"While I think they all adore you so much they have collectively decided to give you a well-deserved break. The fact that I hiss anytime they get too close might be helping too."

With that, her hands found the hem of his jumper and sneaked beneath, her small fingers ice-cold.

"Hell Cat," he growled, then rubbed her hands through his jumper to warm her up.

"Big Boy," she said, batting her lashes. Then tipped her chin for a kiss.

He kissed her softly. Then more thoroughly. Then, in the kind of silent agreement that happens between two people who had multiple love languages, with needing to get naked together and often being one of them, they hotfooted it back to Laila's bookshop, where they turned the sign to read The Happily-Ever-Afters Will Resume Tomorrow, and locked the door behind them.

* * * * *

If you missed the previous story in the
Italians of Vermillion duet, then check out

Dating Deal with the Italian

And if you enjoyed this story,
check out these other great reads from Ally Blake

Always the Bridesmaid
Secretly Married to a Prince
Cinderella Assistant to Boss's Bride

All available now!

CINDERELLA'S BARGAIN WITH THE BILLIONAIRE

MARIAH ANKENMAN

MILLS & BOON

To electrolyte drinks, compression socks,
and doctors who listen.

CHAPTER ONE

"I CAN'T BELIEVE you did this to me, Abby. You are in big trouble, young lady," Marissa Webb hissed into her cell phone as she stepped inside of Bean Basin.

A blast of cool air conditioning hit her, causing her to sigh in relief. Though it was only May, it was unseasonably warm in Pine Creek, Colorado. The ski area up in the mountains usually stayed cool all year long, but this spring they'd seen temperatures as warm as seventy. Which was high for them.

"I said I'm sorry like a million times." Abby's voice came over the line. "And may I remind you, you're my sister, not my parent."

"I know," Marissa said. But she felt like a parent most days. Had to. Ever since she was thirteen and their mother died, leaving her alone with her four-year-old sister and their father, who was useless when it came to taking care of his kids. "But it's my job to look out for you as your big sister, and I've clearly failed considering where I am and what I have to do."

"Come on, is it really that bad to go on a date?"

She rolled her eyes up to the ceiling, counting to ten, reminding herself she loved Abby and didn't want to strangle her. Most days. Today was looking iffy.

"Abby, you made a profile for me on Just Vibes and catfished some poor man. Yes, it's a big deal!"

An angsty snort sounded in her ear as Abby responded.

"I didn't catfish anyone. The app won't let you use names or pics, remember?"

True, the Just Vibes app was unique in that you matched with people based on interests and hobbies. No identifying information allowed. Their motto was: "Just vibes, where you date a heart not a part. The dating site with no pictures, no names and no identification. Match based on hobbies, interests and vibes. Make a deeper connection."

When she had first heard about the dating app, Marissa had convinced her bestie, Nora, to sign up as a joke. Didn't quite pan out like she thought, as Nora was now dating the love of her life. Funny how life worked out.

This situation, however, was so far from funny she wanted to cry.

"It doesn't matter. You created a profile and chatted with men and women while pretending to be me. That's lying, Abby. It's not right."

"Well, I wouldn't have had to do it if you'd take two seconds for yourself and go get some action."

"Abby!" She cupped her hand around the phone. Not that anyone in the coffee shop could hear her conversation, but having her fifteen-year-old sister talk about her sex life was something she never wanted anyone to ever be privy to. Herself included. "I'm fine. I don't need anyone."

"I know you don't *need* anyone, but you deserve someone. Someone to make you happy, Missy Sissy."

Her heart squeezed hearing the melancholy in her little sister's voice as she used the old childhood nickname.

"Abs, I am happy. I promise. I don't need anyone's help with that. Besides, I have enough on my plate right now with opening the business. I don't have time to date anyone."

Was she stressed? Yes. Overworked? Burning the candle at both ends. Constantly exhausted? These days she needed a caffeine IV just to get out of bed, but that didn't mean she wasn't happy. Her dream of opening her own event-planning business was coming true. She had happiness bursting out of every worn-out pore of her body. Adding in dating to her already full plate was out of the question.

"Just meet the guy and keep an open mind," Abby said, refusing to back down on this.

"My mind is open." She glanced around the coffee shop, looking for someone who might be waiting to meet a date. "It's so open I'm going to tell him everything and hope he isn't crushed by it."

Dating was hard. One of the reasons she didn't do it anymore. Her heart felt for the poor guy who was duped by her sister's sweet but ill-thought-out plan to get her a date.

"What is he wearing again?"

A heavy sigh filled her ear as Abby answered. "He said he'd be wearing a black suit with a light blue tie, and you're taking all the fun out of this."

A suit? Who wore a suit to a coffee date?

"Lying is never fun," she replied. She should know. She'd had to deal with her father's lies for over ten years now.

She scanned the room. Bean Basin wasn't as busy as it got during the ski season, but tourists loved to visit the mountains in the summer for hiking and zip-lining. Weddings were also big at all the ski resorts during the summer. Something she was banking on for her new business. Her eyes finally landed on a white man with light red hair sitting alone at a table in the back wearing a dark suit. She squinted to see the color of his tie. Yup, light blue. That had to be him. Everyone else in this place was in shorts, leggings or jeans.

"I think I see him, Abs. I gotta go. I'll be home for dinner. Make sure you finish your homework."

"Yes, *Mom*."

The teenage angst was in full force today. She sighed,

remembering how hard it had been to be a teenage girl and giving her sister some grace.

"I'll pick up sushi for dinner. I love you."

At the mention of her sister's favorite food, her entire tone changed.

"Yes! Get extra wasabi. Love you too."

"Homework," she reminded Abby, but the line had already gone dead.

Slipping her phone into her pocket, she took a deep breath and headed toward the back table and the poor man she had to deliver very unfortunate news to. Her heart pounded with each step she made toward the table. Sweat gathered on her palms as she planned out what she was going to say, how she would apologize. She hoped he wouldn't be too disappointed.

As she approached the table, she noticed how handsome he was. Strong square jaw, bright blue eyes and a full bottom lip peeking out from his facial hair. He had a neatly trimmed beard. The light red hair on his face matched the hair on his head. She'd never dated a redhead before.

And you won't now, because you're not going on a date. You're here to explain and apologize.

Right. She had no time for dating. Even if this man did make her stomach flutter. Probably just the nerves of ruining his day.

"Excuse me," she said as she stood at the edge of the table. "Are you PuzzleMaker32?"

He looked up at her and smiled. Well, almost smiled. It was hard to tell as his lips didn't fully curl up, but one could consider it a smile of sorts. Maybe he was nervous. Weren't most people nervous on a first date? It had been so long for her she had forgotten.

"Yes," his voice, deep and rich answered as he stood and held out a hand. "And you are GrannyCrafterGirl?"

A sharp stab of annoyance pierced her. She could kill

her sister for that stupid username. Yes, she liked old-fashioned hobbies like knitting and puzzles. That didn't make her a granny.

"That's me," she replied, reaching out to shake his offered hand.

The moment their palms touched a shock of awareness shot though her entire body. Warmth radiated from where his skin caressed hers, enveloping her like a cozy blanket on a rainy day. If this had been a real date her hopes would have skyrocketed. As it was, she cursed her baby sister under her breath for putting her in this uncomfortable situation.

"Please sit," he said, pointing to the chair across from him.

She slipped into the chair, wondering how to do this. Ease into it or just rip the bandage off? He seemed like a nice guy. She hated to hurt his feelings. Maybe she should keep the sister thing to herself and let him down gently. She could claim they had no chemistry in person?

"Can I get you a coffee? Pastry?" His gaze dropped to the floor before he bent and picked something up. "Here, I believe you dropped these."

He handed her a ring of keys. Her keys. The ones that were always falling off her purse because the clip was broken. She really needed to get a new one. As she took the keys from his hand their fingers brushed. Again, that zap of electricity coursed through her entire body. She glanced up to see his nostrils flare, a flicker of heat filling his eyes.

Yeah, no way could she claim no chemistry. If this was a real date, she'd be back at his place before their coffee got cold. Shoot! She'd have to rip off the bandage.

"Um, thank you. And no thank you to the coffee. I'm afraid I need to discuss something with you."

The heat in his eyes vanished, replaced with wariness. He stepped back and slowly took his seat, motioning for her to continue.

"Well, you see, the thing is…um…my sister, I have a little sister. Not little, little—she's fifteen, not a baby or anything. Her name is Abby and she's very sweet, but sometimes she gets these ideas into her head, and you know how impulsive teenagers can be."

He blinked at her rambling. "I'm afraid I don't have much experience with teenagers."

This wasn't working. Dang it, she had to go at this another way.

"Do you have any siblings?"

He shook his head. "Only child."

There went her angle to try to gain understanding by pulling the sibling card. Anyone with a younger sibling would know how frustrating they could be at times.

"Oh, okay, well, sometimes sisters can do things out of love, that are really, really…stupid."

He frowned. "Perhaps it would be easier to simply tell me what the problem is?"

Right, rip off the bandage. Here it went.

Taking a deep breath, she opened her mouth and let it all out. "It wasn't me talking to you on the Just Vibes app. My sister, Abby, made an account for me to try and get me a date because she has some silly notion in her head that I need someone to make me happy. I'm so sorry."

His frown turned into a dark scowl, eyes filling with storm clouds. "You lied to me?"

Clearing her throat, she winced. "Technically my sister lied, but she did it out of love. She meant no harm. She wasn't trying to trick you or anything—"

"But she did." He leaned back in his chair, arms crossing over his broad chest. "She deliberately falsified information to achieve her goal, unrepentant of the consequences of her actions."

Falsified? Unrepentant?

Who talked like that? Who was this guy?

"She intentionally misled me."

That was a bit much. The guy was acting like her sister had pulled a diamond heist on him.

"You had one conversation."

She knew because after Abby spilled the beans, she made her sister show her everyone she had talked to on the app. Thankfully it had only been the man in front of her and a woman who liked knitting and horror movies. Abby knew Marissa well enough to nope her out of that convo. She was a scaredy-cat when it came to horror.

"One deceitful conversation," he said, eyes narrowing.

"Now, hold on one minute." She raised a hand, pointing a finger in the guy's face. Rude? Maybe, but he was being a bit of a jerk. She understood he might be upset at the situation, but it wasn't like Abby tricked him to be mean. It was a sweet, misguided gesture by a little sister looking out for her big sister. Maybe he couldn't see that as an only child, but that didn't give him the right to be so rude. "My sister may have misrepresented who was speaking to you, but all the things she said were true. I mean, were true about me."

His head tilted, stern expression dissipating slightly. "You read our chat?"

A half laugh, half snort left her at his ignorance. "Of course I did. My baby sister was talking to strangers on the internet. I demanded to know what happened."

He nodded in approval. She brushed away the warm feeling filling her belly. She didn't care about his approval.

"I promise you this was all a very innocent mistake."

The stern expression returned. He shook his head. "It wasn't innocent or a mistake. Your sister intentionally impersonated you and deceived everyone on the app. Whether or not her intentions were pure, the result was wrong."

"She's not a bad kid." Anger fueled her gut as her protective instincts rose.

"I didn't say she was, but what she did was wrong, and I do not tolerate liars."

The dark way he said that, tinged with a hint of pain, made her pause.

"My sister is not a liar. You don't even know her."

"And apparently I don't know you either, but judging from the actions of your family I do know it's best we end our acquaintance."

Seriously, who did this guy think he was? The morality police? Like he'd never done anything wrong in his life ever? He was a guy. She bet his mess-ups could fill this entire coffee shop. Embarrassment, anger and offence swirled inside her, creating a tornado of pain that needed to lash out. She'd tried being nice, explaining things, softening the blow, but if he wanted a fight, she wasn't afraid to get her hands dirty.

"Look, buddy, I don't know who you think you are with your fancy suit and superior morals, but us lowly humans make mistakes sometimes. We do things that aren't very smart when we're trying to help the ones we love. Something I bet you know nothing about because no one could love an uptight, stick-up-his-butt, better-than-thou snob like you. Get bent, jerk."

With that she stood and flipped him the bird before turning and heading out of the coffee shop, thanking her lucky stars she would never have to see his handsome, arrogant face ever again.

CHAPTER TWO

THIS PLACE WAS PERFECT.

Rory Thorson stood in the grand library of Stonebridge Castle. Bit of a silly name, but it fit. The home did resemble a castle, with its stone exterior, multiple turrets, over twenty-five bedrooms and the large stone bridge leading into the seventy-five-acre property from which the castle got its name. It was huge and grandiose.

Perfect.

If all went as planned, by next summer his camp would be up and running—giving children who had never had the camp experience a chance to get into nature, learn wildlife skills and hopefully find a place where they were loved and accepted. Something he'd never had until the Thorsons adopted him after his mother ran off. He'd be forever grateful to the older couple who took in a traumatized kid in need of a little love and understanding. Not only had he gained loving parents, but an entire extended family including his cousins, who never treated him like an outsider because he was adopted. They treated him like one of their own. He hoped this camp would be a way to honor their memory and keep them alive in some small way.

Damn, he missed them. Some days the pain was so fresh and raw it ate at him. Hard to believe almost a decade had gone by since he lost them.

"I hope this makes you proud, Mom and Dad."

His words echoed off the high ceiling of the library. No response except for the tweet of the birds outside and the musty smell of the book-filled room. He made a mental note to open some windows and air out the place. He was the first owner in three years. While he planned on living in the smaller groundskeeper house on the property, the main house needed to be ready for the campers and counselors. The place could do with an airing out and deep clean. Another task to add to his ever-growing list.

Maybe he should listen to his cousin's advice and hire an assistant. He shook his head at the idea, knowing he was far too stubborn and controlling to ever let anyone else handle his plans. Better that he accomplished them himself. That way he knew for a fact they were done right. Some might call that uptight—like his ex—but Rory preferred to look at it as rigid independence.

Had a nicer ring to it.

Slipping his phone out of his pocket, he unlocked it. A ping of anger churned his gut as his gaze fell on the Just Vibes app. What a disaster yesterday had been. His fault really. He never should have let his cousins talk him into downloading that ridiculous app. Dating was a fool's errand that only led to heartbreak. He knew that better than most. The three of them had not let it go until he downloaded the damn thing and created a profile. At least he'd get the satisfaction of telling them "I told you so." One thing he loved being was right. Though, a small part of him wished he hadn't been in this instance.

Selecting his contacts, he touched the screen, calling his eldest cousin.

"So do you love it, or do you love it?" Kellen Thorson asked.

"I love it, Kell." He chuckled, not at all put off by his cousin's lack of greeting. "It's perfect for the camp."

"I told you it would be."

One thing Kell had been right about. Not surprising. Kell and his brothers had one of the most successful real estate businesses in Colorado. Kell had an eye for knowing exactly what a person needed in a home. Or castle, in his case.

"I'm always right," Kell said.

"Hardly." His happy mood soured as he remembered the other thing he wanted to talk about. "You were very much wrong when you told me to download that ridiculous app."

"What app?" A pause filled the air before Kell spoke again. "The secret dating thing?"

His fists clenched as memories of yesterday assaulted him. The embarrassment at being tricked yet again burning a hole in his stomach.

"It's not secret, it lacks identifying information, but yes, that one."

"I thought you said you met someone nice on there. Had a good chat."

He thought so too. But the one pleasant conversation he'd had with GrannyCrafterGirl hadn't been with the twenty-seven-year-old woman he'd thought, but her fifteen-year-old sister impersonating her. The conversation had been very innocent. They'd talked about enjoying puzzles and nature. All stuff you would say to someone in line at the grocery store. Nothing inappropriate for him to worry about. It was the deceit that pained him.

"We met in person, and she was…not exactly who she portrayed herself to be." Sort of. Not really though. The woman he chatted with in the coffee shop was exactly who he thought he'd been speaking to online. Not only that, she'd also been beautiful, with shiny blond hair and the most enchanting pale brown eyes he'd ever seen. Almost golden in hue when the sun shined properly on them. He'd never seen such eyes. They wouldn't leave his mind, haunting him with their beauty.

No matter how beautiful she'd been, she had been a liar.

Or, her sister was, technically. He was still trying to wrap his head around why someone would lie like that. It was all so confusing. As much as he had hated ending their contact, he did not suffer liars.

"That sucks, man. I'm sorry. But that's online dating for you. My buddy met a nice guy through that app, thought it might help you get back on the horse."

"I don't need to get back up on the horse. I'm fine on my own two feet."

Silence filtered over the line before Kell spoke in a soothing tone. "It's been four years since Britney. Maybe it's time to move on."

Easy for him to say. Kell didn't wake up in the middle of the night with a cold sweat reeling from the nightmare of finding out his ex-fiancée had been embezzling from the charity foundation he ran. No, that fun little gem was reserved for Rory.

All those times she'd told him she loved him "for him." Her reassurances she would sign any prenup he wanted because she wasn't after his money. Just his foundation's money, as it turned out. He doubted a single thing she had told him was the truth.

Could you blame a guy for being a little gun-shy to hop back into the dating world?

"I'm sorry, Rory," Kell said after a minute of silence. "You do you, man. I just think you should give love another chance."

"This coming from the man who hasn't had a significant other in—" He paused, thinking over his cousin's dating history. "Have you ever had a girlfriend?"

"Whoa! Enough with the labels. You know I hate those." Kell cleared his throat. "Besides, this call is about you and your grand plans for Stonebridge. How goes the fundraiser gala planning?"

He let Kell off the hook. This time.

"I don't know. The event planner I hired should be arriving any minute."

He'd spent time online researching all the event planners in Pine Creek, of which there were very few. In the end he went with a brand-new company, Eventful Occasions. Every other event planner was booked through the summer because it was wedding season.

"Don't let me keep you, but do think about giving that app another chance," Kell said.

He grunted in place of a response.

Kell laughed. "And try to be pleasant to the event planner. You don't want to scare them off and have to plan the whole gala by yourself."

"I'm always pleasant," he said, realizing he was scowling as he spoke.

He ended the call to the sound of Kell's laughing. Relaxing his face, he took a few deep breaths. Maybe his cousin was right. Not about the dating app. That thing was getting deleted today. But he could stand to try to be a little… cheerier to people. It would help if people weren't so duplicitous. Over the years he'd discovered his grumpy demeanor weeded out the people trying to take advantage of him. Unfortunately, it ran off the friendly people too.

"Hello? Mr. Thorson?" a soft, feminine voice called out from the front hall. "It's Marissa Webb from Eventful Occasions. We have an appointment."

"In the library," he replied.

The click-clack of heels on the hardwood floor echoed through the large mansion. A few moments later, a tall white woman with ash-blond hair twisted up into a bun on the top of her head stepped into the room. She wore a maroon pantsuit and was carrying a black leather satchel. His heart stopped for a moment as recognition fired in his brain.

"I'm so sorry for barging in like this. I knocked, but no one answered and—"

Her rambling cut off as she saw him and the same recognition hit. Her pale brown eyes widened before narrowing with rage as she stormed over to him.

"You! What are you doing here? Are you stalking me or something? I told you I was sorry about the app thing yesterday at the coffee shop. Is this some weird revenge thing? Come here and mess up my meeting?" Her face paled as she glanced around the room to see they were alone. "You should know I'm meeting someone here and also I know Krav Maga, so if you're planning on trying anything I'd think again, buddy, because I can—"

"Stop." He held up a hand, wondering how anyone got in a word around this woman. "I'm not here to hurt you or seek out any type of revenge."

Her eyes held suspicion as she looked him up and down. "Oh really? You just happened to be here, at the same time I'm here. What a coincidence. Wait, are you the—" she looked him up and down again "—butler or something?"

He chuckled, wondering if he should drag this out to see how flustered she got. This wasn't going to end well for her—hell, it wasn't ending well for him either. If she was who she claimed to be when she called out, they were about to find themselves in a situation more uncomfortable than yesterday's had been.

"No, I'm not the butler," he responded, taking great satisfaction in watching her face as he spoke his next words. "I'm Mr. Thorson. Owner of the house and the person who hired Eventful Occasions to plan my fundraiser. Ms. Webb, was it?"

Her face turned white as a sheet, eyes going impossibly round as her mouth hung open in horror.

"Well, this day just went to hell in a handbasket," she muttered.

His feelings exactly.

CHAPTER THREE

IF THE UNIVERSE had any pity for her at all it would open a cavern in the ground and swallow her whole right now.

Marissa waited… Dang it! No luck. She was still here. Standing in front of the man her sister had tricked. The man she'd insulted not once but twice. The man who held the future of her business in the palm of his hands.

"You're Mr. Thorson?" Maybe she'd heard him wrong. Or she was hallucinating. Had she taken her sodium tablets today? Perhaps she hadn't and she'd had a POTS flare, passed out, and this was all a fever dream.

"Yes." He nodded, face grim. "Rory Thorson."

"Mother fudger," she muttered.

His brow furrowed at her censored swear. A habit she'd gotten into to try to keep Abby from getting in trouble at school when she was little and parroting everything Marissa said. What was it they said? Old habits die hard.

"Do you greet all your clients with threats and accusations?" Rory asked, arms crossing over his chest as he stared at her.

No, because she didn't have any other clients. He was her first. And possibly her last.

Please don't let him be my last.

She really needed this business to work out. Going back to her old job was not an option. Not after the very demonstrative way she quit. Companies didn't tend to hire back employees who told their boss to shove it where the sun don't shine. Not that her old boss didn't deserve it, but it did not bode well for her as far as references went.

"I apologize, Mr. Thorson. I didn't realize—"

"That I was who I said I was?" he interrupted.

Taking a fortifying breath, she pasted on her brightest customer service smile. "This house is very large. I could have sworn I heard your voice come from a different room."

"But I said I was in the library."

He had her there. She had no excuse as to why she had come in and gone off on him, not realizing he was her client. Of course he was. Looking back now it was ridiculous to think anyone other than Mr. Thorson would be here. Her brain had short-circuited. That was her only excuse.

"I know, and I realize how unprofessional it was of me to raise my voice like that."

"You mean yell at me?" One pale red eyebrow quirked.

Her temper was starting to rise. This guy really needed to relax. Could he not see how someone could get confused and make a mistake? Mr. Perfect was getting on her last nerve. But she needed him. Needed this event. She swallowed her pride and pushed on.

"I'm sorry. My actions were out of line. Would it be possible to start over?"

A second eyebrow joined the first. "Start over? I'm afraid I'm not in the habit of hiring people who insult me."

"But you already hired me." She slapped a hand over her mouth as the words poured out. *Play nice, Marissa!* Clearing her throat, she put her hand down and tried again. "What I mean to say is, you signed a contract. As stated in the contract, the deposit is nonrefundable."

Literally, because she had already spent the money to keep the bank from repossessing her family home. The meager deposit helped, but she'd need more. A lot more. That's why this job had to go well. If it did, it would open so many doors for her. The Thorson Foundation had connections. He could send so many clients her way. *If* he agreed to keep working with her.

He shrugged. "I can afford to lose a deposit."

Of course he could, because he was rich. Rich people thought the world revolved around them. They moved through life without a care for who they crushed under their preposterously expensive shoes. He could afford to lose this contract, but she couldn't. She had to find some way to convince him to keep her on.

"That may be the case, Mr. Thorson." She straightened her spine, throwing her shoulders back as she spoke with a confidence she in no way felt. "But Pine Creek has a limited number of event-planning companies. And this time of the year, wedding season is ramping up. I'm sure every single one of them is booked solid until fall. Your event is in two months, correct?"

A growl escaped his clenched jaw. She took extreme satisfaction in the knowledge that she had hit the nail on the head. If she was his only option, she had leverage. Still, she needed him to like her work, so he'd recommend her to his other rich, snooty friends who wanted to hold parties or fundraisers or whatever the heck rich people threw their money away on.

He relaxed his jaw, looking her up and down with a challenging expression as he spoke. "I could do it myself."

She couldn't stop the laugh from leaving her lips. "Really? You can organize a gala for three hundred people? Research and hire catering companies? Oversee staff? Decorate a mansion ballroom? Keep track of a guest list? Hire security? Book entertainment? Not to mention the dozens of other details a party like this calls for?"

"Fundraiser," he said, doubt beginning to creep into his eyes as she listed all the duties of an event planner.

Fundraiser, party, what was the difference? To be honest, she wondered if any of those funds ever got to the places they claimed to be going. Not her problem. She was here to plan a party—*fundraiser*—and do it well enough that her business got the boost it needed to save her family.

"That does sound like a lot of work," Rory said, hand coming up to stroke his trimmed beard.

She liked the contemplative look in his eyes. Hope rose inside her. She latched on to that feeling and ran with it.

"It is a lot of work. Too much for someone like you to accomplish on his own."

He paused, hand dropping as his eyes narrowed. "Someone like me?"

Shoot! She had to stop putting her foot in her mouth around this man. He was her lifeline. Or his event was, anyhow.

"What I mean is someone as important as you must have so many things on his plate. Planning this par—fundraising gala would take up all your time. Time that I'm sure is better spent on business matters."

Whatever that business was. She'd done as much research as possible when booking this job, but information on Rory Thorson was scarce on the internet. Odd, since everything seemed to be on there these days. Not him. All she had discovered was that he was the CEO of the Thorson Foundation. A charity that provided aid to children in the foster care system. A billionaire philanthropist, his money came from his parents who had done something in stocks or trading. She had a hard time understanding it, to be honest. Investing wasn't something you did when you were barely keeping your head above water.

As far as trust fund babies went, at least he was doing something good with his money. She supposed that didn't make him a totally terrible person. Hopefully his spirit of giving extended far enough to give her a second chance.

"Let me show you what ideas I have so far," she said, crossing her fingers as she gripped her satchel tight.

He stared for a moment before nodding and motioning to two chairs in the middle of the library. A cheer of victory screamed inside her head. She had another shot. Now she had to make sure not to mess it up this time. Making her way to the seating area, she waited for him to sit first, then took the seat across from him. The large chairs were a dark oak with red velvet padding on the seat and backs. As far as comfort went, they left a lot to be desired. When she read, she preferred to do it in her bed snuggled under a mound of cozy blankets.

"Show me what you have," Rory instructed.

Forgetting about the chairs, she opened her satchel and took out her planning binder. This was it. Her chance to shine. Placing it on the small coffee table between them, she opened it.

"You mentioned in your email that you are planning a gala and expect three hundred people in attendance."

He nodded, motioning for her to continue.

She launched into her presentation, explaining her plans for the catering, entertainment, decor. His email hadn't included much information. Only that he was planning a gala to raise money for a camp for foster youth. Skiing in the winter, hiking and outdoor skills in the summer. It sounded amazing to her.

She'd never been to camp. They could never afford it even though her father was a doctor. It wasn't until her mother died that she discovered why they were always struggling to pay the bills. Her father's gambling problem had bled them dry over the years. He refused to get help or even admit he had an issue. No matter how much she pleaded with him.

But she was determined to make a better life for her and Abby. And that started with this moment right here. This account. And the man sitting across from her.

"So that is the basics I have right now," she said as she finished her presentation. "Of course, more details will come as we plan out more. I like to save specifics for the client to decide on. At Eventful Occasions, all the magic of the night is up to you, and we see it through."

A silly tagline, but it got the best reaction in the event groups online.

Rory sat back in his chair, gaze focused on her open notebook with sketches, ideas and estimated prices. She held her breath as she waited to see if her future was about to come crashing down around her.

"And how many clients have you had, Ms. Webb?"

"Marissa, please." Using your first name built familiarity. A trick she learned in her business classes. She needed all the tricks up her sleeve to seal this deal.

"Marissa," he nodded. "How many clients has your company successfully served?"

She didn't like the way he said *successfully*. And she really didn't like that she had to answer this question. He waited, the large room filling with silence as she pondered if she should lie. In the end she knew it would do no good. She'd already messed up big time with this account. No need to add lying in the mix.

Taking a deep, steadying breath, she stared him straight in the eyes and answered truthfully. "You are my first client, Mr. Thorson. But I hope to show you how dedicated I am to making sure your function is everything you dreamed of and more. I promise to go above and beyond to make sure every infinitesimal detail is not only to your satisfaction, but beyond it. In fact, I am so confident in my skills that I'll make a deal with you. Let me plan your gala, and if you're not completely satisfied with the end result, I will refund all your money, including the nonrefundable deposit."

A risky move. One she could in no way afford, but she was running out of options. She had to get him on board and agree to let her plan this event. It was her last hope, and she was confident enough in her skills to risk it all.

The ticktock of a clock filled the air as she sat, waiting for his response. Her heart pounded in her chest, fear and hope causing every nerve of her body to be on high alert. Her smartwatch vibrated, letting her know her heart rate was rising, but she ignored it. Nothing new for her. She was fine. Or she would be if he would just freaking give her a yes or no.

"Rory."

She blinked, not understanding his response. "What?"

"You can call me Rory. If I'm to call you Marissa while we're working together, we should both be on a first-name basis."

Joy leaped in her chest as she felt her mouth curl into a huge smile. Did she hear him right? He wasn't firing her?

"I have the account?" she asked, needing to hear the words before she believed them.

He nodded. "You do. You are correct in that there are no other companies available, and I am not…equipped to plan such a large event myself."

Wahoo! Logic and luck for the win.

"But," he continued, his voice serious and stern. "My expectations are high. This gala must go off perfectly. There's a lot riding on it. I expect nothing but your best, Marissa."

She nodded. "And you'll get it, Mr. Th— Rory. I promise."

He stood, extending his hand. Hope bursting inside her, she quickly rose and immediately regretted it. Her vision tunneled to pinpoints, body wavering as the woozy feeling took over. She reached back to steady herself on the chair's arm only to feel the strong grip of a pair of large, warm hands envelop her waist, holding her steady.

"Are you alright?" Rory asked, concern etched on his face as he stared at her.

Shoot! Not now. This was so unprofessional. She'd just secured this account after almost losing it—she could not faint in front of her client and risk him deeming her unable to do the job.

"I'm fine, thank you." She smiled up at him, ignoring the whirlwind of butterflies taking flight in her stomach at his touch. It was just because she hadn't dated in a while, that was all. She wasn't used to someone touching her in such a protective, caring way. "Just stood up too fast, you know how it is."

Not technically a lie, but she generally didn't discuss her POTS with anyone outside her family and best friend. Certainly not with a client.

He searched her face, finally nodding and releasing his hold on her. She sucked in a breath of air, immediately regretting it when his woodsy scent surrounded her, intoxicating and comforting.

"Alright, Marissa. Let's start planning."

Shoving the strange feelings of the past few minutes deep inside, she smiled and prepared for the hardest job of her life.

CHAPTER FOUR

SMELL WAS A funny thing. Once he was adopted by the Thorsons, Rory accompanied them on their international travels. He was exposed to new cultures, amazing foods and a vast array of sights and smells. Each one cemented in his brain, creating memories that lasted a lifetime. But the one smell that always filled him with longing was pine.

He sucked in a deep breath, the crisp scent of the forest of towering pine trees surrounding him invading his senses. A memory filled his mind, painful and joyful at the same time. The one time he could remember being happy with his birth mother. She'd taken him on a camping trip to some forest, he couldn't remember where. They'd slept in the back of the car, cooked hot dogs over a campfire and watched the stars until he fell asleep in her arms as she stroked his hair, promising to always take care of him.

It had been perfect.

Then she'd abandoned him.

Her false promise was etched into his soul. A lesson at the tender age of eight on how a lie could destroy the happy, secure life you thought you had.

A bird cawed in the air, pulling him from his jumbled thoughts. He glanced around the vast forest that surrounded the castle. When he bought the place, he had also purchased the seventy-five acres surrounding it. The previous owners had set up a rope course a few yards away from the home as well as a large tree house. More of a fort, really, with how large it was. He stared up at the structure as a hint of child-like excitement coursed through his veins.

It looked safe enough. The wood was stained a dark brown, no visible cracks or splinters on the ladder or railings that he could see from here.

"I should probably test it," he mused to himself. "To make sure it's safe for the kids."

Reaching out, he placed one foot on the bottom rung of the ladder and put his weight on it. When the wood didn't creak or buckle, he slowly climbed up. There was an open porch surrounding the enclosed part of the tree house. He breathed out a sigh of relief as the wooden planks held him firm. Whoever had constructed this had done an excellent job. Moving to the door of the tree house, he ducked to avoid hitting his head as he stepped inside. Much to his surprise and delight, once inside he was able to fully stand up.

"Wow."

The inside was as nice as the outside. A large open room with multiple windows let in natural light. Tiny sparks of dirt and dust hovered in the air like blinking stars. It was clear that, while the structure was sound, no one had been in here in a while. He made a mental note to do a thorough cleaning and add some pillows and cushions for seating before the kids arrived.

"Mr. Thorson?" a voice called out from below. "I mean, Rory? Are you out here?"

He moved to one of the windows, impressed that there was actual glass enclosing them. He popped the handle on the bottom of the frame and pushed. The window opened on its hinges, moving outward and allowing him a bit of space to glance down and see Marissa walking the property, head swiveling this way and that as she looked for him.

"Up here," he called out.

He watched as her head turned up, eyes going wide with shock when she spotted him.

"Come on up."

"Seriously?"

"Yes."

He had no idea why he didn't just come down. Maybe he wasn't done assessing what needed to be done in the tree house yet, maybe he wanted to push her off her game a little, or maybe he just wanted more time amongst the pine trees. Whatever the reason, he left the window open and moved to the door. Marissa was halfway up the ladder by the time he opened it. Her satchel slung across her back as she took the steps one by one.

"Here," he said, extending his hand as she reached the top.

She placed her hand in his, soft palm gripping tight as he helped her up onto the porch. A zing of awareness zapped like lightning, striking his body and setting every neuron on fire at the contact. He heard her suck in a sharp breath as she quickly dropped his hand.

What the hell was that?

"Um, thank you." She gave him a professional smile, glancing around as her brow drew down in confusion. "What are you doing up here?"

He turned toward the door and ushered her inside. "I was checking out the tree house, making sure it was still in good condition for the campers. Come see."

He followed her in, watching as she turned around the room with awe.

"Whoa, this place is bigger than my entire bedroom. I would have killed for a tree house like this as a kid."

He chuckled. "Yes, it is impressive. My tree house was nice, but it wasn't nearly this large."

She turned to face him. "You had a tree house?"

He nodded. "My parents built me one just a few months

after they adopted me. I only made mention of the desire for one once, but they took it to heart and got started on it right away."

Her head tilted, brow furrowed. "You were adopted?"

He paused at her question. It wasn't a secret. Most people who knew his family were aware. It wasn't something he liked to advertise, especially with people he didn't know well. He had no idea why it slipped out like that. Something about this woman tilted his careful control, made him lose focus.

"Yes."

No sense in backtracking now. Besides, a deep enough internet search and she'd find a story or two on the generous older wealthy couple that took a young, abandoned boy into their home and raised him as their own. Puff pieces that his mother and father had always hated. They never saw what they did as saving. Time and time again they reminded him that he was the one who saved them. Gave them new life and love.

"My mother abandoned me when I was eight." He had no idea why he was telling her this story. His mouth opened and words kept pouring out. "She had some…problems. She wasn't a bad mother, but she realized one day that she couldn't care for me and dropped me off at the fire station."

So much for her promise.

He'd learned back then that even those who swore they loved you had the capability to tell the most harmful lies. A lesson that had been reinforced later by his ex.

Every lie felt like another knife in his already wounded back. Was it a wonder he didn't suffer falsehoods? Who could blame him with his past?

"At age eight?" Marissa gasped, her hand going to her chest. "That must have been so scary for you."

He frowned. Usually when people found out what his

mother did, they condemned her. He'd done it himself at his lowest, but truthfully, taking him to a safe space when she realized she couldn't care for him had been the kindest thing his mother had done. Even if he did harbor anger at her broken promise, deep down he knew she'd done it out of necessity. No one had ever heard the situation and commented on his feelings. A strange sensation filled his chest as she stared at him, compassion in her warm brown eyes.

"I don't remember clearly," he lied. The terror he had felt that day still haunted him in the darkest hours of the night. "But there was a news piece on foster children in which I was featured. The Thorsons saw it and... Mom always said the moment my face came across the screen she knew I was theirs."

Marissa smiled, tears welling in her eyes. "That's the most beautiful thing I've ever heard."

He cleared his throat, unsure of what to do with her emotions. Emotions for him. He hadn't told her this story to garner sympathy. He was simply stating facts.

"Sorry," she said as she sniffed and swiped at her eyes. She turned away from him, dipping her head.

He waited as she composed herself. When she turned back, her cheeks were flushed with embarrassment. He watched with curiosity as she pulled herself together. She straightened her shoulders, professional mask back in place as she explained.

"I'm not usually this emotional. It's just... I lost my mom when I was a kid too. Ovarian cancer. She died when I was sixteen."

"I'm sorry." He took a step forward, feeling an inexplicable pull toward her. Toward their common grief. "That's awful."

She lifted one shoulder in a small shrug. "Yeah, Abby, my sister, was only four. Sometimes I think she has it worse.

I have a ton of wonderful memories of our mother, but she barely remembers her. I've been taking care of her ever since. Most days I feel like her mother instead of her big sister."

She let out a small laugh filled with stressful humor. "So, you're planning to make this tree house part of the camp?"

He recognized her subject change, but since he didn't know how they got on this personal past-sharing adventure anyway, he gladly accepted the out.

"Yes." He turned, gazing around the tree house as he spoke. "I'm not entirely sure what its purpose will be as of yet, but I hope the children will enjoy it."

She laughed softly. "Any kid would die to hang out up here for a summer. I think it's really amazing what your plans are for this camp, Rory."

He didn't put much stock into what other people thought of him, but her praise had his chest puffing up with pride.

"And speaking of which," she continued. "We should probably head inside to discuss plans for the gala. Unless you want to do that up here?"

He felt a small smile tick up the corner of his mouth. "No. As lovely as it is in here, I believe chairs and a table would help in our planning."

They headed out of the tree house door. He took the ladder first, stepping aside as she followed him down. She teetered a bit on the last plank, her slick dress shoes slipping on the wood. He reached out, grasping her hips to steady her as he helped her down to the soft dirt. His hands burned at the contact, something inside him screaming to pull her closer.

Shocked by the intense feeling, he pulled his hands away and took a step back. "I should see that the campers wear sneakers. Dress shoes do not seem like appropriate footwear for this structure."

She looked up at him with a playful smile as her eyes

took in his appearance. "Says the man wearing a suit in the middle of the woods."

He couldn't stop the grin from curling his lips. Something about her calling him out intrigued him. He liked it. Maybe a little too much.

CHAPTER FIVE

THIS WAS WEIRD.

Marissa stared at Rory, standing at the counter of Sweet Treats Bakery in his dark blue suit, inspecting the glass case filled with mouthwatering-looking cupcakes. He wasn't weird… Okay, he was a little weird. Did the man own anything besides suits? Even yesterday in the tree house he'd been in a black suit. Who wore a suit in a tree house?

The situation they were in was weird. In her last job with the event-planning company she had worked for, they had brought potential caterers to the client. Not the other way around. But Rory had insisted on coming into town and seeing the bakery himself.

"I could have brought samples to you," she said once again, rehashing the argument they had had in the car on the way here. "Most of the time we bring the vendors to the client. Especially a client as…important as you."

He glanced at her over his shoulder, one reddish eyebrow arching as the corner of his mouth ticked up in a small grin. "You were going to say rich, weren't you?"

Maybe, but it was considered rude to comment on a client's monetary value, or at least that's what her old boss had always said. He'd also said women should always wear makeup and smile, so maybe she should stop taking his advice into consideration.

"I'm simply trying to be conscious of your busy schedule," she replied, avoiding the accusation.

He made a humming sound, nodding before going back to stare at the desserts. "Very kind of you, but at the moment my schedule revolves around the gala, and I like to be involved in every aspect. That includes seeing the vendors in their element. Many people pull out all the bells and whistles to impress a client in a private setting. I like to see how the everyday customer is treated to ensure I'm employing the proper company."

See, weird! Never had she worked with a client who had such an odd moral compass. Most of the time they didn't care as long as their event was the best of the best. Worthy of one-upping their other rich snotty friends. Rory was the strangest rich person she'd ever met.

He wasn't always rich.

Right. She'd forgotten he'd spent his early childhood with a single mom, struggling to get by according to the small bit of information he'd shared with her yesterday. Her heart broke for that sweet little boy and his mother. She couldn't imagine the pain of abandoning your child. Whether his mother did it out of love or neglect, it had to have hurt either way. Lucky for Rory he'd found a safe place with the Thorsons.

"Got that sample order for you, Marissa," a cheerful voice called out.

Monica, the Korean woman who owned the bakery, came out from the back with a smile on her face and a tray filled with delicious-looking treats.

"Please have a seat," Monica said as she placed the tray on a nearby table.

Rory pulled out her chair before taking his own seat. Her heart did a stupid flutter. He was just being polite. But she couldn't remember the last time someone had pulled out a chair for her. Never, maybe.

"I've gathered a selection of my favorites as you requested, Mr. Thorson. Here we have chocolate lava cupcakes, raspberry tarts, lemon shortbread cookies and *Yakgwa*, which is a traditional Korean honey pastry. This recipe comes straight from my *halmeoni*, my grandmother. It's the best you'll ever taste." Monica beamed with pride as she pointed to the small yellow square-shaped treats.

"Enjoy. I'll be back to check in later."

With that Monica left them alone to sample her product. Rory picked up the layered honey pastry first, so Marissa did the same. As she placed the sweet in her mouth, flavors exploded on her tongue. Sweet honey mixed with the slight spicy hint of ginger to create a flavor more delicious than anything she'd ever tasted.

"This is amazing," she moaned, reaching for another.

A flicker of heat burned in his eyes as he watched her, but then he blinked, and it was gone. She shifted in her seat, wondering if she'd imagined it.

"It is quite amazing," he agreed. "I wonder if the other desserts are as delicious."

They were. After they'd sampled the entire tray, Monica came back and preened under their praise. They still had a few other dessert vendors to check out, but based on Rory's compliments to the desserts, she'd bet he wanted to go with Sweet Treats for the gala.

"Our next appointment is just down the street at—"

"Missy!"

Marissa turned at the shouted nickname to see Abby barreling in the door of the bakery, with Marissa's best friend, Nora, just behind her.

"Abby? Nora? What are you two doing here?"

She rose from her seat as they made their way to her table.

"Nora is helping me with my report today, remember?" Abby smiled. "My brain gets fried with research, so we ordered some cupcakes and gluten-free cookies to pick up on our way to the library. What are you doing here?"

"Rory, I mean, Mr. Thorson and I are interviewing vendors for his gala event." She turned to see Rory had risen from his seat, a polite, not smile, but expression on his face. "Mr. Thorson, this is my best friend, Nora, and my sister, Abby. Abby, Nora, Rory Thorson."

Abby's face paled at the introduction. Dang it! She'd forgotten Abby heard her talking to Nora the other day about how the guy from the Just Vibes app turned out to be her new client. The embarrassment had died down for her, but Abby must be feeling it tenfold based on the tightness of her body.

"A pleasure, Nora, Abby," Rory said with a small nod.

To his credit, he didn't chastise her sister for her actions or even acknowledge them in any way. She could tell Abby was struggling. Just as she was about to say goodbye and rescue her sister from this awkward situation, a chime sounded from Rory's pocket.

"Excuse me," he said, pulling out his phone and glancing at the screen. "I need to take this."

Rory moved off to the far end of the shop, thumbs flying across the screen as he responded to whatever text he'd gotten.

"Holy smokes, he's hot," Nora said in a hushed voice, sliding up to her side.

"Nora! He's a client."

"And he's hot. Two things can be true."

She shook her head at the ridiculous statement. Yes, Rory was attractive, and yes, he was her client, and therefore that meant he was off-limits. She didn't like that mischievous twinkle in her best friend's eyes. Falling in love had clouded Nora's vision with rose-colored glasses. She was happy for her friend, but that didn't mean she saw love around every corner.

In her experience, all that was around the corner was more work for her.

She looked past Nora to see Abby staring across the room at Rory, a pinched expression on her face.

"Abs, sweetie." She placed a hand on her sister's shoulder. "Are you okay?"

Abby turned her head, eyes filling with guilt as she asked, "That's him, right? That's the guy from the app I…tricked?"

The weight of failure crushed her as she pulled Abby into her arms. "Yes, but it's okay. He's not mad. Everything is fine, Abs, I swear."

Raising a teenager was no joke. The past week Abby had waffled between intense guilt and nonchalance over her actions. Marissa suspected the latter was a front to assuage the former.

Rory ended his task, slipping his phone into his pocket. As he started to walk back to them, Abby pulled herself from Marissa's arms and rushed away.

"Be right back!"

"Abby, what are you doing?"

She moved to go after her sister, but Nora's gentle hand on her arm stopped her.

"Let her go," Nora insisted. "I think she needs to apologize."

"No, she doesn't. I already did that." Her throat clogged, heart pounding in her chest. Logically she knew Abby did need to apologize, but big sister protection instincts reared up. She hated seeing her sweet baby sister face any situation that caused her stress. Marissa wished she could wrap Abby in a big fuzzy blanket and never let anything in the world cause her pain or discomfort.

Realistic? No, but it was how she felt.

"Let her do this, Marissa."

Nora moved into her line of sight, blocking Abby and

Rory from her view. She arched her neck, peaking around her friend. Which wasn't hard to do considering she had a good four inches on Nora.

"Tell me what it's like working for Mr. Gorgeous."

Her attention snapped back to Nora. "Mr. Thorson."

"To-may-to, to-mah-to," Nora said with a shrug.

A chuckle escaped her. "It's…fine. He's not what I was expecting."

"You mean hot as sin?"

He did put all sorts of sinful thoughts into her mind, late in the dark of the night. But that wasn't what she meant.

"No, I mean yes, he's attractive—"

"Hot as hell."

"Nora!"

"What?" Nora bobbed her eyebrows. "Tell me I'm wrong."

She wasn't. Nora was spot-on, in fact. Didn't change the situation at all.

"He's my client. My *first* client. I need this to go well, and that doesn't include hooking up with him."

Nora shrugged. "Why not? Might get you a better review."

She smacked Nora playfully on the shoulder. "I can't believe you just said that. Zane is a bad influence on you."

"Don't I know it." Nora's smile turned serious. "But really, how's it going?"

A sigh left her as she contemplated the question. "Fairly well, actually. He's a bit more stubborn than I expected. He insists on being involved in the process instead of delegating everything to me, which is both good and bad."

"Ah, control freak?"

She chuckled. "Yes. Very. But it's helpful to know exactly what he wants so I can make this event amazing, and I really need it to be amazing, Nora."

"It will be." Nora grasped their hands together, giving

her a reassuring squeeze. "Because you, Marissa Webb, are amazing, so everything you do is too."

"You have to say that because you're my best friend."

"No, I get to say that because I'm your best friend."

She pulled Nora in for a tight hug, warmth filling her as gratefulness for her friend washed over her. A ping sounded again, this time from Nora's pocket. She pulled away as Nora pulled out her phone and smiled.

"Our order is ready. Abby," she called out. "Time to get back to it."

She looked over to see Abby smile as Rory nodded to her. It took everything in her to stand still and not rush over there and demand to know what was happening. Abby was fifteen, on the brink of adulthood. It was a good thing she wanted to face up to her mistake and apologize. It meant Marissa did a good job raising her, right? Or maybe not. Abby not making the mistake in the first place would have been better. She couldn't help but feel like her sister's mistake was her failing.

With a smile on her face, Abby hurried back over to them, giving Marissa a quick hug. Abby refused to look her in the eye, raising concern.

"Bye, Missy, see you at home later."

Heart pounding, all sorts of awful thoughts flew about in her head as to what Rory had said to her sister. He wasn't a cruel person, but he was…direct with his thoughts. It could come off as abrasive.

"What did he say to you—"

"Gotta go!" Abby bulldozed over her question, grabbing Nora's arm and rushing them off to the counter to grab their order. Nora shrugged with a smile, letting Abby drag her along. "Bye, love you!"

"Love you too," she called out as the two left the store, two bags in hand.

"Shall we move on to our next appointment?"

She gasped, whirling around as Rory's deep, rich voice boomed behind her. "Don't sneak up on me like that."

He frowned. "I didn't sneak, merely walked from there to here."

She scowled, emotions going haywire at her sister's hasty exit. "What happened back there? What did my sister say to you?"

The unspoken question hung in the air: *What did you say to her?*

If he had upset Abby in any way, client or not, she was going to hurt him.

Rory tilted his head, staring at her with a strange expression.

"Your sister simply wanted to apologize for the Just Vibes fiasco."

"Oh." She blinked, her anxiety dissipating as pride filled its place. "That's good"

"And she invited me to an apology dinner at your home tomorrow evening."

Shock had her silent for five seconds as his words flew about in her head. "I'm sorry, what? My sister invited you to dinner? At our house?"

Wasn't the "I'm sorry" enough? Why had Abby asked him to dinner?

Rory nodded. "Yes. She seemed quite insistent even when I told her it was not necessary."

A spark lit up in her brain. Oh no. Was her sister still trying to play matchmaker?

"Abby, I'm gonna kill you," she muttered under her breath.

"Pardon?" Rory asked.

"Oh, nothing. Shall we continue?"

She moved toward the exit, all the while wondering what the heck she was going to do when Rory Thorson stepped into her home.

CHAPTER SIX

RORY LIFTED HIS hand to knock on the faded storm-gray-colored door. He hesitated before his knuckle made contact, assessing the strange situation he'd found himself in. His nerves jittered inside his body, wriggling around like worms searching for a pile of fresh dirt. He felt…nervous. Which was ridiculous. It wasn't like he was some pimply-faced teenager heading to his date's house to meet her parents for the first time.

Then why does it feel like that?

He shook his head, brushing off the strange feelings. He was simply going to dinner at the house of his event planner. Hmm, it didn't sound any less strange when he put it like that. He'd been surprised when Abby had come up to him, asking to talk. Based on the poor girl's pale complexion when Marissa introduced them, he didn't think she'd want to address the incident at all. But she had. Abby had been quite apologetic and mature as she invited him over to apologize for her actions with a meal.

Rory hadn't known what to say other than yes, so here he was, standing on the stoop of a modest one-story house with faded paint and a cheery welcome mat declaring all who enter as friends. His fist finally made contact with the door as he knocked twice. The late spring sun was setting over the mountains, casting a hue of reds and golds across the sky. The porch light above brightened the fading light around him, allowing him to see the vision who opened the door.

All the air left his lungs as the door swung open and there stood Marissa. She wore a sky blue dress that flared just above her knees. Thin straps tied in bows rested on each of her shoulders. The bodice was scoop-necked, showing just a hint of tempting cleavage. Her blond hair was down, pinned back on one side with a jeweled clip. She'd done that smoky eye makeup women did that always astounded him. The gold tones she used made her brown eyes appear end-less. Her lips were painted a deep red, full and tempting. He had the strongest urge to see how stay proof the lipstick was.

"Wow." The words escaped him before he could stop them. "You are absolutely stunning."

Marissa blinked, mouth falling open as shock covered her face.

Damn! Why had he said that out loud? This was not a date, no matter what his confused brain thought.

"Thank you," she said, smiling sweetly. "I figured I bet-ter dress up to try and see if I could outdo you."

He frowned, puzzled by her playful response, but grateful she didn't take his unprompted compliment the wrong way. "Outdo me?"

She laughed softly, motioning to him. "I knew you'd show up for a casual dinner in a suit, because when are you not wearing a suit, so I decided to beat you at your own game and get as fancy as I could."

The pulse beating at the base of her neck implied there was more to it than that, but he knew inquiring would only lead down a path he wasn't sure they should explore. So in-stead, he asked, "What's wrong with wearing a suit to din-ner?"

His ex had insisted he *always* wear suits to dinner. Said it made him look distinguished and handsome. Then again, she'd also said she loved him, then stolen hundreds of thousands of dollars from his charity, making her words as reliable as a rumor spread on the internet.

Marissa leaned against the open doorframe, casually crossing her arms over her chest. "Us mortals usually wear jeans and T-shirts to friends' houses. Suits are reserved for business dinners."

But they weren't friends. Still, this wasn't a business dinner.

"I'm afraid I didn't know the dress code for an 'apology for catfishing you' dinner. Slacks and a button-up, perhaps?"

Marissa stood, arm falling to her side as her face lit up with surprise. "Why, Rory Thorson, was that a joke?"

He felt the corner of his lips curl up at her surprised pleasure. "Maybe."

"I knew there was a funny guy inside all those stuffy suits," she said, pointing a finger at him.

He didn't know about that, but something about this woman made him feel…light, playful. It was an entirely new feeling that he wasn't quite sure what to do with.

"Here," he said, lifting the gift he'd been holding in his hands out to her. "For you and Abby."

Marissa took the potted plant with a puzzled expression. "A jade plant?"

He nodded, the confidence he had earlier at picking out the gift slipping at her perplexed expression.

"My parents always insisted on bringing a gift for the host. Since Abby is underage, wine was out, and flowers start dying the moment you pluck them. I never understood the appeal of gifting someone a dying plant. Jade plants are very easy to care for. They also help purify the air and bring good luck and fortune."

She stared at him as he explained his thought process in getting the plant. It felt silly now. He could have arrived empty-handed, but the idea of disappointing his parents even in thought had him visiting the garden store on his way here. Now he wondered if he even should have come. This entire night was a disaster, and it had barely started.

"You're a very strange man, Rory Thorson," she said with a smile. "Good strange."

How could something be *good strange*?

"Come on in," Marissa said, stepping back and motioning for him to enter.

He moved into the house, immediately entering a cozy, warm living room. The walls were a creamy white color with pictures hung across the room of Marissa and Abby in various stages of adolescence. A plush brown couch sat against one wall with a leather recliner off to the side. In front of the couch was a coffee table with a partially done jigsaw puzzle. A TV sat on a credenza along the opposite wall. The room looked like one of those TV sitcoms he used to watch as a child. Homey and inviting.

"Mr. Thorson, you made it!" Abby exclaimed, coming into the room.

Unlike her sister, Abby wore casual jeans and a T-shirt. Her gaze went back and forth between him and her sister, something mischievous sparking in her eyes.

"Call me Rory, please," he insisted. "And thank you again for the invite."

Abby grimaced. "Yeah, well, I owed you after the stunt I pulled. I really am sorry. I just wanted to help Marissa. I didn't think about how my actions would affect others."

"That's very mature of you to admit." He nodded. "We all make mistakes, it's what we do after we make them that shows our character. I'd say your character is very strong, Abby."

She blushed under his praise, but he was merely speaking the truth. Marissa had done a very fine job helping raise her sister. She should be proud. A quick glance revealed she was as he observed her watching her sister with love and pride.

"You have a lovely home," he said to the sisters.

Marissa smiled with a small shrug. "It's no castle, but we love it."

"You live in a castle?" Abby asked, jaw dropping wide.

"Not exactly. I bought Stonebridge Castle."

Abby's eyes grew wide. "That place is huge! I heard it's haunted by the ghost of the guy who had it built. They say he had it built for the love of his life, but she ran off with some duke from Spain or something. The guy got so depressed he walled himself up in the castle and starved to death. And now his spirit roams the halls at night waiting for his lost love to return."

"Abby!" Marissa admonished her sister. "That's awful and not true at all."

Abby shrugged. "Just what I've heard."

Rory chuckled. Kids did like to spread tall tales. "I haven't heard any wailing at night, but I'll keep an ear out. Might be a fun story for the campfires though."

"Oh, right, you're turning it into a camp or something, Marissa said."

"Yes, a summer and winter camp for foster youth. I hope to have it up and running by next year."

"That's so cool." Abby smiled. "If you need any camp counselors, I've been a YMCA camp counselor assistant for the past two years."

"Good to know." He inclined his head. "I'll keep that in mind."

Marissa smiled at him. The sight stole the very air from his lungs. Her smile was radiance itself. Pure happiness and light, shining from behind her eyes and all directed at him. He wasn't sure what to do with that brilliance. A second later the moment broke as a small chirping sound filled the air.

Marissa broke eye contact, pulling her phone from the pocket of her dress. She glanced at the screen, her smile slipping into a frown. Tiny lines of frustration marred her forehead. He hated it. Hated whatever took her joy and replaced it with distress. At least this time it wasn't him.

"Dad's…working late." The words fell from her lips, dull and monotone.

"Again?" Abby let out a heavy sigh. "I really wanted him to meet Rory."

Marissa slipped her phone back into her pocket, shoulder stiff and tense. "Yeah, well, he had something come up at the hospital and can't make dinner. He's a doctor at County General," she explained to Rory.

There was an acidic tang to her words. He didn't know Marissa well, but if he didn't know better, he would think she was lying to her sister about where their father truly was. He tilted his head in question, but she pasted a smile on her face. Not the brilliant smile that stole his breath earlier. This was her fake smile. The one she'd given him when trying to convince him to keep her on as event planner.

Didn't matter. Her home life was not his concern. Even if he was in her home at the moment.

"Dinner is almost ready," she said, pushing past the moment. "Rory, please make yourself at home. Feel free to try and find a few pieces in that puzzle. It's a tricky one."

Considering all the pieces were rainbow colored with no discernible pattern, he assumed it was a challenge.

"Abby, can you help me in the kitchen?"

"Yup."

The sisters moved out of the room, leaving him alone with the puzzle and a million questions racing through his head.

CHAPTER SEVEN

"DID HE BUY you a plant?"

Marissa turned to Abby once they were in the kitchen. She glanced down at the jade plant in her hands. "No. He bought *us* a plant."

Abby's nose scrunched up as her head tilted to the side. "Why?"

Marissa set the plant on the counter, moving over to the oven where the casserole was baking. "Because it's the polite thing to do. Bring a gift for the host."

"It is?"

She shrugged. Seemed so. The only time she'd ever bought a plant for someone was at a housewarming. It was kind of sweet that Rory brought a gift for them. Especially considering this was an apology dinner. He didn't have to bring anything at all and yet he'd been so thoughtful, not bringing wine because of Abby. He really did have a soft heart under all that gruff, proper exterior.

Good thing too, considering how she'd acted the other day. Embarrassment flooded her at the memory of how she'd lost it at his story about his mother abandoning him. She couldn't believe she'd cried like that. In front of a client! Thank goodness he'd been understanding and kind. Giving in to her emotions like that had been incredibly unprofessional. She still cringed thinking about it, but Rory had been sweet and understanding and...surprised, it seemed. Shocked that she would feel so deeply for his pain.

It hurt her heart to think that he'd shared his painful past with others and hadn't received any compassion. What was wrong with people?

"I can't believe Dad has to work late again," Abby complained. "He's never home for dinner anymore."

"Can you grab the salad from the fridge?" Marissa asked, glossing over the comment.

Their father wasn't at work late. He never worked late. What he did was head to the ski resorts' casinos and lose himself—and his paycheck—at the poker table. But she couldn't tell Abby that. She couldn't tell anyone. The embarrassment and shame of having a gambler for a father was something she could shoulder, but she would not put that burden on Abby. Better that her baby sister think their father was dedicated to the job. That his hard work ethic was what kept him away from his daughters. Stopped him from seeing school plays and science fairs. Neglect was easier to deal with if Abby could see their father in a noble light instead of the harsh reality Marissa had to face every day.

Her father was an addict, and his gambling addiction was more important to him than she and Abby were.

"We're out of ranch dressing," Abby said, pulling Marissa from her dark thoughts.

"Check in the pantry. I just bought a bottle yesterday at the store."

The oven beeped, letting her know dinner was done. She and Abby set about placing the food on the table in the dining room. Less of a room and more of an area right off the kitchen. Nothing like the grand dining hall in Stonebridge Castle. But it worked for them, and Rory had seemed genuine in his praise of their house, which made her insides go all warm and fuzzy. She took a lot of pride in making their modest home feel warm and welcoming. Nice to know she'd succeeded at it.

"Can you go grab Rory?" she asked Abby, setting the chicken casserole down on the hot pad in the center of the table.

A few moments later Abby returned with Rory, who sniffed the air with a pleasant expression.

"The dinner smells delicious, Marissa."

Heat rose on her cheeks at the compliment. "Thank you. It was our mom's recipe. Please sit."

They sat at the table, Abby and Marissa on one side with Rory on the other. They ate in silence for a few minutes before Abby started asking Rory about the camp he planned to start. Marissa sat back, enjoying the food and the way Rory's eyes lit up as he talked about his plans. He truly seemed to have a passion for this camp. Now that she knew he'd been in the foster system himself, she understood his drive to help these kids. It was nice to see someone give back in such a significant way. She had to make sure the gala was a rousing success. She wanted to help provide this space for the kids as much as he did.

"And what about you, Abby?" Rory asked. "What are your plans for the future? Are you looking into colleges yet?"

Abby nodded. "Yeah, I mean I'm only a sophomore, so I'm still weighing my options, but I really want to study biochemistry and go into cancer research."

Her heart ached listening to her sister's dream. Rory's gaze found her, a wealth of understanding filling them.

"That's a very honorable goal, Abby."

Abby shifted in her seat, eyes dropping down to her plate as some of the joy left her. "Yeah, well, our mom died of cancer when I was four. I don't remember her much, but I do remember her laugh. It was magical, wasn't it, Missy?"

Tears gathered in her eyes, but she blinked them back,

nodding to Abby. "Yes, Abs. It was the most beautiful laugh in the entire world."

"It's difficult losing your mother," Rory said softly.

Abby's head snapped up. "Your mom died too?"

He cleared his throat. "My adopted mother and father have both passed, and I lost my birth mother long ago."

She sucked in a sharp breath, the pain of his abandonment piercing her chest as she watched him comfort her sister.

"You were a foster kid?" Understanding lit Abby's eyes. "That's why you want to do the camp?"

He nodded. "Much like you want to do cancer research. I think we all try to do our best to help others survive what harmed us in our past."

Marissa pondered his statement. While she agreed that Abby wanted to go into cancer research because of their mother and Rory wanted to help foster kids because of his past, it didn't line up for her. She helped people plan parties. A party had never harmed her before. After her mom died, she hadn't really had any time to celebrate anything. She'd been too busy caring for Abby. Maybe that's why she went into event planning. To make sure every celebration, big or small, received the attention it deserved.

"You know," Rory continued, "I know a former classmate who is a professor in the chemistry department at Stanford. I could make a call, get you in touch in case it's one of the schools you're interested in?"

Abby's mouth dropped open. "Interested in? That's my dream school!"

Rory nodded. "I'll make the call then."

Abby turned to her, eyes wide, silently mouthing, *Who is this guy?* She shrugged. Rory was constantly surprising her. Abby took their plates to the kitchen. She leaned in close, lowering her voice since her sister was only a dozen feet away.

"Thank you, Rory."

The corner of his mouth ticked up in that almost smile he always gave her. "My pleasure. We need more dedicated people in the field of cancer research. Abby shows great passion and intelligence. I believe my former classmate will welcome her enthusiasm, and it's never too early to start planning for college."

Never too early to start saving either. Unfortunately, Marissa hadn't been able to squirrel away nearly enough for a place like Stanford. Maybe her sister could get a scholarship, or she could take on a second job? Anything to help Abby succeed.

"Should we have dessert in the living room?" Abby asked as she stacked the plates in the dishwasher. "We could work on the puzzle. Or play a tabletop game?"

They decided on the puzzle. After grabbing some bowls of chocolate chunk ice cream, which Rory insisted on carrying, they made their way to the living room. Abby plopped down on the floor, placing her bowl on the coffee table to the side of the puzzle. Marissa took a seat on the couch next to Rory. She was a good six inches away from him, but she could feel the heat radiating off his body. His woodsy scent surrounded her, heady and intoxicating. Needing to cool down, she shoved a spoonful of ice cream into her mouth, immediately regretting it when she got a brain freeze.

"This puzzle is quite complicated," Rory mused as he picked up a piece to examine it. "Do you have the box for a reference picture?"

Abby shook her head. "We play on hard mode."

He frowned, turning his head to glance at Marissa. "Hard mode?"

She nodded, grateful the ice piercing her skull had died down to a dull hum. "We do so many puzzles that we started playing what we call hard mode. We put all the pieces out and hide the box so we can't see what image it creates when finished. Makes it more fun."

Abby snorted. "She says fun, I say annoying. Now do you see why I wanted to get her a date? She needs to get out more if this is her idea of fun."

"Abby!"

"What? Too soon to joke about it?"

She held her breath, glancing over at Rory. He'd said he understood about the whole Just Vibes fiasco. He was here, accepting an apology dinner, but it seemed risky to bring it up so casually. The last thing she wanted to do was anger her only client.

Rory stroked his trimmed beard, an actual smile curling his lips as he responded.

"I'm afraid your plan backfired, as the profile you built for your sister attracted other puzzlers such as myself. This is our idea of fun."

Abby laughed. "You guys are such grannies."

Rory joined in with a small chuckle of his own. She let out the worried breath she was holding, joining in the frivolity—even if it was at her expense. The rest of the night went by pleasantly. They made good progress on the puzzle that she was sure would end up being a gradient rainbow wash. The vague pictures were some of the hardest puzzles, and the most fun in her opinion. So what if that made her a granny? There was a lot to be said for simple hobbies. Besides, like any good Pine Creek resident, she also skied in the winter. Nothing granny about that.

She glanced over at Rory, wondering if he ever got up on skis, or a snowboard. She couldn't imagine the suit-wearing man decked out in snow gear flying down the side of a mountain. Then again, she hadn't expected him to offer to help her sister get an in with Stanford. The guy was full of surprises.

"I should be getting back home," Rory said after they called it quits on the puzzle for the night. "Thank you, Abby, for the invitation and thank you, Marissa, for the delicious dinner and delightful puzzling."

"Thanks for coming, Rory." Abby stood, throwing her arms around Rory and giving him an enthusiastic embrace. "And thank you so much for talking to your friend at Stanford for me."

Marissa watched with amusement as he stood there, unsure what to do with her sister's grateful excitement. He patted her back awkwardly, but she saw a flicker of happiness light his pale blue eyes.

"Happy to help."

Abby pulled away and grabbed the dessert bowls. "I'll clean up so you can walk Rory out."

She arched one brow at her sister, but Abby just smiled and headed into the kitchen. Walk him out? The door was twenty feet away and he was a grown man. He didn't need her to walk him out. She swore if Abby was still trying to play matchmaker her sister needed to think again. He was her client. Ergo, off-limits. Still, she didn't want to appear rude.

"Thank you again, for coming," she said as she walked with him to the door.

"I'm grateful for the invitation. You have a lovely home, and you've done a very fine job raising your sister, Marissa. She has a good head on her shoulders and a kind heart. I hope you know that."

Emotions clogged her throat, preventing her from saying anything in response to his praise. Most days she felt woefully unprepared for the task of caring for Abby. She constantly felt like a failure with each mistake her sister made. Logically she knew everyone made mistakes, but it was hard not to see Abby's mistakes as her own failings. It was nice to have someone reassure her she wasn't totally screwing up her sister's life.

"Thank you, Rory."

He opened the front door and turned to face her, the brightness of the moon shining high in the sky as the porch light illuminated them in a soft glow.

"And thank you for being so understanding about…everything with the app and all."

He stared at her silently, gaze roaming over her face as heat burned in his eyes. A small gust of wind picked up, blowing a few strands of hair across her face. His hand reached out to brush the strands away, tucking them behind her ear. Her skin tingled at the contact as his fingers brushed her cheek softly before dropping.

"I can't say I don't often wonder what would have happened if it really had been you who I spoke to on the app."

She sucked in a sharp breath, unable to admit she wondered the very same thing. What would have happened if she met this man in truth? Would this simmering attraction she felt for him develop into something real? Or explode in her face?

"Marissa."

Her name, low and dark, uttered from his lips as he took a step closer, sent a shiver of need coursing through her entire body. She found herself leaning forward, eyes closing as she felt his hands grasp her hips and tug. Her hands fell on his chest, head tilting as she felt his warm breath caress her lips just before—

"Marissa, where's the dish soap? Are we out again?"

Abby's voice calling from inside the house broke the spell. Her eyes snapped open, face flaming as she realized what she'd almost done. She took a step back, lamenting the loss of his touch as Rory's hands fell to his side. He blinked, as if coming out of the same spell she'd been under.

"Um… I should…" She pointed inside the house.

"Yes, of course." Rory nodded, taking a step back. "I'll see you tomorrow when we go over the decor for the gala."

"Yup, yes, sure, tomorrow it is."

With that he turned and got into his car, leaving her to mire in the awkward and embarrassing realization that she had nearly kissed her client.

CHAPTER EIGHT

"I REALLY THINK you're going to send the wrong message with this decor."

Rory stared at Marissa as she scrolled through the Pinterest board filled with ideas he had for the fundraiser. They'd been disagreeing over the decorations for the event for the past ten minutes. He'd thought visual examples would help her see his point, but he'd been wrong. The stubborn woman wasn't seeing his vision at all.

"This all feels very cowboy cliché," she said, shaking her head. "This is supposed to be a fancy gala for a kids' camp, not a hoedown for a dude ranch."

He huffed out a breath of frustration, not used to people arguing with him. The last event planners he'd hired had done nothing but say yes. He wasn't used to opposition. Had to say, he didn't care for it.

"I do not understand how you can't see the tie-in. The vision," he stated, pointing to the tablet in her hand with endless hours of carefully thought-out ideas pinned in a folder.

She gave a small chuckle. "And I can't believe you know how to use Pinterest. The only people I've ever seen use it are brides and moms-to-be."

His spine straightened at her teasing words. He never quite knew what to do when she mocked him. People generally didn't tease him. It wasn't entirely unpleasant.

"We used to have an in-house event planner for the foundation's fundraisers. Kenny used Pinterest for all the events. It was a fantastic way to showcase his ideas for the events so I could get a clear picture and adjust when needed."

She glanced up from the screen, a hint of worry in her eyes. "Where's Kenny now?"

Was she worried he disagreed with Kenny's ideas and fired him? He could keep her in suspense, do a little teasing back, but he wasn't very good at that sort of thing so instead he went with the truth.

"He got married and moved to Norway to be with his husband's family and work for their family business. I hated to lose him, he was a very diligent, *agreeable* employee."

She narrowed her eyes at his emphasized word. Maybe he could tease a little.

"Do you want a yes man, or do you want to throw the best gala ever?" she asked.

Couldn't he have both?

"And no, you can't have both."

He frowned, wondering if he'd spoken out loud without realizing.

"I saw the question written all over your face." She set down the tablet on the coffee table in between them and let out a heavy sigh. "Look, Rory, I know you're used to getting your way and everyone saying yes to you, but that is not how I work. I want to provide my clients with the best possible event I can. Sometimes that means I have to push back when their ideas are…less than ideal."

"But it's my event," he insisted. "Shouldn't you do everything in your power to make the client happy?"

"Yes, but I know to make you happy we need to bring in as many funds as we can from these people, and I am telling you, this theme is not the way to go. We need to make them feel important, special. And I just don't think this will do it." She waved to the Western-themed pictures on the table. "Then again maybe I'm wrong. They're your friends. Maybe they do like cheesy cowboy stuff."

He wouldn't call anyone attending the gala "friends." Acquaintances, business associates at best. In his world one didn't really have friends. He glanced down at the screen, knowing what he was going for, but seeing her point. It wasn't like a board Kenny would have made. This lacked the charm and elegance. She was right—an event with this decor would entice very few funds.

"Perhaps you are right," he said slowly.

A victorious smile lit up her face. He sucked in a sharp breath, reminded again how beautiful she was. A fissure of guilt wormed its way into his brain as he remembered last night and how he had almost kissed her. What a colossal mistake that would have been. He was lucky she hadn't slapped him.

She'd been going in for it too.

He shook away the thought. It didn't matter. He had hired her to plan his gala. They couldn't…cross any lines. It would be inappropriate. He was just glad they both seemed to silently agree it had never happened.

"I think you have a good jumping-off point here," Marissa said. "I can see what you're going for, but I think we need to hone it in a little."

He frowned. "What do you mean by that?"

She leaned back against the plush reading chair. They'd decided to have their meeting in the library. The large floor-to-ceiling windows allowed the natural light to brighten up the entire room. The massive bookshelves lined the other walls, filled with row upon row of books from every genre available. The air smelled of paper and ink. He'd always been a reader as a kid, escaping into books when things got rough. The smell soothed him. He had to admit this was his favorite room in the massive home.

"You want to highlight that the gala is to help with the cost of the camp, right?"

He nodded. "That's why I went with all the outdoor things here."

He pointed to the pictures on the screen of the Southern Rockies, large pine trees, horses grazing in a pasture. They didn't have any horses on the property yet, but he had big plans for the future. Providing they could raise the funding.

"I like that, but we don't want to appear tacky. People like this like to be reminded how much money they have and how great that makes them. They're much more likely to open their wallets when you make them feel important."

The slight sting of acid in her words made him wonder just who she'd planned events for in the past. He knew he was her first client with her solo business, but she'd worked for other event-planning companies before, she'd said. He wondered how difficult those jobs had been for her. And how he compared.

Needing her to see that he was in this not to feel important about himself, but to help kids like the one he'd been, he stood up. "Come with me."

She blinked up at him. "What?"

"I think I need more than a visual demonstration. We need hands-on examples to get our brains working."

She stood with a shrug. "I suppose it couldn't hurt."

He led her out of the house off to the side of the property, where a large ropes course had been set up by a previous owner. He'd tested it the other day, deeming it safe for use. Secretly he'd had a blast making his way across the various rope challenges. He hoped the kids would love it too.

"A ropes course?" She frowned. "What does this have to do with decor for the party?"

"I know the type of people coming to this thing, and you're right. They need to feel important and special to open their wallets. But I also want to show them why they're giving. I want them to see this isn't going to be a fancy place, it's going to be a real place. A place where kids can come to let out steam. Learn life skills. Just be a kid for a little while. We can have the fancy crystal champagne flutes and fresh floral garlands, but I also want them to see this. The reality of the place and what their money is doing to help."

Her gaze moved over the ropes course, a contemplative look in her eyes. Finally, she nodded.

"I think I'm beginning to understand what you mean, and I have some ideas. Maybe I can noodle about on Pinterest tonight and make a board that will encompass your ideas while appealing to your target audience?"

A warm sense of pride and something else he couldn't identify filled him as they found their compromise. "I think that is an excellent idea."

She smiled, taking his breath away again. Damn, he needed to get his head on straight and remember this woman worked for him.

"How sturdy is this ropes course?" she asked, reaching out a hand and tugging on a thick rope suspended between two large pines.

"I completed it myself the other day in under twenty minutes."

She let out an adorable snort of a laugh.

"Twenty minutes? Was it because you were wearing a suit while trying to finish it?"

No, he'd been in jeans and a T-shirt. Did she truly think he wore nothing but suits? Suits were appropriate for business attire, and since their entire relationship was business, he had no reason to be around her in anything else. But he did own other clothing.

"You think you could do better?" he challenged, unsure where this playful side of himself was coming from.

She looked at him with a teasing grin.

Her. It was coming from her, and he had to say, he enjoyed it.

She kicked off her black pumps, grasping the first rope with both hands. "Time me."

A chuckle left his lips as he lifted his wrist and brought up the timer on his smartwatch.

"On your mark, get set, go!"

He touched the screen to start the timer as she raced across the ropes. The brown slacks she wore allowed her the freedom to move quickly across the course. She went on to the next obstacle, after accomplishing the first. He watched as she wobbled back and forth on the tightrope-like obstacle, arms above her head as she held on to the rope above her to steady herself.

"Five minutes," he called out, unable to keep the humor out of his voice.

"I don't need updates," she called back tersely, her face a mask of concentration.

He stifled a laugh, watching as she moved on to the next obstacle, a rope climb over a wall. She planted her feet on the wood, sweat gathering on her brow as her arms strained, pulling her up the plank of wood. He frowned as he noticed her breath becoming labored, limbs quivering slightly with each movement.

"Marissa? Are you okay?"

He barely got the words out before he heard her swear softly. Horror filled him as he watched her grip slip. Running as fast as he could, he reached out his arms to catch her as her eyes rolled back and she fell unconscious.

CHAPTER NINE

No, no, no!

Marissa knew the exact moment she'd made a mistake. The ropes course had looked fun, and when Rory had challenged her she hadn't been able to refuse.

Big mistake.

Her heart had started to pound after the first obstacle, but she'd ignored it. Sweat gathered on her brow starting the second obstacle, but she'd pushed it away. Once she had started to climb the wall and her limbs began to shake, she had known she was in trouble. Then her vision had started to tunnel out and she'd cursed the competitive nature that had goaded her into doing this. As her grip slipped, body giving up, she'd muttered a soft curse. Consciousness left her for a brief moment as she fell backward, fully expecting to slam into the hard earth below.

"Marissa!"

The shout of her name brought her back around as she fell into a pair of strong, comforting arms. She blinked, vision still doing that blacking in and out thing it did whenever she had an episode. Her head stopped spinning as reality came back into focus.

"Are you alright?"

She glanced up to see the worried face of Rory as he gazed down at her. Shoot! This wasn't good. If she'd thought last night had been embarrassing, dial that number up to a hundred and that was the situation right here.

"I'm fine," she muttered, trying to shift out of his arms, but he just pulled her in tighter to his chest.

"You are most certainly not fine," he insisted. "You passed out."

Not really. She waved away his concern. "Only for like a second."

He frowned, scowling down at her dismissal. "You fell and nearly cracked your skull open."

Wow, someone was Mr. Dramatic.

"I would have gotten a tiny bump at worst. Besides, I didn't get hurt at all because you saved me." She batted her eyelashes overtly. "My hero."

"This isn't a joke, Marissa." His scowl deepened. "You could be seriously ill."

She let out a heavy sigh as her attempt at humor fell flat. Suddenly they were propelled forward as Rory started walking toward the house, still holding her tight in his arms.

"What are you doing?" she shrieked, throwing her arms around his neck to steady herself as his long strides ate up the space between the ropes course and the house.

"Getting you inside."

"I can walk, you know."

He gave her a stern look, tightening his hold on her in answer. She could have sworn she also heard a low growl escape his lips. Okay, so he didn't like the idea of her walking back to the house. Whatever. He could strain his back carrying her if he wanted, no skin off her nose. Only it didn't seem as though he was under any undue stress supporting her body weight. She had no idea what he looked like under those stuffy suits he wore, but based on the muscles she felt holding her, she would guess Rory was no stranger to working out.

She gave up protesting his overprotectiveness and snuggled into his chest. Why fight it? Besides, she had to admit, she rather liked being held in his arms. It was warm and comforting. To be perfectly honest her legs were still a bit mushy feeling. Not having to walk back to the house was probably the best thing for her right now.

Rory took them inside the side door that led to a small solarium off the kitchen. She hadn't been in this room yet. It was beautiful. The glass-enclosed room was smaller than other rooms in the house, but big enough to house a large green chaise longue and two matching reclining chairs. Various plants, flowers and small trees lined the octagonal room. Floral and earthy smells permeated the air, filling her lungs with a calm sense of serenity.

Rory placed her on the soft, velvety lounge, crouching down in front of her. His hands gently grasped her face as he turned her head, staring into her eyes.

"What are you doing, weirdo?"

"Checking you for a concussion."

"I didn't even hit my head."

"How many fingers am I holding up?" He lifted two fingers in the air inches from her face.

"Two. Rory, I promise I'm fine. I just got a little winded."

He raised one eyebrow, clearly not believing her. Fine. Guess she was going to have to do this. Taking a deep breath, she prepared to share a part of herself she rarely shared with those outside her inner circle.

"I swear I'm fine. I…have POTS. I overexerted myself and had a small episode, but I promise you I'm fine now."

"POTS?" He frowned. "I'm afraid I'm not familiar with that."

Most people weren't. Even she had had no idea what it was until she fainted one day in gym class in tenth grade. It had taken almost a year to figure out what was wrong with her, and she had a doctor for a dad.

"Postural orthostatic tachycardia syndrome."

His frown deepened. "Tachycardia is heart related, correct? Should I call an ambulance?"

He started to stand, but she grabbed his wrist and pulled him back down. The last thing she needed on top of all her troubles was an ambulance bill.

"No. I mean yes, it is heart related, but not like a heart attack or anything. I don't need an ambulance."

He stared at her for a moment before nodding and motioning for her to continue.

"It's not life-threatening. Basically, my automatic nerve system is a little wonky, and sometimes when I do things like stand up or exert too much energy my heart rate goes wild, and I can pass out. But I promise you I'm fine now."

"You're sure?"

She nodded.

"Is there anything I can do to help? Do you need water or food?"

Her stomach was always a little iffy after an episode. "If you have anything with electrolytes that would be great, but water sounds amazing."

He nodded, standing and pointing to her with a stern expression. "Do not move from this spot."

She gave him a sassy salute. "Yes, sir."

The corner of his mouth ticked up as he turned and headed out of the solarium and into the kitchen. Darn it. One of these days she would get a full smile out of this man. She swore it, if it was the last thing she ever did.

A few moments later Rory came back into the room with a bottle of red Gatorade.

"I found this in the pantry. Best I could do. I hope you like fruit punch."

She took the bottle with a grateful smile, twisting the cap open. "My favorite flavor. This is perfect, thank you."

She took a deep sip of the drink, sighing in relief as the liquid soothed her parched throat.

"How long have you had POTS?" he asked, taking a seat in the chair across from the lounge.

"High school," she answered, taking another sip, feeling her strength return slowly as she rested and rehydrated. "I had a nasty virus that kicked my butt for about two weeks, and afterward, I couldn't seem to get my energy level to where it was before. I was always so tired and thirsty, craving salty foods. My dad thought I might have diabetes, but the glucose test came back normal. Then one day I passed out in gym class, and it was months of testing, scans and finally a tilt table test to confirm POTS. I'm usually pretty good at managing it, but some days it just sneaks up and kicks me on my butt."

"Why didn't you tell me about it earlier?" he asked.

She saw the question in his eyes. Knew he was remembering that moment in the library a while ago when she had almost passed out.

Lifting her shoulder in a shrug, she stared into her bottle at the bright red liquid, avoiding his piercing eyes. "It's not something I like to talk about, especially with clients. When people find out, they treat me…differently. As if I'm less. I don't want anyone thinking I can't do my job because I have POTS."

"I would never think less of you, Marissa."

His warm reassurance made her head snap up. Bright blue eyes stared at her with sincerity.

"To be honest, I believe you are one of the most amazing people I've ever met. Nothing could take that away from you. Nothing."

She swallowed, hands gripping the bottle tightly to keep

herself from throwing her arms around him and kissing the ever-living daylights out of him. How was she supposed to keep her head on straight when he said things like that to her?

"Thank you, but I probably should listen to my body more and not push myself when teased into a challenge."

A flicker of guilt filled his eyes. "I'm sorry, I shouldn't have—"

"Stop." She held up a hand. "You didn't know. It was my fault entirely. Besides, going out to the ropes course was a good idea. I think I'm starting to see what you mean by incorporating the nature aspect of the camp for the gala decor."

He rubbed a hand over his head, red hair mussing slightly with the motion. "No, maybe you're right. We should go fancy and important."

"Hey, now." She held up a finger and pointed it at him with narrowed eyes. "Don't give in to my idea because you feel sorry for me. I will not accept a pity win."

"There are many things I feel for you, Marissa, but *sorry* is not one of them," his deep voice spoke, gaze never wavering from hers.

She swallowed hard, wondering what exactly those other things he felt for her were, but too chicken to ask. They were dancing a fine line here. She wasn't sure if she wanted to keep on toeing it or take the risk to cross it. After a moment of silence, he cleared his throat and broke eye contact.

"Perhaps we can come to some mutual agreement on the decor as you mentioned earlier?"

Trying to find her words, she nodded. "Um, yeah, yes. I think we can find a way to incorporate your ideas and highlight the more rugged aspects of what the camp will be, but make it elegant so your guests feel important enough to open their wallets."

He leaned back in his chair with a thoughtful expression. "Yes, I believe we can."

"And if that doesn't work, we can challenge them to the ropes course. If they don't complete it in ten minutes they have to donate ten thousand dollars."

His head tilted as he stared at her. "I must say, Marissa. You do have the most creative ideas of anyone I know. I don't think the guests will go for that, but it is amusing to think about."

"I aim to please, cowboy," she teased, affecting a silly Western accent.

He chuckled softly, gazing up at her as his lips curved into a full-blown genuine smile. The sight stole the breath from her lungs. She swore the room got brighter as Rory's joy lit up the solarium. Holy cow! Scowling Rory was handsome. Stoic Rory was hot. But nothing could have prepared her for how panty-melting sexy, happy Rory was. Her heart started to pound in her chest, but this time it had nothing to do with her POTS and everything to do with the man in front of her.

CHAPTER TEN

WHY AM I HERE?

Rory grimaced as someone to his right let out a loud, eardrum-shattering cackle. Bright lights flashed red and yellow from the ceiling as the thumping bass blared from speakers set up on the small stage in the front of the room where a band was tuning their instruments.

The club scene had never been his preference for a good time. Not that one could truly call this venue a club. Bar might be a more accurate description. It was a good-sized room, but not overly large. It felt smaller with the amount of people stuffed into it. Normally he would never voluntarily spend his evening in a place so…overstimulating, but Marissa had mentioned a band she thought would be perfect for the gala. They just so happened to be playing at a bar in town tonight so here he was.

"This was a mistake," he muttered to himself as he glanced around the room, trying to spot Marissa. They'd agreed to meet here at seven forty-five. The band was scheduled to go on at eight. He glanced at his watch. Seven forty-five exactly. Where was she?

The crowded room and less than helpful lighting made his search difficult. The throng of people moved like choppy waves in the ocean, ever changing, making his search impossible. He spotted half a dozen blondes, but none of them were Marissa. Pulling out his phone, he went to text her when he spotted a familiar smile out of the corner of his eye. There, standing at the far end of the bar was Marissa, smiling and laughing while talking to a tall white man with brown hair. The guy had his back to Rory so he couldn't see his face, but something ugly and dark rose up inside him as he watched Marissa playfully punch the man on the shoulder.

If he didn't know better, he'd say it was jealousy, but he did know better, so he said nothing. They weren't an item. It was no concern of his if she flirted with a man at a bar. Wasn't that what bars were for? Flirting and hooking up? Hell if he knew. He hadn't been with anyone since he found out his ex had stolen from his foundation. Hard to be intimate with anyone when trust was broken so monstrously.

He wasn't jealous. No, he was simply worried her focus was distracted. After all, she was on the clock. Sort of. They were here to see if the band performing was a fit for the gala entertainment. He needed her to focus, not make googly eyes at some guy all night. He was thinking of the gala, nothing more. Determination set in place, he made his way through the crowd to Marissa and the mystery man.

"Marissa." He called out her name as he reached their side. If he'd said it a bit too loud it was only because he wanted to be heard over the noise in the room. Nothing more.

Her gaze turned to him, eyes lighting up as her smile grew. The sight eased some of the raging storm inside.

"Rory! You made it."

"Naturally."

"The band's warming up now," she said, motioning toward the stage where a group of people dressed in a strange combination of Western and goth-style clothing were setting up. "They are perfect for what you're looking for, I promise. They have this kind of country gothic mash-up sound with a hint of classical thrown in. It's so unique and awesome."

He nodded, noticing a tall Black woman in a dark Victorian-style dress tuning up a large cello. Not the instrument he would have expected in this type of band. He had to admit he was intrigued to hear their sound. But he was more interested in the man beside Marissa, who had turned to face him but still had not spoken.

"I look forward to hearing them." He glanced over at the man, wondering if he should start the introductions. Before he could decide, Marissa spoke again.

"Oh, how rude of me. Rory, this is Zane." She pointed to the man with black-rimmed glasses and a smile on his face. "Zane is my best friend Nora's fiancé."

Immediately the tension in his body released at her words. This wasn't a bar hookup. He was a friend. Again, not that it mattered to him; Rory had no claim on Marissa. She could date or be intimate with whomever she pleased.

"Nice to meet you," Zane said, extending his hand.

Rory took the other man's hand and shook it, noticing the guy seemed friendly enough.

"Rory is my current client," Marissa said to Zane. "We're working on a gala fundraiser for the children's camp for foster youth he's starting at Stonebridge Castle."

Zane smiled, releasing his hand. "Really? That's cool. Hey, if you plan on doing any winter stuff, my fiancée owns a ski resort, and I'm sure she'd love to work something out with you so the kids can hit the slopes. She just went out to take a call, but she should be back in a minute."

No sooner had the words left his mouth than the woman Rory recognized from the pastry shop the other day walked up to them, shoving her phone in her pocket.

"Sorry, sorry, I promise I am free for the rest of the night. Oh, hi, Rory." She smiled in welcome as she spotted him. "You made it."

"I did." He nodded.

Zane wrapped an arm around Nora's waist, kissing her

temple. "I was just talking to Rory about how you might want to do something for the kids at his camp if they do winter stuff. Like a free ski day. Would be great publicity and a good tax write-off."

The guy knew his stuff. Rory knew all the tricks to get businesses to donate to the foundation. Tax rebates were one of the biggest, along with good public image. He had planned on having a winter camp session, and a ski day would be a fantastic experience for the kids. Skiing had become so expensive these days; he doubted any of the kids coming to the camp would experience it otherwise.

"Thank you, Mr. Marketing Majesty, but he's here to see the band, not talk winter sports," Nora said, snuggling into Zane's side as she turned her head to face Rory. "I would love to discuss it with you at another time if you're interested. Always happy to help the kids."

He nodded, already planning ideas for a ski-themed camp in his mind. "I would like that very much. Marissa can put us in touch, I assume?"

Marissa nodded. "Can do."

"Can I get anyone a drink?" he asked, motioning to the bar.

"Potato vodka martini," Nora said.

"Gluten-free beer," Zane added.

"Come on," Marissa said, placing a soft hand on his arm. "I'll go with you."

His body sparked like live wire at her touch, but he ignored it and moved with her to the bar a few feet away.

"I didn't know they made vodka from potatoes," he said to distract himself from the strange feelings coursing through his body.

"Yup," Marissa answered. "Nora is celiac. Zane too. That's actually how they met. On the Just Vibes app, funny enough."

He chuckled, things clicking into place. "I see. Is she the reason Abby knew about it?"

"Yeah. The funny thing is, I was the one who encouraged her to sign up as a joke, and she ended up finding the love of her life. I guess Abby thought the same would work for me." Her gaze focused on the bartender rushing back and forth across the bar, avoiding looking at him. "Teenagers think the most ridiculous things."

They did. But he had to wonder, if Marissa had been the one to contact him on the app, if they hadn't been working together...would things be different? There was no denying there was *something* between them. A spark they both felt but danced around. If circumstances weren't what they were, would that spark catch fire?

"What can I get you?" the bartender asked, making it to them.

Marissa ordered her friends' drinks, adding a vodka cranberry for herself and turning to him. "What do you want?"

"Old-fashioned," he said, ordering his standard drink.

The bartender nodded and set about making the drinks.

"Of course you drink an old-fashioned," Marissa chuckled.

He frowned. "What's wrong with an old-fashioned? It's a classic."

"Like you," she hummed, looking him up and down. "At least you're not wearing a suit. Though the slacks are cutting it pretty close to suit territory."

He glanced down at his outfit. A pair of tan pressed slacks and a light blue polo shirt. "You threatened me if I came in a suit."

Mouth opening in a mock gasp, she placed a hand on her chest. "I did no such thing. I simply suggested if you came in a suit everyone would think you were either an undercover cop or a talk show host who got lost on the way to set. You'd stick out like a sore thumb."

He scowled, but felt the corner of his mouth tick up at her teasing. "And how about now?"

She gave his body a long perusal, her gaze so intense, he swore he could feel it on his skin.

"You look like you got lost on your way to the golf course, but it is what it is."

He chuckled. "Maybe you should pick out my outfit for me next time."

"Happy to." She grinned. "We're a full-service operation at Eventful Occasions."

The bartender returned with their drinks. Marissa started to reach into her pocket, but he quickly whipped out his credit card and passed it over to the bartender.

"Hey!" she complained, lip sticking out in an adorable little pout. "I was going to get those."

"I offered," he said simply, grabbing his drink and Zane's beer.

"Sneaky," she muttered, grabbing her and Nora's drinks. "I'll allow it this time, but the next round is on me."

He shrugged, agreeing to no such thing. After they returned to her friends with their drinks, the band started to play. She was right, they were good. Their sound was exactly what he'd imagined for the gala. It had the country sound that incorporated the area, along with the dark haunting vibes of gothic and classical music that would add elegance to the event.

An hour and a half into their set, the band started up a hauntingly beautiful slow song. The crowd on the dance floor dissipated as people went off to refresh their drinks or visit the restrooms.

"Come on, sweetheart," Zane said, tugging Nora onto the dance floor.

Nora went willingly, looking at them with a knowing smile on her face. "Come on, you two, join us."

Marissa glanced over at him, hesitation on her face and longing in her eyes. It was the eyes that got him. He held out his hand, waiting with anticipation as he watched the myriad of emotions flash through those beautiful brown eyes. After a moment of hesitation, she smiled, slipping her warm palm into his.

He walked them to the dance floor, pulling her into his arms and swaying with the beat as the lights dimmed around them. He stared into her beautiful face, the world around them disappearing. The music became a low hum in the distance, time dropping away as everything in his world zeroed down to this moment, this woman.

"Rory." Her soft voice carried to him as she stepped closer, so close he could feel the heat of her body burning him.

"Yes?"

"Do you think…if it had actually been me on the app and our meetup had been real that we…"

"Yes." He had no doubt in his mind that this amazing woman would have been the one to finally break his lonely solitude. To cut through the doubt and suspicion his ex had placed there. She would have been the one he took a chance on. He knew it in his soul.

Her eyes widened, mouth dropping open in shock at his admission. He saw something pass through her eyes, a decision she'd reached. Before he could contemplate what it was, she leaned forward and pressed her mouth against his. Shock held him immobile for all of zero point two seconds before a low growl escaped him. He tightened his grip on her waist, tugging her closer until he could feel every inch of her soft body against his.

She moaned softly, mouth opening slightly, and he took advantage, sweeping his tongue inside to taste the most glorious heaven he'd ever experienced. Her fingers threaded into his hair, tugging slightly as she kissed him back with a fevered passion. The consequences of what they were doing could wait—right now all he could feel, all he could think, all he could consume was Marissa.

Just as sudden as it started, it stopped. Marissa pulled away, eyes round as saucers, and she brought her hand up to her lips. Harsh breaths panted out of him as he stared at her, still feeling the tingle of her lips on his.

"Oh, Rory, I'm sor—"

He held up a hand, stopping her apology. She had nothing to apologize for. They both simply got lost in the moment. A moment he wished hadn't ended.

The song died down and a loud buzz sounded from the pocket of her jeans. Pulling out her phone, she glanced at the screen and looked back up at him with an apologetic grimace.

"It's Abby," she said, waving her phone in the air. "I need to…"

She pointed to the exit. He nodded, not trusting himself to speak right now. If he opened his mouth, he might beg her to kiss him again. Her sister needed her. He had to respect that.

With a small wave, she turned, calling out to Nora and Zane on her way out of the bar, leaving him there more confused and aching than he'd ever been before in his life.

CHAPTER ELEVEN

It was all a bad dream. She was going to wake up in her nice warm bed, having received the deep restful slumber of a woman who hadn't kissed her client last night…

"Dammit!"

Marissa muttered out the curse as she placed a finger to her lips, the tingly feel of Rory's mouth still there. A phantom kiss haunting her with her bad decision. She had no idea what had possessed her to kiss him last night. It hadn't been the booze. She'd only had one drink, and that bar did not make them strong. She could blame it on the music, the dancing, the atmosphere. But when all was said and done, she had to admit to herself, she'd wanted to kiss him.

It had been a slow simmer beneath the surface every time they met. That nagging voice in the back of her head that grew louder with each second in his presence. Their attraction to each other was undeniable, no matter how much they'd tried to ignore it. What had she been thinking inviting him out to a bar? They could have asked the band to come audition at Stonebridge.

Except that Rory liked to see people in their element. Which was why they were running all over town, checking out caterers and entertainment, instead of having those people come to them. And look how that turned out. With them lip-locking in the middle of a dance floor.

"How is this my life?" she said, rolling over to muffle a groan into her pillow.

As much as she wanted to play hooky today to avoid the embarrassment of facing Rory, she had no other employees. Rolling back over, she tossed the covers off and sat up. Her head spun a touch as it always did when she first got up in the morning, but after assessing her body, she rose and made her way to the bathroom. A quick shower did nothing to wash off the memories of last night, but it did help her feel refreshed and ready to face the day.

Now if she could only find the courage to face Rory.

After putting on her favorite dark blue pantsuit that always boosted her confidence, she grabbed a quick breakfast of toast and coffee. Mornings were hard on her stomach. She usually didn't like to eat until ten, but she had to take her sodium chloride pills, and taking them on an empty stomach was awful.

"Abby, time to go!" she called out to her sister, grabbing her bag and keys.

When no response demanding five more minutes came, she paused, noticing for the first time this morning how quiet the house was.

"Where is everyone?"

Dad being gone wasn't a surprise. If he didn't leave his dirty dishes in the sink for her to clean, she wouldn't even think he lived there anymore. It sucked to admit it, but her father had been more like an absentee roommate for the past decade. Between work and the casino, she rarely saw him. A sharp pain twisted in her chest. For Abby, not for herself. She'd resigned herself to the fact that she didn't have a real father long ago, but poor Abby still believed their dad loved them so much he worked outrageous hours to provide for them. Her sister had no idea Marissa had been keeping the house afloat for years.

And she never would know. No reason to burden Abby with the sad realities of life. Better to let her sister live in blissful ignorance about their dad's problem for as long as possible.

"Abby?" she called out again, but only silence returned.

Pulling out her phone, she checked to see if her sister had texted her. She had. Abby messaged that she was riding to school with a friend today. Dang it. She'd been hoping to avoid heading over to Stonebridge for as long as possible. School drop-off only took ten minutes, but it was ten minutes she didn't have to spend in Rory's presence, wondering if he was going to can her for kissing him.

"Come on, Marissa," she chided herself. "Put on your big girl panties and do your job. He's not going to fire you. He kissed you back. Just go to work and talk to him like a rational adult. Admit it was a mistake and move on."

Right, she could do that.

Only…she didn't want to move on. What she really wanted was to kiss him again.

"No! Bad Marissa, we cannot hook up with our first client. Or any client," she added after a moment's thought. "That's a bad look. No more kissing Rory."

Repeating the mantra to herself, she headed out the door and got into her car. As she pulled onto the road, her phone rang. Using the button on her steering wheel, she answered through her car stereo so she could talk hands-free.

"Did I see you suck face with Rory on the dance floor last night?"

She groaned as Nora's voice filled the car. "What ever happened to 'Hi, Marissa' or 'Good morning, Marissa, how are you today?'"

Nora chuckled. "That's a yes."

"Noraaaaa," she dragged out her best friend's name, earlier determination to remain professional slipping away. "What was I thinking?"

"That he's hot and sweet and your sister matched you with him for a reason."

All solid points she couldn't argue, but there was one big red flag her bestie was missing.

"He's my client," she stated. "It's unethical."

"Not really," Nora replied. "He's not your boss, and either of you can end your contract at any point, so there's not really a power dynamic. I saw him kissing you back, very enthusiastically I might add. It was two people who were attracted to each other exploring that attraction. What's wrong with that?"

"We're in business together." Seemed like a pretty big problem to her.

Nora laughed. "Sweetie, you're talking to the woman who found out she was online dating her business competitor and created a D&D loophole so she could keep doing it."

"You are such a nerd," she teased.

"Hey, you're the one with the granny hobbies, Ms. Knitter."

She chuckled, anxiety easing slightly as the warmth of her best friend's love filled her. She should have called Nora last night after she got home instead of lying in bed for hours going over what happened and oscillating between joy and worry. Talking with her best friend always made her feel better.

A heavy sigh left her as more worry crept in. "What am I going to do, Nora?"

"You're going to talk to him," Nora said as if it was the easiest thing in the world. "Maybe this isn't as big a disaster as you think. Maybe he even wants to do it again. He sure looked like a puppy who'd lost his favorite toy when you left."

"He did?" She shouldn't be happy about that, but knowing Rory might be as into her as she was into him made butterflies take off in her stomach. "But no, we can't. It's—"

"Pot to kettle, sweetie," Nora interrupted. "I'm not here to judge you."

But others might and that's what she was afraid of.

"I promise this isn't as bad as you think," Nora continued. "Just go in there and have an open, honest conversation. If you decided to keep it professional from here on out, that's fine, but I'm voting for getting your groove on."

"That sounds like something Zane would say. He's a bad influence on you."

Nora giggled. "Indeed he is."

She smiled, even though her friend couldn't see it. Zane wasn't a bad influence, not really, but he had helped Nora loosen up since they got together, and he made her happier than Marissa had ever seen her best friend. She loved the guy for that alone.

"Okay, I'll talk to him," she agreed, pulling up to Stonebridge. "Thanks, Nora."

"That's what I'm here for. You better call me tonight with all the details."

She snorted. Nora's imagination had gotten far too salacious lately. The likely outcome of this conversation would be admitting a mistake and moving on. That tiny tug of disappointment pulled at her again, but she pushed it away. This was the right thing to do.

"I'm here. I have to go."

"Call me!" Nora insisted.

"Got to go, love ya," she said in lieu of a promise.

"Marissa Webb, you better call me or I'm coming over to get the—"

"Oh no…bad…can't…breaking up…" She made static noises with her mouth as she chopped up her words.

"Nice try, but the cell towers in Pine Creek are all working just fine," Nora laughed. "Fine, you don't have to call me back…tonight. I love you. Good luck with your talk."

The call disconnected, and she turned off her car. Stone-bridge Castle stood before her, a towering mass of stone and bricks. Intimidating in size, but more intimidating was the man inside. She had to be professional. Go in there, apologize for her actions, admit it was a mistake, and hopefully move on without any more embarrassment.

Taking a steadying breath, she exited her car and headed up to the front door. After knocking twice with no answer, she turned the knob. "Hello? Rory?"

No answer.

Stepping inside, she closed the door and made her way to the kitchen. She usually found him in there making a pot of coffee in the mornings. But today the kitchen was empty.

Yes!

Perhaps she could avoid this embarrassing confrontation for a day or two. She had no idea where the man was, but if she couldn't find him, she couldn't talk to him. She could still work on the gala. Contracts needed to be written up and sent to vendors. Decorations secured. All things he gave her the go-ahead to start on.

Reaching into her bag, she pulled out a pad of paper and a pen. Scratching out a quick note, she ripped off the paper and placed it on the marble countertop. Perfect. Now he would know she was doing her job, but she didn't have to talk to him and—

"What are you doing?"

A screech of surprise left her as she whirled around to see Rory standing in the kitchen doorway.

"Don't sneak up on me like that!" she accused. Her heart pounded in her chest, watch beeping, letting her know her heart rate was elevated. A few deep breaths and it settled down.

He frowned. "This is my house. I wasn't sneaking, I was walking."

"Well, wear a bell or something. Jeez, you're the quietest walker in existence."

He arched one eyebrow. "Is that note for me?"

She glanced back at the paper on the counter. "Yes. I was… I mean, I'm going to… I… Nutcrackers, I was avoiding you."

"Because of the kiss."

The man did not mince words. Guess they were doing this.

"Yes." She nodded. "I'm embarrassed and ashamed I acted so unprofessionally. I apologize for kissing you. It won't happen again."

Rory stood there silently, his eyes assessing her. For the life of her she couldn't decipher what he was thinking. He was like a brick wall sometimes. Totally unreadable. Finally, after what felt like an eternity, he spoke.

"Is that what you want? To forget about it?"

No, but it was the right thing to do.

Right?

"I think it's for the best," she said, ignoring the voice in her head screaming at her to grab him and kiss him again. "We should keep things professional."

Rory nodded. "Then I will abide by your wishes."

"Great, that's good," she said with a forced smile. But it wasn't great or good. It was torture to be so close to this man, knowing the heaven of his lips and not being able to have another taste. "Then let's get to work."

CHAPTER TWELVE

THIS "KEEPING THINGS PROFESSIONAL" was exceedingly difficult. Rory closed his laptop, rubbing a hand over his face as exhaustion settled in. It had been three days since he and Marissa had their discussion in the kitchen about their kiss. Three days, and ever since, every interaction between them had been rife with awkwardness. She no longer disagreed with any of his demands. Whatever he said she acquiesced to. He never imagined he'd miss someone arguing with him, but here he was, longing for her to roll her eyes at one of his ideas and inform him why it was ridiculous.

The teasing was gone too. He had to admit he missed that more than he realized. Something about the fun yet sweet way Marissa had teased him whenever he wore a suit to an appointment that didn't call for it made him want to wear a suit everywhere. As strange as it was to say, he liked her teasing. It wasn't malicious. It felt playful, like one would do with a friend or loved one. He didn't have many friends. Only his cousins really, and while they occasionally teased him, it didn't feel the same as when Marissa did it.

Had done it.

A heavy sigh left him. If only he knew how to put things back to the way they were before he'd lost his head and kissed her back. If he could take it back…hell, he wouldn't. No way he could ever give up the memory of what it felt like to kiss Marissa. Truth be told, he wasn't sure he would ever forget it. Every time he saw her it dominated his mind. His body burned with the need to kiss her again.

Kiss her and more.

"Dammit," he muttered into the empty library.

This was not helping anything. Maybe he needed to take a break. Get some coffee. He'd been going over the budget proposals all morning. Larkin, the foundation's finance officer, had sent over some figures for him to review. Going over numbers always gave him a headache. A caffeine fix would help.

Pushing up from the desk, he left the library and headed into the kitchen. He paused as he entered the room, noticing Marissa sitting at the counter, reading glasses perched on her adorable pert nose, gaze focused on the tablet in front of her. He took a moment to study her, unnoticed. Her hair was clipped back, allowing him to see the soft curve of her jaw. His palm burned with the memory of how silky smooth her cheek felt under it. Body tightening with need, he silently cursed himself for where his thoughts traveled. She'd made her stance on them clear, and he would not violate that.

Clearing his throat to indicate his presence, he stepped fully into the room. Marissa glanced up, relaxed posture immediately stiffening. He regretted his desire for coffee now. Disrupting her peace was the last thing he'd wanted to do.

"Sorry," he apologized. "I didn't mean to disturb you. I needed a cup of coffee."

She glanced over at the half-full pot. "No need to apologize. It is your house, after all."

"What are you working on?" he asked as he moved to grab a mug from the cabinet.

"I'm finishing up the contract for the caterers. I'll send it off tonight. Once we have it signed, we can move on to the contract for the entertainment."

"Good, good." He poured the dark liquid into a mug, motioning to the pot. She waved off his offer, pointing to the blue water bottle he'd noticed she was never without.

"Yes, we're, um, moving along swimmingly and…" She grimaced, pulling her glasses off and setting them on the counter. A small groan left her lips as she rested her head on her arms, noise muffled by the countertop.

Concern immediately filled his body. Shoving the pot back in its holder, he rushed to the fridge. He pulled the door open and scanned the sparse contents until he saw what he was looking for. Grabbing the silver bottle, he rushed to her side, placing it on the counter next to her. She turned her head, looking up at him with the side of her head still resting on her arms. Confusion marred her brow.

"What's that?"

"An electrolyte drink." He pushed the bottle toward her. "It's a new brand I recently discovered. Specially formulated to help people with POTS. I ordered a box of it just in case."

"Just in case… I needed it?"

He nodded, glancing at the bottle and back to her, wishing she would drink it. He hated seeing her struggle.

A smile—the first real one he'd seen in days—lit up her face. She sat up, staring at him with awe as she finally picked up the bottle.

"You bought this for me?"

He shrugged, suddenly feeling very uncomfortable. "I was doing some research and read that overexertion can exacerbate POTS symptoms. Having electrolytes on hand can help manage symptoms. I also purchased some electrolyte gummies if you'd rather."

She clutched the bottle to her chest, eyes glistening with moisture. Dammit! He hadn't meant to make her cry. He'd been trying to help.

"You researched POTS?"

He nodded, not sure what to say, not wanting to upset

her further. She dipped her head down, avoiding his gaze. Damn! He was an idiot. What had he been thinking, bringing attention to her condition. She was probably furious at him. She told him she didn't want to be treated differently and here he was, insinuating that she needed help.

Soft laughter interrupted his mental berating. When she lifted her head again, her eyes were free of tears. She smiled up at him so brightly he feared he might lose sight of everything in the world save her.

"You really are a sweetheart, Rory Thorson."

Sweetheart? He'd been called a lot of things in his life, but never a sweetheart. He wasn't sure how to feel about that, but at least she was smiling and not taking his head off.

"Thank you for this, but I wasn't groaning because of my POTS. I was groaning because…of the weirdness," she sighed.

"What weirdness?" What was she talking about?

One pale eyebrow arched, and she pointed back and forth between them. Oh, that weirdness.

She nibbled on her lower lip. He knew the move was not intended to tempt him, but it did. He yearned to pull that lip from her teeth and soothe the ache with his kiss. But he wouldn't. No matter how much his body screamed at him to do so.

"Can I admit something to you?"

He nodded, afraid that if he opened his mouth the only thing that would come out would be a plea to kiss her again.

"I really liked kissing you."

Damn! How was he supposed to abide by her wishes and resist her when she said things like that to him?

"Me too." The confession left him in a low growl.

An odd realization. He never thought he'd be able to feel this yearning for another person's touch after what happened with his ex. He was beginning to think Britney had ruined his chances at ever trusting another person enough. Then Marissa had stormed into his life with a fierce attitude and a kind heart. Slowly chipping away at his reservations on relationships.

They stared at each other, eyes locked, bodies still. He could feel the heat radiating off her, smell the sweet floral scent of her. His hands twitched, needing to grab hold of her and sate this ever-growing need inside him to taste her again. But he didn't move. It had to be her decision. He would not do a damn thing unless she specifically asked for it. She was in control of what happened next.

The silence in the room was so loud he couldn't even hear his own breathing. If he was breathing. He might have stopped while waiting for her to make a decision. As he watched a million decisions pass through her beautiful brown eyes, the room was suddenly filled with a bright light followed by an ear-shattering boom of thunder.

"Mother fletcher!" Marissa swore.

He blinked, a small smile curling his lips at her creative curse.

The pounding sound of raindrops hitting the roof of the conservatory off the kitchen filled the air, erasing the tension-filled silence from before.

"Oh nutcrackers," she sighed, standing from her stool and gathering her things. "I should probably go. This looks like it's going to be a heck of a storm."

Indeed. The day was nearly over anyway.

"Will you be alright to drive home?" he asked, worry for her still churning inside.

She smiled, slipping the strap of her satchel over her head and placing it on her shoulder. "I'll be fine, thank you. Rain isn't so bad to drive in. It's the black ice in the winter that's really dangerous."

She gave him a small wave and turned to head toward

the front door. Glancing to the counter, he noticed the silver bottle of electrolyte drink still sitting there, unopened. Picking it up, he called out to her.

"Marissa."

She turned, stopping just at the kitchen doorway. "Yeah?"

"Take this." He held out the bottle. "Just in case. Try it. If you like it, I can send you the information on where to buy it."

She stared at him, something passing across her face. A decision. Confident, determined strides brought her back to his side. Pulling the bottle from his hands, she smiled up at him.

"Thank you."

Rising on her toes, she placed a hand on his bearded cheek and gently brushed her lips against his. The kiss was soft, sweet and over far too quickly for his liking, but the potency was just as strong.

"Bye, Rory," she whispered, turning and hurrying from the room.

He stood there in the now empty kitchen, the sound of rain a melodic soundtrack to the roaring inside. A smile curled his lips, lips that still burned with her taste.

"Goodbye, Marissa," he answered to an empty room and a full heart.

CHAPTER THIRTEEN

MARISSA JUMPED INTO her car, a squeal of joy leaving her. She couldn't believe she had just kissed him, again! It might not have been her smartest idea, but she couldn't be sorry for doing it. Holding herself back the past few days had tested every ounce of her willpower. When he'd said he enjoyed kissing her too, it had shattered into a million tiny pieces that even she, the jigsaw puzzle master, wouldn't be able to put back together.

She turned on her car, blasting the defrost as the cold, rainy weather immediately fogged up the windshield. Her hair was dripping wet from the short run to the car. Thankfully her satchel was waterproof, as her tablet was inside, safely protected from the rain. As soon as her windshield was clear, she put her car in Drive and pulled away from Stonebridge.

A tiny voice inside whispered at her to stay, see where these stolen kisses with Rory would lead, but she knew better. A kiss or two was one thing. Spending the night with the man would get her into murkier territory. She wasn't completely discounting the idea, but they should at least have a conversation about it before crossing a line they couldn't come back from. Marissa watched a lot of rom-coms. She knew what happened when two people were stranded alone together in a storm.

The rain pounded her little car, the drops so loud and forceful they blocked out the soft music playing from her radio. The sun hadn't set yet, but the storm clouds blocked out any of the colorful rays of sunset, leaving nothing but darkness, pierced only by her car headlights. She flicked the wiper speed, ticking it to full blast. The long pieces of rubber and plastic swished back and forth at a blurring pace. Her hands tightened on the steering wheel, tension filling her body.

All the joy from Rory's kiss evaporated as distress took its place. She hadn't been lying earlier. Driving on black ice was much worse than rain, but this storm was no picnic either. Her tires hydroplaned for three seconds. Not long, but long enough for her heart to skip a beat and a swear she would never utter in front of Abby to slip out.

"Get it together, Marissa," she scolded herself. "Pump the breaks gently. Don't slam."

The stress of the drive had her sweating and freezing all at once. Temperature regulation was a problem in normal situations thanks to her POTS, but under stress it jumped tenfold. She could do this. All she had to do was slow down, drive safe, and once she hit town, she'd be fine. She just had to—

"Oh crap!"

She gently pumped the breaks until the car came to a stop a few feet in front of a sight that made her heart plummet to her toes.

"No, no, no!"

Putting the car in Park, she slumped in the driver's seat, staring at the washed-out road in front of her. Literal waves of water rushed over the dip in the road, completely blocking the way. Maybe if she had a huge SUV, she might consider trying to cross the temporary river, but no way would her thirteen-year-old sedan make it through that.

"What do I do now?"

Silence answered her. Not that she'd expected anything

else, but she'd been hoping something would come to her mind at the question.

Abby.

Right. She had to call Abby. Check in with her sister to make sure she was alright. Storms usually hit the mountains worse than in town. She hoped everything was okay and her sister was safe and dry at home.

Pulling her phone from her pocket, she hit Abby's face in her contacts, putting the phone to her ear.

"Hey!" Abby greeted enthusiastically. "You almost home?"

Not even close. A heavy sigh left her. "Um, not really."

"What's wrong? Are you okay?"

Abby's tone immediately changed. Concern and worry filled her sister's voice. She cursed herself for causing Abby unease.

"I'm fine, nothing is wrong." Not true. "But the storm is really bad up here. The roads are a mess."

"Oh, it's coming down pretty hard here too. My weather app says it supposed to last all night. Are you still at Stone-bridge?"

"No. I left when the storm started, but the road is washed out a mile out."

"Do not cross that road, Marissa!" Abby insisted. "I saw a video where someone tried to cross a water-blocked road and their car got caught up in the current and washed down the river. Flash floods are nothing to mess around with."

She smiled at the warning tone in her baby sister's voice. Usually, she was the one to give warnings. It was strange to hear it coming from Abby. Warmth eased her panic at her sister's concern. She was becoming a very mature and thoughtful young lady.

"I'm not going to cross the road," she assured Abby. But she had no idea what she was going to do.

"Guess you'll have to go back to Stonebridge and spend the night with Rory," Abby said, voice tinged with innuendo.

What was that she'd been thinking earlier about her sister maturing?

"I can't stay at Stonebridge."

"Why not? The place has like fifty bedrooms, right?"

More like twenty-five, but that wasn't the point. Hadn't she just been convincing herself that staying the night with Rory was a bad idea?

"I…can't impose on my client like that."

Abby's snort came over the line. "Pretty sure it's not an imposition with all that room, and based on the way he was looking at you at dinner the other night, I don't think he'd mind."

"Abby!"

"Missy," Abby threw back with a small chuckle.

"He's my client."

"And you're both adults. Don't you always tell me that what consenting adults do behind closed doors is nobody's business but theirs?"

She could not believe she was having this conversation with her baby sister. On the one hand, she was glad all her talks about consent and safety were getting through, on the other hand, talking about her love life with Abby was not something she ever wanted to do. Embarrassment heated her cheeks.

"Nothing is going to happen." Maybe. "If I do go back and stay with Rory, it's only because I can't cross the road and sleeping in my car is dangerous."

"Do not sleep in your car! I saw a video about that too. The couple nearly froze to death."

What kind of videos was Abby watching? Did she need to start monitoring her sister's screen time again like she had when Abby was a toddler?

"I'm not sleeping in my car," she assured Abby. "I'll go back to Stonebridge. I'm sure Rory won't mind putting me up in a room."

"I'm sure he wouldn't mind having you in his room." Abby snickered.

"Abby! It's not like that."

"Whatever you say, sis, but I saw the way he looks at you. He'll only be your client for another month, right? After that…"

She refused to respond, but her mind whirled with the possibilities.

"Stay at home tonight," she said, instead of answering.

"Duh, I'm not going out in this."

"There's a frozen pizza in the deep freezer in the garage and salad in the crisper."

"No need," Abby said. "Dad's on his way home and bringing sushi from Sushi Mango."

Shock had her pulling the phone from her ear in surprise. It was rare that their father came home for dinner. Rarer still when he brought home one of their favorites. Sushi wasn't cheap when you lived in a landlocked state. He must have had a good night at the casino. She wondered how much he'd wasted to win tonight.

Rage and disappointment had her gripping the phone tight. She put her anger at her father aside, grateful he would at least be home tonight to keep an eye on Abby.

"Good. Enjoy the sushi and tell Dad I'm safe and I'll be home tomorrow." Not that he would even notice or care.

"Okay, have fun with Rory."

She did not appreciate the teasing way her sister said his name. "Nothing is going to happen," she insisted.

"Not with that attitude."

"Abby!"

"Love you, Missy. Bye."

She sighed, rolling her eyes even if her sister couldn't see it. "Love you too, Abs. Bye."

Hanging up, she slipped her phone back into her pocket. Carefully turning the car around, she drove back to Stonebridge. As she pulled up to the castle-like home, she noticed all the lights inside were off. Huh, had he gone to sleep already? It was barely six thirty. There were a pair of lanterns powered by motion sensors that illuminated as her car drove up, but the large house was completely dark.

"Maybe he's in the back of the house?" she muttered to herself.

The place was huge—it made sense not to leave every light on and waste electricity.

Grabbing her satchel, she turned off her car and stepped out. The rain had intensified. Large drops hammered into her, stinging her skin as the cold water seemed to slice right through her. She clutched her bag to her chest and ran to the front door. Thankfully, there was a portico over the door, allowing her a respite from the downpour.

"Rory?" she called out, pressing the doorbell. The peel of ringing sounded from inside the house, but no footsteps followed. "Rory? Hello?"

She pounded on the door with the large brass knocker. Still nothing. Could he not hear her? Maybe he was in the theater—and yes, this massive place had its own theater with surround sound, reclining seats and a freaking popcorn maker.

"Rory? Hello? Are you in there?"

Nothing.

Shoot! Where was he? What was she going to do if he didn't answer? She couldn't get home. She couldn't risk sleeping in her car. Maybe she could sleep in that decked-out tree house? She thought she'd seen a blanket or two.

A bright flash of light followed by a loud crack of thunder

had a scream ripping from her throat as she cowered closer to the door. Okay, tree house idea was out. Not a smart idea to be around trees in a lightning storm, unless she wanted to get struck. And she did not, thank you very much.

"Rory!" she called his name again, pounding on the door as fear and frustration mounted. "You get your butt down here right this minute and open this door!"

"Marissa?"

She turned at the sound of her name, confused to see Rory standing behind her. How did he get there? Why was he outside? Her questions soon flew out the window as she took in his rain-soaked appearance. She always thought it was silly whenever movies had romantic scenes in the rain. What was so appealing about being sopping wet?

She took back her criticism.

Mr. Darcy coming out of Pemberley Lake had nothing on rain-soaked Rory. Her mouth dropped open as she gazed at the chiseled muscles of his chest and abs, defined by the nearly translucent white button-up shirt currently plastered to his body. His hair was dripping wet, red strands curling with the moisture, giving him a roguish appearance.

"What are you doing here?" he asked, hurrying to her side.

Once she found the ability to put her tongue back in her mouth and speak again, she explained. "The road is washed out a few miles down. I can't get past, so I figured I'd come back here and stay in one of the rooms, if that's okay with you? I could just sleep in my car if—"

He grasped her hand, pulling her to him. "You are not sleeping in your car," he said firmly. "That is extremely dangerous. Especially in weather like this. Come with me."

She allowed him to tuck her into his side as he led them away from the main house off to a small cottage a few yards away, lights humming warmly from the windows. How had she missed that, and why was Rory staying in the caretaker's house and not the main one?

Another bolt of lightning and crack of thunder ripped through the night air. Rory tugged her closer to his side as they ran through the pelting rain.

All questions that could be answered later when they were safely inside and warm. Though she had to admit, tucked up to his side, she was warmer than she'd been in a long time.

CHAPTER FOURTEEN

THE WOMAN WAS going to shave ten years off his life from sheer worry.

Rory did his best to tuck Marissa into his side, protecting her from the rain as they hurried over to the small caretaker house just off to the side of the main house. When he had heard her calling his name, at first he thought he'd been dreaming. But he hadn't been asleep. Then her yells became frantic shouts, and he'd run out the door, heart in his throat.

"Wait here," he said, closing the door behind him. He left her in the small mudroom entrance, rushing to the hall closet where he kept his towels. Grabbing one, he hurried back. He tucked the towel around her. "I have some sweats you can change into if you would like. They might be a bit big, but you shouldn't stay in those wet clothes. I can toss your clothing in the dryer."

A cheeky grin lit up her face as she stared up at him, shivering slightly. "I can't believe you own a pair of sweats."

He chuckled. Even with fear still coursing through his body she managed to make him laugh. She was amazing.

"Yes, I own sweats. I don't live in suits, you know."

"No, I don't know." She shrugged. "Because I've never seen you in anything else."

"The bar," he insisted.

She huffed out a laugh. "Slacks and a polo are suit adjacent. It's suit light."

He laughed along with her. As another shiver racked her body, his humor died. Bending down, he scooped her into his arms as she let out a small shriek of surprise.

"Rory! What are you doing?"

"The floor is wet," he answered, walking carefully to the main bathroom down the hall. "I don't want you to slip. You need to get out of those wet clothes before you catch a cold."

"That's just an old wives' tale." She rolled her eyes.

"Okay, then you don't want to catch hypothermia."

She frowned. "Okay, you got me there."

He set her down gently at the entrance of the bathroom. "Stay here. I'll grab you something to change into."

Leaving her, he headed to the far end of the hall where his bedroom was. He quickly grabbed some thick socks, a long-sleeve shirt and a fleece-lined pair of gray sweats he used when snowshoeing in frigid temperatures. They would engulf her, but it was all he had. He glanced to his closet, seeing his bathrobe hanging on the door hook. He grabbed that too, roaring inside at the thought of Marissa wearing his clothes, covering herself in his scent. The caveman inside him pounded his chest at the idea.

Quickly making his way back to her—being careful not to get any rainwater on the clothing—he handed the items over.

"My apologies if they don't fit. I'm afraid it's all I have."

She smiled up at him. "I'm sure I can make it work, Rory. Thank you."

He nodded. "Just leave your clothing there after you change, and I'll dry them for you."

She closed the door, and he stood there for a moment, staring at it. Frozen.

"Rory?" Marissa called from behind the closed door. "Are you standing out there waiting like a weirdo? You need to change too, ya know."

He chuckled, shaking his head as her teasing words pulled him out of whatever fog he'd been in.

"Worried, not weird," he called back.

"I'm fine. Go change," she said with a laugh.

Turning, he headed back to his bedroom. After shucking off his wet clothing, he changed into a pair of gray sweatpants and a black T-shirt. He'd show her he could dress casually. Grabbing his towel from his bedroom bathroom, he ran it over his hair, drying the short strands as much as possible. He wondered for a moment if Marissa would like a hair dryer for her hair. Dammit, he didn't have one. He didn't have need for a hair dryer, so he hadn't thought to purchase one when he moved into the home.

He grabbed his pile of wet clothing and headed out of the bedroom to check on Marissa. She was already standing outside the bathroom door, waiting for him with a smile on her face. His robe swallowed her small frame, sleeves rolled up several times and cuffed at her wrists. The towel he had given her earlier was now wound around her head in that twisty wrap thing all women seemed to know how to do. In her hands she held out a small pile of wet, matted clothing.

"I rung them out in the tub first so they wouldn't drip as much," she said as she handed him the pile.

"I'll get started on the dryer." He lifted his chin, indicating with his gaze toward the living room. "Go ahead and make yourself at home. There's a fire going in the living room. Get warm, and I'll be right out."

The laundry area was just past the bathroom in the back of the house. The caretaker house was not nearly as large as the main house. At just shy of two thousand square feet, with three bedrooms, two and a half bathrooms and a finished basement, it more than worked for his needs.

After tossing the clothing in the dryer and starting it up, he made his way back to the main area of the house. The living room and kitchen faced each other in a wide, open-room concept. A small eating area sat off to the far left in the back of the kitchen, though he preferred to eat at the kitchen island most days. He spotted Marissa sitting on the soft, hand-woven rug in front of the crackling fire.

"Feeling warmer?" he asked as he came to sit beside her.

She glanced over at him. He was relieved to see her cheeks were pink, lips no longer blue as they had been when he found her pounding away at the main house's front door.

"Much, thank you. And look at you in sweats and a T-shirt. You do own normal people clothing. I have to say, Rory, casual looks good on you."

He snorted but grinned at her observation.

"I didn't realize you lived in the caretaker's house," she said, moving on from his apparel.

"Why would you think I lived in the main house?" he asked, arching a brow.

"Because you bought it. Why buy a house if you're not going to live in it?"

Lots of reasons. People wanted to be landlords. Run vacations rentals. Flip houses. His cousins did it all the time. Some of the homes they flipped they donated to the Thorson Foundation for those in need. His cousins had helped the foundation house over thirty-five families in the past ten years.

"I bought it for the camp," he said. "The campers and counselors will stay in the main house. I plan on keeping this as my home, as I won't always be around to help with the camp."

He planned to be as involved as possible, but the foundation did more than support foster youth. As the CEO, he had to oversee everything, and unfortunately that meant he wouldn't always be able to focus on his pet project.

"Oh, I see." She nodded. "Well, it's a lovely home."

He was glad she thought so. He'd put a lot of thought and care into filling this place with things that reminded him of his parents. It would never feel like a true home without their love, but he was working on it.

"Truthfully…" She leaned in closer to whisper. "The main house is a little too hoity-toity for me. I'm always afraid I'm going to break or stain something. You might want to think about changing some of the decor in the home before the kids arrive. If you want them to feel comfortable, that is."

He did. She had an excellent point. He hadn't realized how cold and polished the main house felt. While his home growing up had been filled with love, his parents had been rich and enjoyed nice things. There were rooms he was afraid to go into as a kid for fear of breaking something priceless. Not that his parents would have punished him for an accident, but still. He made a mental note to look into redecorating the main house after the gala.

"I think that's a wise decision, thank you." He nodded. "Speaking of children, have you contacted your sister? Informed her you can't make it home?"

She chuckled. "Abby would rip you apart for calling her a kid, not literally, but you'd need to watch out for your coffee, because it might have hot sauce in it."

Hot sauce? Did siblings really taint coffee when upset? Since he had none, he had no idea. The closest he had were his cousins, and while they liked to rib him every now and then, they never messed with his food.

"Yes," Marissa continued. "I called Abby and let her know I was, um, staying with you."

A pink blush rose on her cheeks. He did his best not to read into that statement, but his body tightened with need at the possibilities of what the night could bring.

"Thank you, by the way." She smiled, gratitude filling

her eyes. "For letting me stay. I can crash on the couch or even right here. This rug is beautiful."

He watched as her hand stroked over the multicolored rug, delicate fingers grazing the wool.

"No need for that. I have a room for you, and thank you." He motioned to the rug. "I'm quite fond of how the rug turned out myself."

Her eyes widened as she looked from the rug to him. "Wait, you made this?"

He nodded. "My parents took me to London on business when I was fifteen. While taking a tour of the city, we stopped at a weaver shop. Very old, but still in business because of its historical importance. I was fascinated by the looms. The way the yarn moved on the old machine. The precision of the weavers. One of the women working the loom noticed my fascination and told me to come back the next day for a lesson. I was hooked." He gave her a small grin.

"Rory Thorson," she giggled. "Was that a crafting joke?"

"I have my moments."

"And you have hidden talents." She looked down at the rug again. "I'm very impressed. This makes my knitted scarfs look like preschool craft time. Though it also makes your hobbies even grannier than mine. Maybe you should change your name on the Just Vibes app to GrandpaCrafter."

Not possible since he deleted the thing already. It had been an experiment, and it failed.

Or had it?

He took in Marissa sitting on his rug, in his home, wearing his clothes. Abby might have set up the profile, but she had filled it with Marissa's interests, and that was what had caught his eye. And now here they were. Could the app have worked?

A small rumbling, too soft to be the storm outside, reached his ears. Marissa shifted on the rug, face flaming with embarrassment.

"Sorry. I haven't eaten anything since lunch and my stomach is reminding me of that fact."

Damn, he hadn't offered her anything to eat or drink yet. His mother must be rolling over in her grave at his rudeness.

"Well, then," he said, standing. "Allow me to make us dinner."

Her eyebrows rose. "You cook?"

"As you said before, I'm a man of hidden talents." He gave her a wink and headed off to the kitchen to make her a dinner that would knock his socks right off her feet.

CHAPTER FIFTEEN

"Holy cow!" Marissa moaned, placing her fork down on her empty plate. "I think that was the most delicious meal I've ever had."

Caring, handsome, rich and he could cook. It just wasn't fair. Rory was slowly knocking down all her carefully constructed walls. Much more of treating her this way and she would take that line she'd drawn between them and erase it. Maybe Nora and Abby were right. Maybe she could start something up with him without damaging her new business.

"Thank you." He stood, taking her plate and his to the sink. "It was my mother's recipe."

"Really? Your mom cooked? I figured the Thorsons would have had personal chefs." Did all rich people have someone else who cooked their food for them?

He paused at the sink, back tense, shoulders stiffening. "No. My birth mother."

Oh. Dang it. Now she felt like a complete jerk. Unsure of what to say, if she should apologize for her assumption, she sat at the kitchen island where they'd eaten the delicious mac and cheese casserole, silently berating herself for her insensitivity.

"I'm sorry," she said softly, unable to stand the silence choking her.

He turned, a soft, sad smile on his face. "Don't be. I don't have many happy memories of my birth mother, but this dish is one of them. We had it all the time because the ingredients were inexpensive, and it saved as a leftover very well. I supposed you could say it's one of my comfort dishes."

And he had shared it with her.

Humbled that he had opened up to her, she took a deep breath and a chance on being vulnerable. "My mom used to make me ice cream soup every time I fell off my bike."

His head tilted. "Ice cream soup?"

She laughed softly, allowing the memories to wash over her. "She was a terrible cook. Takeout and those box dinners that you add meat and veggies to were a staple in our house. Once she tried to make cookies and nearly burned the kitchen down."

"That does sound dangerous," he chuckled.

"She was creative though." She smiled as her mother's loving face filled her mind's eye. "One time I got stung by a bee and to make me feel better she said I could have ice cream for dinner. But being the rule-following four-year-old I was, I told her ice cream was a dessert, not dinner. So she stirred it up with a spoon and called it ice cream soup because soup could be a dinner."

"Sounds like she was an amazing person," Rory said, gracing her with a gentle smile.

"She was." Her smile dipped as she realized she couldn't say the same about his mother. For one, she didn't know enough, but it sounded like as much as she loved her son, she'd also hurt him very badly with her abandonment.

"And I don't doubt for a second that four-year-old you followed every rule set before her," he teased.

"Excuse me." She pointed a finger at him. "Mr. Pot are you calling this kettle black?"

He laughed. "Fair point. Maybe we should start a club."

"The stiff-shirt, rule-following, stubborn-people's club?" she offered with a grin.

"That's quite the mouthful. I don't think it would fit on a member's jacket."

He had the oddest sense of humor. She loved it.

"I don't have any ice cream," he said, moving over to the pantry. "But I do have chocolate chip cookies and milk if you're interested."

"One of my favorite desserts." She grinned.

The storm had died down during dinner. Rain still fell, but the pounding had dwindled down to a steady beat. The lightning and thunder had moved past them. Only a few miles away, based on her counts of flashes to booms. The roads were most likely a mess still. The washout would last until tomorrow at least. But if she had to be stuck for the night anyway, she had to admit, being with Rory wasn't too bad.

"Would you like to enjoy dessert in the living room?" he asked, a package of cookies tucked under his arm and two glasses of milk in his hands.

She rose from the table and moved over to him, gently grabbing the cookie package to reduce the risk of it falling. "Sure. Do you want to..." She glanced over to the living room, trailing off when she noticed something odd. "You don't have a TV."

He shrugged. "I don't care much for television. I prefer to read or spend time on hobbies."

She wasn't a big screen addict herself, but she did enjoy the occasional movie and watched murder docs with Nora sometimes.

"Do you have any puzzles?" she asked as they made their way to the living room. "Or board games?"

He glanced over at her, a wide grin curling his lips. "I may have one or two."

He placed the glasses down on the coffee table. Moving over to a dark, oak credenza along the back wall, he crouched down and opened the door. A gasp left her as he turned with a proud smile. One or two, her butt. The thing was packed with games and puzzles galore. There had to be at least fifty boxes in there.

"No wonder you don't have a TV." She moved over to him, inspecting the games, recognizing a number of the titles. "Some of these games take hours to play."

There were a lot of games that could be played solo, but also a number of co-op games requiring three or more people. She wondered if he had a monthly game night with friends. Did he have any friends? Come to think of it, she'd never heard him talk about a friend. Not once. He mentioned his cousins occasionally, but she didn't even know where they lived. She looked over at him, watching as he stared at the games with an eager smile on his face. For the first time since she met him, she noticed something.

Rory was lonely.

She had Nora and Abby and a few other friends to keep her company in her off-work hours, but who did he have? No one as far as she could tell. And based off the number of single player games he had, she wondered if that was a standard in his life. Did he live a mostly solitary existence? That did not sit right with her. No one should be all alone. You needed people to laugh with, cry with, play games with.

"Which is your favorite?" she asked, waving a hand over the stacked games.

He blinked, hesitating as he answered. "I enjoy all of the games I own. We don't need to—"

"Which one, Rory?" she insisted.

He reached out and carefully extracted a brown box with an island and treasure map drawings on it.

"It's a very strategy-heavy game," he said with warning. "Long too. Almost impossible to win. Most people don't care for it."

"But you love it?"

He nodded. "I enjoy the challenge."

She grinned, grabbing the box from his hands and standing. "I've never backed down from a challenge. Let's play."

She heard his soft chuckle as he followed her to the coffee table. As he set up the game, she pulled the very thick instruction book from the box and began to read.

"I can explain the rules if you like."

She shook her head. "Thank you, but I prefer to read them myself to make sure I don't miss anything."

"Rule stickler?" he asked, smiling.

She nodded. "Rules are important. They keep things fair and safe. Abby says I'm a stick-in-the-mud, but I just don't like crossing lines. Things get…messy when that happens."

A dark humming noise caused her to raise her gaze to him. Rory stared at the board game he was unboxing, a pensive expression on his face. He glanced to her, and she knew in an instant what he was thinking. The line they'd crossed the other night at the bar and just earlier in the kitchen. When she'd kissed him.

Shoot! She was sending mixed signals. The problem was she was mixed up. A part of her knew it was best to keep things professional. Toe the line. Another part of her, a very big part, wanted to throw caution and rules to the wind and see where this attraction took them. She had two wolves inside her and neither of them knew what to do.

"Rules are important," he said, turning his attention back to setting up the game.

The rest of the setup happened in silence. It took a good fifteen minutes to organize. Once she'd read through the rule book, they started. Rory had been right in describing the length and difficulty of the game. Two hours later, they died and lost.

"This is not a game," she huffed, picking up a game piece and glaring at it. "This is torture."

He laughed. "I told you most people don't like it. It's why I play on my own."

"Have you ever won? Has anyone?"

He shrugged. "I did come close once."

She was all for challenging games, but to play one you never win sounded awful. Then again, a lot of people found her knitting to be boring, so who was she to judge.

They packed up the game, a large yawn escaping her as Rory tucked it back in the credenza. He glanced to his watch with a frown.

"It's late. We should turn in."

After the events of the day, she couldn't wait for her head to hit a pillow. She stood, following him as he led her down the hall past the bathroom. He opened a door on the left and ushered her inside.

"There's a bathroom past that door on the right there, feel free to use any toiletries you need. I believe I have a few spare toothbrushes in their packages under the sink."

She glanced around the room, noting the closet full of suits, the picture of an elderly couple on the dresser and the large king bed with the dark blue bedspread. The pillows had a slight indent that looked like someone had slept on them last night.

"Wait." She turned to face him. "Is this your room?"

He nodded.

"I thought when you said you had a bed for me you meant a guest room."

"I'm afraid I haven't had time to set up the guest room yet. But I insist you stay here. I'll be fine on the couch."

Not likely. The man was over six feet. His couch was big, but not big enough to hold a man of his size comfortably for the entire night.

"Rory, I can't—"

"You can," he said, holding up a hand to stop her protest. "You need your rest."

"And you don't?"

He shrugged.

She glanced back at the bed, an idea coming to her mind. One she should absolutely not be thinking and in no way speak. But it was late, and her body was tired of fighting her mind. She was tired of always following the rules. Even when you did, there was no guarantee you'd win. Like the game they had played. They had done everything right, played exactly as instructed, and still they'd lost. Why not bend the rules a bit, cross that line, take what she wanted for herself for once? What was the worst that could happen?

"We could…" She hesitated, glancing up at him, allowing all the need and desire she felt every time she was around him to show in her eyes. "Share the bed."

Her heart pounded as she waited for his answer, lungs burning as she held her breath in anticipation. She watched as desire, raw and hot, burned in his eyes. Excitement rose within until he blinked. The fire snuffing out. He frowned, shaking his head.

"That would be…inadvisable."

Mortification heated her cheeks. She backed away toward the bathroom, wishing the floor would open up and swallow her whole.

"Right, of course. Forget I asked. That was stupid of me. I don't know what I was thinking. Just forget I said anything. It's late. I'm tired. Um, yeah, I'm just going to…"

She backed into the bathroom, shutting the door forcefully as her embarrassed ramblings died out. Covering her face with her hands, she let out a silent scream. Why had she asked that? What was she thinking, propositioning her client? She'd let Abby and Nora's silly notions get into her head and now she'd gone and humiliated herself in front of Rory. In the game of life, she was definitely losing.

CHAPTER SIXTEEN

I AM AN IDIOT!

Rory backed out of his bedroom, closing the door softer than Marissa had. She hadn't slammed it, but the force of the bathroom door shutting had been enough to rattle the painting of a mountainscape at sunset hanging on the wall. He continued to curse himself all the way down the hall and into the living room.

He had said no. Why had he said no?

All evening he'd been dreaming about what would happen between them if their desires took over. No. Scratch that. All week he'd been fantasizing about turning the kiss they'd shared into more. He'd held back out of respect for Marissa and the line she'd drawn. The line she just asked him to step over and he'd said no!

"Idiot," he muttered to himself again.

What had he done?

The right thing.

A heavy sigh left him as he sat on the couch facing the dying embers in the fireplace. He had done the right thing. Just earlier this evening, Marissa had been talking about boundaries, keeping things in place. He knew her business was brand-new. A lot was riding on his gala. She didn't want to be known as the event planner who slept with her clients, and he didn't want to be known as a man who took advantage of the people working for him.

"I did the right thing," he spoke into the silent room.

Then why did it feel so wrong? Why was he berating himself for the embarrassment he saw in her eyes, the pain? Rejection was difficult no matter who you were, but he hated that he'd been the one to stir that emotion in her. He didn't want to be the one who caused her to break her rules. It would only lead to regret, on both their parts, and he had enough of that to last a lifetime.

He grabbed the throw blanket from the back of the couch and lay down. The small crocheted blanket wasn't nearly big enough to cover his body, but that didn't matter. Rory knew he wouldn't be getting much sleep tonight. He only hoped Marissa could find some rest. She'd see things his way in the morning.

"Or she'll quit and never want to speak to me again," he muttered.

A sharp pain stabbed his chest at the thought of never seeing her again. No. She wouldn't do that. She couldn't do that. The contract he signed ensured protections for both parties if the job wasn't finished. If he pulled out she would still get paid, but if she quit she'd be out the rest of the money. He knew, with her business being so new, she needed this job. Yet another reason not to mix business with pleasure.

"Dammit," he growled into the night air, knowing how much pleasure he could have given Marissa had things been different.

Best not to think about it or he really would be up all night and in unpleasant discomfort.

He shifted on the couch, feet hanging off the end awkwardly. Preparing himself for a long restless night, he closed his eyes and tried to take deep, calming breaths, pulling up the meditation techniques his cousin Cash taught him. He tried to quiet his mind. It didn't work. The damn thing still raced at a hundred miles an hour. Playing back the entire night, making him doubt himself.

Resigning himself to a sleepless night, he threw back the blanket and sat up. Maybe he could get some work done. He stood, intending to grab his laptop, when a loud thud sounded from down the hall. His heart leaped into his throat, knowing there was only one place that sound could have come from. He rushed to his bedroom, worry clouding his mind as all manner of tragedy fill his imagination.

"Marissa?" he called out as he threw the bedroom door open. His heart stopped beating as he spied the empty bed, covers tangled, but no Marissa. Where was she? "Marissa!"

"Stop shouting," her voice sounded from somewhere beyond the bed. "I'm right here."

He stepped into the room, moving around the bed to see her sprawled on the floor. He was at her side in an instant, crouching down low as his gaze roamed over her.

"What happened? Are you hurt? Did you have a POTS episode?"

She snorted. "No, I had a stupidity episode."

He frowned. The bedside lamp was on, casting a dim glow around them. She sat on the floor, his sweatshirt engulfing her, pale legs bare. Desire rose inside at the sight of her smooth skin, but he pushed it down. Now was not the time.

"I was going to get some water from the bathroom, and I tripped on your stupid blankets. Why are they tucked in so tightly? It's like trying to escape a cocoon."

He hid a smile, grateful she wasn't hurt. "My apologies. I spent a summer working in hotel housekeeping as a teenager, and I suppose the skill never left me."

Her eyebrows rose. "You worked in housekeeping as a teen?"

"As I told you, my parents thought it was important for

me to learn life skills and the value of working hard for your money. They weren't always rich, you know."

She tilted her head, staring at him. "One of those real-life rags to riches stories?"

He shrugged. "Maybe not rags, but they worked hard for what they had. Life skills were very important to them, and they wanted to make sure I had them as well."

She snorted. "Well, you can check off 'make a bed no one can escape from.' Though I have to say, it's a weird life skill. I can't remember the last time I even made my bed."

He laughed softly. Reaching out a hand, he cupped her cheek, staring into her beautiful brown eyes. "Are you sure you're okay?"

"Physically? Yes." She sighed, pulling away from his touch. "Emotionally? I just want to crawl into a hole and disappear."

"Why?"

"Why?" Eyes growing wide, she shook her head. "Why? Because I basically threw myself at you and you rejected me. 'It's inadvisable' were your exact words. I was so stupid to think you wanted me and I—"

"Marissa." He grasped her face again, compelling her to look at him as he explained. "Listen to me because this is very important. You are not stupid. You are the smartest, kindest, most stubborn person I know."

A sputter of laughter escaped her lips. "That last one isn't a compliment."

"Yes it is," he insisted. "There is nothing I want more in this world than to lay you down on that bed and worship your body all night long."

He heard her sharp inhale as her eyes grew wide.

"But," he continued, "as you said earlier, rules are there for a reason. I would not want to do anything to jeopardize your business. I would hate if anyone thought crass thoughts because we were together."

White teeth came out to bite her plump lower lip. He wanted nothing more in this world than to soothe that small mark with his own lips, but he wouldn't. He had to stay strong.

"What…what if we don't tell anyone?" She stared up at him, desire burning in her eyes, need on every inch of her face.

"Is that truly what you want?" he asked, gazing deep into her eyes, wishing for one answer and fearing another.

"I want you, Rory," she whispered softly.

Screw it.

Scooping her up into his arms, he stood. She let out a small squeak of surprise.

"What are you doing?"

"Something *inadvisable*," he said with a grin.

Her arms tightened around his neck as a giggle of excitement left her lips. He planned to turn that giggle into a scream of pleasure later. Gently, he placed her on the bed, rising above her to take in the moment. She looked like a goddess laid out on his bed. Golden hair sprawled on his pillow, cheeks flushed pink, his sweater covering the heaven he knew awaited underneath.

Kneeling on the bed, he grasped the edge of the sweatshirt. "May I?"

She nodded, lifting to help him remove his garment from her. A curse left his lips as he realized she wore nothing underneath. Of course she wore nothing. Her clothing was still in his dryer. Still, he had not been prepared for the absolute beauty of her body.

"This is feeling a little one-sided here," she complained with a smile.

"My apologies." He reached back, pulling off his shirt in one fluid movement. "Better?"

She sucked in a sharp breath, eyes darkening as she stared. "Getting there."

He chuckled, climbing on the bed and crawling up her body. "Patience, sweetheart."

She started to protest, but he cut off her arguments with an all-consuming kiss. Her arms wrapped around his neck, pulling him closer. His body hardened at the feel of her soft, bare skin against his own. He memorized her lips, savoring the sweet taste of them, reveling in the fact that they were both taking what they wanted.

But he wanted more.

Pulling away, he kissed his way down her neck, worshipping her body with his mouth until she was screaming with rapture.

"Holy guacamole," she sighed, sinking into the pillow, eyes closing as a satisfied smile curled her lips.

He chuckled at her refusal to swear, even in the bedroom. Sliding off the bed, he stood and turned, but before he could walk away her hand reached out, grabbing his wrist. He looked down at her worried face.

"Wait, where are you going?"

"Don't worry. We're not done yet, sweetheart."

One eye cracked open as she stared up at him. "We're not?"

He shook his head. "Not by a long shot."

A giggle escaped her. "Oh goody."

"I just have to get something."

Nodding, she released him. Hating that he made her worry, he quickly went into the bathroom, crossing his fingers that he had what he needed under the sink. It had been a while since he'd been intimate with anyone, but he liked to be prepared at all times. Searching through the cabinet, he let out a soft exclamation of triumph as his hands closed over the protection they needed.

When he came back to her side, she smiled up at him. The sight nearly stopped his heart. Never before had he seen anything as beautiful as Marissa's smile. Something inside his chest cracked, but he ignored it. This was about pleasure. Nothing more.

"Now," he said in a low, growling voice. "Where were we?"

She laughed softly, the laughter turning to screams of pleasure as he joined them together, their bodies entwining in pure bliss. And when exhaustion claimed them, he slipped into the first peaceful slumber he'd had in longer than he could remember. Marissa warm and sated in his arms, he succumbed to the heaven of holding her through the night, leaving tomorrow's worries for the harsh rays of the morning sun.

CHAPTER SEVENTEEN

MARISSA WOKE UP feeling more rested than she ever had in her life. Why was her bed so comfortable? She hummed softly, rolling over and snuggling deeper into the comfy pillows and blankets.

Wait.

This wasn't her bed. She hadn't been able to go home last night because of the storm so she'd driven back and stayed with—

With a gasp, she shot up in bed. Clutching the blankets to her chest, she glanced around the room. Rory's room. Because last night she'd come back to Stonebridge. Rory had invited her into his home. Not the big mansion, but the smaller caretaker house. He'd given her dry clothes, cooked her dinner, introduced her to the world's worst game and then…

Oh, and then.

Her body still tingled with the memory of what they'd done last night.

"Something inadvisable," she giggled to herself.

It may have been a bad idea, but oh how right it felt. She didn't even know her body could feel like that. Rory must have some secret map to erogenous zones because the man had turned her into putty last night. Probably why she slept so well. That and this amazing bed. Not only was it huge, but she was pretty sure the blankets were made of pure clouds. So soft and fluffy, it was hard to believe they were real. Her blanket was at least ten years old and hanging on for dear life. She believed she'd got it on sale at an outlet store.

Lying back down, she burrowed into the coziness of the bed. A girl could get used to this. No! Sitting up again, she gave herself a little pep talk.

"This is just a little harmless fun," she reminded herself. "Nothing more. I don't have time for that. I don't want that."

Did she? No. She wasn't in a place in her life right now to devote time to a relationship. Especially one with a man who was all wrong for her. Okay, not all wrong. They had a lot in common, but their lifestyles were complete opposites. She had her new business on top of caring for her sister and making sure their dad didn't financially sink them due to his gambling. Rory had… Honestly, she didn't really know what he did besides work on the foundation. But that sounded like a big responsibility itself.

And speaking of Rory.

She glanced around the room, noticing his absence. A small pang of worry constricted her chest. A quick glance to the bathroom revealed the door open, but no one inside. Had he left? Did he regret what had happened last night and snuck out in the wee hours of the morning? No. That didn't make sense. This was his home. Why would he leave instead of kicking her out? She laughed at herself for the thought. Rory might be a bit direct at times, but he wasn't cruel. No way would he have kicked her out, even if he did regret what happened between them last night.

Her stomach churned. The thought of him having any remorse did not sit well with her. She didn't feel guilt over a single thing they'd done. They'd both consented and had an amazing time…right? Doubt began to creep into her happy mood. Maybe she'd been the only one to see stars. Rory might not have enjoyed their time together. Maybe he faked it. She didn't know if guys could do that, but now that the uncertainty invaded her brain, it was all she could think about. After all, if he'd had a good time he'd still be in bed with her, right?

Good mood eviscerated, misgiving and mortification began to overtake her. How could she have been so stupid to think a man like Rory would have a good time with her? He was probably used to dating supermodels and women of the world who knew all kinds of ways to make a man's eyes cross in pleasure. There was no way she could compete with—

"Oh good, you're up."

Her whirling mind paused its worries as she glanced up to see Rory coming in through the bedroom door, a tray filled high with goodies on it.

"I didn't want to wake you. You looked so beautiful and peaceful sleeping. I wasn't sure what you liked for breakfast, so I whipped up a bit of everything. There's eggs and bacon. Bagel and cream cheese. Fruit and yogurt. Oatmeal and of course coffee. Two creams one sugar."

He knew how she took her coffee? Of course he did—they had midday coffee all the time at Stonebridge. But he remembered. And he made her a literal continental breakfast to make sure she had something she liked. He hadn't left. He'd gone above and beyond the standard breakfast in bed.

It's just fun! Don't read into it.

She repeated the words in her head as her heart started to fall. He was just being a conscientious host. Good manners instilled by his parents, she was sure of it.

"How long have you been up?" she asked, staring at the mound of food.

He shrugged. "A few hours."

She groaned, grabbing her coffee mug from the tray. "Oh gross, you're a morning person, aren't you?"

He chuckled at her tease. Setting the tray down on the

bedside table, he sat facing her. "Indeed I am. I assume you are a night owl?"

Shaking her head with a grin, she answered, "Nope. Permanently exhausted pigeon."

He threw his head back, letting out a boisterous laugh. The joyous sound reverberated through her chest. The man had a great laugh. The kind of laugh that warmed you from the inside. She wanted to hear it more.

"You better help with this." She motioned to the food-filled tray. "No way will I be able to finish it all. It all looks and smells amazing. Except the oatmeal."

"Not a fan?"

"Of congealed snot? No. No I am not."

With a small chuckle, he grabbed the oatmeal off the tray and began eating it. She went for the eggs and bacon, plucking a grape from the fruit bowl and popping it into her mouth as well. They ate in silence for a few minutes, enjoying the morning rays peeking through the curtain, warming up the room. After she'd finished half her coffee, she decided it was time to bring up the elephant in the room.

"So…last night…"

He tilted his head, not offering any follow-up to her open-ended words. Dang it. She really hoped he'd take the wheel on this. Maybe she should try again.

"It was…"

Again, he said nothing. Simply stared at her with a curious expression.

She let out a small huff. As good as this man was in bed that's how infuriating he was out of it.

"This is usually the part where you interject to say how amazing it was."

He arched one pale red brow. "It is?"

Irritation rising, she crossed her arms, thankful he'd given her his T-shirt last night to wear to bed after everything.

Having this conversation naked would be more than she could handle.

"Yes." She paused, uneasiness entering her mind. "Unless it wasn't amazing for you, and this is a pity breakfast, in which case I'm going to drive off a mountain pass to avoid the embarrassment of—"

Her words were cut off as he grasped the back of her neck with his large hand, pulling her to him and silencing her with a toe-curling kiss. She eagerly kissed him back, reveling in the warm feel of his lips against hers. When he pulled back, he placed his forehead against hers.

"It wasn't just amazing, sweetheart," he said on a deep whisper. "It was astounding. The best night I've had in as long as I can remember. This breakfast is a meager offering of thanks to the rapture of last night."

Wow. Okay then. Guess she could put her doubts about how he felt about last night aside. The man had a way with words, she had to give him that.

"You liked it then?"

He laughed softly. "Yes, very much, and I hope you did as well."

Needing to tease him a little for the scare he gave her at being absent on waking, she shrugged.

"Eh, it was okay." At his stricken look she laughed, cupping his face in her hands. "I'm kidding, Rory. It was wonderful. My toes are still tingling."

"Just your toes?" He waggled his eyebrows.

A giggle escaped her. She liked this teasing side of him.

"Finish your oatmeal," she said, grabbing half of the bagel. "You need to build up your strength for later."

He cocked his head, eyes gazing into hers. "Are we continuing our liaison?"

There was that way with words again. Liaison? Such an odd way to talk, but she was getting used to it.

"If you want to." She certainly did. "We'll have to keep it quiet because of…our working relationship, but I'm game to keep having fun if you are."

He frowned, a contemplative look crossing his face. "I understand the need for discretion, and I'm not opposed to it. I would like to clarify one thing."

They should probably clarify a lot of things. Communication was key in situations like this.

"Shoot," she said, popping another grape in her mouth and chewing.

"While we are having…fun, I would like to request that neither of us have fun with others."

He wanted to be exclusive in their secret hookups? Worked for her. She barely had time for one secret affair.

"That works for me. I'm a one-person gal anyway."

He smiled. "Excellent. Any other rules we should discuss?"

She paused, thinking through everything in her brain, calling up possible issues they might face. "Yes. As we said before we should keep this between us. No telling friends or family."

"Not even your sister?"

Her jaw dropped in horror. "Especially not Abby! That girl cannot keep a secret. Plus, I don't want to hear any 'I told you so's' from her or Nora."

"'I told you so's'?"

She waved a hand in the air, not ready to talk about how Nora and Abby had been pushing her to start something with him since the get-go. "It's nothing. Never mind."

He grinned but let the issue drop. "No disclosing our relationship to others. Agreed."

"Also, we should probably keep the bedroom stuff separate from the work stuff."

"How do you mean?"

"No hanky-panky during working hours."

His eyes darkened, gaze roaming over her. "Agreed, but I must warn you, the temptation of spending all day in your presence, not being able to touch you, will make for some very wild nights."

She swallowed hard, her body heating at the sensual promise in his words.

"Guess you'll have to practice restraint then."

"Sweetheart, you test my restraint to the breaking limit."

Okay, now it was boiling in here. This man could set her on fire with nothing but a glance and words. It wasn't fair.

"Keep it to ourselves and keep work separate," he nodded. "Anything else?"

Her brain had stopped working about five minutes ago, but something tickled in the back of her mind, reminding her of a very important scenario they had yet to discuss.

"Yes." Taking a deep breath, she forged into the topic no one wanted to discuss with their new lover but was of upmost importance. "Once we stop having fun we end things. No harm. No foul. No repercussions for either of us."

The heat in his eyes died. She knew it wasn't fun to talk about the end of things, but everything ended eventually. They agreed this was for fun, so it made sense to stop when things weren't fun anymore. An easy-out clause. She held her breath and waited as a million thoughts passed over his face. None of which she could read. Finally, he nodded.

"Agreed. To all of it."

Oh. Well…good. She supposed that was good. They were both getting what they wanted, and no one would get hurt in the end. This was all very good. She was happy with their agreement, despite the unease working its way into her gut—feeling suspiciously like disappointment.

"Now," he said, taking the plate from her hand and setting it on the tray. "I've built up my strength again from that deliciously filling oatmeal that in no way tasted of snot."

She giggled, scooching down against the pillows as he came over her.

"Shall we proceed to the fun?"

"By all means." She smiled, pushing down that last bit of foreboding and focusing on the man above her who made her feel like she was the only thing in the world that mattered.

CHAPTER EIGHTEEN

THE GALA WAS less than a month away. Rory scrolled through the latest numbers the foundation's accountant had sent him. They were looking good, but it could be better. He wanted to provide a space for as many kids as possible. Hopefully the gala would ensure every child that wanted to come to the camps could for years to come. He planned to provide as much security and happiness for these kids as he could.

And speaking of happiness...

It had been a week since he and Marissa had agreed to the terms of their liaison. A week filled with hard working days and glorious, pleasure-filled nights. She refused to participate in anything physical during the day per their separation of business and pleasure rule. So professional. He found it admirable and adorable. Everything she did was adorable. Even when she was teasing him. Especially when she was teasing him.

His smile started to fade as he wondered if he'd fallen too deep. No. He promised himself he'd never do that again. Never be vulnerable enough with another person to give them power over him. He couldn't handle a repeat of his ex. Not just the theft—that had been a difficult betrayal to deal with. What hurt more was the lies. He had truly believed Britney loved him. Some might find it strange, but it hurt more to know she'd been lying to him than finding out she embezzled thousands.

Good mood eviscerated, he focused back on his laptop, promising himself he wouldn't let this situation become more than it was. Fun. She'd said as much herself. They were having fun, and when the fun stopped, so did they. It was what they agreed on.

So why did the thought of it make him sick?

The ringing of a phone interrupted his dark musings. He checked the screen, heart rate elevating as he hoped it would be Marissa. She was checking on some things with one of the caterers today. He would have gone, but she'd insisted he stay here and work. The fact that he was missing her after only a few hours sent a wave of unease through him. He needed to lock these feelings up. Never again, he'd said, and he meant it.

A sigh of relief and disappointment left his lips as he saw the caller ID. Not Marissa.

"Hello, Kellen," he said answering the phone.

"Whoa, did I call at a bad time?" his cousin asked. "What's with the full name? Am I in trouble?"

He huffed out a small laugh. "No. Apologies. I was… going over the foundation's financial reports."

Kell hummed in understanding. "I get that. The numbers can be a nightmare. I'm so glad Mal deals with that for our stuff."

Their stuff being the homes they flipped and gave to those in need. The Thorson Foundation had many branches of service, which was why the dollars didn't always stretch as far as he wanted them to. Still, he was glad his parents had built something that helped so many and that he could continue their work of helping others.

"Did you need something?" he asked, scrolling through the report.

"Not really, just had a break in my day and wanted to catch up, see how the gala planning is going."

"Very well. The event planner has done phenomenal work." A fact that nothing could erase. Marissa truly was excellent at her job.

"That's great, man. I can't wait to see it."

"Are Mal and Cash coming as well?" His cousins always supported his endeavors with the foundation as he did with theirs, but he never presumed anything.

"Yeah," Kell answered, the grin coming through in his voice. "They're finishing a house up in Boulder, but they said they'd be there no matter what."

Grateful warmth filled his chest. He could never truly hate his mother for abandoning him. Though her broken promise would always sting, deep down he knew she'd done what she thought was best for him. He'd always harbor some anger and sadness, but a big part of him understood she had been trying to give him a better life. And she had. The Thorsons had welcomed him with open arms and given him a life he never dreamed of. He wished he could find his birth mother and show her how loved and cared for he was, but no amount of money and private PIs had ever been able to find her.

"We get a plus-one, right?" Kell asked. "I think Cash wants to bring the woman he's seeing."

Rory chuckled. "You do, but the event is still a few weeks away. Will he still be seeing her?"

His cousin Cashel was a notorious playboy. He never stayed with a woman for more than two weeks.

"We'll see," Kell laughed. "And speaking of dates, any chance you'll be bringing one?"

He paused. Technically no, he would not be bringing anyone, because Marissa would already be there. But per their agreement this was a work thing, so they wouldn't be there together. Even if they were technically there together.

"Rory? You still there?"

Shaking the confusion from his mind, he answered, "Yes, I'm still here."

"Holy crap, you're seeing someone, aren't you?"

How did his cousin do that? Kell always seemed to root out the truth in people. He'd been the one to discover Britney's deception. He was awful to play poker with. The bastard always won.

"No…um…it's complicated."

Kell's snot came over the line. "It always is, man."

He had no idea. And it would stay that way. Rory had made a promise to Marissa to keep this thing between them a secret, and he had no intention of breaking that promise.

"What's she like?"

He paused, thinking about Marissa and the way she made him feel. They had agreed to keep their relationship secret. No reason he couldn't share vague things with Kell.

"She's amazing," he said, unable to keep the grin off his face. "Smart, determined, beautiful and funny."

"That great, Rory. I'm glad you're getting back in the dating game."

It wasn't a game, and he wasn't back in anything. "It's not like that. We're just…having fun."

A loud disbelieving bark of laughter came over the line.

"Sure, whatever you say. But those are some famous last words of a man who is about to fall and fall hard."

No, he was not. He'd already had this conversation with himself. No need to have it with Kell too. No falling. Just fun.

"I promise you it's not like that," he insisted.

"Sure, okay, just make sure you—"

Kell's words were drowned out by the front door opening and slamming shut. The force reverberated all the way into the kitchen, where he sat at the counter.

"Kell, I apologize, but I'm going to have to call you back."

"Everything okay?"

He had no idea, but he was about to find out. "Yes, everything is fine."

"Okay, see you in a few weeks."

He ended the call, slipping his phone into his pocket as Marissa came storming into the room.

"What's wrong?" he asked, concern rising in his chest.

She looked up at him and blinked as if surprised to find him sitting there. No idea why she would be shocked. It was the exact place he was in when she had left a few hours ago. Had she expected him to leave while she was out?

"How did I...?" She glanced around the room. "Do you ever get so angry you get in the car and drive, but once you arrive at your destination you can't remember driving there at all?"

He shook his head. "No. I can't say that I have. Sounds dangerous."

She shrugged. "I made it here safe."

And for that he was grateful. Standing, he went to her side, gently grasping her elbow to guide her to one of the high-back chairs at the kitchen counter. She sat with a sigh of exhaustion. Worry filled him as he took in her dejected expression.

"Let me get you some tea," he said, moving around the counter to the electric kettle.

The coffeepot was full, but judging by her body language, caffeine was not what she needed right now. A soothing chamomile would better suit her nerves. He set the water to boil, grabbing the tea bag and putting a teaspoon of honey in a mug, just how she liked it.

Once the kettle clicked, he poured the steaming water into the mug and brought it over to her. She smiled softly, taking the cup.

"Thank you."

He inclined his head. "May I ask what's wrong?"

She hesitated, stirring her tea, avoiding making eye contact. "Just a bad day is all."

It wasn't even noon and her day was already difficult enough to have her shoulders stooping that low? He didn't like it. Not one bit.

"Did the caterer give you trouble?" It was the only thing he could think of since she'd left to see them and come back like this. "If that is the case, I will fire them on the spot, I don't care what the contract says."

She glanced up at him with a mixture of warning and warmth. "No, it wasn't the caterer, and even if it was, remember our deal. I can handle my job no matter what. That includes dealing with vendors. I've dealt with plenty of rude and dishonest vendors in my previous job. I can handle things. I don't need you to run in and try and protect me."

He held up his hands in surrender. "I wasn't doing that."

She arched one eyebrow.

He shrugged. "Okay, maybe I was. A bit."

She laughed softly. "It's okay, but honestly it wasn't the caterer. Both caterers you picked are amazing and right on schedule with all the tasks assigned to them."

He was glad of that, but it begged the question of who had upset her and why. A question he was determined to get to the bottom of. Someone had to pay for putting that look of despair in her eyes. And he'd make sure it happened.

"I'm just…" She let out a heavy sigh. "Having some issues with home stuff."

Home stuff. Did that mean…? "Is Abby okay?"

He'd become quite fond of the young girl. She was smart, funny and clearly loved her sister more than anything. He remembered how hard it had been being a teenager. Emotions ran haywire and everything felt like life or death.

She graced him with a genuine smile this time. "Yes, Abby is great. It's...just stuff with my dad."

Her dad. She didn't talk much about her father. He hadn't even met the man. All he knew was that her dad was a busy doctor and rarely home. He had no idea what could be wrong, but a large part of him wanted to know so he could help fix it. Erase the sadness he saw in her eyes. Marissa should never be sad.

"Nothing for you to worry about," she said.

Right. Nothing for him to worry about because they didn't have that kind of relationship. The kind where you shared your problems and leaned on one another. They were just having fun. Like they agreed. His insides warred with wanting to know more and grabbing at the out. His brain screamed at him not to tip this into something it wasn't supposed to be while his heart pushed for more.

He ignored his heart, building up that brick wall again. Focusing on other ways he could make her smile.

"Should we take a break? It's almost lunchtime."

She looked at the clock hanging on the wall. "It's eleven ten."

Walking over to the clock, he plucked it down from the wall. Thumbing the tiny wheel on the back, he turned the hand until they were both pointing at the twelve.

"There," he said, putting the clock back. "Now it's lunchtime."

She lifted her wrist, pointing to her smartwatch. "You can't change time with a flick of your fingers, Rory."

He grinned. "Maybe not, but I can do other things with them. And since we're off the clock..."

She smiled, as he intended her to.

"Are you suggesting an afternoon delight?"

He lifted one shoulder in a small shrug. "You said no intimacy during working hours. It's not working hours right now, and I hear a good release helps cure a bad mood."

She threw her head back and laughed. The sound warmed his chest. Watching the misery leave her face made him want to roar with delight.

"Okay, mister, you win this time." She placed her hands around his neck, pulling him close.

He whisked her up into his arms, the smile on his face a complete opposite to the small whisper in the back of his mind warning him he was falling for this woman and there was nothing he could do to stop it.

CHAPTER NINETEEN

MARISSA WOKE IN the dark of night to an empty bed. The sharp pine and woodsy scent that was unique to Rory still lingered on the pillow next to her. Reaching out, she touched his side of the bed. Still warm. He might have gotten up to use the bathroom, but a quick glance over revealed it to be dark and empty. He couldn't have gone far.

Sitting up, she tossed the covers off and got out of bed. Normally she didn't sleep over after they had their fun at night, but it was Friday and Abby was staying at a friend's house so she could stay the night without questions as to her whereabouts. Grabbing the robe hanging on the hook on the closet door, she slipped it on and went in search of Rory.

Peeking out into the hallway, she saw a dim light coming from the living room. Making her way down the hallway on silent tiptoes, she entered the front area of the house to discover the light was coming from the crackling fire. They hadn't lit a fire before bed. There was a large shadowy figure sitting in front of the fire, shoulders slumped, red hair glowing like the flames licking the wood in the hearth.

Rory.

Her heart clenched, worry tightening her chest as she took in his morose posture. Wanting to do something to help—because he clearly needed a little cheering up for whatever reason—she made her way into the room.

"Hey, you," she said softly, coming to sit beside him.

Rory glanced over in surprise, his dark expression melting away into a gentle smile as she sat next to him. "Hello. I didn't wake you, did I?"

She shook her head. "No. What's up? Couldn't sleep?"

He made a noncommittal grunt. He was shutting her out. She could feel it. The logical part of her brain reminded her they were just having fun. They weren't in the type of relationship where you shared and tried to fix each other's problems. She should get up and go back to bed. Let him sort out whatever was bothering him on his own.

But another part of her, a much larger part, reminded her that this was the man who had offered her a second chance on a job when she had screamed in his face. The man who had researched her chronic illness to make sure he had things on hand to help her through bad days. The man who had wound her up so tight and held her gently afterward. This was Rory, and just fun or not, she cared about him.

"Bad dream?" she asked, scooting closer until their shoulders were touching.

He glanced into the flames, expression darkening. "Bad memory."

She slipped her hand into his, giving it a reassuring squeeze. "Wanna talk about it?"

Talking didn't always help, but sometimes it was just what a person needed.

She waited, exercising patience as they sat in silence. The only sound was the pop and crackle of the logs in the fire. He was quiet for so long she wondered if they would stay like this all night, silently staring at the fire until the rays of the morning light broke the darkness surrounding them. But then, he spoke.

"Have you ever been engaged?"

She blinked, not expecting that question. That was something you asked a girlfriend, not your secret lover. "Um, no, I haven't."

Her longest relationship had been six months, and that had been her high school girlfriend. They broke up when Brooke went out of state to college. Since then, it had been short-term relationships that fizzled out quickly. Most people didn't want to marry a woman who came with the responsibility of a teenage sister.

"I was," he said darkly.

She blinked in shock. It wasn't that she thought Rory wouldn't be a good husband. To someone. Someday. But the thought of him having a previous fiancée never crossed her mind. He always seemed so…isolated.

"What happened?" She wasn't sure she wanted to know. Based on his mood, she'd guess it didn't end amicably. She hoped his ex hadn't cheated on him. She'd had an ex who cheated once. The pain and embarrassment haunted her to this day. Cheating was the worst.

"She embezzled from the foundation."

"What?" She took back her earlier thought. Stealing from charity was way worse than cheating.

He sighed, gaze still focused on the fire, but his hand tightened in hers, seeking comfort. She leaned against him, offering all the reassurance she could. The following story would not be a happy one, that was for sure.

"I met Britney at a fundraiser gala. We matched well."

Matched well. What a Rory way to put it. She smiled, squeezing his hand in encouragement to continue.

"After six months of dating, I proposed. She seemed to care about the causes the foundation supported and even offered to help with some of the functions."

"What did she do?" she asked when he paused. "For work, I mean."

His jaw clenched. "She told me she was a trust fund baby

whose parents had died. We…commiserated on the loss of our loving parents. But I later found out none of that was true."

How awful! What an evil person to lie about losing a loved one. Having lost a parent herself, she could never imagine invoking such a terrible falsehood to gain someone's trust.

"We had been engaged for two months when the foundation's accountant brought some missing funds to my attention."

"That troll," she hissed. Rory glanced over at her with an amused smile. "Sorry, jumping to conclusions, but I'm assuming she was dipping into the honeypot?"

He nodded. "Yes. We did some digging and discovered someone was misappropriating funds from the foundation to a secret bank account she controlled. I confronted her about it, but she denied any knowledge."

Not surprising. People like that never admitted to their wrongdoing. How awful for her to take advantage of Rory and all the people whom the foundation had helped like that. That was truly evil.

"I told her our engagement was on hold while I had a PI conduct an internal investigation into the missing funds," Rory said, gaze going back to the flames. "She was understandably upset, but insisted she had nothing to do with it."

"What did the PI find?"

A scowl darkened his face. "Evidence that she was embezzling hundreds of thousands of dollars from the foundation."

Awful! Simply an awful human being to do something like that.

"What did she say when you showed her the proof?"

The crackle of the fire filled the room as Rory remained silent for a moment. When he finally spoke, his voice was tinged with anger and pain. So dark and deep, it cut her.

"I never got the chance. She took off in the dead of night."

"She ran like a coward." Ire burned in her chest. For Rory and everyone who benefited from the foundation.

"Yes." He nodded, jaw clenching tight. "But not before she stole all the cash and jewelry I had in my personal safe. The money I could care less about, but she took my mother and father's wedding bands, which were heirlooms. Been in the family for generations. I planned to use them for our—"

His words cut off, anger and pain etched on every inch of his face. It hurt to see the agony radiating off him.

"Rory, that's awful. I'm so sorry." She hugged herself to his side, wishing she could take away the misery she still heard in his voice. "Did they catch her?"

Please let them have caught her.

He nodded. "Yes. They caught her trying to withdraw the funds from her account and flee the country. She was tried for embezzlement and is currently serving a ten-year sentence."

"Did you get the rings back?" The dark expression on his face made unease squirm in her gut. She knew the answer even before he said it.

"No." The growled word sounded as if it was torn from his very soul. "She sold them online. Already shipped them off before they caught her. I tried to find the buyer but…"

Her heart broke for him. She knew the value of the rings meant nothing to Rory. It was the memories behind them. The importance of them. They had belonged to his parents, who had passed them down to him. It was a connection to the family that chose him. A symbol of his belonging and love. His ex had stolen that from him. For that she would never forgive the woman.

"I'm glad she's locked up, but I am so sorry that happened to you."

He turned his head, gazing down at her with a curious expression. "It was four years ago. I haven't… You're the first person I've been with since."

The confession hit her like a ton of bricks. Four years.

Four years! No wonder the man was so stiff and closed off. She would be too after an incident like that. But to go four years without engaging in another relationship? The gravity of how much trust he put in her weighed on her shoulders. It wasn't a heavy burden. In fact, she welcomed it. It made her feel special. She wanted to take his trust and wrap it up in a blanket, protect it, protect him from anything else in this world that could hurt him.

Silly. Rory was a grown man who clearly could look after himself. But she was humbled that she had been the one to draw him out into the world again. A role she would not take lightly.

"Thank you for telling me," she said, kissing him softly, pouring all the love she had for him into the kiss. Because it was at that moment she realized the truth.

She loved Rory Thorson.

She hadn't meant to. Nowhere in her plans for her life did "falling for a rich philanthropist" appear, but here she was. Somewhere in the course of their time together she'd fallen head over heels in love with this man. Her initial assessment of him being a rich, selfish snob had been wrong. For that she was ashamed. Getting to know him, who he was inside, this past month and a half had opened her eyes and her heart.

But now, she had no idea what to do with that love. She couldn't confess it. Not now after he revealed his painful past. Plus, there was the matter of their agreement, keeping this thing fun.

She had no idea what to do about her revelation, but she did know one thing she could do. Standing, she held out her hand, breathing a sigh of relief as Rory placed his palm against hers and let her lead him back to the bedroom. Confession could wait, forever if necessary. Tonight, she was going to give this man all the love he deserved from a cruel world who had denied him so much.

CHAPTER TWENTY

"IF YOU KEEP scowling at the camera, I'm putting one of those creepy tooth smiling filters on you," Marissa threatened.

Rory frowned, wondering how he'd even let her talk him into this. They were outside at the ropes course, where he was demonstrating how to cross the various obstacles. She'd said it would be a good idea to have visual examples of the activities the kids would experience at camp playing during the event. He wasn't sure he agreed, but one look at her determined face and he'd agreed.

He'd discovered Marissa made him do a lot of things he'd never thought he would before. Like share himself with another person, physically and emotionally. It still surprised him that he had shared his past with Britney a few nights ago. The only people he'd talked to about her other than the authorities were his cousins. So why had he shared with Marissa?

Because she makes me feel hope again.

Hope that he could learn to trust another person again. Maybe even…love again?

"Yes! That's it! Perfect, hold that smile."

He glanced over to her, not even realizing he was smiling. He wondered what she would say if she knew the reason for his unintended grin was her.

Probably gloat about it and tease him mercilessly.

His smile grew at the thought.

"Okay, move onto the cargo net. Wait!" She hurried around him to the other side of the net. "That's better."

He grumbled. "But if you would have stayed back there, I wouldn't have had to smile."

He wasn't opposed to smiling, especially around her, but he found the forced smile for pictures disingenuous and painful.

"Yeah, but if I would have stayed back there it would all be butt shots. As amazing as your backside is in those jeans, I don't think we want that to be the message here."

He chuckled, "You seem to like it just fine."

Tilting the camera down, she waggled a finger at him. "We're working here, mister. Keep your head out of the gutter."

He nodded, hiding another laugh when she quickly blew him a kiss. Their line was getting fuzzier by the day. He knew that should worry him, but it didn't. Since the night he had shared his painful past with her, things had been different. He couldn't explain it, but everything felt…more. Kell would congratulate him for finally opening up his heart again. Maybe that was what was happening, maybe not. All he knew was that it felt good, right.

And yet…

A small voice in the back of his head screamed out a warning. Insidious whispers of doubt. Fear that things were going too well, a shoe was about to drop and knock him right over.

He brushed the feeling off, determined to enjoy the pleasantness of the moment and the person he was sharing it with. As his hand hit a bit of frayed rope, the bristles scraping away the top layer of skin, he swore. Okay, maybe it wasn't all pleasant. He made a mental note to have someone come out and recheck the entire ropes course for issues. It had to be in safe condition before the kids arrived.

"Good," Marissa said from behind the camera. "Now give me a thumbs-up with a big smile."

He frowned.

"That's the opposite of what I asked for, Rory."

Sighing, he gripped the rope with one hand, lifting the other in a thumbs-up. He pasted what he hoped looked like a genuine smile on his face. Judging by the grimace Marissa made, he'd say he failed.

"This is supposed to be a camp for kids, not serial killers. Try again."

His hand dropped. Hopping down from the net, he came around to her side. "I feel ridiculous."

"Well, you look great." Her nose wrinkled as she scrunched up her face in thought. "Actually, you look stiff and uncomfortable in a lot of the shots, but I got some good ones we can work with. I only need a few more, I promise."

"I still don't see how this will get us donations at the event."

"A lot of people are visually focused," she explained. "Plus this lumberjack vibe you have going on will definitely open a few wallets."

He grunted. "I'm a piece of meat then?"

"Sex sells, baby." She grinned, before sobering. "Besides, you said you didn't want to show videos of the kids in their foster homes."

He nodded. There were many reasons he did not want to go that route with the video. A host of legal reasons for one, but the bigger issue was he hated how people often exploited the kids they were supposedly helping. Before the Thorsons had adopted him, he'd been subjected to a number of news segments where they trotted out the "poor abandoned" kids. Put on damn display like shelter animals to tug at the heartstrings of those looking for "good deeds" to make themselves feel better.

He knew his parents had found him through one of those

segments, but they never treated him as anything other than their own son. Loved and accepted. Some of his other foster acquaintances weren't so lucky. He would never do that to another person. Exploit their bad situation in the name of helping. They could raise the funds without the pity propaganda.

"I think people will really love seeing the man behind this camp idea showing off how much fun the kids will have," Marissa continued. "It'll bring out the childhood fun in the adults to see you playing on the ropes course. That will make them want to donate more. I bet some might even ask for a turn out here themselves."

Ha! He'd love to see some of the rich and powerful people the foundation called upon for donations slough off their highbrow attitude and complete a ropes course. Not that he thought any of them would. Sadly, most of the people who ran in his circles kept their extracurricular activities to games like tennis and golf. Boring games he had no idea why anyone found interesting.

"Trust me, Rory." She smiled, placing a hand on his arm. "This will help."

"Okay." He nodded. Because surprisingly, he did trust her. It astonished him to realize it. He didn't trust many people, but somehow at some point Marissa had found her way into his small circle of trust. And not only in business. "I'll try again."

He went back around the net. Stepping onto the ropes, he hoisted himself up, remembering why he was doing this. Who he was doing it for. Not only the children who needed this, but also for himself. For that sad, scared, angry little boy who had never understood why his mother lied and left him. Who had just wanted a place to belong, to be loved. He'd found it eventually, but he knew not every kid was so lucky. Maybe, for a few weeks out of the year, this camp could be that place for them.

Lifting one hand, he gave a thumbs-up and thought about the kids who would find joy here. The life his parents gave him. The way his cousins accepted him. And most of all, the happiness the woman in front of him made him feel.

"Oh wow!" Marissa exclaimed, behind the camera. "That's perfect, Rory. We got it."

He hopped down, the smile still on his face as he moved to her side. "I hope you got enough, because I'm afraid I'm done with the ropes course for the day."

"We got it." She glanced down at his hands. "Oh no, are you bleeding?"

Holding his palms up, he examined the raw redness of them, seeing a few scratches here and there, but thankfully no blood.

"No, but those ropes are a bit rough. Perhaps I should provide gloves for the children or replace the ropes entirely with softer ones."

"They do look a little on the old side. Replacement might be a good idea, but do you have the funds for that?" She frowned. "Replacing an entire ropes course must be expensive."

He shrugged. "I'll see to it."

If they didn't get enough donations for course repairs, he would gladly take the money out of his personal finances. Not like he had any grand plans for it anyway.

She hummed, giving him a knowing grin. "I'm sure you will, you big ol' softie."

Rolling his eyes at her ridiculous assessment of him, he pulled her into his arm, bending his head down to capture the lips that had been tempting him all morning. She put a hand up, covering his mouth with a small tsking sound.

"We're on the clock, remember?"

Gently moving her hand down, he rubbed the tip of his nose against hers. "Thirty-second break."

She giggled, the sound filling his soul with warmth.

"That's not a thing," she insisted.

"Okay, then five-minute break." He bobbed his eyebrows. "We can do a lot in five minutes."

"Oh, can we now?" She smiled up at him, leaning in close.

Before their lips could connect a buzzing sound filled the forest air.

"Shoot." She pulled back, reaching into her pocket and pulling out her phone. "Hold that thought."

Glancing at the screen, a frown marred her face.

"Who is it?" he asked, a sense of unease filling him.

"It's Abby's school. I have to take this."

"Of course."

She stepped away, answering the call and bringing the phone to her ear. He watched as she paced the forest floor, dirt crunching under her sneakers. She'd insisted they dress casual for today's shoot, so they were both in jeans, T-shirts and sneakers. She pulled on the hem of her shirt as she listened to whoever was on the line.

"Yes, this is Marissa Webb."

She paused, lips turning down in a worried frown at whatever the person said. His chest tightened as unease morphed into full-blown trepidation.

"Oh no!" She placed a hand on her chest. "She did mention something this morning, but insisted she was fine." Another pause. "Yes, thank you. Thank you for letting me know. I'll be right there."

She ended the call, chewing her bottom lip. Her obvious distress was gutting him. Rushing to her side, he grasped her hand.

"What is it?"

She glanced up at him, worry and guilt glazing over her eyes. "Abby threw up at school. She mentioned she wasn't feeling well this morning, but said it was probably just nerves about a big test. I knew I should have made her stay home.

There's been a stomach bug running rampant in school this week. Guess it finally got her."

He pulled her into his arms, wishing he could wash away the worry radiating off her body. A stomach bug didn't sound overly troubling, but being sick was never a good time. He'd become very fond of her little sister. It pained him to know Abby was suffering.

"I doubt you could have stopped her," he said, rubbing her back in a soothing manner. "Much like her sister, she's stubborn."

Marissa glanced up at him with narrowed eyes. "Determined."

"To-may-to, to-mah-to." He shrugged, hoping to inject some playfulness and ease her fear. He knew she felt guilty for letting Abby go to school unwell.

She chuckled softly before letting out a weary sigh. "I'm sorry, Rory, but I need to cut today short and—oh, son of a biscuit eater!"

He blinked as she cut off her own statement with yet another creative curse.

"Oh no, no, no," she moaned, covering her face with her hands.

"What is it?" Worry started to rise in his own chest at her crestfallen look.

"My car is in the shop," she answered, dropping her hands. "I took a rideshare here this morning. What do I do? It will take forever for the driver to get up here and then back to the school, and Abby is in the nurse's office feeling awful, needing me and—"

"Sweetheart, it's okay." He cupped her face in his hands, stopping her worried ramblings. "I'll take you into town. We'll get Abby together."

"What about work?" She blinked, her mind clearly still

jumbled by the news. "You have a ton of things to do. I can just wait for a ride. You don't need—"

"Screw work," he said. "As you said, a rideshare would take too long. I'm here for you, Marissa. Both of you."

Her eyes closed, a few tears leaking out. He hated those damn tears. Wished he could make sure she never felt their cold sting on her cheeks ever again. When she opened her eyes, he sucked in a sharp breath at the wealth of emotion swimming in them.

"Thank you, Rory."

She rose up and placed a soft kiss to his lips.

Knowing time was of the essence, he kissed her back briefly before taking her hands and escorting her out of the forest to his car. His heart pounded as he realized this thing they'd started had gone far beyond the fun zone. At some point in their dalliances, Marissa had cemented her place directly in his dead heart, bringing it back to life again.

CHAPTER TWENTY-ONE

SHE LOVED HIM.

Marissa closed the door to her sister's bedroom. She'd picked Abby up from school and tucked her into the back of Rory's car. He gave her his sympathies and promised to drive slowly so as to not upset her stomach further. How could she not love him after something so sweet? When he said he was not only there for her, but her sister as well, the last bits of her jaded heart fell away, replaced with something she'd always desired.

Acceptance.

Rory didn't mind that she came as a package deal. In fact, he seemed to care for her sister as if she was his own. He was truly something special. She didn't know what she had done to deserve him, but she was seriously thinking about having a conversation with him after the gala. Seeing if he'd be open to taking their "fun" and turning it into something real.

Abby was resting in her bed with a bowl by her side and a glass of water on her nightstand. Thankfully she didn't have a fever. The school nurse said it was a twenty-four-hour bug that was going around and to keep her hydrated and rested. Marissa crossed her fingers that it wouldn't hit her next. The gala was next week, and even if it was only a day-long sickness, she could not afford to lose a day right now.

She made her way back into the living room where she

had left Rory, determined to thank him profusely for his help today. When she arrived in the room, she saw him sitting on the couch, crouched over the coffee table working on the puzzle.

"Hey," she said softly, smiling at the warm fuzzies filling her seeing him so comfortable in her home.

He glanced up, standing as his face pinched in concern. "How is Abby?"

"Resting." She moved over to his side, kissing him briefly before wrapping her arms around his waist and snuggling into his chest. "Thank you. For helping today."

His arms encircled her, squeezing tightly. "My pleasure, sweetheart."

She chuckled. "I bet it wouldn't have been a pleasure if Abby upchucked in your car."

"Cars can be detailed," he said casually. "I'm happy to offer my help."

Pulling back, she smiled up at him. "And I'm happy to offer you a drink. What would you like? Coffee? Tea? I should check to see if we have ginger ale for when Abby feels up to drinking something."

"If not, I can run to the store for you."

Cupping his bearded cheeks in her hands, she placed a very thorough kiss to his lips. "You, sir, are too wonderful. Let me go see what we have in the garage first."

She walked into the kitchen with Rory following.

"I can start some coffee if you would like, while you search for the soda," he offered.

If he didn't stop being so sweet she was going to say screw the gala deadline and tell him she loved him right then and there.

"Thank you." She nodded. "That would be lovely."

She went out the door connecting the kitchen to the garage. Rooting around in the pantry they kept out there for overflow staples, she let out a cheer of success when she found a six pack of ginger ale. Grabbing the cans, she made her way back into the kitchen.

"Did you find the coffee grounds? I forgot to tell you where they were." She glanced up to see Rory, his back to her, shoulders stiff and tense. "Rory?"

A sinking dread filled her stomach. The coffeepot sat, filled with water on the counter. Machine open, waiting for the liquid. It looked like he stopped mid-task. But why? What was going on?

"Rory? Are you okay?"

"I feel I should ask you that question," he said as he slowly turned. "What is this?"

She glanced to the paper he held in his hand with bold red letters on it. Her heart jumped into her throat, vision tunneling at the sudden spike of adrenaline. Rory swore, rushing to her side and pulling the soda cans from her hands. He placed them on the counter and helped her over to the table. After gently helping her into a chair, he sat next to her, placing the letter on the table.

"Marissa, what is this? Are you in trouble?"

She blinked, vision coming back as she took a few deep, calming breaths.

"Where did you get this?" she asked.

"It was open on the counter."

Dang it! Why had she left it out? She meant to hide it away this morning after she got the mail, but she was in a rush. At least Abby hadn't found it. Thank goodness.

"It's a foreclosure notice," Rory stated plainly.

She scowled at him. "I know what it is."

He arched one eyebrow at her terse words.

"Sorry, I... I'm just a little behind on the mortgage payments right now, but I'm fine. I have it handled."

Now it was his turn to scowl. "Why are you paying the

mortgage? I thought this was your family home. Does your father not pay the bills? Or at least help with them. He is a doctor, correct?"

She sucked in a sharp breath, the secret she held so close to her chest for so many years begging to burst free. But she couldn't let it. It was her problem. Her shame. Anger started to build within her, covering up the humiliation.

"It's really none of your business who pays the bills in my household."

He reared back at her words, a spark of hurt in his eyes. She cursed herself for putting it there. She hadn't meant to hurt Rory, but he shouldn't have been looking through her mail.

"I'm sorry," she said, shaking her head. "I promise it's all fine. It's just a warning letter, but I'm not losing the house so don't—"

"We're losing the house?" a soft voice called from the edge of the kitchen.

She glanced over to see Abby, looking miserable, standing just inside the kitchen, horror on her face. Crap! Why was her sister out of bed?

"No," she insisted. "Not yet. We still have thirty days to make the payment, and I have—"

"But why?" Abby's voice asked softly through tears. So childlike and painful it cut Marissa in two. "Why are we so far behind on payments? Dad's a doctor! He works all the time. Shouldn't he make enough to cover our mortgage?"

And here it was. The dark secret she'd been hiding from her sister. From everyone. She glanced back at Rory. Taking a deep breath, she explained.

"Yes, he should, but Dad… He's… I lied about him working late. He isn't at the hospital at night. He's at the casino. Dad has a gambling addiction, Abby."

Abby blinked, fear replaced with shock. "What?"

She could feel Rory's presence behind her, feel the shift in the air around them. Something was wrong. But she couldn't deal with whatever it was right now. She had to focus on Abby. She had to explain.

"For years now, even before you were born. I didn't find out until Mom died. She managed to keep him in check, but once she passed…it got worse. It's why I started working part-time in high school. He'd pay the bills but then lose the rest. I had to use my paychecks to buy us groceries and clothes. Eventually he stopped paying bills altogether and it was up to me."

Abby shook her head. "But…why didn't you tell me?"

"I didn't want you to worry."

"You lied to me!" Abby accused.

She held up her hands in surrender. "No, I was protecting you."

"By lying to me!"

"No… I…" She looked back at Rory, but his face was blank. Completely devoid of emotion. "Rory… I was protecting her. You get that, right?"

He stared at her, eyes cold. When he glanced over at Abby, they softened with empathy. "Sometimes," he said slowly, "we think we're protecting someone when really we're taking their choices away."

"Rory." Her voice cracked at his harsh condemnation.

His eyes pierced her. "I know my mother thought she was doing the right thing by abandoning me, but she never talked to me about it. Never gave me a chance to say how I felt or even process the goodbye. She promised to never leave me, yet she broke that promise. She lied to me. Her intentions of giving me a better life might have been good, but the action was still a betrayal."

Did he really just compare her keeping their dad's addiction a secret to his mother's abandonment? What happened to the sweet, supportive man who had rushed to her side to help her with her sick sister? Where was he? Why was everyone against her? She'd only been trying to protect her sister.

"This is ridiculous," she muttered to them both. "Abby, I'm sorry I didn't tell you about Dad and the house, but I promise you I have everything under control. I'll have the money next week to pay the bank."

"You will, won't you," Rory said, giving her a knowing look.

Oh shoot! He knew the money she needed was coming from her fee for planning the gala. So what? She'd earned that money. The past two months she'd worked her butt off and proved herself. The gala was a week away and everything was perfect. He couldn't back out now. Could he?

Looking into his face, she noticed emotions she hadn't seen before: mistrust, anger, hurt. The last one crushed her, like a weight on her chest. The very last thing she wanted to do was hurt Rory. Poor man had been hurt by enough people in his life—she never wanted to add to that.

"Okay, so say you do save the house," Abby said, pulling her attention back. "What about everything else? My college fund? Did Dad burn through that too?"

She sucked in a sharp breath, knowing this was going to look bad, but she needed to be fully honest with her sister if she ever hoped to regain her trust. "Yes and no."

A soft sob left Abby's lips, and she hurried to reassure her sister.

"Dad ran through the one he and Mom started for you. Mine also. There was nothing I could do about mine." Which was why she had a mountain of student loans she'd be paying off until she died. "But I opened a secret savings account that Dad doesn't know about or have access to."

"A secret account," Rory's voice growled with accusation. She turned her head to glance at him, knowing what he thought, the memories it most likely brought up about his ex to hear her talk about stashing away money. But this was different! She was different!

"I had to," she said, staring him straight in the eyes. "To protect her future."

"Then why not tell me?" Abby cried, completely unaware of the undertones passing between Marissa and Rory.

She looked back at her sister. "I'm sorry, Abs. I was waiting until…you were older, I guess. I just wanted you to enjoy your childhood without worry. It's my job to look out for you."

Abby glared. "You're my sister, not my mother. It was Dad's job to look out for me and your job to be honest with me. Whatever, it doesn't matter anymore. I just came to get some ginger ale, but I'm not thirsty anymore."

Abby stormed past her, stomping down the hall and slamming her bedroom door. Glancing up, she saw Rory, anger and hurt in his eyes. Oh goody. Guess it was "be angry with Marissa" day.

She stared down the hall and then back at Rory. Mind wavering between the two people who meant the most to her, lamenting the fact that through her actions both of them currently hated her. What in the world was she going to do?

CHAPTER TWENTY-TWO

SHE LIED.

Rory gripped the back of the kitchen chair tight, his knuckles turning white, as hot, bitter betrayal ate a hole in his gut. How could Marissa keep such a huge secret like this? He understood her desire to protect her sister when she was younger, but why hadn't she shared her struggles with him? He thought they were… Didn't matter. She lied.

It was unforgivable.

Dark thoughts swirled in his brain, a storm cloud blocking out all logical thought. All he could see was Britney, her betrayal. It wasn't the same as what Marissa had done, but the similarities were close enough to have red flags waving. No wonder she tried so hard to convince him to keep her contract. Now he knew it wasn't just about her new business. She needed the money to save her home.

She's working fair and square for it. Not stealing like Britney.

He shook off the logical voice in his head, too furious to see the truth. Since Britney, he'd never let another person— no matter how close they were to him—have access to the foundation's funds. There was no way she could be stealing from him. He knew that. But the wounded part of his soul whispered that Marissa had found a way. He'd been duped again. A sucker, just like before.

He debated going back home. Leaving the sisters to their

argument and betrayals. But he'd been betrayed too. He wanted answers or at least an explanation.

"Guess that means she doesn't want to talk to me," Marissa said with a sigh, staring down the hall where Abby had slammed her bedroom door.

"Can you blame her?" The words were out of his mouth before he even thought, but he didn't regret saying them.

She turned to him, a mix of guilt and anger etched on her beautiful lying face.

"Look, I understand that I may not have done the right thing by not telling her about Dad's gambling, but—"

"You lied, Marissa."

She shook her head. "No, I didn't, I—"

"You did," he insisted. "You lied to her, and you lied to me."

Her shouldered stiffened. "My family life is none of your concern, Rory. I had no reason to tell you anything."

"I told you about my ex." The words tore from his throat, raw and pain filled. "I told you what she did to me. How she lied to me, to everyone."

"That's not at all the same." She shook her head in disbelief. "Are you really comparing me to your ex who embezzled from your charity? What the hell, Rory?"

He shrugged. "A lie is a lie. How do I know you aren't after my money too? You seem to need it."

It was a low blow. One he didn't truly believe, but pain and anger were ruling his thoughts. Every ugly fear he had was lashing out.

She blinked. "Wow, you really are a jerk deep down, aren't you?"

She stormed away. He followed, not sure why he didn't just leave. But he couldn't. The pain was too raw, too visceral. He needed a place to put it all, and since she was the cause of it, it only seemed logical that she should face the consequences of her actions.

"Why didn't you tell me you were losing the house?" he demanded, following her to the sink.

She grabbed a glass from the cabinet, filling it with water as she glared at him.

"Because it was none of your business. And I'm not losing it. I can pay what's due once…"

She trailed off, gaze going to the rushing water as her words trailed off.

"Once I pay you the rest of the money," he finished for her.

She shut the water off, taking a small sip before answering.

"Yes. Once the gala is finished and I get the rest of my fee." Her eye snapped up to his, full of fire. "I planned a perfect event, just like I promised. I earned my fee. You signed a contract."

He barked out a sharp laugh. "Yes, but I also remember you saying if the gala did not go off one hundred per cent to my liking you would relinquish your fee and pay me back the deposit. Remember?"

Her face paled. A sharp stab of regret filled him. It was a terrible thing to say, even if it was the truth. He would never be so petty as to call her bluff like that. Besides, she was right—barring any unforeseen circumstances, the gala would go off without a hitch and be a huge success. She deserved her fee.

But he deserved someone who didn't lie to him.

"You wouldn't," she whispered.

No. He would never. Rory Thorson was a man of his word. If he went back on their deal, all because his feelings were hurt, his parents would roll over in their graves. He could never disappoint them like that. But he also couldn't be with someone who lied to him. Not again.

"I won't," he agreed. "Despite your personal moral code, your professional actions have been satisfactory."

"Wow," she deadpanned. "Such high praise."

"I will fulfill the payment at the end of the contract as promised after the gala, but this—" he pointed between them "—is over."

She sucked in a harsh breath. "What do you mean?"

"We're through, Marissa," he said, speaking with a calm demeanor as his insides raged. "From now on our relationship is strictly professional."

She snorted out a sardonic laugh. "So that's it then? One fight and you say it's over, so it is?"

"Did we not agree to an easy-out clause?"

She shook her head, setting her water glass on the counter. "Nothing about this is *easy*."

On that they could agree.

"You lied to me, Marissa." He shook his head. "And I don't tolerate liars."

Her eyes glared at him, agony and fire filling their dark depths. "Why are you making this about you? It has nothing to do with you!"

"Precisely!" He took a step forward until he could feel the heat coming off her body. His hands ached to grab her, crush her to him, hold her in his arms and forgive everything. But he couldn't do that. "You made sure of that, didn't you?"

"What?" She shook her head, brow scrunching in confusion.

"I shared with you. I told you about my ex, my mother. I shared my past, my pain."

"I told you about my mother too," she countered.

"But you held back." He stared her down. "I thought we were…"

He didn't finish his statement. It was too painful to put

into words what they could have been. What she ripped away from them.

"Rory, we were. I—"

She reached out a hand to his face, but the thought of her touch was too much right now. He wasn't sure he was strong enough to resist it. And he had to be. He pulled back. She flinched, his refusal of her touch clearly wounding her.

Join the club, sweetheart.

He stared into those beautiful eyes. Eyes he thought might be his second chance. Now they only reminded him of his naivety. How, after all these years, had he forgotten his most important rule? Never trust anyone. Somehow over the past two months she'd wormed her way through all his defenses. Broken down that wall of ice he built around his heart and planted herself inside. It was going to kill him to push her back out, but he had to do it. To protect himself.

"You're really doing this?" she asked, voice soft and small. "You're really throwing away everything we had because, what? I didn't share my dad's gambling problem with you?"

"You lied to me, Marissa." He sighed, wishing things could be different, but knowing it was impossible. "I told you I don't suffer liars. Goodbye."

Taking one last look at her—memories to hold on to in the dark of night—he turned and made his way out of her house for the final time. A sharp four-letter curse and demand for him to do something physically impossible to himself followed him out the door. Her words had been laced with pain, the same pain he felt consuming his entire being. The fact that she used a curse word at all, and in such close proximity to her sister, let him know that any hope of reconciliation between them was destroyed.

For the best.

He got into his car and drove back to Stonebridge. Once he arrived, he thought about going home, but instead he made his way inside the main house. His sneakers made no sound on the marble floor. He swore he could hear the echoing click-clack of Marissa's heels in the library. He made his way into the kitchen, glancing about the room, feeling lost, adrift. A terrible feeling. In the past four years he hadn't felt adrift for one second. But now, he had no idea what to do.

Looking about the room, his eyes fell on the conservatory off the kitchen. He spied the edge of the soft lounge, memories of taking Marissa there rising up in his mind. Memories that would now haunt him forever.

"Dammit!" he swore, slamming his hands down on the dark oak table. "I'm a fool."

He cursed himself as the pain washed over him, his mind going back and forth. Was he a fool for trusting her or for cutting her off so swiftly?

"She lied," he growled to the empty room. "I can't… The trust is broken."

The storm raged inside him, but a small spot of calm burst through the dark clouds. He had done the right thing. As much as it ripped his heart out to do so, he knew he could never trust her again knowing she held back something so big from him. The part that hurt the most was that he would have helped her, helped her father. If only she would have shared with him. If only she would have asked.

But it was too late.

Marissa had sealed their fate in hiding things from him, and now he had to pick up the pieces of his shattered heart and try to move on alone.

I am always alone.

And he always would be.

CHAPTER TWENTY-THREE

MARISSA SAT AT her kitchen table, working hard on her laptop.

Okay, she wasn't actually working hard. She was procrastinating by messing with the fonts on her website. A necessary task? No. But the alternative was to sit here and think about how screwed up her life was lately. No thank you.

It had been two days since Rory stormed out of her life, accusing her of all manner of wicked deeds. Guilt pinched her side even as her anger rose. How dare he call her a liar? She had never lied to him. Withheld information, maybe, but it wasn't like she blatantly lied.

I only did that to Abby.

A heavy sigh left her as she clicked on Comic Sans then grimaced and clicked Cambria. Her sister had recovered and was barely talking to her, and honestly, she couldn't blame her. The whole thing was such a mess. And the person responsible for all of it, her father, hadn't been home in days. She called the hospital and discovered he'd picked up a coworker's shift and been on call for the past forty-eight hours. No doubt in exchange for cash he could blow at the poker tables.

Dammit! How was she supposed to talk to her dad about the mortgage if the man was never home? And what was she going to do about Rory?

Nothing. He said we're done.

She rubbed at her chest where a sharp stab of pain sliced right through her. How could he throw everything they were away, just like that? Yes, she'd stipulated an easy-out clause when they started this whole thing, but she never thought she'd fall this deep. Yet here she was, down the deepest, darkest hole she'd ever been in with no sliver of light to help her find her way out.

"Good grief," she muttered to herself. "Pity party, table of one. Get it together, Marissa. You're a freaking adult. Act like it."

Only, she didn't want to act like it. She wanted to run to her room screaming about the unfairness of life. Wrap up in a cozy blanket and watch sappy rom-coms. Cry her eyes out while being held by her mom.

"I miss you, Mom," she whispered into the empty room, warm tears sliding down her cheeks.

The sound of the front door opening pulled her out of her morose thoughts. Sniffling, she wiped her face, hands flying over the keyboard as she adjusted the background colors on her site. Two familiar feminine voices filled the air, getting closer until she glanced up to see Nora and Abby, arms full of grocery bags, come into the kitchen.

"Told you she'd be in here pretending to work," Abby said with a small snort of laughter.

"Holy cow, sweetie, when was the last time you showered?" Nora grimaced. "Or brushed your hair?"

Marissa reached up to the tangled topknot she'd put her hair into this morning. No, wait, it had been last night...yesterday morning? She couldn't remember. Whatever. It wasn't like she had anywhere to go or anyone to look presentable for. Why bother looking good when she felt like hot garbage. Have the outside match the in, or whatever the saying was.

Nora set her bag down on the table and snatched the laptop. "Let me just take this from you."

"Hey!" she protested. "I was working on that."

Nora raised one eyebrow in disbelief. "Were you? Or were you redesigning your website for the five hundredth time? I know you, bestie. You do unnecessary busywork when you're upset."

"Do not," she grumbled.

Abby set her bag down, pulling out three pints of ice cream. She passed the pistachio to Marissa.

Grabbing the offering from her sister, she gave a tentative smile. "Does this mean you're not mad at me anymore?"

Abby shrugged. "No, I'm still PO'd at you, but I also hate seeing you sad. Eat your disgusting ice cream while we figure this out."

She opened the lid, hiding a smile. "It's not disgusting, it's yummy."

"It's nasty," Abby insisted. "It's nuts. Ice cream shouldn't be a nut flavor."

Nora set a spoon down in front of her, giving her an encouraging smile. The pain in her chest eased slightly as she dug into the cold, creamy treat. As much as she wished she was strong enough to handle this mess she'd gotten herself into on her own, it was nice to have Nora and Abby here. The ice cream was a bonus.

"How are you doing?" Nora asked.

She'd called Nora the night everything went down. Explained the whole situation. Nora had also been upset with her. Years of friendship and she'd never shared her dad's addiction with her best friend. But, she'd let Marissa get out the whole story, up to Rory accusing her of being a liar. She'd had to admit to their secret relationship and subsequent breakup. It made everything hurt more, admitting it out loud. What she had, what she lost. The pain sliced though her, leaving rivers of agony in its wake.

"I'm fine," she lied.

Abby snorted, digging into her chocolate fudge brownie ice cream.

"Okay, I'm not fine. I'm…upset and sad, and so very sorry I kept things from you, Abby." She turned to Nora. "From both of you."

Abby sniffed, shrugging one shoulder. "You should have told me about Dad. Maybe not when I was a kid, but like, this year at least."

"I know." She nodded, placing her spoon in her ice cream and pushing the bin away as she focused on her sister. "I guess I was just so used to protecting you, my little sister, I forgot you've grown into quite the capable young lady."

Abby glanced up with a small smile.

"I just…didn't want to burden you, either of you, with this." She looked over to Nora. "It's my responsibility to take care of it."

"No, Missy, it's Dad's," Abby said with a shake of her head. "He's the one who has the problem. He's the one who got us into this mess."

"Oh, sweetie." She grabbed Abby's hand and gave it a small squeeze. "I don't think he can fix it. He won't even admit he has a problem."

How could he admit anything when he barely saw his daughters? He rarely responded to her texts these days.

"That's what addicts do," Nora said with a sad smile. "They refuse to see the trouble they're in until they hit rock-bottom. But that's not *your* problem. You're not responsible for your dad and his issues. You have to take care of yourself and Abby."

"I can take care of me just fine," Abby insisted.

She shared a look with Nora. Oh, to be a teenager again and know everything.

Taking a deep breath, she dug down deep and admitted her true fear. "I don't know what to do. How to fix this."

"You can't fix it," Nora said, gently taking her other hand. "Not every problem in life has a fixable solution. Sometimes you just have to let go."

What did that mean? Let go. Let go of cleaning up her dad's money messes? Let go of parenting her sister? Let go of Rory?

The last one slammed into her, eviscerating any happiness her favorite cold treat had given her. She didn't want to let go of Rory. Even as he pushed her away, she still ached to run to him, beg him to reconsider.

Pathetic.

She had never begged a man before in her life, and she didn't plan to start now. Besides, she hadn't done anything wrong.

"Have you spoken to Rory?" Nora asked, somehow knowing where her mind was.

She huffed out a humorless laugh. "Uh, no. Pretty sure Mr. High And Mighty doesn't ever want to speak to me again."

Silence filled the air. She glanced up to see Nora and Abby exchange a look. Uh-oh, she didn't like that.

"What?"

Nora winced. "Nothing, it's just…"

"You were kind of a jerk to Rory," Abby said without hesitation.

She blinked, not sure she heard her baby sister correctly. "Excuse me?"

"I can understand not wanting to tell me about Dad, but why wouldn't you share it with your boyfriend? Isn't that what relationships are for? To help each other with problems?"

"He's not my boyfriend," she mumbled, grabbing her ice cream and shoving a spoonful in her mouth. She immediately regretted it when a brain freeze had her wincing in pain. "We were…casual."

"The way he looks at you doesn't feel casual," Abby said with wisdom far beyond her fifteen years.

Again, the pain of loss bored into her soul. "Doesn't matter. It's over now."

"Nothing is over until you're dead," Nora said with a nod.

"He called me a liar." She shoveled another scoop of ice cream into her mouth, a smaller one. "I never lied to him."

Nora gave her a stern look. "A lie of omission is still a lie."

"He's a jerk," she muttered.

"He was hurt," Nora insisted. "We all were. When you find out the person you care for is holding back their problems, refusing to let you help them, it hurts."

Well, great, now she felt even worse than before. If they'd come to cheer her up, they were doing a terrible job.

"I was trying to—"

"Missy, I swear if you say you were trying to protect me one more time I'm going to dump the rest of my ice cream in your bed." Abby glared, holding up her pint as she threatened. "I know I'm still a kid in your eyes, but even I know that when you care about people you let them help you with your problems. Share the load, ask for help."

She sniffed as tears threatened to fall. "Yeah? And how do you know that?"

Her sister's face softened, love filling her green eyes she'd inherited from their mother.

"Because you taught it to me."

She sucked in a breath at the admission.

"You always encouraged me to come to you with anything," Abby continued. "You told me it's what you were there for. To help me with anything because you're my sister and you love me."

"I do… I am… I…"

Nora wrapped an arm around her shoulder and gave her a hug. "See, sweetie? Sharing your problems isn't a burden for the people who love you. That's why we were so upset. That's why Rory felt so betrayed. When you love someone, you want to help them."

"But he doesn't love me," she whispered, revealing her darkest fear. How could he when he gave up on them so easily?

"Are you sure about that? From what I hear, the man thinks you hung the moon."

Yeah, and he'd argue with her about the placement, insisting she move it a little more to the left. She chuckled. They were a pair for sure, but she had to admit, they brought out the best in each other. Every small disagreement they'd had about the gala was only to make sure it was the best it could possibly be. He'd listened to her ideas, even when he hadn't initially agreed with them. They'd learned to compromise over their time together, and by the end they were a well-oiled machine.

Until I ruined it all with my lies.

"Oh no," she sobbed, face dropping into her hands as the truth finally broke through her fog of pain. "He's right. I lied to him. Just like his ex."

She glanced up to see Abby and Nora exchange a look of confusion. That's right, they didn't know about Rory's ex. It wasn't her place to share, but the realization of what she'd done, the pain she caused him, stung deep.

"What do I do?" she asked in a hushed whisper.

"You talk to him," Nora said, pulling her in for a hug. "You explain. Let him listen. Apologize and hope you can move past this."

"Also make him apologize," Abby said, crossing her arms over her chest. "You might have lied, but he was a bit jerky if I remember correctly. I don't know, I was kind of spacing out. But I hold the right to be a little mad at him for making my sister cry."

She laughed through the tears, reaching over and pulling Abby into the hug. Surrounded by two of the people she loved most in this world, things started to click into place. She could do this. Now that she understood she didn't have to face her problems alone, she could learn to lean on those she loved.

And she loved Rory more than she thought humanly possible.

The only question now was, did he love her in return, or had she ruined her shot at happiness forever?

CHAPTER TWENTY-FOUR

EVERYTHING REMINDED HIM of her.

Rory stared into his closet at the row of dark suits. They were all different shades of blues and blacks. It didn't matter which one he picked to wear this morning. Any would be fine. But as he stood there, staring at the clothing he wore daily, all he could hear was Marissa's voice in his ear. Teasing him about his stuffy suits.

Dammit! He couldn't get the woman out of his mind.

His bed still held her scent. No matter how many times he washed the sheets, the subtle smell of her lavender lotion clung to the mattress, haunting him in the middle of the dark and lonely nights. It was driving him mad. How could he miss someone who had betrayed him?

"Get it together, man," he grumbled to himself, grabbing his dark charcoal suit and pulling it off the rack.

He dressed, determined to put his mind off thoughts of women who deceived him and onto more important matters. Like the upcoming gala. It was less than a week away. Everything was set. All the contracts signed, decorations set, staff hired. There was nothing more for him to do, but that didn't mean he couldn't go over the checklist one last time. What the hell else was he going to do with his time?

He made his way into the kitchen, starting the coffee and making a bowl of oatmeal. As he ate his breakfast, he went over the guest list RSVPs for the gala. Nearly everyone he'd invited was coming, save for a few who had prior engagements but sent along sizable donations because that was what was expected in his world. Sometimes it paid to be privileged, but only when you used that privilege to help others.

He remembered what it was like to have nothing. As long as he had the means to do so, he'd make sure to do everything in his power to help kids like he had been.

A knock on his door had him glancing up from his laptop, heart jumping in his chest, anticipation running through his veins. Not many people visited him. No one in fact. Only one person had been out here.

Marissa.

He hesitated. Indecision held him immobile. Did he want to see her? Yes. No. He didn't know. A part of him wanted desperately to see her, touch her, hold her in his arms and never let her go. But a larger part was still hurting, still angry. Why was she here?

Another knock sounded, followed by a deep, cheerful voice that in no way matched Marissa's.

"Rory? Come on, man, open up. I drove like three hours to get here, and I need coffee stat. I can smell it from here."

"Kellen?" What in the world was his cousin doing here?

He rose from the table and made his way to the front door. Opening it, he saw his tall, dark-haired, blue-eyed cousin with his trademark grin on his face.

"Rory!"

Suddenly he was engulfed in a classic Kell embrace. Fierce and forceful, it nearly knocked the wind out of him every time. His cousin was a gregarious man who never passed up an opportunity for a hug. Rory indulged him, squeezing him back, not realizing until now how much he needed the comfort of his cousin's embrace after the awful week he'd had.

"Kell, what are you doing here?" he asked, pulling away and motioning for Kell to come inside.

"I finished up my work in Denver and decided to head up a bit early for the gala. Cash and Mal will be up in two days. They're still working on getting permits for a new house the foundation is giving to a recipient."

He got Kell a cup of coffee.

"Thanks." Kell smiled, taking the cup as he glanced around the house. "The place is working out for you?"

He nodded.

"I knew you'd like the caretaker house. You're planning on having the counselors stay in the main house with the kids, right?"

He nodded. His cousins knew all about his plans for the camp. They'd even helped with their own bits of advice when he was planning the idea.

"Everything set for the gala?"

He nodded again.

Kell put his coffee down, face filling with suspicion. "What's wrong?"

He shrugged. "Nothing is wrong. Why would you assume something is wrong?"

Kell stared, eyes boring into his very soul. After a beat he swore. "Dammit. You screwed up with your woman, didn't you?"

How the hell did the man do that? Ever since Rory had joined the family, Kell had been able to sniff out bull from a mile away. He was like a damn human lie detector. Nothing got past the guy.

"Why do you assume I was the one to mess things up?"

Kell laughed. "Because you're a guy. We always screw things up."

Not always.

When he remained silent, Kell sighed.

"Okay, tough guy, go change."

Confused by the abrupt change of subject—Kell never let things go, he was like a dog with a bone when ferreting out secrets—he frowned.

"What?"

"Change out of the stuffy suit into some jeans and a shirt and let's hit that ropes course you've been telling me about. I just drove for hours, and my muscles are all stiff. I need a workout, and you need some fresh air."

The stuffy suit comment reminded him of Marissa all over again, worsening his mood, but Kell was right. It would do no good to sit inside and stew. After a quick change into jeans and a T-shirt, he led his cousin outside to the ropes course. They worked the first half in silence except for the sounds of their grunts and the chirps of the forest birds. Once they reached the platform in the middle of the course, Kell motioned for him to sit.

"This place is beautiful," his cousin said, panting slightly from the exertion.

"It is," he agreed.

"Makes you realize how big the world is looking at all these tall trees," Kell continued.

He glanced at his cousin from the corner of his eye, suspicion rising. "I suppose."

"And how small we are." Kell picked up a leaf that had fallen from an aspen, twirling it around in his fingers. "How maybe the problems we think of as huge, really aren't that big a deal. Especially when we share them with our family."

"Very subtle, Kellen," he deadpanned.

Kell chuckled. "Hey, man, I'm just letting you know I'm here to listen if you wanna talk."

"Thank you, but there's nothing to talk about."

"Really?"

He looked over at Kell, emotions boiling over inside. Pain,

sadness, anger all swirling until they became a vortex of sensations he could no longer hold back. Hands clenching into fists, he glared at his nosy cousin.

"You want to know what's upsetting me? Fine!"

He launched into the story. The whole story. From meeting Marissa under false pretenses to finding out she was the event planner, to the dinner at her house, growing closer and the eventual culmination of their secret relationship all the way to discovering her lies of betrayal.

"So that's it," he said, harsh breaths coming out as his lungs burned for air. "She lied to me, even after everything I shared with her. It's over."

Kell sat in silence, a contemplative expression on his face. The warm sun heated Rory's back. A cool breeze whipped through the trees, chilling the sweat that had gathered on the back of his neck. The tweets of the birds in the trees seemed to echo off the distant mountains with an ostentatious shrill. Everything felt larger, deeper…more in the silence between them. Finally, Kell spoke.

"Do you think she's after your money?"

He flinched, offense rising at his cousin's words even though he'd thrown the accusation out himself. "No. Of course not. I mean…the idea did cross my mind briefly."

"Can't blame you for that." Kell nodded. "Considering."

He let out a heavy sigh, shoulders slumping with the weight of everything. "I know she's not Britney."

"Do you?" Kell asked, genuine concern on his face.

"Yes." He nodded. "But when I found out she lied about her father, that she was struggling financially, I admit for a moment my brain went there. I feared she…was using me like Britney did."

"But she's not?" Kell prompted.

"No. But that doesn't excuse the fact that she lied. Don't

you see? It's the lie I'm upset about. How can I be with some-one if I can't trust them?"

Kell sucked in a deep breath. "Look, man, you know I'm not the best person to give relationship advice."

That was accurate. His cousins were as bad in the love department as he was. Cash flitted from date to date, Mal was a secluded hermit, and Kell was everybody's best friend and nobody's boyfriend. Poor guy was a stepping stone for women to find their one true love after they dated him. Count in Rory's lying ex and they sure were a group.

"But," Kell continued, "people make mistakes. We're human. It's what we do."

"A mistake is using baking powder in a recipe instead of baking soda," he scoffed. "Not deliberating lying."

Or embezzling.

Or abandoning your kid.

He didn't say the last two things, but judging by the look on Kell's face, he knew what Rory was thinking.

"Rory, I know people have screwed you over in the past, but you have to look beyond that. Recognize the people in your life who love and support you."

His jaw clenched as Kell's words tried to permeate the thick cloud of rejection in his brain.

"Your parents loved you. So much. And so do me, Cash and Mal. You're our family, man. Blood or not, we're family."

He knew that. They'd never treated him otherwise, but there was a part of him that always felt…less than. Unwor-thy. And he didn't know how to shut that part of him up.

"Now, I know you're stubborn as hell—"

"Hey!" He glared at Kell.

Kell arched one dark eyebrow. "Tell me I'm wrong?"

"Shut up," he grumbled, knowing he could do no such thing.

Kell chuckled. "Listen, she might have lied, but she didn't

steal. She's not Britney. Even if your conscious brain knows that, I bet your subconscious is still telling you to run, that it's happening all over again."

He glared, hating that his cousin was right in his assessment.

"She messed up. Made a wrong choice in not sharing her problems with you. We all do that sometimes. You included."

He wanted to argue, but Kell was right. He often held back his problems from his family so as not to burden them.

"But what really matters is the reasoning behind our choices," Kell said.

He frowned. "What do you mean?"

Kell shifted on the wooden platform, tossing the aspen leaf off the side and watching as it caught a breeze and twirled in the air toward the ground. "Well, there's two reasons to lie. Selfish and selfless. Was her lie out of malice, to hurt you or someone else? Or did she do it out of love? To protect those around her?"

The second one. She'd said as much. Insisted numerous times when he and Abby had accused her. Reality finally broke through the wall of ice around him. Dammit! How could he have been so blinded by his past? Marissa hadn't shared about her father's struggles because she wanted to protect Abby, protect him. She probably thought if she told him, he would assume she was with him for his money. She knew about his past, didn't want to make him think she was just another grifter out to take from him.

And I accused her of it anyway.

Dammit, he was a grade A jerk.

Glancing up at Kell, he frowned. "Does it get annoying being right all the time?"

Kell grinned. "I'm used to it."

He laughed softly, feeling the weight of a lifetime of suspicion and fear slip off his shoulders. A sunbeam poked through the trees and landed on his face, warming it without overheating his body.

"I love her," he whispered to the trees, the animals, Kell.

"I know, man. But what are you going to do about it?"

He had no idea. A lot of groveling and apologies needed to happen in addition to talks about honesty and openness. For now, he needed to come up with a plan to talk to her. The gala was four days away. That gave him four days to come up with his apology and try to convince the woman he loved that they were worth a second chance.

CHAPTER TWENTY-FIVE

"Okay, everyone," Marissa called out to the serving staff in the kitchen at Stonebridge. "The video presentation is in ten minutes, so let's start circulating the trays of champagne. You're all doing a wonderful job. Just a few more hours."

The staff in the kitchen nodded, hustling to grab the champagne flutes and fill the trays. The gala had started two hours ago and was running like a well-oiled machine. Mostly. There'd been a few hiccups, but nothing major that she couldn't handle. Everything looked amazing.

She thought.

Since she arrived this morning, she'd been holed up in the kitchen supervising. Some might say she was hiding out, but this was just what management looked like. She'd made sure everything in the ballroom was set for the gala before sneaking—slipping—away to the kitchen. It's where most of the action for tonight was anyhow. She needed to be in a centralized place where the staff could come fetch her if any problems arose.

Please don't let any problems arise.

Making her home base in the kitchen was smart. It wasn't because she was hiding from Rory or anything. Yes, she needed to talk to him, apologize, but this was not the night to do it. This night was too important. This camp and the kids were too important. Their issues could wait until to-morrow. Besides, she didn't think she could handle seeing him all dressed up in a tux right now. As much as she liked to tease him about his suits, she had to admit they made him look temptingly dashing. Rory in a tux? No way she could hold herself together seeing that deliciousness.

"Ms. Webb?"

She turned to see one of the servers, a young Latina woman named Carla, pointing toward the kitchen door.

"Yes?"

"There's a man outside asking to see you."

"Thank you, Carla."

Her heart leaped into her throat, pulse pounding as she glanced at the door wondering if Rory was on the other side waiting for her. No, that was silly. The entire staff knew Rory, as he came to every interview she'd done. If it had been him, Carla would have said Mr. Thorson. Then who was it?

Oh no, she hoped it wasn't a guest angry about the fact that they'd run out of *yakgwa*. Monica had been right about it being delicious. They'd disappeared in the first hour. Good things tended to go quickly, and rich people loved to complain about it. Straightening her shoulder and pasting on her most accommodating smile, she made her way out of the kitchen into the hall.

Music filtered in from the ballroom just beyond. The band was on fire tonight. Everyone seemed to love them. She gave herself another gold star for picking the right entertainment for this crowd. Everything was perfect. Then what in the world could this mystery guy want to complain about?

She glanced around the hall, noticing a tall white man with dark hair in a black tux standing just outside the ballroom doors across from the kitchen. He stood with his back to her so she couldn't see his expression, but his posture was relaxed. She crossed her fingers for an easy request from whatever this rich guy wanted.

"Excuse me, sir? You wanted to see me?"

The man turned and graced her with the friendliest smile she'd ever seen. He was handsome. Clean-shaven with a sharp jawline and piercing blue eyes. A few months ago, this guy would have made her stomach take flight with his handsome looks. But her heart did nothing, stomach remaining firmly in a tight knot as she anticipated his complaint. Rory had ruined her for all other men.

"Ah, so you must be the magician who made all this possible." He took a step toward her. "Marissa Webb, owner of Eventful Occasions and planner of this gala?"

She gave a polite laugh. "I don't know about magician. I plan every event with the client's requests in mind, so it's as much their success as mine. Mr. Thorson has excellent taste."

He stared at her for a moment before doubling over with laughter. Confused, she frowned.

"Oh, you are good. I have to say, I've heard a lot of people say a lot of…creative things about my cousin, but excellent taste has never been one of them."

"Wait." She held up a hand as his words sunk in. "Rory is your cousin?"

He nodded, pointing into the room. "Yup, and I know a lot of this was your doing. Rory is as stubborn as the Rockies are high. We all thought when Kenny left the foundation this gala would be a flop. It's the first one Rory had full control over. I was worried he'd fill it with hay and cowboy boots or something."

He'd tried. Thank goodness she'd been able to talk him down from going full Wild West theme.

"But this is…" The man lifted his glass to her. "Well, I think it's the best gala the foundation has ever had."

She preened under the compliment, brain still trying to wrap her head about the fact that this was Rory's cousin.

"I'm sorry, I didn't catch your name."

"How rude of me." He held out a hand. "Kellen Thorson, but everyone calls me Kell."

"Wonderful to meet you, Kell."

His handshake was warm and friendly. For some odd reason she immediately felt comfortable, like she was meeting an old friend for the first time.

"Rory has nothing but nice things to say about you and your work," Kell said, dropping her hand and leaning against the doorframe. "He's very impressed by you, and my cousin is not an easily impressed man."

The hair stood up on the back of her neck. Something about the way he said that made her pause. Just how much had Rory told Kell about her? What did he know? The warm smile on his face never wavered, but his eyes held a spark of secrets.

"I strive to make my clients happy. It's good to hear Mr. Thorson is satisfied with the gala."

Kell arched a dark eyebrow. They were playing a cat and mouse game. As an avid tabletop player, she usually loved games, but not this kind. It wasn't like she could come out and ask Kell what he knew about her and Rory's relationship. Not right in the middle of the gala. But the fact that the man wasn't cussing her out for hurting his cousin had to be a good sign, right?

"He's a hard man to please." Kell took a step toward her, his smile falling as genuine emotion crept into his eyes. "He's also had a lot of hurt in the past, which I'm sure you know. It made him a bit protective when it comes to matters of the heart, but he's working on being more open with the people who love him."

He gave her a pointed look. She nodded, dropping her professional facade and allowing all the whirling emotions she'd been feeling the past week to show on her face.

"Don't give up on him, okay?" Kell patted her shoulder softly. "I think you're just what he needs."

With that, he moved toward the ballroom, gently guiding her with him. She went, brain trying to catch up to what he had revealed as they stepped into the gala.

"My brothers and I are planning a gala fundraiser for our housing charity in the fall. We'd love to have you plan it for us."

"You would?" She blinked, trying to get her brain to focus back on work. "I can give you my card."

She started to reach into the pocket of her dress, but Kell held up a hand.

"No need. I got Rory's email."

Confusion had her brow pinching. "Email? What—"

"Expect a lot of inquiries into your services in the next week," he interrupted her with a grin. "Like I said, Rory has been singing your praise. To everyone."

She had no idea what that meant, but she had an inkling ten minutes later after Kell left and she was approached by half a dozen more people praising her work on the gala and promising to contact her for their own events, from weddings to fundraisers to retirement parties. At this rate she'd be booked up for the next year. Relief and happiness filled her, also confusion. Why had Rory told all his rich friends about her business if he hated her?

Maybe he doesn't hate me?

She crossed her fingers, almost too afraid to hope.

The band stopped playing, informing the crowd they were taking a break to allow for a special presentation. A large screen came down from the ceiling covering the stage. Right on cue the AV guy played the video she and Rory had prepared with the information on how tonight's donations would help fund the camp. A soft touch on her arm had her pulling her gaze away from the image of Rory crossing the ropes course. She turned, fully expecting to see another guest inquiring about her services.

Shock had her immobilized as she came face-to-face with the man himself. Rory looked unfairly gorgeous in his tux, red beard trimmed, hair slicked up into a fashionable pompadour style.

"Marissa."

Her name on his lips nearly made her cry. She'd been so worried she'd never hear it again.

"You look unequivocally beautiful," he said with a soft smile.

She glanced down at her plain black dress. It was cocktail style, fancy enough to blend in but not stand out, and best of all it had pockets.

"Thank you. You look amazing too." Suddenly nervous, she glanced around the room. "The gala seems to be a success."

He nodded, holding out his hand to her. "May I speak with you in private?"

A million scenarios flooded her mind. He hated the gala and wanted to fire her and ask for all his money back. He loved the gala but was still angry at her and wanted her to leave. He loved the gala and her and wanted to whisk her off to the tree house for a make-up session.

Okay, none of those sounded accurate, but she was hoping for something more like the latter and less like the former.

Slipping her hand into his, she shuddered when that spark of awareness shot through her body. She followed him out of the ballroom, across the hall and through the kitchen to the conservatory. Most of the staff was passing out champagne, but the few that were in the kitchen didn't pay them any mind as they made their way into the glass-enclosed room.

Moonlight filtered into the room. The sweet smell of the flowers and earthy plants filled her lungs as he led them to a secluded corner where no one could see.

"Did you send out an email recommending Eventful Occasions to all your rich friends?" she asked, unable to keep the words inside.

He sighed, rolling his eyes to the glass ceiling. "Kell talked to you, didn't he?"

She nodded. "He seems very nice."

"He is. He's also a nuisance who pokes his nose in where it doesn't belong."

She chuckled, thinking about Abby and Nora. "I know some people like that."

He glanced down at her, expression serious. "Marissa, I'm sorry. I shouldn't have accused you of being a liar or wanting me just for my money. I…let my past control my emotions in the present. My judgment was clouded because of it, and that wasn't fair to you. I had no right to demand you share things you weren't comfortable with sharing."

Stepping forward, she grasped his hands in hers, needing to touch him, hoping it wouldn't be the last time.

"No. I'm sorry. You were right. You shared your pain with me, and I held mine back. I didn't want to burden you with my problems, but I should have trusted you. I should have shared. I swear I'm not after your money—"

"I know," he interrupted, pulling his hands free and cupping her face. "I never thought that of you, I swear. I was simply lashing out, and I am so damn sorry. I'm a fool, but I promise, if you give me another chance I'll do better."

Tears streamed down her cheeks as a week's worth of heartbreak and worry left her.

"I love you, Marissa." He stared into her eyes. "You're smart, supportive, brave, have the most beautiful heart of anyone I've even known. And you're possibly even more stubborn than me."

She laughed between her sobs. "I love you too, Rory. You try to hide it, but you're one of the kindest people in the world. You care about people, and even though you have terrible taste in board games, I still want to play them with you."

He grinned. "I'm going to pull you around to that one, you wait and see."

"I talked to my dad," she said, sucking in a deep breath. "Told him he either gets help or I'll go to court to file for custody of Abby and the deed to the house."

Rory blinked in surprise. "What did he say?"

She shrugged. "I have no idea. It was a voicemail because he's still at the casino."

She highly doubted her father cared enough for her or her sister to stop gambling, but she was tired of cleaning up his messes and shoving things under the rug. No more. She was done hiding the shame that should be his and his alone.

"I'll help, any way I can." Rory nodded. "I'll hire you the best lawyer and—"

She placed a finger over his lips, stopping his sweet offer. "Thank you, but I got this. I just wanted to share it with you so you know. But I promise if I need help, I will ask."

He nodded, kissing the tips of her fingers. "And I'll be here, whatever you need. No more one-day-at-a-time or easy-out clause. With you I'm all in, Marissa."

She smiled up at him, wrapping her arms around his neck and rising on her toes. "I'm all in too, Rory."

His dipped his head, brushing his lips against hers. Too starved for the man she loved to be gentle, she deepened the kiss, squealing with delight when he growled and tugged her flush against him. What a pair they were, so different yet so alike. There in the moonlight with the sweet smell of flowers around them and the endless possibilities of the future before them, Marissa finally let all her worries go and surrendered to the moment and the man she loved.

* * * * *

If you enjoyed this story, check out this other great read from Mariah Ankenman

Accidentally Dating the Enemy

Available now!

MILLS & BOON®

Coming next month

HOW TO FAKE DATE HER BILLIONAIRE
Clare Miles

'Ready to practice, Nic?'

'Always,' he said with a bravado he hoped to be true, mentally rolling his shoulders and tightening the reins of his control.

The instant Eleanor placed her palms against his chest, he hissed out a breath and jack-knifed like she'd scorched him.

Finally, she pressed her lips against his, and like a fuse igniting, heat roared between them. It was no polite, pretend kiss. It was hot and demanding. Linking her fingers behind his neck, she gripped his hair. He wrapped his arms around her waist, pulling her fully against him.

Eleanor moaned, then stilled and reared back, pushing against him.

'Stop!'

Disoriented, he opened his eyes, bringing her into focus—her lowered lids, flushed face and puffy lips devoid of gloss. A primal beat of satisfaction curled through his veins that he'd caused that.

'That should convince everyone,' she said flat and firm, her words penetrating the roaring in his head, and—like a bucket of ice had been thrown over him—reality hit. *Hard*.

This was an act.

Continue reading

HOW TO FAKE DATE HER BILLIONAIRE
Clare Miles

Available next month
millsandboon.co.uk

COMING SOON!

We really hope you enjoyed reading this book.
If you're looking for more romance
be sure to head to the shops when
new books are available on

Thursday 18th December

To see which titles are coming soon, please visit
millsandboon.co.uk/nextmonth

MILLS & BOON

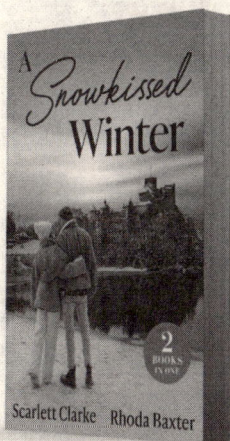

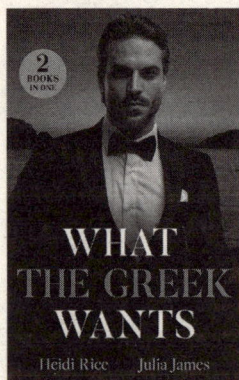

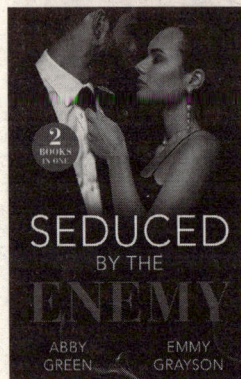

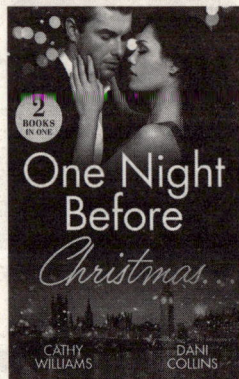

OUT NOW!

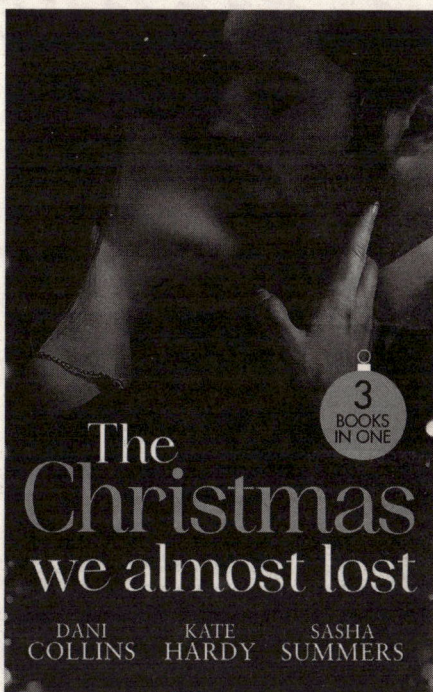